THE SOUL DWELLER

STEPHEN PAUL SAYERS

Hydra Publications

Praise for Stephen Paul Sayers

The Soul Dweller:

"The Soul Dweller grips you from the first chapter and refuses to let go until the heart-stopping end." -Darcy Coates, USA Today bestselling author of THE CARROW HAUNT and CRAVEN MANOR

"A terrifying tale of demonic possession that is perfectly paced and will have you hooked. One you do not want to miss!" – Lee Mountford, bestselling author of THE DEMONIC and HORROR IN THE WOODS

"The Soul Dweller has everything you'd want in a riveting supernatural horror story. Crisp writing, engaging characters, and a brazenly refreshing plot pitting good against evil that will keep you turning pages late into the night. Don't miss the Caretakers series." – Jeremy Bates, USA Today bestselling author of SUICIDE FOREST and MOUNTAIN OF THE DEAD

A Taker of Morrows:

"A page turner in every sense of the word." – The Falmouth Enterprise

What readers say about *A Taker of Morrows*
★ ★ ★ ★ ★ "This book was a work of art. Absolute perfection…"

★ ★ ★ ★ ★ "A thrilling thriller from the beginning – couldn't put the book down…"

★ ★ ★ ★ ★ "Enticing from the very first page!"

★ ★ ★ ★ ★ "A real original thriller. Best book I've read in years…"

★ ★ ★ ★ ★ "…the quick pacing and high tension kept me hooked until the very end."

★ ★ ★ ★ ★ "…vivid prose and surprising plot twists had me reading late into the night, and left me wanting to know what happens next."

★ ★ ★ ★ ★ "…keeps you guessing till the end."

★ ★ ★ ★ ★ "The suspense was amazing and the imagery made me feel like I was in the book…at times I forgot I was reading a book."

★ ★ ★ ★ ★ "…believable characters, perfect pacing, and a nice twist at the end. Who could ask for anything more?"

★ ★ ★ ★ ★ "Do yourself a favor and read A Taker of Morrows!"

★ ★ ★ ★ ★ "…you get deeply involved in the storyline and everything around you ceases to exist."

★ ★ ★ ★ ★ "Stephen Paul Sayers really stands out in the world of fiction. I can't wait to read his next book!"

Author's Note

All introductory chapter notes are the original epitaphs from Burial Hill Cemetery, obtained from Bradford Kingman's "Epitaphs from Burial Hill, Plymouth, Massachusetts, from 1657 to 1892: With Biographical and Historical Notes." New England Illustrated Historical Publishing Company: Brookline, MA, 1892.

ISBN: 978-1-937979-35-5

Hydra Publications

Hydra Publications
Goshen, Kentucky 40026
www.hydrapublications.com

Chapter One

'Stop traveler and shed a tear
Upon the fate of children dear.'

In memory of Four Children of Mr Zacheus Kempton &
Sarah his wife (all died between the years 1802-1820)
-Epitaphs from Burial Hill

June 14, 2019

RG

You wonder sometimes. About a face.

Someone passing you on the street, in the subway or airport, a face you've never laid eyes on before and will likely never see again.

So many different ones, with welcoming eyes, maybe an intimidating scowl…or a false smile, a distracted glance, a courteous nod, a lustful once-over.

A face can communicate some things…but not everything. No face reveals the true world lurking behind it. It hides things no one could ever see.

No one but Robert Granville, that is. "RG" could see it all.

The thoughts of unsuspecting strangers streamed through their well-constructed facades and into RG's mind like blinding sleet in a winter storm. Their truths…*well, don't you look like shit today, honey*…their sins…*you still have time to hide the body where no one will ever find it*…their pleas for help…*don't let him track me down again. Don't let him find me here, please God…*

Who would have guessed looking into RG's face that he sheltered some of the darkest secrets of the universe behind his brown eyes and kind smile, secrets nobody could possibly fathom.

Who would have guessed that he had discovered a battle between good and evil raging outside life's boundaries, one determining the fate of earthly souls, where 'caretakers' protect the living and 'jumpers' hunt them as prey; that his loving wife, Kacey, could glimpse the future in her dreams and change it, and transport herself into otherworldly dimensions; that his long-dead father and caretaker, Morrow, had saved him from a collision course with a ruthless and vengeful jumper from the afterlife.

No one could glimpse that in his face.

RG stared at the familiar curves and lines reflecting in the bathroom mirror as he braved another day, another chance to mull over the abrupt, life-altering events that had upset his world, turned him upside down and inside out, redefined his life, his existence, his relationships, his life goals and purpose. And he was nowhere near wrapping his head around it. Life had tried to settle back into some variance of normal, the entire last year shifting him back to a steady acceptance of lost ground, unfavorable notoriety, and the need to claw his way back out of the trenches.

Shuffling into the bedroom, RG ran a hand through his thick hair to flatten it down, what Kacey lovingly called his wavy brown garden of weeds, then stretched through a silent yawn. He glanced at the glowing red digital numbers on his bedside clock, a five-minute window remaining until the alarm's expected intrusion. He calculated whether a few more minutes of sleep would provide enough benefit to counter a restless night. Probably not, but he dropped into bed anyway, settling in gently beside Kacey's limbs splayed akimbo, trying not to disturb her. He pressed his head deeper into the memory-foam pillow, wishing sometimes it had supernatural powers to extract and delete disturbing historical sequences from his mind.

RG paused a moment and traced his wife's face and body contours with an appreciative gaze, part of his waking ritual he had yet to kick. With a spate of freckles across her nose and a river of near-auburn hair spilling over tan shoulders, Kacey Granville could send his heartbeat rocketing with a simple glance, or laugh, or a million other things she drew from her arsenal to paralyze his senses. And each passing day brought with it something different, something else to trip the switch and increase the palpitations. If a cardiologist wired him up and monitored him throughout the day, the wild swings in rhythm would force the doc to send for an ambulance before he had finished his first cup of morning coffee.

He slipped out of bed and eased himself to the carpet. Rolling onto his stomach, he readied himself for the hellish, daily stretching regimen keeping him pain-free. A warm, sun-spattered patch of thick carpet reignited a sleepy moment, but he resisted the temptation to climb back onto the beckoning pillow-top mattress. At thirty-seven he wasn't getting any younger, and his back would never be the same after an explosion snaggled his vertebrae and jumbled four lumbar discs.

Getting blown through a house wall will do that to a person.

Eighteen months ago, RG found himself thrust into a place between worlds no theology or doctrine could have prepared him for, the target of a jumper's burning vengeance. But with help from Kacey and Morrow, RG found a way to defeat an unrelenting evil unleashed upon the earth, nearly dying in the fiery Armageddon he sought to prevent.

So, now he had to stretch every morning, a small price to pay to be alive with his wife and child beside him. RG never took for granted how lucky he was to have a wife who really followed the better or worse wedding vow stuff. How many wives would have stayed by his side through that mess? But then again, Kacey's powers didn't make her an ordinary wife.

Keeping his pelvis glued to the floor, RG pressed his body upward and arched his spine as his face twisted into a grimace. A popping sound ripped the air, as if he had gripped a bendy straw and yanked on opposite ends.

"One," he grunted.

"Oh my God. What was that?" Kacey woke, peeking over the edge of the bed, eyes half-lidded.

"Just what's left of my backbones," he replied, pressing up again to the staccato pop ripping across the room. "Two."

Kacey threw the covers off and slipped out of bed. "That can't be doing you any good." She gave his face a playful nudge with the sole of her foot. "We'll have to come up with a more productive exercise to help your lower back." Grinning, she stepped over him and ambled toward the master bathroom.

RG's heart rate spiked as he rolled onto his side and gazed at his wife's lithe form glide across the carpet. After giving birth to Robert Jr. last year, Kacey's daily workouts had more than transformed her body to its pre-pregnancy tone. RG's injuries and increased couch time had steered his body in a different direction. He put a hand over his sagging belly and sighed.

How life had changed in the past eighteen months.

RG's involvement in a high-profile, double murder of a Boston University colleague and a lifelong friend had forced them from their life in Beantown, a crime the national media had dubbed the 'Fugitive Professor' case. The publicity, his flight from law enforcement, telltale physical evidence at both murder scenes, and a rumored inappropriate relationship with a co-ed had created a relentless firestorm of protests from Boston University's parents, alumni, and donors, ensuring his dismissal. Most figured he had gotten off easy. If someone asked the Boston locals, they would say he got away with murder, despite law enforcement's clearing him of the two crimes. His reputation had taken a hit, and university colleagues, as well as his and Kacey's friends, had abandoned him. With few professional prospects, he had settled on a part-time position at Cape Cod Community College in Barnstable, teaching health sciences courses.

Now he couldn't even support his family.

Kacey glanced back at him as she strode across the carpet, pulling her tee shirt over her head in a mock striptease, twirling to give him a quick peek. She turned her back as she dropped different articles of clothing onto the floor, like a trail of breadcrumbs. Wiggling a raised eyebrow, she entered the bathroom and left the door open a crack, the shower's hiss whispering her unspoken invitation.

He stared at the carpet as he prepared for his next rep.

Concentrate.

"Three," he groaned, dropping onto his stomach. He tilted

his head and peered through the sliver of steamy bathroom light, Kacey's outline a blur through the shower's frosted glass. But as he gazed at her, a familiar silhouette crept toward the bath. The man had RG's same patch of unruly brown hair, but he was younger, leaner. He resembled the man Kacey had met and fallen in love with, who bought her things and took her out just because it was a Tuesday night, who didn't worry about whether her treasures impacted the week's food budget.

As he pressed his eyes shut, a ping from his cell interrupted his daily self-wallow.

Struggling to his knees, he lunged toward the bedside table and grabbed the device. Tapping the mail icon, RG scrolled through his email accounts until he came to the one he and Kacey shared, a bolded '1' displayed in the inbox.

RG released a heavy sigh and mumbled, "Great."

The email account represented a last resort for those with nowhere else to turn, the only earthly help against an evil most could not comprehend. When Morrow had revealed himself as RG's father, he had transferred his powers into RG's wedding ring, bestowing upon the couple the universe's power to share. The three had made a pact to combine forces and protect the living from the next world's threatening evil. But, the couple had come to realize their mission would comprise long stretches of downtime—and their efforts wouldn't come with a paycheck to help with the bills.

RG squinted at the device, re-examining the cryptic message Kacey and Morrow had composed and released to the deep web months ago.

You can't explain it. No one believes you, but we will. It exists. The other place. We understand, because we've been there. The others exist, too. We've seen them. Need help? Email.

RG scanned the inbox message with a scowl.

My child is gone. The other one took him away, the one inside him. Please get back to me. It's been twenty years and I miss my boy. Please contact me as soon—

RG hit delete. *To hell with this! Who waits twenty years?* How many false leads would they have to endure before they agreed to shut down this whole ridiculous scheme? It may have been a good idea in the beginning, but...well, it didn't seem to be going anywhere. "Bunch of nut jobs out there."

He glanced toward the steamy shower, his heart jumping in his chest. Struggling to his feet, he aimed his body toward the bathroom, hunched over and shuffling across the carpet like Quasimodo to the bell-tower.

————

Mike

It happened at least once a day...sometimes more.

It just took one misstep, a toe stub, a shoe scuff, or an awkward footfall. Either one was sufficient to aggravate the Glock 9mm slug embedded in Detective Mike Stahl's hip and rouse millions of eager pain sensors. And then it would come, an explosion of steel daggers hurtling across his neural networks and into every forgotten nook and cranny of his body. Stahl wasn't bothered much by the pain anymore. He could block that out. But the pain triggered *the rush*—that's what the department shrink labeled it—the dark memories he couldn't block out.

Hard to imagine how hip pain linked to heart-stopping brain flashbacks, but that's the funny thing about trauma and stress.

It's all connected.

Stepping into the interrogation room, Stahl winced as his pain sensors unsheathed the daggers. A psycho cop with a gun and a demon on fire, swaying in Stahl's living room, emerged from his memory, rocking him, caving his knees. He reached for the doorjamb to steady himself as he struggled to breathe, a pair of hands gripping his windpipe. He swiped sweat beads off his forehead once the episode subsided.

He never knew when it would come, but it was always just one step away. If only he could figure a way to stop moving, maybe his brain would leave him alone, give him peace.

Today, there would be no peace as he stepped across the interrogation room's chipped, gritty tile. He squinted through the dim light of the single 70-watt bulb dangling from the ceiling fixture, its full capacity failing to penetrate the basement room's deep shadows. Decades of sweat, nicotine, and cleanser leeched from the humid, stained walls and floors, a room as ugly and corroded as the soul of the man resting on the other side of the scarred, wooden table.

Stahl took a seat and faced the child killer, Abner Stennett.

He thought he had witnessed some gruesome deaths investigating the 'Fugitive Professor' case, but nothing could compare to eight-year-old Nathan Stennett's broken body folded like a deflated tent on the rocks below the windswept bluff in Eastham, his sightless eyes staring upward from his shattered skull. Stahl, one of the Cape's handful of forensic investigators, had been forced to stomach countless murders throughout his years as a detective for the Chatham Police Department, but this one would haunt him.

He produced a digital audio recorder from his pocket, placed it on the table, and triggered the on switch. "You've waived your right to counsel, and you've agreed to have your statement recorded, is that correct?"

Abner Stennett nodded.

"I need a verbal confirmation." *You piece of shit!* He wanted to add…but didn't.

He eyed the Chatham Card & Candle proprietor, a respected Cape Cod citizen, former city councilman, and unrepentant Boston sports fan as he recounted how he and wife, Maria, had weathered two miscarriages until Nathan's birth blessed them, how he had coached his son's hockey team, took him to Red Sox games, and walked him to Sandi's diner every Saturday afternoon for milkshakes.

"…he'd always get chocolate and I'd stick with vanilla. We used to be close…best friends, even, but then…"

Detective Mike Stahl thrust his chair back from the table and struggled to his feet, shadowing the man who had once been a pillar of the community. He leaned close to the murderer's pale and strained face, bracing one hand on the table and the other on the back of Stennett's chair. "Do you think a jury gives a shit about what flavor ice cream you like? Just tell me what you did to your son. Quit the bullshit."

"That boy wasn't my son." Stennett tapped his fist against his lips. "He looked like him…he even moved like him. But it wasn't him. I'm not sure…*what* it was."

What the fuck?

"How could *you*…a father, for God's sake…*ever* kill…Jesus Christ…"

Stahl shoved Stennett's chair with a pained and flinching heart, picturing the boy's indelible, lifeless stare. He could only hope Nathan's eyes would be the first thing Stennett would see when he lay down to sleep and the last thing he would see when he rose upon awakening. And if they jolted him from his hellish dreams in between, all the better. It would serve him right but would never be punishment enough. No, Stahl wished he had never answered that 911 call.

He dropped into his chair, releasing the coiled fingers pressed into his palms. "Help me understand, Mr. Stennett, because I don't." He leaned forward, wincing as he rested his elbows on the table—the other slug buried in his shoulder vying for attention now—"I need the *why*. Why throw an eight-year-old child off a cliff?"

"Nathan hadn't been…" Stennett trained his eyes upward, grasping for the right word. "…present…for a long time." He swiped a pudgy hand through his thinning hair. "The boy replacing him, well, he wasn't gonna do."

Stahl positioned the digital recorder closer to the killer. "Replacing him?"

Psych eval, anyone?

Stennett clasped his hands together on the table, as if in prayer. "Nathan left us about three weeks ago. He didn't want to leave. In fact, he begged us to help him. But Malachi had gotten too strong, too persistent. Malachi wanted life, and Nathan had it."

"Wait. What are we talking about here? Who's Malachi?"

Stennett surveyed his surroundings with eyes unfocused, smirking at the one-way glass panel against the adjacent wall. "Malachi would peek out from the back of Nathan's eyes." He turned his head in a slow arc toward Stahl. "You know, eyes are like windows. If you look deep into them, you can spot all sorts of things."

Mike leaned forward, eyeing Stennett. "Well, I'm looking real hard, but I'm not seeing much."

Stennett pressed his eyes shut. "I saw things in Nathan's eyes I'd never imagined, flashes... shadows. You see, Malachi was quick. He would hide." His jaw muscles rippled as he clenched his teeth. "It wasn't long before he turned mean."

Stahl stopped doodling on his frayed notebook and raised his eyes.

"Maria took the brunt of it. She'd have these unexplained bruises, scrapes. She wouldn't tell me much, but I figured it out." He tapped his fingers against the table. "We even took the boy to the doc to see if there was something triggering his outbursts."

Stahl filled his cheeks with air before releasing. "And?"

Stennett grinned. "Well, Malachi made sure Nathan was on his best behavior that day. We looked like fools. But afterward, the real changes came. It started with the odor...like something died inside him. I'd smell him from his bedroom, this rancid stench wafting off him, hanging in the air, stopping me in my tracks as if I'd marched into a brick wall."

A vein twitched in Stahl's temple. "Well, maybe you should have bathed him once in a while before you killed him."

Stennett's eyes lost focus, as if Stahl's words hadn't reached past his ears. "And when you looked at Nathan real close, he didn't even resemble a little boy anymore. He had these blood-shot eyes and thin, blue veins fanning out along his pasty skin. Sometimes you'd see them; sometimes you wouldn't. Ropy muscle chords protruded from his neck and arms," Stennett said, bristling, "as if something inside pulsed against Nathan's skin, pushing, trying to get out."

Something inside him? This guy has lost his—

Stahl's throat tightened as he found himself back in his old living room, bleeding out...a wall of flame barreling toward him. As fingers around his neck squeezed harder, he struggled to shake the images from his head—*the rush* in full effect.

Pushing back from the table, he stumbled toward the bubbler for a gulp of water. *What the fuck…must have tweaked my hip somehow.* Sitting in a chair? Stahl shook his head, no arms manufacturer in history having gotten more mileage from a pair of bullets than the ones whose slugs remained lodged inside him.

"And he would laugh sometimes in this raspy bark. Sounded like an old man."

Fucking lunatic. This is bullshit. Next, he'll be telling me the boy was possessed by a demon. Maybe he should have called a priest, not kill the poor kid. Now he was on fire, a detonation hurling him into the air. His knees jackknifed as he ripped at his flaming shirt, stumbling backward into the cooler. He steadied himself against the wall, shutting his eyes as he blindly reached toward the bubbler to fill his cup. He gulped down the cooling fluid. The fire died out, and the musty basement walls resumed in his vision. He emitted a slight groan as he crushed the paper cone and tossed it in the garbage.

"You okay there, detective? Hope I didn't scare you."

"Just a little dehydrated, that's all." Stahl's arm remained draped over the bubbler.

Stennett leaned back, raking a hand across his two-day stubble, a slight tremor flitting across his fingers. "You got a smoke? I think the both of us could use one."

Stahl smirked through his mind's foggy haze. The discomfort pulsing through the man's nicotine-starved body provided a welcome distraction. He never interfered with a suspect's need to light up, despite recent changes in policy. A well-timed butt established rapport and relaxed a perp, helped uncover details someone jonesing for a nicotine fix would never reveal otherwise. With anyone else, Stahl would have found a match, struck it against the table's edge, cupped his hand around the flame, and ignited the man's tobacco. But he was content to prolong Stennett's suffering.

Stahl nodded toward the 'no smoking' sign on the wall as he hobbled to his seat. *Just get through this.* "Where's Mrs. Stennett? Why didn't she come with you to make your statement?"

Stennett waved his hand, dismissing the detective. "After the doctor's visit, we took to locking our bedroom door at night. I'd wake in the darkness to the floorboards creaking outside the room. I'd glimpse his shadow beneath the door. He'd be standing in the hallway. When the doorknob would jiggle, Maria would lunge for me, wrapping her arms around me to stop me from getting up and unlocking the door, because it wasn't Nathan. It wasn't my son out there."

Mike leaned back and pressed his eyes with his palms. He had sat across from countless psychopaths and listened to their stories, but this one would have the mental health professionals scratching their heads. *Time to call the Wacky Ward and book a nice long vacation.*

"Frankly, Mr. Stennett, your story's pretty out there." *Like Mars, out there!* His gaze darted to the wall clock, its second hand hammering out each painful moment of the interview. "Anything else you want to tell me?"

Stennett deliberated a moment before lifting his gaze to Stahl, meeting his stony gaze. "That boy wasn't my son."

Mike leaned forward, a few careless strands of hair tumbling over his lined forehead. "Can you wife corroborate any of this? It would go a long way toward—"

"Maria…?" Stennett tilted his head to the side. "I don't think so…not anymore."

Stahl dropped his pen, the tumblers clicking into place. He burst from his seat, pressing his fists into the table's grooved wood surface. "Mr. Stennett, where's your wife? Tell me she's okay."

Stennett's empty stare met Stahl's stony gaze.

For the second time, Stahl's throat tightened, the images building behind his eyes. "Where the hell is she, Stennett!"

"She's back at the house…" He leaned forward and whispered, "…in the basement. Malachi killed her a few days ago."

———

Malachi

Before Nathan Stennett hit the rocks at the bluff's base, Malachi had jumped from the body, back to the far corner of darkness, in a hidden place somewhere between this world and the next. Malachi had been dead for over seventy years but never ascended to his designated realm, forever longing for the previous world's magnificence and majesty. Each body he found to inhabit resurrected him, granting him a stay in his preferred domain.

He hadn't expected the man to throw Nathan from the cliff, but human emotion's irrational and unpredictable nature never surprised him. Thankfully, he had been alert and escaped his host before he died, or he would have died along with him, a lapse in focus responsible for the majority of jumper deaths.

Malachi could jump into the many different parallel existential planes throughout the universe. A quick jump through the veil and he could instantly emerge elsewhere, past worlds, as well as present. He had worn the shells of diverse hosts, too —men, women, old, young. In some hosts, the older boys mostly, uncomfortable developmental changes disturbed him, hair growing in strange places, a deepening voice, or the arousal of different curiosities. Malachi would jettison these bodies quickly, preferring the frames of young boys from the world he had once inhabited.

They fit better, and he understood how they worked.

Malachi wasn't a typical jumper, maybe because he died at such a young age. He didn't possess a typical jumper's rage, slipping back and forth between worlds to prey on the living, killing for sport or to avenge an unfulfilled earthly life. Malachi spent time with his hosts, getting to know them. The host vessel allowed him to live again, so he loved and treasured them.

At least for a while.

Malachi would search for a body with a kind-spirited boy inside, or someone needing a friend, welcoming hosts with whom he could play. Malachi cared deeply for these boys. But after a while, even the friendliest of hosts turned, disappeared deep inside themselves, unable to find their way back. Malachi learned over the years the human body could only accommodate one owner at a time, discarding the other.

And Malachi was never the other.

When he observed the turning, witnessed his new friends go away, he ached for them, but he couldn't bring them back. Instead, he would end things humanely. Permanently.

He owed them that.

Some hosts weren't as friendly. They battled him for control over their own bodies. These hosts Malachi didn't care for, and he took pleasure in *making* them go away. Malachi would bury them so deep inside themselves, they would never get out.

Like he did with Nathan.

Like all jumpers, Malachi had learned to be wary of caretakers from different realms. They spoiled his fun, and Malachi didn't much care for them. But, he found great pleasure frustrating them with his guile. Like a child, Malachi would trick them, hide buried within a host where they couldn't find him, laughing at them all the while. Sometimes, an exceptional caretaker could discover him and expel him from a host but only if he lingered inside too long, when the body fought back and oozed the unpleasant odor—impending death's telltale signal. Malachi had learned to enter and use up the host long before the body turned, then move on to the next.

Malachi reclined against the dwelling's stone wall buried beneath the earth, naked branches scraping and clawing against the building's exterior, snapping with a percussive backbeat to the howling wind's orchestra outside. Burning torches lit the tomb-like darkness but did nothing to alleviate the blanketing chill. Malachi's ears picked up faint wails and moans coming from below, a churlish sneer snaking across his lips at the thought of his keepsakes, his precious companions he could relive and cherish, restrained in basement cages, abducted from the world he had loved before they had turned.

His favorite hosts.

A memory transported Malachi to his youth…a day at the Franklin Park Zoo. He had been hanging onto his mother's hand as they strolled by the huge cages, afraid of the gorillas, bears, and big cats.

"What's that smell? It stinks!" He pinched his nose and held his breath.

"Now don't get too close, Malachi." His mother let go of his hand. "You don't want to frighten them."

He inched closer to the cages with cautious steps. *Frighten them?* "I won't, Mother."

Malachi's eyes widened as he stared at the caged beasts. He wondered what they were thinking while they paced back and forth across their cells. Their jet-black eyes made it seem like they wanted to eat him up right then and there, if they could, maybe shake him back and forth by the neck like a rat in a dog's mouth. He was small and weak, and that scared him. But when he stood next to their cages, and they couldn't do anything to him, his feelings changed. *They* were the weak ones…stuck behind bars.

Now, relaxing above his own human zoo, Malachi relived those same sensations of power. He remained in ultimate control of whether the boys lived or died. He brought them food and drink, nourished them, cleaned their cages. It pained him to witness the revulsion seething behind their eyes, the ungratefulness.

Don't they appreciate all I've done for them?

Sometimes he would leave them without food or water and wallowing in their filth for days at a time to reassert his dominance. Upon his return, well, that's when they would show their appreciation for him again.

Malachi descended the ancient stone steps into the cavernous clearing and surveyed his flock. Boys huddled together, sharing their warmth to thwart the pervasive chill radiating from their cells' stone floors. Others stood against the bars, staring at him with venomous eyes.

Malachi reached into the back pocket of his tattered brown knickers and withdrew his slingshot, a treasured remnant from his childhood. He bent down and picked up a stone, positioning it in the weapon's leather pouch.

I'll wipe that look from their eyes.

Aiming at the center cage, he pulled back his elbow and extended the rubber tubing, releasing the stone with a snap. The projectile pinged off the cage's vertical bar and deflected away, scattering children across the dank, dusty floor.

A grin creased Malachi's face. It had gotten a bit crowded in the cages, and he would need to make room for his new arrivals. Not everyone would be able to stay.

He would have to make difficult decisions.

Chapter Two

'Early Bright Transcint Sweet
As Morning Dew They Sparkled
Were Exhaled And went to Heaven.'

In memory of **JAMES HERSEY THACHER**, died 27th April 1793 (Aged 1 year, 4 months) and **CATHERINE THACHER**, died 10th Febry, 1800 (Aged 3 years)
-Epitaphs from Burial Hill

June 15, 2019

Kacey

Kacey palmed a circle in the steamy bathroom mirror, revealing a once familiar woman staring back at her. She secured the bath towel and leaned forward to take inventory.

She looks like me, but I'm not sure where the hell she came from.

She grabbed the magnifying mirror off the sink for a closer

inspection. The faint beginnings of crow's feet extended from the corners of her eyes, and the first wisps of gray now sullied her locks. At thirty-six, Kacey hadn't yet come close to slowing down, maintaining a rigorous schedule of boot camps and beach runs, but she sensed her supernatural encounters somehow hastened the sand through her hourglass. She grabbed the mirror's base in a death grip, jamming it into the upper drawer of the bathroom vanity.

That's right, girl, blame the mirror!

Kacey threw on jeans and a Sox tee shirt and headed down the stairs, appreciating the weekend respite from Chatham Elementary School. Despite having more than a year under her belt in the new job as vice principal, Kacey sensed she didn't quite fit there yet. It wasn't the move to Chatham. She had grown up here; the Cape fit her like a glove. It wasn't the whispers in the staff room or stares in the hallway. She could understand those. Everyone had their own opinion about her husband. Maybe meeting the jumper responsible for the 'Fugitive Professor' killings had something to do with it, or maybe learning she herself had supernatural DNA played a role. By teaching her to embrace frightening and mysterious powers she had repressed, Morrow had prepared her for her destiny as a caretaker, the job of protecting earthly lives from the reckless, vengeful souls in the unpredictable afterlife.

How does teaching in an elementary school measure up once you've glimpsed the realm of the unknown and helped take down a supernatural force bent on destroying the world?

It doesn't, but somebody's gotta pay the bills.

Entering the kitchen, she spied RG lounging at the kitchen table, skimming the *Boston Herald*, his laptop open in front of him. The early summer Cape Cod sun blazed through the open, wood-framed window, a salty breeze drifting through the flowing curtains tickled her nostrils, triggering a salvo of memories from a thousand other dazzling June mornings in Chatham. Kacey relished living in the place where she had grown up, her parents only a few miles down the road, a few hundred barefoot steps away from the Atlantic's swell. The Granville's new house surrendered at least half the square footage and an additional fifty years on their previous suburban Boston dwelling, but Kacey didn't mind.

Change required adaptation.

She glanced across the table at her husband, still in his pajama bottoms and white tee, a man without the day-to-day regimented life defining him for so long. She had never seen him so lost. He had paid a tremendous price for heroic actions no one would ever recognize or celebrate. It cost him every-thing, including the one thing he loved more than anything—his career. She had never considered how his career had defined him, and when he had lost it, it had emasculated him, affecting everything they had become.

But amidst the previous year-and-a-half's strife, fate had delivered a blessing in the form of Robert Jr., a boy named after his father. Over time, he had evolved into 'Junior,' history repeating itself as the second Robert in the household to relin-quish his first name.

RG pored over his laptop while shoving the second of three Dunkin' Donuts powdered sugars into his pie hole, not once taking his eyes off the screen to ensure proper hand-mouth coordination. RG's penchant for junk food hadn't posed a problem when he worked out regularly and kept himself active, but, since his injury, his trips to the gym had grown rarer than a harvest moon. He would joke how he deserved a break after saving the world from the apocalypse, but he had also been eating enough for the family of three, and Kacey continued to remind him he only counted as one.

"Goddamn Sox dropped their second in a row to the Twins."

Kacey threw her hands over Junior's ears and shot RG a disappointed glare. "Um, language? We have impressionable ears now."

"Damn...oops! Sorry, Junior." He ran a hand across the boy's head.

Kacey shook her head as the powder from his upper lip and cheek sifted onto his keyboard like a gentle snow. She stretched across the table for a napkin, but RG waved her away. Instead, he lowered his face to the table's edge and whistled for Baron. The German Shephard loped up beside him and licked the sugary mess from his chin.

Kacey's mouth hung open, her tongue pushing forward. "Ugh! You are disgusting."

"Just 'going green.'" He grinned as Baron's tongue graduated to the crumbs along his mouth.

"I don't have to kiss that face anymore, you know..."

"But you can't help yourself." He flashed his best headshot smolder.

"Have you checked messages?"

"Not today."

"Here, let me see." Kacey pulled the laptop across the table and spun it in her direction, logging in to their joint email account. She straightened in her chair as she spied the bolded '1' blinking at her from the trash icon. "Goddammit, RG!"

This time RG threw his hands over Junior's ears. "Um, language?" The boy squealed and pressed his father's hands against his head.

She folded her arms. "Not funny. There's a message in there from yesterday morning. Why didn't you tell me?"

"It's just another nut job looking for attention." He grabbed the third donut.

Kacey scowled as she snatched her readers off the counter and leaned over the table. "Six-one-seven area code, from a Molly Buckholtz." The silence pressed between them as Kacey read the message. "This doesn't sound so crazy to me."

"Kacey, trust me. It's another dead end. I don't even know why we keep that account."

"We haven't had a nibble in months, it's not like we don't have time to at least make contact and see what's going on." Kacey rose from the table. "Did you even read it?"

"I skimmed it."

"Well, she says 'the other one took him away. The one inside him.' What does she mean…took him away?"

RG reached into the donut box and pressed his finger against the powdered sugar layer lining the cardboard base.

"Could you at least try to work with me on this?"

"Okay, then." He licked the sweetness off his finger. "Demonic possession? An exorcism would probably do the trick, but that's above our pay grade."

"But she says 'it's been twenty years.' Could it be a jumper?"

RG gave a dismissive wave. "She probably means figuratively." He pushed back from the table, grabbed the donut box, and tossed it into the garbage. "The kid could have had some psychotic break, multiple personality or something, and has been gone…mentally for twenty years."

"Then why contact us? She could find help for a child with mental illness at any hospital."

"He could have wandered away twenty years ago, too. We don't know." He folded his arms. "Either way, she should call a psych ward…or the Catholic Church."

Kacey pressed her hands against her hips. "RG, here's a

woman in pain, reaching out after twenty years. Anyone answering our ad is at the end of their options. Could you be any less sympathetic?"

"What do you want from me?" he replied with a shrug. "I'm just being realistic here."

"Why won't you even consider it could be a jumper who took him away?"

"Because it's not likely." He collapsed into the kitchen chair, his eyes drifting back to his laptop.

"How do you know? You've had experience with one jumper."

"And I saved the world, don't you recall?" He blew a breath onto his fingertips before wiping them on his chest.

Kacey rolled her eyes. *Have another donut, Ironman!*

He tapped away on his keyboard.

"Is it too difficult to give me a moment of your attention?"

RG filled his cheeks and exhaled, closing the laptop. "All right, Morrow told me sometimes jumpers take their hosts back to their world to…well, take their time with them. But that's rare."

Kacey shuddered, recalling the time Victor Garrett, the burning man, had kept her captive in his filthy cave, the jumper they had defeated. "But it's possible?"

"Well, anything's possible, but——"

"Well, what if someone took him twenty years ago…"

"Then he's been dead for twenty years!" RG reached across the table for the *Herald*, snapping the paper open. "Nothing we can do. It's not like we can bring him back."

Kacey placed her fists on the table and leaned toward him, imagining the pain this woman must be enduring. "Why are you so hesitant to get involved here?" She had lived with the fear of losing her own unborn child when the burning man had been determined to kill her. Kacey's angst had lasted only weeks, but this Buckholtz woman had lived two decades grasping at a vague thread of hope, nurturing a glimmer of faith her son still lived or might return home. The depth of the woman's suffering and unanswered longing staggered Kacey like a slug to the chest.

"Someone's reaching out to us, someone in pain. We can at least call her and tell her—"

"And tell her what?" RG interrupted, pushing his chair back from the table and springing to his feet. "That we can find him? That we can discover what happened to him after all this time? We got lucky with the burning man, and you think we can walk on water."

Kacey clenched her teeth with a slow shake of her head. "She's been waiting twenty years to hold her boy again, and you don't seem to give a shit." Kacey grabbed her cell and stabbed at the keys. "Molly Buckholtz, this is Kacey Granville. We got your message. Tell me your address." She shot RG a burning glance. "We'll be right over."

———

Mike

Mike Stahl inched the Crown Vic down Main Street in Chatham, his eyes fixed on the road, but his mind a thousand miles away. He couldn't get that boy's face out of his mind, a face as innocent as his own stepson's, his future guillotined in the most violent, brutal way, not even an animal deserved. In his deepest anguish, Mike envisioned a softer, less frightening ending for the lively youngster forced to his death…he prayed his heart ceased and released his soul before his body ever broke against the pallet of rocks bearing the water's powerful surges. An early summer invasion of tourists and workday commuters clogging the roadway usually brought Stahl's blood pressure spiraling, but today it didn't register. Funny how tragedy deemed the mundane inconsequential. But Stennett consumed his thoughts. He clenched his teeth and pressed his head against the headrest, gripping the steering wheel the way he'd like to work Stennett's neck.

What affliction turns a man's heart to cold and brittle hate? After last night's discovery, he may not want to know.

Mike's thoughts drifted back to the previous night, when he had heard Stennett finally confess to the senseless murder. He had flown from the claustrophobic room and nicotine stench to assemble another team for the crime scene investigation awaiting them on Queen Anne Road. He had moved through Stennett's pitch-dark Cape-style home with detective Chris Daniels beside him. The recent heat and humidity had amplified the decaying fetor sifting through the living room floorboards from the cellar. As they descended the creaky wooden basement steps, small light halos from their flashlights pierced the dark and danced off the floor and walls, reflecting a blizzard of dust particles suspended midair.

And a cloud of buzzing flies.

Training their lights upward, they found what they had come for. The horrific images Stahl had conjured in his head from Stennett's revelation bore little resemblance to the one before his disbelieving eyes.

Maria Stennett's nude body dangled from the ceiling. A jump rope, duct tape, and garden hose tethered her arms and legs to the ceiling joists, sagging limbs reinforced with a nail gun. Her body slumped downward in places not secured with either, her head and stomach protruding at impossible angles, gravity and time exerting their effects. Her face wore a mask of pain and terror, left eye still open, mouth frozen in an eternal scream.

Stahl glanced at the youthful Daniels, a blonde brush cut

framing an honest face. He had put in a word for the former Falmouth detective over at the Bureau of Criminal Investigations, recommending him for Criminal Investigations Officer training and eventually recruiting him to the Chatham Police Department. Now the pair investigated crime scenes throughout the Cape and islands.

Mike had become his mentor and friend, despite the pair of bullets Daniels' former boss, Chuck Brennan, had slammed into Stahl's body a year and a half ago, moments before the police chief's horrific death. He had never talked to Daniels about it, and the detective had never asked. Searching his face for a reaction to the grisly scene, Mike observed nothing but a slight twitch at the corner of Daniels' mouth, the profession already reinforcing the thick shell needed to guard emotions.

"Looks like the bruising patterns in the knees, elbows, and neck resulted from the trauma, but I'm seeing older patterns, here…and here. Smaller bruising, too." Daniels shone his light along the body. "It looks like she had a rough go of it over the past few weeks." He pressed his lips together, shaking his head.

"Good eye, Chris." Stahl knelt on the floor, transferring a small penlight to his mouth. He opened up his kit to process the scene.

As they initiated the grueling work, footsteps tapped across the living room floor above, heading toward the basement. Russ Randle, the chief medical examiner in the County Coroner's office, snapped on the light at the top of the stairs.

"Some crime scene investigators you guys are."

"The best the state can afford," Stahl replied.

"State must be deep in the red." Russ joined the two in the shadowed substructure. "It helps to actually see what you're investigating."

"Depends…" Daniels stared upward.

Randle took a step back as his eyes followed Daniels' track. "Jesus...."

The three men stared in silence at the lifeless form hanging above them.

Stahl put a hand on Randle's shoulder. "Glad you're here, Russ."

"Not sure I am."

"Let's photograph the body and get her down," Stahl groaned.

The men struggled to untangle the corpse from the ceiling, the tightly sheathed body parts flattened against the ceiling joists' thick wood. Dark purple blotches swelled on the corpse's skin at the ligature sites. In several joists, they had to wrench the nails from the wood to extricate the body, while others remained embedded upon yanking her limbs and appendages free.

Stahl supported Maria Stennett's torso as Daniels and Randle pulled and tugged at her limbs. His head rested inches from hers, a frozen eye staring directly into his. No matter how he positioned his body or twisted to escape it, the eye followed him like one of those creepy posters in an old Cape Cod joke shop.

"How did he get her up there?" Daniels scratched his head. The three men had combed the basement for additional ropes or pulleys Stennett could have used to leverage the body but had found nothing. "It took three of us just to get her down."

Over the next several hours, they collected physical evidence. The team performed blood spatter analysis on each drop or smear sullying the basement floor. They recorded and measured finger and footprints; diagrammed, photographed, and video-recorded the position of all evidence. They had recovered and catalogued biological samples for subsequent lab work and had interviewed sleepy neighbors. They had laid Stennett's mangled corpse on the open body bag as Randle positioned the limbs inside and yanked the zipper, making the call of homicide as cause of death.

"I'll give you a call in a couple days, Mike. We'll have a clearer picture when the autopsy has been—"

A blaring car horn jolted Stahl from his daydream, a yawning empty road in front of him and a frustrated sea of motorists building behind him, a few gesturing with their hands and revving their engines.

Jesus, Mike, get a grip!

He gave a remorseful wave out the window as he accelerated down Main Street, surprisingly empty for both a workday and the start of the tourist season.

Chapter Three

'The tender Parents have scarce time to wipe
Their weeping eye loe heaven cauls and the other dies.'

In memory of ICHABOD SHAW HOLMES, died Nov. 1st,
1802 (Aged 1 year, 4 months) and CHANDLER HOLMES,
died Nov. 6th, 1802 (Aged 4 year, 10 months)
-Epitaphs from Burial Hill

June 15, 2019

Kacey

Kacey struggled to keep the Outback poised within Beacon Street's white lines as the squelching wipers thumped full speed, trying to keep up with a pounding summer rain. RG scrutinized Brookline's building facades across the sidewalk through a hand-cut circle in the fog-laden passenger-side window, trying to discern the faded numbers stenciled into brick and brownstone.

Kacey raised her voice above the hammering rain. "What do you see?"

"Sixteen-fourteen, sixteen-sixteen. What are we looking for again?"

"Sixteen-forty-six."

"Okay, coming up. Pull over wherever you can."

With no metered spaces in sight, Kacey banged a right at the next street and skidded into a 'Resident Permit Parking' space along the road. "What are the chances I won't get a ticket?"

"Zero percent."

Kacey rubbed her chin. "I'm comfortable with those odds." She glanced at RG, his jaw clenched, sensing his mentally preparing a check to the City of Boston's Parking Clerk.

Kacey killed the engine as the rain continued its assault. They both leaned back in their seats as they waited out the storm, optimistic for a break in the summer squall.

"Was Morrow upset when you showed up with Junior?"

"How could he be? He loves his grandson." Unable to find a babysitter on short notice, RG had paid a surprise visit to his father in the next world, delivering an unfed, cranky eighteen-month-old to an older man in a pristine and tastefully appointed, non-child-proofed home. "Besides, it'll be a couple hours, tops. How hard could it be?"

Kacey raised her eyebrow. *Really?*

"Okay, how do you want to do this?"

"Well, I'm gonna probe her, right away," Kacey replied, "confirm her story through her mind's images and memories. I don't want to waste time, like the last guy we visited."

"Ah, the old salt from Nantucket."

"Uh, no. The *loony tune* from Nantucket, told us he was Jonah, from the Bible."

"Well, he could have been legit. Nantucket *was* a whaling town…"

Kacey rolled her eyes. "The guy ogled my chest the entire time. Remember when he tried to…touch them."

"Can you blame the old guy? I'm guessing he hadn't been face-to-face with a set of ta-tas like yours in over half a century. I wonder if he ever got his nose to stop bleeding."

Kacey curled her hand into a fist, wiggling her eyebrows.

"At least we got a nice weekend out of it. And that lobster…to die for. We need to go back."

Does he ever think of anything but food? "If the only way I can get you to take me to Nantucket is by letting an aging Hobbit grab my boobs—"

"I know, I know, we should get out more." RG glanced upward as a rising rain crescendo swept over the Outback. "How 'bout we just tell Molly you need to verify things, tell her you're going into her mind?"

"The mind will resist, to protect itself. If she's aware what I'm doing, I won't get much from her. Just keep her occupied. Use a bit of the roguish charm you once had."

RG flinched like she had slapped him into a previous decade.

"I'll be in and out in seconds. Her memories will tell me all I need to know."

"Fair enough."

While most jumpers and caretakers had the ability to read thoughts streaming from someone's head, others could perform brief, split-second scans, probing the entire mind's history, moment by moment. RG had yet to refine this talent, but Kacey's abilities rivaled the best caretakers from the next world and beyond.

"We want to earn her trust before we reveal too much. The things we've seen would cause even the most desperate soul to question our sanity. Be patient, don't just go blurting things out."

"I'm the king of patience. Trust me."

Kacey grabbed his face and squeezed. "Just let me do most of the talking." She gave a quick kiss to his fish lips.

The two bolted from the car, sloshing through ankle-deep puddles collecting against the steep curb. After Buckholtz buzzed them into the building, they stepped into the birdcage-style elevator and closed the accordion gate with a crunch. With a whirr and drumbeat of concerning clunks, the platform ratcheted to the fourth floor.

At the apartment door, a woman's weary face filled the narrow space above the hanging chain, a vertical worry line indelibly etched between her eyebrows.

"Ms. Buckholtz? We're the Granvilles. We called earlier."

"Call me Molly." She closed the door to unfasten the chain and welcomed them into the tight apartment. "Let me grab a couple of towels for you. You're both soaked to the bone!" Kacey pegged Molly to be in her early fifties, a smattering of grey in her flowing blonde hair, a woman with the functional physique of a longtime city dweller.

After toweling off, Molly guided Kacey and RG through the apartment toward the living room couch. "Please, sit." She parked herself opposite them in an overstuffed chair.

The warped floorboards resting underfoot and patterned wallpaper peeling from the living room's ceiling corners dated the apartment. From what Kacey could gather, the woman had somehow managed to cobble together a comfortable living space. The sofa sat a little worn around the edges, its cording fraying at the corners, but the bright yellow patterned pillows offered a small token of optimism—something hard to come by in this woman's life. Kacey couldn't imagine how she would survive if something happened to Junior.

As RG initiated conversation, Kacey closed her eyes. She hesitated, reluctant to enter the woman's mind and witness her pain firsthand. She already sensed it, like a tumor growing from inside and bursting through her body's seams, enveloping her in a gloomy shroud. The room pulled away from her as she fell headlong into the woman's mind and tapped into her memory, learning about her, a burst of images flying past her like confetti in a breeze. Kacey slowed them down, latching onto the ones in the forefront of Molly's mind.

She visited a younger Molly as she ushered the last group of drunken frat boys from the Hammond Lounge, closed the door, and hoofed along a soggy Washington Street toward home. A grimy film layer clung to her skin, the combination of smoke and sweat embedded in her pores. The skies had opened during the evening, Beacon Street's rain-filled potholes projecting the blinking traffic signal's shimmering reflection. The May night's air already had a humid quality, but the early morning breeze brought with it summer's peaceful anticipation.

A heavy sigh burst across her lips; flavored alcohol smells permeated her clothes. On Friday nights, Molly wore everything a bit tighter and undid the bun corralling her frenzied blonde hair, letting it fall to her shoulders. Anything to help pry more money out of those college boys' tight fists. It hadn't been long ago she had given higher education a try, but academia had picked her bones clean like a lost doe in a coyote pack. A decade later, the life of a single mom on the opposite side of thirty had hardened Molly, who had scratched to make ends meet with a ten-year-old boy in tow.

To her friends, Molly described her boy, Gunnar, as a 'looker,' and Kacey couldn't help but agree—fire-red hair like his father's with matching dimples tucked into the crease of his cheeks, marking a smile destined to make the girls melt. But it was Molly herself who melted with each grin he flashed.

Kacey had sifted through a lifetime of memories in the time Molly and RG had blinked their eyes: Gunnar holding his mother's hand as he waded in the gentle Cape Cod surf, a cold, white foam flowing over his suntanned feet; the boy giving a spirited yawp atop a blue-saddled plastic horse on a carnival carousel, one hand grasping the pole, the other wind-milling his cotton candy as Molly watched from beyond the metal perimeter fence; mother and child playing pitch on the worn rug of their Brookline apartment as a sultry breeze parted the open window's curtains, the Sox game drifting from a portable radio on the window sill. Kacey fast-forwarded through the collage of images in her head, a subtle change overtaking the boy, his eyes going from a seawater blue to midnight onyx. She sensed a darkness prowling behind them. A presence lingered beside him, an odor she couldn't pinpoint permeated him, as if death had staked a claim on him, patient and waiting. She could tell Gunnar was disappearing, wearing his body's shell, but having relinquished the soul beneath it.

Kacey joined Molly as she slipped into Gunnar's room the night before he disappeared, nestling beside him on his bed, her gaze dissecting her son's delicate features like a surgeon. She traced his jawline's curve and upturned nose as a soft snore chafed his throat, admiring her little work of art, the one thing in her life she had done right. The nightlight cast a dull glow across the room, exposing comic books and toys littering the floor, clothes draped across the dresser drawers. Kacey swooned at the murky smell emanating from within the boy. A pair of tears surprised Molly, winding down her face and disappearing into his down comforter. Maybe she sensed the darkness, too. She had leaned over and whispered into her son's ear, kissed him on the cheek. She rose from the bed, tiptoed across the floor's obstacle course, and closed the door, glancing back once more to solidify the image to take her through the night.

The next morning, Molly burst into Gunnar's room with two chocolate covered sprinkles from Dunkin' Donuts. When she reached to wake him, the bed lay empty.

Molly never saw him again.

Kacey discontinued the probe, voices fading in from the background. "…Well, thank you, Mr. Granville."

"Please, call me RG…"

"And call me Kacey," she interjected, hoping she had reinserted herself into the conversation at the proper moment.

"Thank you both for coming." Molly deliberated a moment, squinting at RG's face. "Hope you don't mind my asking, but have we met before? You look familiar."

"I don't think so. I must have that kind of face."

Molly stood and circled the couch as they fell into an awkward silence, her eyes fixed on RG. "Your name sounds familiar, too. Are you the guy from BU…? The one who got away with murder a couple years back? The 'Fugitive…Teacher?'"

"It's 'Fugitive Professor,'" RG corrected her, still oddly protective of his one-time criminal moniker.

Kacey shot RG a glare. "The police cleared my husband of all—"

"Doesn't mean he didn't do it," Buckholtz interrupted. "I've watched those murder shows on *20/20*."

"The only thing I've ever killed is a good joke…and the moment," he snickered. "Ask anyone."

Molly continued circling. "I read about a financial scheme with your murdered friend. How can I be sure you're not here to scam me somehow?"

"Scam you how?" RG asked, his palms raised.

"Take my money, what else? Convince me you can find my son, play on my emotions a bit. Easy to prey on the weak and desperate, isn't it?"

"Have people done this to you?" Kacey inquired.

"Well, not like they could get much out of me," Molly waved an arm around the apartment, "but it doesn't mean they haven't tried. I've had your type call me before. Psychics. Telling me they've been in contact with my son, that he wants to come home. They know where to find him. If you just pay me—"

"Don't forget," RG cut her off. "You contacted us."

Kacey glared at him, using her powers to communicate with him in silence. *"We need to earn her trust."*

"She thinks I'm a murderer."

"We don't want money, and we're not psychics." Kacey stood and faced Molly. "I understand you're wary, but we're both blessed with powerful gifts. Let us help you."

"I could have invited a murderer into my apartment. Your husband could be crazy. How would I know?"

Kacey's eyes softened. "Sometimes you have to trust."

"Have they charged anyone else yet, for the murders?"

"No one ever will be," RG offered.

"How come?"

RG threw his hands out to his sides. "Because a supernatural killer from the next world committed the murders!"

"You *are* fucking crazy." Molly scampered across the room to the front door and flung it open. "Out with the both of you, now!"

"What the fuck, RG? The king of patience?"

"She's gotta hear the truth or we're gonna sit here all day."

Kacey glared at him, his damn attitude driving a wedge between them and the person they were trying to help. How would she ever earn this woman's trust and get to the bottom of Gunnar's disappearance if she was the only one committed to this?

"Molly, just wait. Hear me out," Kacey pleaded.

"Why should I?" Molly's hand hung on the open door.

"Because your son Gunnar's missing, and we're your last chance to find out what happened to him."

"Okay, if you're as special as you say, wow me. Show me your gifts. Tell me something you couldn't possibly know about us."

Kacey sifted through the woman's memories. "Well, someone took Gunnar from his bed twenty years ago, in this very apartment."

Molly scoffed. "Common knowledge available in any police report or newspaper article. What else?"

Kacey took deliberate steps toward Molly. "You dropped out of Emerson your sophomore year after you got pregnant. You ended up tending bar at the Hammond Lounge."

"You talk to any of my neighbors, they'll tell you the same thing."

"After work each night, you'd go into Gunnar's room. You'd lean over and kiss him, whisper in his ear."

Molly continued to hold the door, tapping her foot.

"You whispered the same words your mother used to sing to you at night. But you didn't sing, you said them… just four words. 'You are my sunshine.'"

Molly's hand dropped from the door as it swung closed with a clunk. She lowered her head, her chin quivering as fat tears toppled down her cheeks.

Kacey stood silent before her, the staccato pop of rain picking up, slapping against the whining window air conditioner.

Molly threw a hand over her mouth as she sprinted into

the kitchen. Kacey and RG eyed each other from across the room, not sure whether to follow. Minutes later, Molly returned, balancing a tray holding three cups of steaming hot coffee and placed it on the coffee table with an audible clink.

"So, you can help me?" Molly lowered herself into her chair.

RG and Kacey returned to the couch. "Why do you suppose we came all this way to see you?"

"I sense a power inside you," Molly acknowledged, resting a hand on Kacey's forearm. "More than I get from him." She shrugged as she turned to RG. "No offense."

"None taken. I'm still kinda the apprentice."

"Something struck me when I read your ad online, a feeling I can't explain. Then, when you opened the door, there it was again. I'm sorry I tested you, but I had to be sure." Molly gazed upward as she dabbed her damp eyes with a napkin.

Kacey leaned forward and took hold of Molly's hand. "Gunnar changed in the weeks before he disappeared. What happened?"

Molly's grip tightened. "He'd been fine until about a week or so before he left me, but then a change fell over him, and it turned more disturbing with each passing day."

"How?" RG probed.

"At first, he'd grown distant, withdrawn, almost overnight. Wasn't communicating at all. But his eyes bothered me most."

"What about them?" Kacey asked.

"Gunnar had these beautiful, mischievous eyes. They revealed everything about him, his heart, his dreams…his deepest secrets. But toward the end, a dark shadow crept in, drawing the life from them."

"So, they changed color?"

"It's more like something had *pulled* the color from them."

Kacey and RG exchanged a glance. Kacey recognized in RG's eyes the first hint of credence to her story, that there might be something there. She had believed it the moment she had entered the apartment.

"Sometimes I'd glimpse a flash of someone through the inky blackness, maybe Gunnar, maybe someone else...I couldn't tell."

"What do you mean by someone else?" Kacey leaned forward.

"Different eyes in my boy's head. Someone else's."

Molly steadied the cup in her hands, slowly lowering it to the table.

"He spent a lot of time alone in his room, and I'd overhear him talking with someone. I used to sneak up close and listen through the door. I chalked it up to an imaginary friend, but it would go on for hours on end. He never talked to anyone else, and he stopped talking to me. Day by day, I watched him disappear inside himself."

"Then he vanished?" Kacey asked.

"Whatever lived inside of him took him away. I'm sure of it."

RG stood and circled the room, rubbing his chin. "What did you tell the detectives? They must have questioned you."

"I couldn't tell them what I suspected. They would have slapped the cuffs on me and measured me for a straightjacket. I kept my suspicions to myself."

RG nodded his head, recalling his own hard lessons learned with law enforcement. "You did the right thing."

Kacey sensed the change in RG's attitude, some empathy finally showing up. "Did they ever find any evidence of an abduction? A kidnapping? Anything at all?"

"The case went cold. The detectives eventually directed

their investigation toward me, but with no evidence…no body…they just gave up. I'm sure they still think I'm guilty."

"Listen, Molly." Kacey arose from the couch. "I'm getting stirrings there could be a…supernatural explanation to this. My senses heighten around these events, and my radar's buzzing. But I have to be frank with you. It's been twenty years, the chance that Gunnar, well—"

"I understand…" Molly interrupted, her voice trailing off. She stood and collected the half-filled coffee cups, hurrying to place them on the tray.

Kacey stepped toward her, giving her an awkward hug. "I'm so sorry."

Molly held the tray to her side as Kacey continued the embrace. She finally whispered, "Just find out what happened to my boy."

Chapter Four

'O ever blest and happy one
Whose little pilgrimage was done.'

In memory of SUSAN EDWARDS, died Nov 22, 1825 (Aged
3 years, 2 months)
-Epitaphs from Burial Hill

July 4, 1946

Malachi

"Now, Malachi, don't be shocked at the way Uncle Bradford, Aunt Millie, and Cousin Elias live." Emerson Alcott Pratt shouted from the front seat. With the car top down, Malachi had to listen hard to hear what he said. "They're only getting back on their feet again after Mr. Ashton's return from the war."

"Yes, Father." Ten-year-old Malachi Pratt nodded and

tugged on his collar. He didn't like the stiff, white button-down shirt and scratchy knickers his mom made him wear. He tore at his shirttails as he scooted into the huge automobile's backseat. He hoped his mother didn't see. He hated when she fussed at him and smoothed out all the wrinkles. And if she spotted the slingshot dangling from his pocket, she might have something to say about that.

"Now don't you pay attention to the cad in the front seat, Mal." Sarah Pratt leaned over and reached a hand over his head. He tried to duck. The way she ruffled his hair and messed it all up again after she told him to comb it would make him have to do it all over again. "My brother and sister-in-law work hard, and they're doing fine down there in Plymouth, you'll see. Plus, the ocean doesn't care how much money you have. It lets everyone swim in it." She kissed the top of his head and wrapped an arm around him, squeezing him. Now he would have that smelly stuff she splashed on herself all over him.

Malachi gawked at all the fancy houses with the leaves growing up the brick walls, kind of like the stadium where the Cubs played. And he would bet you could just about fit an entire baseball diamond inside the fenced-in yards, too. He and his friends could get lost on those lawns. He felt lucky to live in such a beautiful neighborhood along Commonwealth Avenue. His father used to be a lawyer until everyone wanted him to help the governor. He wasn't quite sure why his father didn't want to be a lawyer anymore, but his mother told him all about how a person doesn't turn down the chance to serve the great people of Massachusetts, which was fine with him because he got to meet a lot of important people. His father even met the president once, so he was really important now.

This July Fourth weekend, Aunt Millie had invited them all down to the shore in Plymouth. His father didn't really want to go, preferring to vacation with the folks on the Vineyard or Nantucket. He would say his aunt and uncle were a bit too 'blue collar,' but Malachi didn't see them wear anything like that. Malachi loved Aunt Millie's family, especially his nine-year-old cousin Elias. He couldn't remember the last time he had been to the beach, and he didn't want to miss a chance to see them again. His parents agreed to drive him to North Station to catch the train to the shore. This would be the first year his family didn't celebrate the Fourth of July together, but even if he stayed, he wouldn't have been with them anyway. The governor had invited his parents to watch the fireworks on the Charles River, with a whole bunch of important people, and he would have had to stay home.

Riding in the car through downtown Boston, Malachi stared at all the sights and sounds around him. The whole city looked like one of those fancy stage productions at the Colonial Theatre his mom and dad took him to, shiny automobiles and bicycles zipping through cobblestone streets. He would laugh the way men and women hopped out of the way, hurrying from sidewalk to sidewalk to keep from getting run over.

He leaned out the window and looked straight up until his neck hurt, staring at men balancing on the iron beams of half-built buildings as high as the clouds. The streets smelled like grilled meat and cheeses from the restaurants' and cafés' open windows. He had never seen so many people eating at the same time, and he could hear the ones who weren't waiting in line for a table bicker and bargain with the old men at the fruit and vegetable carts lining the sidewalks.

When the Rolls pulled up in front of North Station, Malachi burst from the vehicle, spinning 360 degrees to take in everything around him.

"Now you be careful, Malachi," Emerson Pratt warned,

jolting him back to reality, "and be respectful of the Ashtons." He raised an eyebrow at his son.

"Yes, sir." Malachi climbed into the backseat and grabbed his valise, then extended his hand.

His father grasped his hand like he was shaking hands with the governor, making him smile. "Give Mr. and Mrs. Ashton our best."

His mother led him down the sidewalk. She put his hand in hers and guided him into North Station, its huge doors like something from a medieval castle. They strolled over to the ticket window and paid the round-trip fare for the 2:20 to Kingston.

With ticket in hand, Malachi took in North Station for the first time. Steam engine trains stood glittering before him, lined up beside each other along row after row of tracks. He threw his hands over his ears as the steam puffed white smoke and the engines hissed. He gazed skyward at the huge riveted metal girders rising from the cement platforms, forming an archway underneath the glassed-in ceiling way up above the tracks. Smoke and steam rose from the tracks like the whole building was on fire, and Malachi could no longer see the sun.

They pushed through the crowds, someone stepping on his toes and another almost knocking him to the ground, but they finally made it to the number four train. His mother kneeled beside him on the platform as the conductor checked his pocket watch and shouted a final boarding call. He counted the shiny brass buttons on the conductor's spotless uniform, thinking one day he would like to work in a train station if they gave you big fancy time piece like that.

"Now the Ashtons will be waiting for you at the station. Stay in your seat and mind your manners. Say your prayers at night, and we'll meet you right here on this spot, Sunday afternoon." She made a small X on the dusty platform.

"Okay." He hugged his mother and held on tight. "I love you, Mom."

"Me too, Mal." She bit down on her lip, trying to hide the way it would shake sometimes.

"Gonna miss you."

"It's only three days. I bet the minute you spot Elias you won't so much as think about us until the train pulls back into North Station." She gave him a slobbery kiss on his cheek as he boarded, but he waited until he got to his seat before wiping it with his sleeve. He pressed his nose to the window, his mother still standing there on the platform as the train jerked forward. She blew a final kiss. He pretended to catch it and put it in his pocket, making her lip do that thing again. He would miss her most.

In less than an hour, the train pulled into Kingston with a high-pitched screech and explosion of steam from the engine car. When he spotted the Ashtons waiting below the platform, leaning against their old jalopy, he had to remind himself to breathe again. Uncle Bradford had his work pants and white tee-shirt on, suspenders hanging below his waist, while Aunt Millie wore her old food-stained apron from the delicatessen, her hair pinned back in a bun—exactly as he remembered them. He couldn't wait to try one of her pies. She had a different one every time he visited, as if she made them just for him. They waved to him through the glass.

With a whole bunch of slow people in the aisles, Malachi figured he had honored his mother's wishes long enough. Grabbing his overnight bag, he leaped over the seat backs until he arrived at the back of the car. He jumped from the train and out onto the platform.

"Malachi!" Elias burst past his parents to reach his cousin.

Malachi couldn't wait to show him the jacks he had stuffed in his pocket. "Elias, look what I brought." He held his hand out to show him the small cloth bag holding the new game, opening it and dumping out the silver pieces and the rubbery ball. "Do you like to play? I bet I can beat you."

Fidgeting in his own pockets, Elias whipped out a handful of marbles, all the bright colors in the glassy balls catching Malachi's eye. He had marbles of his own, but these looked different. Then Elias opened his other hand. "I got some new shooters, too."

Before long, Malachi had traded his New York Yankees Joe DiMaggio baseball card for Elias's Ted Williams, but that was about all he wanted to give up. Maybe he would change his mind before he went back home, but he didn't think so.

"Bet you don't have one of these," Elias said after sticking his baseball cards in his back pocket. Out came a penknife, but Malachi quickly took out his Swiss Army Knife his dad had given him for Christmas and watched Elias's hand hover over it as if he were afraid to touch it unless he had permission.

"And wait until you see this," Malachi said, poking his hand into his back pocket for the best thing of all. Proudly, he showed off his slingshot, happy his mother had not found it and taken it from him. Elias's eyes grew wide.

"That's swell! Where'd you get it?" Elias beamed.

"Made it myself from the maple tree in my front yard."

Elias pulled on the rubber tubing, nodding his head. "How'd you get it so stiff? I bet this thing won't ever snap."

"I heated the wood to remove the moisture. That's what makes it harden." He ran his fingertips along the grip's jagged indentations and turned it over to show Elias the crude 'M' he had carved underneath the handle. "We'll knock some birds out of the trees when we get home."

Uncle Bradford and Aunt Millie leaned against their motor car, waiting. He sensed they wanted to come up and give him a hug, but they probably figured he and Elias had a lot of catching up to do, so they waited their turn. Still, he would have blathered with his cousin until nighttime if the Ashtons hadn't climbed the platform to gather them up.

"Malachi, it's a privilege to have you under our roof for the next few days. I'm sorry your father wasn't feeling well enough to join us." Uncle Bradford tousled his hair the way his mother did. He never could figure out why grownups always rubbed the top of kids' heads like that. "We have all sorts of adventures planned for you."

Aunt Millie knelt and hugged Malachi like a python, squeezing the breath from his lungs. "Well, you've been growing like a weed, haven't you?" she announced, her eyes all glossy like Elias's marbles.

"There she goes again." Uncle Bradford turned and gave Malachi a smirk. "It doesn't take much to get the waterworks flowing." He reached his arm around his wife and pulled her close, planting a peck on her cheek. "We've missed you, Son."

Mr. Ashton grabbed Malachi's valise as he and Elias scrambled into the backseat, gibber-jabbering nonstop on the bouncy drive to Plymouth.

For dinner, the Ashtons boiled lobsters and steamers with fresh corn on the cob. Malachi couldn't quite figure out how to get at all the meat out from under that hard shell, but when he did, it wasn't worth the effort. It tasted like rubber dipped in seawater. He filled up on corn and slipped most of the chewy meat to Elias's dog underneath the table. The Ashtons were amazed old Rexy showed anyone so much attention. He usually just lay by the door and slept.

In the evening, they strolled to the waterfront for the fireworks display, the deafening explosions sounding like they were in a war. Uncle Bradford was the strongest man Malachi had ever seen; but, for some reason, each blast made him close his eyes and reach for Aunt Millie's hand. Still, Malachi had never seen anything as beautiful. Colorful streaks lit the night sky over the harbor, casting eerie shadows over the wooden fishing vessels moored below. Afterward, they waited in line for ice cream at Mr. Brigham's diner, just down from the Ashton's delicatessen. They slurped their melting cones as they strolled through town, Mr. and Mrs. Ashton pausing every few feet to greet friends and neighbors coming from all directions to tell them what cold cuts and cheeses to add to their store's display case and to compliment Aunt Millie on her breads and muffins. How could anyone know so many people? The Ashtons had to be the most popular family in all of Plymouth, maybe all of Massachusetts. Malachi wondered if the governor might need his uncle's help, too.

He played along the harbor's rocky shore with Elias and his schoolmates, searching for hermit crabs and climbing in and out of the drainpipes running under the road. Later, Uncle Bradford unlocked the deli and served up the sherbet and Boston cream pie Mr. Brigham had dropped off at the store earlier in the day. On the walk home, it was so late Malachi could hardly keep his eyes open. He almost wished Uncle Bradford had picked him up and let him fall asleep on his shoulder, but he was too old for that now.

"We kept you out much later than we told your parents we would," Mr. Ashton said. Then he winked. "But we can keep a secret if you can."

"Yes, sir!" Malachi pumped Mr. Ashton's extended hand.

The next morning, Malachi and Elias sprang from their beds as the hazy sun climbed above the waves, eager to hit the shore, not too happy they had to do morning chores first.

"Can we go now?" Elias would ask every time they finished a task.

"Did you make your beds?"

"Then can we go?"

After they had swept the kitchen and washed the last dish, they piled into the back of the beat-up car for the short trip to White Horse Beach.

All morning, Malachi and Elias built sand castles, leaped and climbed across slick rocks, raced each other into the surf, and tasted vendors' snacks along the boardwalk. Malachi's gritty hands put as much sand in his mouth as cotton candy and popcorn, but it tasted great all the same. At noon, they hitched a ride into Plymouth to the deli. Malachi's empty stomach groaned, and he downed two of Aunt Millie's thick roast beef sandwiches and a huge piece of pie...and he was still hungry. Afterward, he and Elias helped Uncle Bradford and Aunt Millie tidy up the store after the lunchtime rush and bolted back to the beach to pick up where they had left off.

On their way home, the late afternoon sun dipped in the sky but was still bright enough to keep Malachi warm. He dragged his exhausted body across a long, grassy field, a shortcut to Elias's neighborhood. If Elias had been game, he would have happily laid down in the field and taken a nap, he had never been so tired. How did anyone have the energy to live near the beach? Malachi peered toward the sky, the warm sun tickling his face. He stuck his tongue out a few times, trying get the salty taste out of his mouth. He brushed the sand stuck to his legs, letting the sweeping grass knock off the rest.

He pressed his fingers against his sunburned arm, giggling as his skin changed from red to white, and back again. Distracted by the show, he slogged a little slower and covered his mouth as he blew out a huge yawn. He stopped long enough to stretch before he plowed ahead, taking a long step to keep up with Elias. But when his foot came down and stomped the tall grass, it kept on going. He waved about, trying to find his balance, but his body dropped from underneath him, like a roller coaster cresting a hill. Tumbling, he fell headlong through wet wooden boards and into pitch darkness. His shrill scream bounced back at him as his back smashed into cold stone, his body falling and rolling through the air like the shooter in Elias's pocket. He gazed about helplessly, unable to make out anything but blackness, even blacker than his bedroom when he woke in the middle of the night. As his screeching voice died out, he slammed into water. He couldn't catch his breath. His chest ached and stung as he splashed about. He paddled his hands to keep from going under. The last thing he heard before the slimy water crept up his face and into his ears was Elias, yelling at him.

"Malachi! Malachi! Hang on! I'm going for help!"

Dizzy from the fall, Malachi swung his arms until his head came up out of the water. He gazed up the long tunnel, barely able to see light at the top. He spat nasty water out of his mouth. "Help me, Elias. Help!" But it sounded more like a whisper. His hands reached out, his fingers brushing soft, mossy walls. He pulled his hand back and cried out again. His arms stopped treading. Too heavy. Too tired. The well too dark. He tried to reach out again, but his hands slipped against the rocky sides. Why couldn't he find something to hold him up longer, just a little longer? If he could stand on the bottom, he would be okay until Elias came back. But the well was too deep. The cold water made him shiver and his lips quivered just like his mom's.

He wanted her now. Elias, get my mom… "I want to go home…"

He inhaled another mouthful of water. He gagged, choked, fought to spit it out, but more water flooded into his mouth. His arms didn't want to move. He couldn't even lift them. All he wanted to do now was climb into his big bed back home, raise the covers to his chin, and have his mom read to him again.

Maybe one last story.

He fell deeper and deeper into the well, wondering whether his feet would ever touch the bottom. He pictured the living room on Christmas morning, the smoldering fireplace embers casting a holy glow across the glittering ornaments dangling from the tree; and his cocker spaniel, Jiggs, sleeping beside him before the hearth, paws resting across his forearm as he practiced his school lessons. His lungs reflexively inhaled a mouthful of water, leading to a brief thrashing. Then another.

Then nothing.

Mom, are you here yet? Hurry, Mom, hurry.

As his world shaded in black, he could see his mother's face looking down at him, but this time she was crying. He reached out to hold her hand, to tell her everything would be all right. She was here now. That's all he needed. His mom. And now he could tell her she'd been wrong. She had said he'd be having such a good time that he wouldn't so much as think about her before Sunday.

Chapter Five

'Alas her tuneful warbling breath,
Is hushed forever, hushed in death.'

In memory of ELIZABETH OWEN, died January 30, 1825
(Aged 3 year & 5 months)
-Epitaphs from Burial Hill

June 15, 2019

RG

RG and Kacey barreled along Route 3 toward the Cape in silence, immersed in the aftermath of the Molly Buckholtz visit, recounting conversations, attempting to put into context events they couldn't fathom. By the time they arrived in Chatham and pulled up to the house, they had a highway's drive worth of questions, but no answers. Only one person could help them make sense of it all.

As Kacey killed the engine, RG pivoted in his seat. "How about I pick up Junior and the old man and we head to the Pancake Man for a debriefing. I'm getting a bit hungry, too."

He could read in Kacey's eyes her understanding they wouldn't be hopping into the car again and braving the Route 28 traffic to the South Yarmouth restaurant. They would be going to the exact replica she had constructed in her mind, the childhood place where she spent her Sunday mornings with her family and where her nightly dreams took her. As she got older, the reconstructed memory would serve as the portal through which she would advance herself to the next world. When RG assumed his powers, he had also learned to use the portal, more as an excuse to sample the breakfast specials than anything else.

"I'll grab a booth," she insisted. "But for breakfast number two today, you're getting the fruit plate."

RG frowned as he spotted her eyes drift to his burgeoning waistline.

They hustled along the walkway toward the front door. The rain had stopped somewhere around Hingham, the hazy Cape Cod sun now piercing the blanketing cloud cover, harbingers of a potential scorcher. Inside the house, he led Kacey to the couch and made a quick detour into the kitchen, searching through the pantry.

"Hey, where did you put—"

"Check the third drawer beside the stove," she shouted.

"Got it!" Hurrying to the living room, he dropped onto the cushion beside her.

Kacey grinned at the package in his hand. "Well, aren't you thoughtful?"

"The word 'wonderful' springs to mind." He grabbed her hand. "Ready?"

"Lead the way."

RG reached over and twirled his wedding ring. In an instant, a yawning chasm opened before them, a fissure between worlds, startling in its absence of sound or light. Through a dark mist, they dropped into the swirling stillness, a gentle tumble along a hazy coiled pathway connecting their world to the next. Through the turbulent calm, the restaurant's familiar outline took shape before them.

As they stepped inside, RG watched nostalgia bloom in Kacey's eyes at the familiar waitstaff bussing tables and clinking dirty glasses and plates; griddle-fried breakfast potatoes and bacon aromas wafting from the busy kitchen; the service bell's metallic ping as orders lined up along the pick-up window; and the dull roar of cheery family conversations. He scanned the bustling restaurant, a younger version of Kacey, her hair in French braids, sat with her youthful parents in a booth in the corner, getting ready to order breakfast.

"It's like returning to your childhood home to find nothing's changed." She grabbed his hand and strolled to an empty booth.

"I'm gonna pick up Morrow and Junior. Don't forget how Morrow likes his fresh-squeezed—"

"Yeah, yeah, I'm on it," she interrupted, waving her hand.

"Be back in a few." He gave her a kiss and strode through the restaurant's front door, dropping back into the abyss.

As RG continued his journey, the darkness dissipated, and his vision cleared. He found himself standing before his father's house, his eyes adjusting to the next world's explosive colors—reality on steroids—staggering his earthly visual field unaccustomed to such extravagance.

Morrow lived in a wooded area at the edge of a field, a churning brook tumbling behind the ranch-style dwelling. RG gazed about in awe at this eventual world's heightened textures and shades, as if with each soul advancement, the existential

designer had refreshed the palette and sweated the details
more. Each blade of grass, swaying leaf, and cloud in the sky
fell upon the eye in vivid detail, viewed through a magnified
lens, the bird and cricket chirps tickling the ear in a cosmic
surround sound, Dolby for the afterlife. Colors hit the cornea
in a Technicolor explosion, the incomprehensible hues falling
outside his own world's limited rainbow spectrum, but
possessing tinctures unmistakably correct in the grand design,
colors meant to be.

RG shook his head as he stepped onto the wraparound
porch and approached Morrow's front door.

And my father picks white with black shutters…

He knocked on the door and waited. Hearing no sound
from within, he grasped the handle and stepped into the foyer.
Turning the corner, his mild concern melted into disbelief as
he beheld Junior gazing at his picture book on the living room
floor. The room appeared as if a tornado had hit, seat cushions from Morrow's handcrafted furniture strewn about the
floor. Spilled food and drinks soaked into the handwoven
carpet, and a toppled lamp rested beside an overturned
end table.

Morrow himself appeared in greater disarray than his
surroundings.

He lay zonked out on the couch, head thrown back on the
decorative back cushions, a soft snore escaping his throat. One
arm rested half in and half out of his dark suit jacket, his tie
hung from the overhead light fixture, his white pearl shirt lay
half untucked over his trousers, and his hat had somehow
migrated to Junior's head.

Next time I call the sitter service.

"Dad!" RG gave Morrow a poke in the ribs. "Hey, slacker,
we don't pay our babysitters to sleep on the job."

Morrow groaned as he snapped back to reality. "You don't

pay your babysitters anything at all as far as I can see…cheapskate."

RG scooped Junior into a bear hug, kissing his stomach to squeals of laughter. "Yeah, but I did bring you something."

Morrow perked up in anticipation as RG tossed the bag of fun-size Kit-Kats into his lap, transferring his hat from Junior's head to his father's. Morrow wasted no time opening the bag and stripping a candy from its wrapper, his eyes closing as he bit into the crispy chocolate-covered wafer. In a world where everything existed but chocolate, RG relished the power he wielded over Morrow's earthly addiction.

Morrow's eager fingers worked at a second wrapper. "Oh, Robert, you shouldn't have."

"Probably not." He reached into the bag and snagged one for himself. *Fruit plate my ass!* He bit into the candy, glancing around the room. "My God, all this after only three hours together?"

"You should have seen it *before* we cleaned up."

"You know, in the future we'll stick with our regular twelve-year-old sitter. She has a bit more stamina than you and runs a tighter ship...kind of like Mom used to." A smile creased RG's face. "You should be ashamed, she would never have let Junior get the best of her. Do you remember how she would—"

Morrow cleared his throat, straightening as he rose from the couch. "What do you say we get this mess cleaned up?" He turned and jammed his hands against his hips as if inspecting the room's damage, lingering for a moment before stepping into the kitchen. He returned after a lengthy absence with a bucket of water and a sponge, dropping to a knee to scrub the stains from the carpet.

RG gazed at the old man in silence as he moved about the room, righting lamps and repositioning seat cushions, contemplating his father's odd reaction to the mention of his mother.

By the time they had finished reassembling the room to its former glory, Junior had fallen fast asleep on the couch.

"Now he goes down…" Morrow scratched his head.

"Listen, Kacey and I need to talk to you about a case. Want to join us at the Pancake Man for a late breakfast?"

"Sounds wonderful. I am a bit famished. I'll just wake the boy and we can——"

"Let's give him a minute," RG interrupted, raising a hand. "Come with me. I need to ask you something?"

He led Morrow through the front door. They settled onto the porch swing, the chain-links tightening against the ceiling joist with a strained groan as it took their weight. They settled into the sway, Morrow resting an arm across the swing's seatback.

"So, I'm talking to Junior this morning, telling him he's gonna see Grampa today, and he turns to me and asks why he doesn't have a Gramma." RG shrugged and turned to his father. "Such a simple question…but I didn't have an answer for him. I've never had an answer."

Morrow sagged as he lowered his head.

"I mention her to you for the first time since…I don't know when, and you turn and leave the room."

Morrow busied himself, wiping his glasses on his shirt to avoid RG's burning gaze.

"I've never pressed, either. I've waited for you to tell me, but you haven't. Why?"

"I had a feeling sooner or later you'd ask." Morrow shifted in the seat. "I never meant to be deceptive. It's just the time was never right."

"I just need to know." RG waited, the breeze ruffling the field grass, sending a springtime pollen aroma wafting toward the porch. "Why isn't Mom here with you?"

Morrow gnawed on his lower lip. "She didn't make it to this world, Robert."

"But this is the next world...where did she go?"

Morrow stood and shuffled to the porch rail, gazing out toward the woods. He rubbed a small spot of peeling paint from the two-by-four he leaned against. "This is *a* next world, not *the* next world."

RG bounded to his feet. "What the hell does that mean?"

"It means we're not all destined for the same existential plane. My caretaker duties took me here. Her destiny was elsewhere."

"But your souls belong together. She mourned you every day of her life. She spoke of you with her dying breath, she—"

"I know, Robert," Morrow said, cutting him off. "I was there."

Of course. "Don't shared souls continue on together?"

"Mmm...not always. But souls have a way of eventually finding each other, especially if they end up in the same place. They're like magnets. There's an attraction that cannot be repelled."

"But what if they're not in the same place?"

"Then it takes longer, sometimes many lifetimes to find each other again. For separated souls, their current life has an emptiness, a hole that's never quite filled."

"That sounds like the definition of hell."

Morrow folded his hands behind his back. "Oh, they get through life okay. They experience joy and happiness, though fleeting. They can sense something's missing."

"Because their shared soul is elsewhere?"

Morrow nodded. "The person doesn't know it, but the soul does."

RG poked him in the chest. "And, so do you. You understand what you have to live without."

"The ongoing curse of being a caretaker," he said, lowering his gaze. "I had to give up one part of my soul to satisfy the other half."

"The other half…?"

"To be with you, Robert." Morrow draped his arm around RG's shoulders and massaged his neck with his palm. "Helen and I will meet again. Our souls will match up one day. I'm sure of it."

RG backed up and sank onto the porch swing. "Did you ever…look for her anywhere?"

Morrow pressed his lips together. "I did once. It took many years to find her." He drew a weary sigh. "She lived in a small village…near the ocean. I found her resting on a bench outside a café, her eyes closed, soaking up the late morning sunshine. I wasn't quite used to the colors of her world, and when they surrounded her, she appeared like an angel."

Morrow gazed across the field, but RG could sense his eyes viewed nothing but the woman projected in his memory.

"I could taste the salt from the misting surf drifting through the air as I approached her. She couldn't see me, of course. All I wanted was to sit with her a while. We used to sit together for hours, hardly saying a word sometimes. I figured it would be like it used to be, just for a little while. Pathetic, right?"

Not at all.

"When I got closer, I could hardly breathe. I did a quick scan and discovered she had a fulfilling life. She had friends and a life filled with purpose. A full life." Morrow turned to face RG, tears balancing on his lower eyelids. "But she had no one to share it with. In that life, she wasn't meant to have another, and won't until we're together again. When I sat down with her, she opened her eyes, a light ignited behind them. She had a moment of profound longing as she sensed something missing inside, something she couldn't pinpoint. Thankfully, it waned after I got up and strode past her."

"You'd spent years searching for her, and you just left?"

"I couldn't stay there and spark her emptiness. I couldn't stand witnessing the sadness I'd caused. The rest of the day I observed from afar. I never went back."

"I'm sorry, Dad." RG rose from the swing and stood next to his father. "I miss her, too."

Morrow turned toward the house, leaning against the porch rail. "But I got to hear her voice again."

"So, we only share souls with one other, and we wait forever for that match?"

"Your world's great poets had it right."

RG shifted his weight from one foot to the other, the porch floorboards squealing beneath him.

"You ever hear the quote by Willie Nelson?"

RG flinched. "Willie's one of our great poets?"

"Universally accepted as one of your best. At least in these parts."

RG nodded, tilting his head with a shrug.

"In his infinite wisdom he once said, 'ninety-nine percent of the world's lovers are not with their first choice. That's what makes the jukebox play.' People get by, but they long for that one percent. Somehow Willie had it figured out."

"Is Kacey my shared soul?"

Morrow grinned. "What do you think?"

"I feel like I've know her for lifetimes."

"You have."

"So, if we're both caretakers, we'll be able to find each other when we die?"

Morrow grabbed the porch rail and pivoted to face the woods. "Maybe."

"Maybe?" RG leaned and peered over his father's shoulder. "What's maybe?"

"Remember, Kacey's a true caretaker. The power flows in her blood. Your powers come from a ring, and the ring won't pass into the next world. If you're fated to be a caretaker, such destiny will present itself to you when your time comes, but it isn't guaranteed."

"So, my powers might end when I die."

Morrow's gaze bore a hole in the floorboards. "There's a possibility."

A dawning reality struck him like a slap to his face, his numbed limbs frozen in place. "Fuck! This is it, isn't it? This is all I get with her."

"Most people in your world accept the fact life is finite, Robert. Just as you did before you learned of me, before you understood Kacey's destiny."

"But now I know different. I've witnessed future worlds; I understand life's continuation. How do I face forever knowing I only have a few years with her?"

"Like I said, the soul finds a way—"

"Well, that's just great!" RG tromped back and forth along the porch. "So, maybe someday she'll walk past me sitting in the sun outside some otherworldly inn? That's what I get to look forward to?"

Junior's waking cry brought the two back into the house, RG's pace impeded by the weighty gloom cloud resting on his shoulders.

Morrow boosted the boy high in the air, plopping him onto the couch with him to Junior's delighted squeals. They turned pages in the picture book as the boy beamed into his grandfather's eyes, riveted to his every word. The image jolted RG from his desolate place, a small grin playing tug-of-war with the corners of his mouth, pleased that Junior could rekindle the joy death had deprived Morrow of with his own son.

Morrow hoisted Junior into his arms as the boy slung an arm around his neck. "What do you say we join Kacey at the portal?"

"Maybe we can share the two-by-four with home fries."

Morrow's eyes crept downward to RG's stomach, a frown creasing his lips. "You might want to consider the fruit plate. You appear to be gaining—"

"All right, all right! Like I need this shit from you, too!" He jammed his fists into his pockets.

Morrow raised his hands over Junior's ears. "Uh, language, Robert?"

He grabbed Morrow's elbow. *And I have a few choice words for you, too!* He turned the ring twice, and they fell into the abyss.

RG

RG, Morrow, and Junior threw open the front door to the Pancake Man, flooding the entranceway with the next world's light and color. They jostled through the crowd, Morrow dropping onto the booth cushion opposite Kacey. RG and Junior slid into the seat beside her. The food sat before them on the table as Kacey snaked a path through her placemat's spiral maze with a red crayon, her tongue poking from the corner of her mouth.

RG kissed the side of her head, a bit longer than usual, attempting to calculate how much time he had with her before his death, before his soul would embark on the eternal journey to find her again.

Not the time for this, RG! He grimaced as he inspected the fruit plate waiting for him.

Morrow grabbed Kacey's hand. "So lovely to see you, my dear."

"How did it go with Junior this morning? He give you a hard time?"

Morrow filled his cheeks with air before exhaling. "Well, 'a hard time' wouldn't come close to—" The old man glanced up as RG shook his head, waving his fingers back and forth in front of his throat, "…being accurate at all," he muttered in a solid recovery. "He's a little angel, well behaved, just a joy." Morrow's eyes darted from Kacey to RG.

"I'm happy he wasn't any trouble." She leaned over and rubbed Junior's hair.

"No trouble at all." Morrow gave a quick wink to Junior from across the table, holding a finger in front of his lips.

Kacey smirked as she cut her silver dollar pancakes to share with Junior. Morrow unwrapped a Kit-Kat from his jacket pocket and placed it on the plate beside his blueberry muffin. RG poked the fruit plate's strawberries and melons with his fork, hoping an undiscovered power in his ring might help them morph into something fried or scrambled.

"So, Robert tells me you want to talk. What's happened?"

"Well, we finally received a response to one of our ads."

"No daytrips to Nantucket again, I hope." Morrow raised an eyebrow.

"Thankfully not."

RG forked a strawberry into his mouth. "We met with a Molly Buckholtz from Brookline, whose child disappeared twenty years ago."

"We're thinking jumper."

"Jumper abductions are rare," Morrow interjected. "Have you ruled out a human crime?"

"I probed her, Mr. Morrow." Kacey tossed more pancake pieces onto Junior's plate. "Not an ounce of deception to her.

The police found nothing at the house, no fingerprints, no evidence of a break-in, nothing. They had pegged her as the prime suspect from day one. No human criminal could leave a crime scene without a trace of evidence, a hair, an eyelash, something."

"Twenty years…" Morrow pressed his eyes shut. "What else did she tell you?"

"She said the boy had undergone changes before he went missing."

Morrow leaned forward, resting his elbows on the table. "What changes?"

"He'd grown withdrawn…distant," RG offered. "She described him as disappearing inside himself."

"Did she mention his eyes?"

Kacey and RG stared at each other. "She said they'd changed, turned black as night," RG added.

"And sometimes she glimpsed someone else behind them."

Morrow removed his hat and combed his fingers through his hair. "The phenomena of host invasions are theoretical at best, since jumpers don't typically remain in the body. But, the body can only tolerate one host at a time. If more than one soul inhabits the flesh, the body will eventually make a choice."

RG put down his fork. "A choice?"

"The body will decide the dominant soul. Since jumpers are always stronger than their human counterparts, the host doesn't stand a chance. But the jumper would have to stay inside a host for a long time for this to happen. They call it soul dwelling."

"What happens when the body detects a soul dweller and has to make a choice?" Kacey asked. "What happens to the host?"

"Well, it's theorized if a jumper remains inside the host

long enough, the host ends up buried inside himself. A child with a buried soul would never recover, and the body would eventually die around him or her."

"But, the Buckholtz woman witnessed these signs," RG interjected. "Why would a jumper stay inside so long?"

"Maybe this one wanted to prolong the agony or possessed a morbid curiosity." Morrow closed his eyes. "I'm not sure."

"When I probed the Buckholtz woman and relived her memories," Kacey recollected, "I met her boy, Gunnar. I had the powerful sensation a childlike presence lived inside him. Sound crazy?"

"A child jumper is most rare." Morrow stroked his chin. "It would have to be a very disturbed child, a child under the impression life had cheated him of his rightful due. Usually children in your world haven't lived long enough to develop such ugly emotions. They willingly move on to the next realm."

RG rested his elbows on the sticky tabletop. "Why would a child jumper seek out another child?"

Morrow took a sip of his orange juice. "Maybe he figured a child wouldn't resist."

"What if a child jumper just wanted to play with a child close to the same age?" Kacey offered. "I mean, a child wants to play, right? Maybe this jumper finds a best friend but can only keep him for a certain length of time before…well, his friend gets buried, disappears."

"So, Molly Buckholtz is watching her son change before her. His eyes turn black, and he begins to disappear inside himself." RG scattered the remaining fruit around his plate with his fork. "Then he's missing. Maybe this jumper couldn't bear to lose a friend and chose to bring him back to his world. Keep him for himself."

Morrow frowned. "Let's slow down here. It just isn't typical behavior. Jumpers don't keep their hosts, they…well." He bowed his head. "You've observed firsthand what they do with them."

They stared at their plates as they ate in silence.

Kacey sighed. "Whether her boy's dead or alive, I promised Molly Buckholtz closure. We owe her whatever answers we can find."

"I'll ask around. Robert, you're the researcher here, find out as much as you can about the Buckholtz case, you——"

"*Was* the researcher," RG said, cutting him off.

"What?" Morrow paused until RG raised his eyes. "Son, just because you no longer work as a researcher does not mean you aren't one. In your field, you may be a pariah——"

"Gee, thanks, Dad," he interrupted. *Kick a guy while he's down, why don't you?* He flicked a blueberry across the table, smacking Morrow in the lapel, leaving an indigo-colored splotch.

"——but don't confuse what has happened professionally with your abilities." Morrow dabbed his napkin into his water glass and rubbed the stain. "You've won prestigious honors and awards in your field based on your research skills, and your discoveries of Victor Garrett's past brought about his downfall. You have much to be proud of."

RG swallowed and gave Morrow a nod. He reflected a moment, considering the father Morrow would have been, a man who would have buoyed him in times of doubt and insecurity.

"I want you to keep digging on this." Morrow pointed across the table with his fork. "Together we'll find the answers to give Ms. Buckholtz the peace she deserves."

RG took a bite from a strawberry, wondering if the answers they would find could bring anything but suffering.

Chapter Six

'*Faded in death now pale She lies*
And fills the parents heart with sighs.'

In memory of AMELIA CHURCHILL, daughter of Capt
JOSEPH CHURCHILL and MERCY his wife, died Sep^t 12th
1807 (Aged 7 months & 5 days)
-Epitaphs from Burial Hill

June 16, 2019

Kacey

Kacey Granville wheeled the Outback into Chatham Elementary School's parking lot. She emptied her lungs and stared through the windshield at parents and children streaming through the front double doors. She checked her watch and raced into the school's side entrance moments ahead of the bell. Navigating the crowded hallways, she sidestepped the throngs of parents giving last-minute goodbye hugs and searching through backpacks for missing homework.

Kacey nearly stumbled, dodging Zach Simpson wandering alone outside Mrs. Pierce's fourth-grade classroom. She corralled the boy with a pair of hands on his shoulders, a grin playing at her lips as she pictured his doting stepfather, Mike Stahl. He spent more time at Chatham Elementary than most faculty, never missing a drop-off or pick-up, a parent-teacher conference, or a school play whose sets he had helped build.

Zach's mother, Claire, had married Mike after nursing him back to health following last year's house explosion. Once, Mike had harbored an inextinguishable flame for Kacey, but watching him drop Zach at school each day, clinging to his wife and stepson's hands, she sensed it had flickered and had finally gone out. The peace and serenity in his eyes communicated what she had already surmised.

But today, the tears welling in Zach's eyes spoke a different story.

She bent forward, her grin melting. "Hey, Zach, what's the matter?"

"I want to go home, Mrs. Granville," he said, voice wavering.

Kacey checked her watch, already late for her first meeting, a disgruntled parent no doubt simmering outside her office. "How come?"

"I just want to."

A single tear spilled onto his cheek. Kacey wiped it away with her thumb. "But, you just got here, and it looks like Mike and your mom already left. Let's get you into class with your friends—"

"I don't have any friends anymore," he interrupted.

"That's not true. What about Jimmy Brody? He's been your best—"

"I don't wanna talk about Jimmy Brody." Zach folded his arms.

"Okay, we don't have to." Kacey brushed an errant hair strand from his eyes.

"I wanna go home."

"How 'bout you give it a try until lunchtime. I'll check back with you then. If you still want to go home, I'll give Mike a call and have him pick you up. Deal?"

"Okay, Mrs. Granville." The words seemed to struggle past something in his throat.

Kacey threw a pleading gaze to Wendy Pierce, who grabbed Zach's hand and led him into her classroom and over to the reading mat, leaving him to his comforting world of books. Kacey mouthed a hurried 'thank you,' then glanced over at Zach.

He'll be fine. Just a tough start to the day.

With an ache in her chest, Kacey raced down the hall to her meeting. She turned the corner to the main hall and bumped into Yvette Brody, Jimmy's mother, her neighbor from down the street. She winced as she took in Yvette's revealing outfit and none-too-subtle fire engine red lipstick.

Oh my God, must be a job fair at the local whorehouse this morning.

Yvette used morning drop-off to lure the single fathers into brief, destructive relationships, sometimes the married ones, too. *Must be recruiting day.*

"Hey, neighbor." Yvette gave her a frazzled wave. "You look like you could use a beer and the sun hasn't gotten over the yardarm yet." Kenny Farley's father, Bill, stood beside her in no hurry to get to work.

Kacey offered her a smirk. *Smells like you've already had a few.* "Hey, Yvette, do you have a sec?" She pulled Yvette away from her disappointed suitor, checking her watch again, preparing the mea culpas she would have to recite to her eight o'clock. "I just bumped into Zach Simpson in the hallway. Did he and Jimmy have a falling out?"

"Well, um," Yvette uttered, pausing a beat, "Jimmy didn't invite Zach to his birthday this year. He's making a lot of new friends on his little league team, and they're all going to the laser tag place over at the mall. He didn't want Zach to feel out of place since he wouldn't know anyone."

"He's kinda feeling out of place anyway." Kacey's stomach dropped. "Any chance Jimmy might let him—"

"When did the vice-principal's job description include matchmaker for nine-year-olds?" Yvette interrupted. "Jimmy wants to be with his new friends now."

"Of course, Yvette." An ache grew inside Kacey's chest, one of life's bitter disappointments arriving unannounced on Zach's doorstep. "Sorry to micromanage. It's just tough to watch Zach—"

"Kids figure this stuff out on their own." Yvette flipped open her compact mirror and pressed her ruby red lips together.

"I guess they do." They stood silent in the bustling hallway.

"But, hey, summer's just around the corner. Hopefully, I'll run into you and RG at the beach one of these weekends."

"I'll look forward to it." Kacey excused herself.

"Ya know, you ought to tell your man to cut out the carbs, or he'll never get his beach body back."

"Yeah, I'll make sure to." *And fuck you very much for saying so!*

After a string of morning meetings, Kacey attacked the next fiscal year's budget and year-end teacher evaluations. Just before noon, she glanced up from her desk onto the playground to witness Zach Simpson leaning back on his swing, hair dusting the ground as he grasped the chain-links. She chuckled, watching him stare at the inverted children swarming the play equipment around him. Jimmy Brody,

Kenny Farley, and the boys from his class threw the football and tackled each other on the patchy grass field.

Before turning back to her work, she glimpsed Jimmy waving Zach over to join the other boys. Kacey's heart swelled as the boy sprung to his feet and raced across the field. But when he arrived, Kenny Farley stuck out his leg, sending Zach sprawling face first into the ground. The other boys cheered and laughed as they strolled away, tossing the football into the grass and leaving Zach in a heap. Jimmy Brody proceeded to step over him as he joined his friends.

"Oh my God." Kacey bolted from her office, down the hall, and out the door. She sprinted across the playground, shouting at staff to round up the boys as she made a beeline to Zach, sprawled on the grass and crying, his shoulders hitching with each sob. Kacey knelt beside him and lifted his chin.

"I want to go home now."

Mike

Mike Stahl pulled up to the tidy beach house on Seaview Road, crushing seashells beneath his wheels. He killed the engine and gazed out the windshield, the house's weathered shingles and white trim straight off a Cape Cod postcard. At just over a thousand square feet, many would consider it small, but Stahl had it pegged as cozy. A white picket fence framed the small yard, the red rose bushes and Hydrangea Claire had planted pushed through the fence slats and cascaded over the top edge. But the cushioned swing dangling from the wrap-around porch's ceiling emerged as the spot his family convened, chain-links squeaking as Claire and Zach leaned against him, swaying back and forth with the gentle, salty ocean breeze.

The house represented an upgrade from the one on the corner of Old Harbor Road where Stahl had grown up and lived until eighteen months ago. A fiery showdown with the burning man had blown it off its foundation and left him with painful burns along his neck and back to accompany lead mementos in his hip and shoulder. He had considered rebuilding, but the house held too many painful reminders of years spent in limbo, alone and dwelling in the past. The house on Seaview not only allowed him to resurrect his life but placed him a few steps closer to Aunt Lydia's Cove, a small piece of heaven located between the Chatham mainland and Tern Island, where the gray seals lounged in the surf along the sandbars just off the beach.

Joining him in his new life was Claire Simpson, a forensic analyst at the Bureau of Criminal Investigations Laboratory, and her nine-year-old son, Zack. He had dated Claire off and on for several years but couldn't fall in love with her until he had exorcised a certain ghost named Kacey Granville. After years alone and closed off from the world, Mike may have surrendered his heart to Claire, but Zach somehow pried off a sizeable piece for himself.

As Stahl sat lost in reflection, he spotted Zach from the corner of his eye, tiptoeing out the front door. The boy stepped carefully down the porch steps and onto the seashells, crouching behind the Crown Vic's left rear wheel. Claire gazed out from the open screen door, her smirk betraying her anticipation of the scene to follow.

As Mike pulled himself from the front seat, Zach took a running leap and wrapped his arms around his neck from behind.

"Guess who's taking us to Carmine's for pizza?"

"Would it be me?" Stahl asked, a grin crossing his lips. He

did a quick spin, attempting to dislodge the giggling boy clinging to his neck.

"Yes, it would." Claire shouted from the porch. She hurried down the steps and gave him a welcome-home kiss, a boy still dangling from Stahl's neck.

"Guess who's taking us for ice cream afterwards?" Zach asked.

"Um, would it be me again?" Stahl extracted Zach's arms around his ever-constricting airway.

"It would." Another kiss.

"Oh, the sacrifices I make for you two." He gave Zach's hair a tousle, then folded his hand around his. The three strolled along Seaview, following the bend around Main Street until they reached Carmine's on the corner. He gazed at the boy beside him, fair skinned with large blue eyes flecked with green, like algae streaks in a swollen summer sea, shielded beneath long eyelashes. His hair had the same enigmatic color as his mother's, fluctuating between chestnut and black, depending on the sun's angle or the season. Sometimes people would stare at him on the street or in a restaurant and tell him or Claire how pretty the boy was. *Pretty.* Zach had told him pretty was for girls.

Yeah, but when the girls take notice, you might not mind as much.

"How'd school go today, buddy?"

Zach remained silent, squeezing Mike's hand a bit tighter.

Claire glanced at Mike, giving him a quick head shake. She mouthed the word 'later.'

Stahl nodded his head.

After a large pepperoni pizza and three ice cream sundaes with whip cream, Mike, Claire, and Zach paid their caloric penance with a stroll along the beach at Aunt Lydia's Cove. While Zach raced ahead, Claire described what had happened earlier on the playground with Kenny Farley and the other boys.

"The sonofabitch."

"Look, Mike, Kenny has issues, but he's still just a boy," Claire offered, holding her sandals in hand as she strode barefoot across the sand.

"No, the sonofabitch is his father, Bill. He beat up both his wives, as well as Kenny. I've seen the reports. The bully has turned his son into one."

"It's the pattern, isn't it?"

"I'm going to have a talk with the asshole. His son comes near Zach again, I'm taking it out on him." Stahl's jaw clenched as he turned away from Claire.

"You can't do that, Mike, and you know it. And it hasn't been just Kenny, either. Jimmy Brody has turned on him, too."

"Why don't you head back up to the house, and we'll catch up with you. I want to have a talk with Zach."

Claire nodded and gave his back a quick rub. She kissed his shoulder and hiked along Shore Road, leaving the two on the beach.

He approached the boy as he threw stones into the surf. "Hey, Zach, watch this." Grabbing a flat stone from the sand, he skimmed it across the water five to six jumps before it disappeared into the sea.

"That's wicked cool!" Zach gazed at him, his eyes perfect ovals.

"And if you hit the wave just right, it'll go straight up into the air."

Stahl searched the sand and picked up a flat, polished white stone. He leaned back, his weight coiled on his back foot as he bent his elbow and cocked his wrist, waiting for the ideal wave.

"Pretty soon...it's coming...I can feel it." Stahl timed his throw as a swell rolled toward the shore. He cast the stone at an angle, causing it to bounce along the surf until it caught the breaking wave's crest. It skipped directly upward and fell back into the water with a plop.

"Awesome!" Zach shouted. "Can I try?"

Against the setting sun's backdrop, they skimmed stone after stone, trying for the same effect. Zach's eyes darted back and forth to Mike for the OK as they waited for the perfect wave. When Mike nodded, the two would throw, blissfully unaware of the sky, the streaking orange and pink chasing the sun toward the sea.

"Rough day today, huh?" Stahl focused his eyes on the water as he tossed his stone.

Zach remained silent, emulating Stahl's posture as he tried to skim another stone off the incoming wave.

"You scared today?"

Zach dropped his stone and blinked back the rising tears. He nodded, wiping his eyes with shaking hands.

Mike stepped beside him and draped his hand across the back of his neck. "You know, Kenny Farley's gonna be spending time after school for what he did."

Zach shook his head. "Won't matter."

"What do you mean?"

"Now he'll have a reason to beat me up." Zach turned and fired his rock straight into the surf.

"No one's gonna let anything happen to you now. Schools don't stand for bullying anymore. You'll be okay."

"He'll find me. Maybe not at school, but he'll find me. It's not the first time—" Zach bit his tongue.

Mike stood, placing his hands on his hips. "What's not the first time?"

"Never mind."

"Hey, listen. The one thing a bully can't stand is when

someone pushes back. When a bully gets a whack in the mouth, that's when they back down."

"But if I hit someone, I'll get in trouble." Zach stared at the sand.

"No, you won't. If someone ever bullies you, you've got my permission to push back and push back hard. You hear me?"

Zach nodded.

"And look at these guns." Stahl ran a hand along the boy's slender arms. "You're like a solid wall of muscle. Don't let 'em forget who they're messing with."

Zach squeezed his biceps to demonstrate his superhero attributes.

"But you don't have to worry because I'm here now, and you'll be safe," Stahl assured him. "I'm not gonna let anything happen to you. Ever. Understand?" He gave Zach's shoulders a squeeze.

Zach raised his head and wiped his eyes. "Jimmy didn't bother helping me up."

Stahl drew a heavy sigh. *Why does childhood have to be so painful?* In a time of firsts—first betrayal, first rejection, first failure—it's no wonder every disappointment felt like the end of the world.

"They wanted me to play today, at least that's what I figured. I was so happy, but then…" Zach glanced down, pretending to search the sand for another stone to skip.

"Zach, listen to me. The friends you have today aren't gonna be the friends you have tomorrow. They change and get better, all the time. You'll see."

"Well, now I don't have any friends."

Stahl plucked a flat stone from the sand. "Well, you got me."

"Yeah?"

"You bet."

Zach let some time pass before speaking. "Is Dr. Randle your best friend?"

"Russ?" Mike hesitated, anticipating where this was going. "Well, he's a really good friend, but I don't think I've ever had a best friend."

"Maybe I could be your best friend." Zach held his hand out as Stahl dropped the stone into his palm. He turned and skimmed it off the surf.

Mike would remember this moment with a fondness and a silent promise. *Always*. "I'd really like that."

"Yeah, me too."

"You know what they say about best friends, don't you? There's nothing they wouldn't do for each other."

Zach tilted his head. "Nothing?"

"Name it."

"Would you jump in front of a car for me?"

"Please!" Stahl waved a dismissive hand. "I'd jump in front of a bus."

Zach crossed his arms. "How 'bout a train?"

He grimaced. "Hmm, might hurt a bit more, but yeah, a train. That's a no-brainer."

"Would you run into a burning house for me?"

Stahl had already been on fire once, but he would gladly do it again. "No sweat."

"What if a monster came after me?"

"Monsters?" Stahl placed his hands on his hips. "Aren't you a little old to believe in monsters?"

"But what if I did, and one came out of my closet and took me away?"

He raised Zach's chin. "Then I'd come get you."

"You promise."

Stahl made an X over his heart. "Hope to die." They

strolled back from Aunt Lydia's Cove in the dwindling twilight, Mike's arm resting across Zach's shoulders.

Malachi

Malachi had observed the young boy on the playing field as he explored Chatham Elementary. Schools, libraries, parks, and playgrounds proved to be the best places to find a host, anywhere children gathered and revealed their passions and sorrows. Malachi regularly visited such places when he looked to jump.

And he had been to this elementary school before.

The boy had rested alone on the swings during recess, needing a friend. When the other boys pushed him to the ground and laughed, the blood had scorched Malachi's racing heart. A deep compassion for the boy grew within him, and Malachi wanted to know more about him.

So, he followed him.

Malachi had stayed close as the boy and his parents strolled into town. They couldn't spot him, of course—no one could detect a jumper outside their chosen realm. Malachi strode with them along the narrow main street, past the tee-shirt stores and gift shops with their sun-blistered shingles, bright, colorful awnings, and window boxes with the bright purple and white petunias in bloom. His parents clutched the boy's hand as they gazed into the ice cream and candy store windows, chattering about all the possible treat combinations they would try someday. He hovered beside the boy and watched him take his pizza slice, fold it in half like his dad, and stuff it into his mouth. The boy's kind parents reminded Malachi of Uncle Bradford and Aunt Millie.

This might be a good place to hang around for a while.

After dinner, Malachi ambled along the beach with the boy and his family. When the boy sprinted ahead, away from the grownups, Malachi performed a quick probe, not a body invasion—not yet—just a gentle mind exploration.

Malachi had concentrated hard and tapped into the boy's consciousness, his thoughts and images, and all the pieces between them. The split-second scan provided a sensory collage—sight, sound, and smell exploding within Malachi's open mind. In an instant, he lived the boy's life through long forgotten images and discarded memory residues. Competing joy and sadness sensations flooded him. The boy's mother and the man, his new father, loved him, but he had no friends, his only one betraying him. Malachi picked out one particular memory and let it unfold before him.

"Hey, pretty boy." The bully with the scar had whispered, sidling up behind Zach in the boys' bathroom.

Zach had stood at the urinal when Kenny Farley's stale breath churned in his ear. He froze, his urine stream squeezing off midflow.

"Don't stop on my account." Farley glanced into the urinal, an ugly grin rolling across his lips. He fixed his stare at his pal, Billy Backus, leaning against the sink.

Zach swallowed.

"If you're done you better wash up. You don't want dirty hands, do you?" Farley hissed, the faded facial scar his father had left him throbbing red with each heartbeat.

Zach zipped his pants and moved to the sink beside the urinals.

Farley clawed Zach's neck in a vise grip, pivoting his head forward. "Not that soap," he growled, guiding Zach's head downward toward the urinal. "Use that one."

Zach eyed the red urinal cake floating in a yellow pool collecting in the basin. "Kenny, please," he begged.

"Shut your mouth! Pick it up!"

"Hey, Kenny," Billy Backus chimed in, edging toward the bathroom door, "we're gonna be late for class. You don't need to waste your time with this little shit. Whatta ya say? Let's go, huh?"

Farley shot him a stare. "You go on. I'm not done here."

Zach's pulse quickened. His glance darted to Backus as the boy gave a half shrug, backed away, and slipped out the bathroom door. The hallway noise dissipated as the automatic door closer slowed the heavy bathroom door's thump against the jamb, leaving the two boys in wretched silence.

Please let somebody come through the door and help me. Zach winced as he picked up the urinal cake from the tepid water. A sharp and sudden odor drifted upward.

"Now make sure you clean your hands good," Farley sneered.

Zach rubbed the urinal cake on his hands until a pungent, slick lather gathered on his hands.

"Don't forget to wash behind your ears." Grabbing Zach's wrist, Farley jerked his soap-clenched hands to his head, ears, and face until the lather dripped onto his new school shirt.

His laugh echoed off the tile walls as he threw open the boy's restroom door. "You tell anyone about this…you die." The sound repeated in Zach's ears long after Farley's boot clomps had faded from the hallway.

Malachi disengaged from the little boy's mind and watched him skim rocks into the surf. He closed his eyes, a visceral ache mobbing his senses.

The boy needed a friend.

———

Mike

Mike and Claire curled beside each other on the queen-size bed, the flat-screen TV's blue-gray light flickering off the darkened walls. Claire's head rested on Stahl's chest, an assortment of different sized decorative cushions scattered across the queen mattress. Stahl had spent his first thirty-six years fluffing a single pillow at night and couldn't comprehend the need for the cushion mountain forever surrounding him. His job responsibilities now included dismantling the collection to access the bed and reassembling them in the proper configuration come morning. But, he would gladly put up with the imposition to have Claire in his bed.

"The man threw the boy off a cliff." Stahl dabbed at his eyes as he recounted the Abner Stennett interrogation the previous night. "I sat across from the guy thinking, 'the man just murdered his own child.' I mean, how many times have we said hello to him in Card & Candle?"

"I know, it's crazy. And Nathan went to Zach's school, in the third-grade class."

"Did Zach know him?" Stahl asked.

Claire nodded. "He didn't want to talk about it, though."

"We found Maria in the basement. She'd been dead a few days. A hard death, and she'd had a rough go of it beforehand, bruises and other indicators pointing to abuse. Abner says the boy did it."

"Oh my God, blaming his son?" Claire squeezed her eyes shut, shaking her head.

"Craziest thing, Stennett kept saying 'he wasn't my son, he wasn't my boy,' this perception something had possessed the kid…like the *Exorcist* or something. In fact, he had a name for him." Stahl wavered, tapping the side of his head with his finger, trying to loosen the forgotten utterance jammed somewhere in his neural network.

"What would have triggered him to kill his wife and son?"

Stahl mulled the query for a moment. "When I heard his story, I figured he had to be crazy. But, he had this super calm demeanor, like he does when he's helping a customer. He came across more relieved than crazy."

They lay together in silence.

"Malachi!" Stahl shouted.

"What?"

Mike banged his palm against his forehead. "The boy's name, the one Stennett said possessed Nathan. Sorry, it just came to me."

"Malachi?"

"Yes, and you wanna hear what else he said?" Stahl tapped his fist gently against his lips. "He could see Malachi behind Nathan's eyes, as if he'd been looking through a window."

"The poor family." Claire sighed. "What the hell happened to him?"

Stahl filled his cheeks, then blew out the air. He turned to hold her gaze but didn't say anything.

Chapter Seven

'And must thy children die so soon.'

In memory of THOMAS PATY, died Oc^t 7th, 1802 (Aged 2 years, 10 months, and 20 days)
-Epitaphs from Burial Hill

June 17, 2019

Kacey

Kacey drifted downward through a cloudless, cobalt-blue sky and into what appeared to be a summer fête along Plymouth's White Horse Beach. She comprehended where she was—but not exactly when—the dream's sepia tones edging the familiar beach in an anachronistic rendition. Hundreds of townsfolk swarmed the crowded boardwalk while vendors in wool suits sold their wares to eager beach-goers dressed as if they had stepped from a Norman Rockwell painting. Despite the scene's nostalgic serenity, Kacey remained wary, the dream's vividness a harbinger of something she couldn't predict, conjuring a familiar dread. But she couldn't stifle her smile as children huddled before the food wagons, hungry eyes darting among the popcorn, hotdogs, and cotton candy, squeezing coins and crumpled bills in their sand-crusted hands. Their wide eyes and laughter offered a cloak of safety, as if nothing could happen to her if they were near.

The scorching sun heated the fine sand granules, forcing her to veer into the surf to chill the rising burn on the soles of her feet. As she traipsed through the surf, two young boys, sunburned and covered in sand, sprinted past her along the shore, splashing each other and diving into the breaking waves. The taller boy, handsome with soft blue eyes and short black hair, kicked up a salty spray as he dashed past her in a dead run, a slingshot protruding from a pocket in the back of his red bathing trunks. Kacey emitted a surprised gasp as frigid Cape Cod Bay water splashed across her heated skin.

The boy stopped running. "Pardon, ma'am, didn't mean to get you all wet."

"It's okay. You don't come to the beach unless you expect to get splashed." Kacey gave a playful kick to the water, sending a water stream cascading over the boy.

He covered up, laughing. "I'm Malachi." He leaned his head toward the boy beside him. "My cousin, Elias."

The other boy nodded. "Ma'am."

Malachi stepped toward her. "What's your name?"

"Kacey. You two sure seem to be having a fun—" As their eyes met, she detected something flash behind them, the boy's eyes transformed into a piercing black canvas, affixing her in place, as if her brain suddenly powered down. When she broke from his gaze, she found herself transported to the middle of a sweeping field, tall grass bending in the late afternoon breeze, the beach hundreds of yards away.

"What are you doing here?" Malachi barked.

"I…I'm not sure."

The boy glared at her. "You don't belong here, caretaker."

Kacey stared transfixed as the boy rapidly aged, wilting like a flower in a time lapse film. His body shriveled before her eyes as blue and crimson spider veins sprouted across his sallow skin. He shed his short, black mane as wispy strands of grey hair pushed through the creature's dry, balding scalp. Thin, ropy muscles protruded from the arms and legs of the cadaverous troll standing before her.

He shuffled toward her. "You're here for Gunnar, aren't you?"

Kacey backpedaled. "How do you know—?"

"You'll never find him," he interrupted. A toothless grin played across his features.

Awakened to the taunting threat before her, she turned in an awkward retreat, half-stumbling, half-sprinting away on numbed limbs unsteady as a newborn colt's. With the ratchet-like movements of a Harryhausen film creature, Malachi loped behind her, gaining on her. A raspy bark escaped his throat, each grunting stride forcing her onward at breakneck speed.

Charging ahead faster and faster, Kacey pounded the ground to build distance between her and the creature's claws, but he jumped ahead of her and burrowed his feet into the grassy meadow in front of her, bracing to break her run, ready to nab her. Reversing her trajectory, she twirled to sprint another direction, but the surface below her shifted and creaked. In her narrowed periphery, she could have sworn she'd witnessed an insidious satisfaction in his glassy eyes, that he had forced her upon this exact spot, manipulating her like a puppeteer would a marionette.

And then he cut the strings.

A rickety platform below her gave way, splitting in two and dropping her from her perch. The opening swallowed her, plunging her into gradual darkness, thrusting her further into a deafening silence. She sank at feather speed, her eyes able to process each jagged indentation of the hidden well's stone surface and alternating granite shades, fat water droplets plopping with such great volume they drowned the silence. A musty breeze prickled her skin, wrapping her in a graduating chill as she accelerated, plummeted downward, faster now, the air growing thinner and thinner, bathing her in darkness. Then, like the random drops, she shattered the water with an ear-popping crack.

Kacey flailed her arms, paddling to stay afloat while she reached outward to grasp something, anything to hold her up. Her fingertips brushed against the silky sidewalls, pulling away slimy moss, no rocky nubs to latch onto, nothing to support her.

"Malachi! Malachi!" Elias screamed from the well's opening. "Hang on! I'm going for help!"

Huh? "It's Kacey, my name's Kacey," she whispered, ears ringing from the fall's impact.

As she treaded water, a gentle tickle caressed her foot. She pictured swampy plant growth carpeting the well's floor beneath her, tendrils undulating below the surface reaching out to her.

Nothing but a vine...

She sensed another gentle tickle against her other leg. Kacey plunged her face into the stale water and gazed downward expecting to see nothing through the inky blackness. But the dream, or maybe Malachi himself, allowed her to discern a hazy silhouette deep beneath the surface, rolling back and forth with the hushed current. Kacey held her breath and jackknifed downward, her heart pounding back against the water's ratcheting pressure. Malachi's bloated body rolled at the well's bottom, his short black hair swaying back and forth, lifeless soft blue eyes wide open and staring at her. Small pea-size bubbles seeped from his mouth and rose to the surface, useless oxygen pockets escaping his water-filled lungs, his hands raised above his head as if reaching for the water's surface.

She snaked her arms around his chest and guided his body to the surface. Treading water, Kacey attempted to resuscitate him but couldn't stabilize herself against the well's slick walls to steady the boy's head, his body slipping from her grip. As she reached below the surface to grab him, the boy's supple limbs turned sinewy and hard, as if she had grabbed a coil of rope.

They jerked against her hands like snakes in the water.

The surface roiled as the troll exploded from the water with a shriek, his hands shooting forward, gripping Kacey's throat.

Her scream ended abruptly as his fingers pressed against her flesh, taking her under the surface. She lashed out against the creature, swiping her nails across his face and leaving jagged grooves across his features. With a colossal effort, she kicked forward, catching the troll midchest, hammering him against the mossy wall. He slipped below the surface with a plop.

Kacey pictured the grizzled creature floating somewhere below her in the dark, her breath hitching in the dark. In the returning stillness, she could hear nothing but her muffled heart's thump roaring in her ears, reverberating off the stone walls.

Where did he go? Her eyes darted back and forth. "Help me!" she shouted to no one.

The well's silence reached a crescendo, overwhelming the smattering plink of water dribbling from the slick walls.

A hand locked onto her ankle, dragging her below the surface.

Kacey's arms shot forward toward the jutting stones, her fingers grasping for purchase, but her nails left nothing but deep furrows in the slippery moss as she disappeared underwater.

Lashing out with her free leg, she kicked the creature's arm away, breaking his grip, but his fist locked onto her other ankle. She inhaled a stream of water and sputtered to breathe, a second violent tug swamping her again. Jamming her heel directly downward, Kacey dug into solid bone, a skull, a shoulder, she wasn't sure, and a grasping claw retracted from her ankle. She bolted to the surface and greedily inhaled the dank, humid air.

Gasping for breath, Kacey whipped her head from the left to the right, awaiting the next assault from below. She took a deep breath and thrust her face into the water, her eyes straining through dark shadows to face the threat head on. A boy's body lay on his stomach upon layered rocks, arms outstretched, unmoving, black hair waving back and forth with the current. She dove, lunging with outstretched arms to turn the boy over.

Malachi's dead blue eyes once again stared back at her.

————

Malachi

"Who's there?" Zach Simpson bolted upright in his bed, eyes blinking open. He rubbed his chest. "Mom? Mike?" he whispered, eyes darting back and forth across the dim room.

Malachi had waited until the boy slipped into his first

dream before he entered his body. He went in as gently as he could, pushing against his chest, then settling inside, as smooth as if he had donned a satin shirt.

"Hi." Malachi's silent voice spoke from deep within the boy's head in a language he had never heard before, an ancient tongue not tethered to time or place, developed in a parallel plane many times removed from the current realm and understood by all living creatures.

"Who's there?"

"Malachi."

"I can't see you." Zach squinted as his eyes adjusted to the dark. "Are you in my room?"

Malachi smirked. *"Not really."* He pushed against the seams of the boy's body, moving around, trying to fit into his shape.

"Are you a dream I'm having?"

Malachi could sense the boy's mind turning, attempting to process the situation. *"I'm your inside friend. Like when you talk to yourself. I listen and answer you."*

"Are you real?" Zach rubbed his eyes.

"As real as you want me to be." Accepting the incomprehensible didn't usually take long for nine-year-olds, especially if you could win them over, make them laugh.

"Ow!" Zach clutched his knee. "What're you doing?"

"Just getting comfortable." Malachi squirmed, stretching his legs. *"What's your name?"*

"Zach."

"Hey, Zach, you want to hear a joke? Why did the basketball coach kick Cinderella off the team?"

"I dunno. Why?" A smile creased his lips.

"Because she ran away from the ball."

Zach attempted to hold in his laugh but couldn't. "Good one, Malachi. Hey, what do pigs take for medicine?"

Malachi waited.

"Oink-ment." The two boys' giggles ripped through the quiet room, but only one could be heard.

"Shhh! Or your mom and stepdad will hear. If you want to keep quiet, you don't have to open your mouth. I can hear what you think."

Zach closed his eyes and spoke in his thoughts. *"Okay."*

"You want to see something cool?" Malachi asked.

"Yeah."

Malachi unveiled a childhood memory, like a movie deep inside Zach's mind. Malachi sprinted along White Horse Beach with his cousin, Elias, kicking the waves and splashing each other, diving headlong into the surf.

"Are you one of those boys?" Zach inquired.

Malachi flashed him a quick image of himself, his blue eyes and jet-black hair shimmering with seawater under a blazing sun.

"I love the beach, too. We go to Aunt Lydia's Cove just about every day."

"Who's Aunt Lydia?" Malachi asked.

"I dunno." Zach shrugged his shoulders. *"I just know she has a beach we go to."*

"I had an Aunt Millie once. She owned a delicatessen with all sorts of pies and cakes." Malachi licked his lips at the recollection.

"I love cake, especially spice cake. My mom makes one on my birthday. I don't have any aunts, though."

"What about Aunt Lydia?"

"She's not my real aunt. She just owns the ocean," Zach clarified.

"Well, maybe she'll let me come and swim there sometime." Malachi understood children; he had been living among them and inside them for over seventy years and spoke to them as a child would.

Malachi stretched out his left arm, making it fit inside the boy. Then his other arm.

"Ow! That feels funny."

"Sorry, Zach."

Zach lay back on the pillow and jabbered inside his head to his new friend. *"You can come with me to my beach if you want. We have seals there."*

"Seals, wow!"

"Yeah, but my stepdad makes me get out of the water when they get too close."

"Why?"

A faint smile played on Zach's lips. *"He says because they're shark food, and I might end up as dessert."*

Both boys chuckled.

"Who's the boy with you at the beach?"

"My cousin, Elias. We'd play there when I visited him. Do you have friends you play with at the beach?"

Zach hesitated. *"Um, not anymore."*

"Why not?"

"My friend Jimmy from down the street—well, he used to be my friend—he doesn't come by anymore."

"How about your friends at school?" Malachi asked.

Zach squeezed his eyes shut. *"I don't have any. They don't ask me to play anymore."*

Malachi rested his arm around Zach's shoulder from within. *"How come?"*

Zach shrugged.

"Well, those kids are stupid."

"You think so?"

"You don't need any of those jerks." Malachi sensed the ache forming in Zach's stomach, spreading like a virus through his own body. Or it may have been Zach's body, he couldn't tell. *"Tell me about...Kenny."*

"How do you know him?"

"I just do."

"I don't want to talk about him." Zach rolled over onto his side.

"There's nothing you could do anyway. Kenny's almost eleven, and he's pretty strong."

"I'm older than him, and I'm pretty strong, too," Malachi bragged.

"How old are you?"

"I'm like eighty."

Zach burst out laughing. *"You're not eighty! You'd be old and wrinkled!"*

"Maybe I am." Malachi giggled.

"You wouldn't be strong anymore. You'd have a bald head and be all stooped over with a cane and no teeth." Zach put a hand over his mouth to squelch a giggle, afraid of waking Mike and his mom.

Malachi folded his lips over his teeth and opened his mouth as wide as it would go. They both laughed.

"Do you want to be friends?" Zach asked.

Malachi grinned as he nodded his head. *"I'll be back soon. There's someone I need to talk to."*

Malachi exited his host, giving Zach his body back.

Chapter Eight

'The infant has resigned its breath,
Sleeps in the arms of icy death.'

In memory of **LUCY TAYLOR COOPER**, died Septe[r] 19,
1803 (Aged 1 year, 5 months)
-Epitaphs from Burial Hill

June 17, 2019

RG

RG woke to the sound of Kacey's scream, rising from the depths of her throat like shrieks from a dying animal. She pulled at her tee-shirt, soaked through with sweat and clinging to her body.

"Kacey?" He checked the alarm clock's glowing face.

1:58 a.m.

Without a word, she bolted from the bed into the bathroom, launching handfuls of water across her face. He dragged himself from under the covers and stumbled to the doorway. "Kacey, what's the matter?"

She breezed past him, collapsing onto the bed. Her breathing stabilized, but tears streamed down her cheeks. She pressed her palms to her eyes.

"Kacey, answer me." He snapped on the nightstand light beside the bed.

She propped herself up against headboard, tossing her pillows behind her. "I had one of my dreams."

RG dropped onto the mattress.

This can't be good.

He had witnessed Kacey's dreams, visions of death for loved ones and friends, deaths scheduled to occur if she didn't intervene. Her actions to thwart these visions had the power to alter destiny. "Did it show you the future?"

"More like the past. The dream wasn't a prediction of something to come, but something already occurring, maybe sixty, seventy years ago." Kacey took a deep breath to quell the last hitching sobs. "Our intuition proved correct. There's a jumper, and he's taking children."

He leaned over and grabbed her hand, squeezing it twice, telling her in their secret language everything would be all right.

"I suspect digging into Molly Buckholtz's mind put me in direct contact with the force responsible for taking her boy, Gunnar."

"Tell me what you saw."

"A boy who died a long time ago. At the bottom of a well. He's a jumper, but he has turned into a monster. I witnessed his death."

"A child jumper?"

"God, what's his name?" Kacey squeezed her eyes shut. "Malachi! He asked if I had come for Gunnar. He said we would never find him."

"So, he's onto you now?"

"Looks like it."

"What else happened?"

"In the dream, I'm at White Horse Beach in Plymouth." She rubbed her temples in tight circles. "I'm in front of all those little shanty houses lining Taylor Avenue…you know the ones. They still had a boardwalk, these old-fashioned cars dropping people off at the beach. It must have been the 1930s or 40s."

"So, who's this Malachi?"

"I end up at the edge of the water, and I meet Malachi and this other little boy, his cousin, he said. He called him Elias. They're racing into the surf, splashing each other, having a great time. But then, Malachi changes right in front of me. First, the eyes. Then, just like Molly described with Gunnar, they faded to black. After that, he transformed into this grizzled old gargoyle-looking thing, more like a living corpse than anything else. But the same size as a boy."

He flinched. "My god."

"The dream showed me what Malachi must be like today, all these years later. I fell into this abandoned well, but he lurked underneath the water, waiting to pull me under and drown me. Before the dream ended, I gazed below the surface. Malachi, the boy version, floated at the bottom."

"So, this Malachi died at the bottom of a well, you think?"

"I'm sure of it," she concluded. "I had to fall into the well, like he did, and relive his death to witness what happened to him."

RG deliberated a moment. "If this happened sixty or

seventy years ago, and he has been abducting children since then—"

"Christ!" Kacey interrupted, a dawning truth lighting her eyes. "He may have taken God-knows-how-many-children from this world."

"Hang on a second." RG stepped from the bedroom, tap dancing around a slumbering Baron sprawled in the hallway. He stumbled into the kitchen to grab his laptop, waking it from sleep mode as he dropped back into bed. "Let's see what we can find out about this kid, Malachi."

His fingers worked the keyboard, entering 'Malachi,' 'well,' 'drowning,' and 'Plymouth' into the search engine. He spent the next several minutes scrolling through several recent drownings, but nothing about a well or anyone named Malachi.

"What year would you guess it was?"

"How would I know?"

He folded his hands. "Well, what did the cars look like?"

"Like big old boats."

RG rubbed a hand across his forehead and pressed his eyelids together. "That's helpful."

"Well, it's not like I'm addicted to every show on *Velocity* like you are! Maybe the forties?"

He let out a breath as his fingers flew across the keyboard and hit enter, pausing to scroll through the revised list. "Well, there's nothing here about a Plymouth drowning in the forties, or a well, or anyone named Malachi. Hold on a second…" He tapped away as he squinted at the laptop's screen.

Kacey grabbed her readers from the end table and jammed them onto RG's face, lining up at least one eye with a lens. "What are you staring at?"

"A hit from the 1950s." He straightened the glasses. "Construction workers found the body of, and I quote, what looks to be an adult and child inside a well about half a mile from White Horse Beach, unquote."

"Two bodies?"

RG continued reading for a moment. "Says here they'd been clearing the land for a new subdivision going in across from the beach when they made the discovery."

She shook her head. "Gotta be a decade later than my dream, and I only saw one body."

"Well, maybe your dream is off by a few years, or it only showed you Malachi."

"Does the article identify the bodies?"

He scrolled through the entry. "Not seeing any names here. Unless someone reported the two missing, they wouldn't have been able to identify them. Back then, they didn't have the technology to ID people from bone fragments, dental records, or skulls."

Kacey rubbed her forehead and frowned. "If it were a parent and child, someone had to miss them. Search for follow-up articles."

RG crammed the Google bar with every conceivable search-word combination, but he didn't get any relevant hits.

"Listen, this'll require a deeper search. I have a friend named Mariel up at Boston Public Library. She'll help me figure this out. Helped her out of a jam a while ago, cost me twenty bucks, but—"

"Another damsel in distress?" Kacey interrupted, raising an eyebrow. "Do I want to know about this?"

"Hmm, probably not."

———

Mike

Mike Stahl rolled up to the Stennett home on Queen Anne

Road, the tires popping over the scattered white shells as the Crown Vic eased to a stop. He jammed it in park and stared out the front windshield at the now-deserted house, a line of police tape delivering its telltale message to those unfortunate enough to view it.

No one had watered the flower boxes in days, and the unseasonably warm weather had taken its toll on its once-vibrant residents. Stahl exited the vehicle, compelled to give them a cool drink of water. Scanning the red-mulch flower beds nestled against the house's perimeter, Stahl searched for something to water the plants.

His stomach fluttered when he recalled why he couldn't find the garden hose.

Jesus Christ!

Standing on Abner Stennett's pearl white shell driveway, his cell phone chirped, jolting him from his recollection.

"Hey, Mike…Russ. I just finished up on Maria Stennett." He paused, concern pulsing in his voice. "Can you come up and take a look."

Stahl checked his watch. "I've got a couple things to do at the Stennett house, but I can swing by after lunch."

"That'll work. Come by 'round—"

"Quarter to one…yeah I figured," he cut him off. He knew the drill, Randle didn't have to tell him he would be out for his lunch-hour run.

Slicing through the crime-scene tape along the front door, he let himself into the death house and stood in the foyer. With their work completed and the scene secured, the house exerted a throbbing silence.

Just the way he liked it.

He often paid a second visit to a crime scene alone, when he could let his mind wander, imagine scenarios, and work things out in his head. With all house occupants either dead or in jail, he had all the time in the world.

He scanned the ground floor. A stone fireplace dominated the far living room wall, a scenic downtown Chatham painting poised above it. The occupants had arranged an array of blown-glass figurines, wood carvings, and polished shells on the mantle with care. He envisioned this room as the house's heart and soul, where the Stennetts entertained family and friends, scanned the Sunday paper, and sipped coffee with the Patriots game droning in the background, or nestled together on winter nights beside the fire. Never to happen again.

Images of Claire and Zach flashed through his head, the two huddled around his kitchen table, Claire dribbling milk into Zach's bowl of Lucky Charms, his hand propping up a sleepy head. How different could the Stennett's mornings have been? He pictured the psychopathic murderer joining his sleepy-eyed son at the breakfast table and trickling milk over his son's cereal the day he threw him from the bluff.

What the hell had happened here?

A thick, soft carpet cushioned his steps as he slipped from room to room. He peered into the shadowed dining room just off the foyer, then crossed through it into the kitchen and flipped on the overhead light. The room appeared neat and tidy and held the faint scent of a recent meal. Backtracking toward the front door, Stahl climbed the stairs to the second floor. The worn carpeting muted his footsteps but couldn't disguise the plywood's groan beneath it.

In the bathroom at the top of the stairs, a SpongeBob towel hung across the shower door, a tube of bubblegum toothpaste beside the sink. Stepping along the hallway, he crept into Nathan's room. On his twin bed, a Star Wars blanket lay rumpled and thrown back—his final day's first act. Red Sox and Patriots' posters hung at angles on the walls, a toy basketball hoop dangled over the fold-out closet doors, and a mini, replica rubber basketball rested on the floor below it, ready for the next game. A hamper sat overflowing with dirty clothes, and a piggybank perched on a bookshelf, a hand-written 'Favorites' label posted beside a pile of children's books strewn across the plywood surface.

Stahl pulled a deep breath as he lowered himself into the undersized chair at the boy's desk, colored pencils and artwork splayed across the desk blotter.

This would be difficult.

Opening the desk's center drawer, he uncovered an eight-year-old boy's junk collection—random artifacts collected during his short stay in this world: bottle caps, marbles, beach glass, batteries, Chapstick, a pair of tattered Red Sox tickets from an earlier season.

Reaching deep inside the drawer, he pulled out a sketch pad. He flipped the cover to the first page, a drawing of a stick figure boy with a lollipop-sized head evoking a smirk. The child in the picture stood in front of his house, holding his father and mother's hands. All three had enormous smiles on their round faces, the grass a brightly colored green, the glowing, yellow sun jumping off the white parchment.

The artwork conveyed a child's comfort, security, and happiness. Page after page of similar drawings followed: the boy zooming in the car, parading along the beach, and frolicking on the playground, always beside his parents, smiling and holding hands.

He returned the sketch pad to the drawer and rose from the desk. He couldn't stomach it anymore, an innocent child drawing blissful pictures of childhood, a monster living under the same roof about to blindside him. Stepping close to Nathan's closet, he palmed the rubber basketball on the floor below the hoop. Stahl rolled the ball in his hands, scanning the room, imagining what landmark Nathan might have used as his three-point line and which NBA player he pretended to be. He placed the ball below the basket with a reverence and gave the room a final glance before padding along the hallway toward the stairs.

Halfway down the flight, Stahl's throat tightened as he struggled to swallow. Ex-partner and former Falmouth Police Chief, Chuck Brennan, burned beyond recognition and clutching a Glock in his blackened hand, stepped from the living room at the bottom of the stairs and gazed upward. The inferno had melted his eyes in their sockets, his charred form still smoldering, his enormous belly split like a brat on a grill, dribbling sizzling fluid down his middle. *"Never got a chance to finish the job, rookie."* The bloated corpse raised the stopper as a blazing shape gyrated behind him. Familiar fingers pressed against Stahl's throat, *the rush* following its playbook to a T. The oxygen pulled from his lungs as a swirling cone of flame shot forward up the staircase, bathing Stahl in a hellish torrent, hurling him backwards against the steps.

Pressing his hands to his dripping temples, Stahl sat up, waiting for the vision to fade against a swelling silence. Reaching for the banister, he pulled himself to his feet, hesitating a moment as his trembling knees fought to obey his brain's demand. An unease in his gut directed him to retrace his steps, unsteady limbs carrying him back toward Nathan's bedroom as if on autopilot. He sensed more than Abner Stennett's evil presence in the house with him.

Finish the job, Mike.

Padding across the carpet, he folded himself once again into the tiny desk chair and removed the sketch pad a second time. He flipped the pages until he had reached a new drawing in the sequence. Happy family, bright sunshine, and giant smiles. Page after page.

Then, changes.

The lines appeared more jagged, drawn in black and white. Stark.

He leaned forward, tapping his fist against his lips. The boy stood expressionless in the barren front yard, alone, no leaves gripping the tree's branches and no sunshine beaming from the sky. Inside the boy's head, another face emerged with dark, piercing eyes and a shock of black hair. Stahl scanned the following entry, again the boy with piercing eyes sharing space inside the young boy's head.

Page after page.

When he surveyed the final picture, he stopped breathing. The lines grew jagged, darker, as if drawn in a different hand. The boy with the piercing eyes no longer gazed out from inside the young boy's head; now, the young boy peeked out from his. The other boy didn't much resemble a boy anymore, but instead something from a B horror flick—ogre-like, with dense, ropy muscles protruding from ancient skin. Gripped in his hand, a slingshot, and beside the boy, a woman lay on the grass with X'd out eyes and a lump protruded from her head.

Stahl leaned closer, squishing his eyebrows together as he scrutinized the sketch.

The woman had an uncanny resemblance to Maria Stennett.

Kacey

Kacey woke early on her last day of school to walk off the Malachi-in-the-well dream from the previous night. She shook RG until he reluctantly rolled out of bed to join her, day one of his supposed new summer exercise regimen. Standing shirtless before the mirror a week ago, he had told her this would be the 'summer of buff,' but he still hadn't followed through on his promise to work out and get his ten thousand steps a day. She worried it could easily turn into the 'summer of buffet' if he wasn't careful. *Oh, and fuck you again, Yvette Brody!* Today, they would kick it off with a thirty-minute walk to her parents' house just past Lighthouse Beach and back, pushing Junior in the stroller. She would have to take a winding route to avoid the two Dunkin' Donuts along the way.

Might be high time to confiscate his DDPerks card anyway.

At the lighthouse, they paused to view the sun-stained ocean, the virgin white sand of Seal's Bay Cove nature preserve amplifying the Atlantic's rich, blue-green swells. Growing up less than a mile away, Kacey had relished this view countless times, filled with the same awe and wonder she had witnessed in others' faces gracing this same vantage point. It struck her how something as *unchanging* as nature had the capacity to profoundly *change* those experiencing it. For Kacey, each viewing created the fleeting, false impression of her own timelessness—she was neither five years old nor thirty-five—nature's indefinable majesty eradicating, in a glance, her own self-perceptions.

She sensed RG's pensiveness and gave him a rub on the shoulders. "Where are you?"

He glanced at his shoes before speaking. "I'm sorry, Kacey, for all this."

"All what?"

"The upheaval. Where we are in life." He raised his arms from his sides. "Everything."

"And where do you suppose we are?"

He didn't answer.

To include 'everything' gave it life, made it real. His career dive had more than halved their incomes, with legal fees draining their savings and liquidating their assets. They now relied on every penny of Kacey's income.

"I recognize we lost just about everything we had, RG, but we came out the other side."

He pivoted to face her. "With what? Let me correct you, my dear. We lost everything! It's all gone, along with our friends and colleagues who abandoned us. Oh, and Johnny D is still dead…"

A hitch in his breath interrupted his rant. Kacey registered his surprise at the reaction, the emotion surrounding his best friend's death at the hands of the burning man still raw enough to blindside him. But why these emotions had also spurred his pulling away from the other members of the Revere gang, boyhood friends, Matty, Donnie, and Walt, remained a mystery. It hadn't accelerated the healing.

"Mike did his best to clear my name, but both cases are still open, and people continue to suspect I got away with murder. I hear the whispers…you know the ones…at the grocery store, the faculty room…but I also get a front-row seat to view the juicy thoughts spilling into my head, the things they don't dare whisper out loud. My career crashed and burned like a Korean missile test. It took you from your job and the home you loved, forced us out of Boston. Now I can barely earn enough for gas money. Quite the example I've set for Junior."

"You're worried about how Junior is gonna view his dad?"

RG shrugged.

Kacey crossed her arms. "Well, he'll be super disappointed in you when he learns you laid everything on the line for us, and you were ready to die for him. You don't suppose that will be enough to 'wow' him?"

Gazing at Junior, fast asleep in his stroller, RG brushed a few errant hair strands from the boy's face.

"RG, we have it all. All this." She gestured toward the ocean. "It's all gravy."

"Gravy…?" He licked his lips.

Food again…gotta be more careful! "Let me rephrase…it's all low-fat, gluten-free topping."

He forced a smirk.

She cupped her hand to his cheek. "Look at what you have. Things you've forever dreamed of, to live beside the ocean, to have a family…to finally know your father. You have all the time you worried you'd miss with Junior, remember? You'd be too busy to throw the ball around. He'd be off the college before you'd blinked, you know, the old Harry Chapin song? If you can't recognize these are the best days of our life, RG, I'm not sure how to convince you."

He turned to his wife. "And for reasons I can't explain, I have you, too." He kissed her as the sun broke through the mist embracing the shoreline.

She rested her arms on his shoulders, her fingers clasped together behind his neck. "Do you want this? This thing we're doing?"

"What thing?"

"The life. Finding jumpers, messing with…other worlds. Evil."

"It's not really a choice anymore."

"There's always a choice. We've been through enough to last a lifetime."

RG disengaged and stared out across the ocean, the breeze sifting through his unruly knot of java-colored hair.

"Morrow and I came up with this idea on our own, we never bothered asking your opinion about it. We *can* stop, you know. We can forget the world's problems and just go through our time here, if you want to. Just you, me, and Junior."

"I wouldn't be honest if I said I hadn't considered it." He lowered his eyes, hesitant to meet her gaze.

"I can tell. I'm not sensing you're one-hundred percent committed to anything right now. And the thing is, I can't do this without you."

"And I can't face losing you again! This may be all the time we ever get…"

"All the time…what?"

"Nothing." RG collapsed on the small bench along the bluff, giving a frustrated whack to the mounted coin-op binocular machine beside him. "If we've chosen this for our lives, how many times will I face a future without you? Or how many times will we face leaving Junior without a father or mother? I've been through it before, and I didn't like it."

"Neither did I." Kacey joined him on the bench, running a hand through his hair. She let it fall to his shoulder.

"Your powers have been with you since birth, Kacey, you have this gift—"

"Trust me, it doesn't always seem like it."

"I get it. But it's your calling. It's what you're born to do." He leaned forward, resting his elbows on his knees. He gazed at the ring choking his finger. "And this hunk of gold may not be coming with me."

"Coming with you where?"

RG waved her off with his hand. "I don't belong here, Kacey. It's like having never held a baseball bat and finding yourself leading off for the Red Sox. Yeah, Morrow dressed me up in the fancy uniform and pushed me into the batter's box, but I'm out of my league. I don't even belong on the field."

"It'll come. But only if you want it to."

At the sound of Junior's discomforting cry, RG undid his stroller's three-point harness and gathered him in his arms. He relaxed for a moment, eyes glued to his boy's face, scanning the familiar contours and shapes. Junior's tiny fingers opened like a flower petal, reaching out to his father and tugging at his lips.

Kacey had lived with RG long enough to recognize the maelstrom swirling behind his disoriented gaze. As he focused on his son, she suspected his mind had turned to Molly Buckholtz and the twenty years she had been waiting to stare into her son's eyes again, wanting to help her, but also longing for his old life again. The one he'd had before Morrow intervened, when he had been the respected university researcher whose star was on the rise, before the national media dragged him through the mud and his friends and colleagues turned on him.

"I understand you can't leave this one alone, Kacey, and I'd never ask you to. If there's a chance we can find Gunnar, or any other child Malachi may have abducted, I guess we have to try." He squeezed out another forced grin.

She leaned over and kissed him, then kissed the top of Junior's head. "You just earned yourself a sugar donut."

"Just one?"

Kacey rolled her eyes.

Welcome to the 'summer of buffet'…

––––––

Mike

Stahl left the Stennett house and slid into the Crown Vic's front seat, cranking the air conditioning to counter the mounting early morning humidity. His imaginings churned as he pulled out into the light Chatham traffic. He didn't like what he'd found inside and had a hunch he wouldn't like what Russ had to show him, either.

He took Route 137 to the mid-Cape highway and sped to the medical examiner's office in Sandwich, pulling in just before one o'clock. As he strode through the front doors, he glanced toward Sarah Bricker at the front desk, the facility's appointed gatekeeper. A telephone embedded beneath her chin, she had a coffee in one hand, the other tapping on her computer keyboard. A barrage of pings erupted from her Outlook email.

Sarah raised an eyebrow when she spotted him. "Livin' the dream," she mumbled.

He flashed a smile and pointed down the hall, mouthing "Russ" as he trotted past her. She gave a quick nod before turning back to her conversation.

He paced along the spotless corridor, footsteps echoing off the tiled floors and walls. The state had built the facility in 2012 with emergency funding to counter the state's huge back-logs in autopsy and toxicology reports, but the cash infusion still couldn't fix the dearth of medical examiners, leaving Russ Randle's team swamped. The fact he had already performed the Stennett autopsy spoke to pressure from above to clear the family killer case.

As Stahl approached Randle's office adjacent to the morgue, he smelled the familiar formaldehyde and death odors seeping through the walls. He glanced at the laboratory door leading to a sterile room housing the deceased inside air-condi-tioned steel drawers, no fan of what lay inside its walls. He respected Randle for painstakingly extracting secrets from the dead, but never understood why he had accepted such a morose calling.

Stahl stepped into the waiting area outside Randle's office and knocked on his door, the shower still running.

"Just a sec. Be right out."

He inspected the pictures displayed on the walls and

bookshelves, a new one of Russ and Sherry with Mike and Claire on their trip to Bar Harbor in March added since his last visit. Framed photographs of Sherry and the girls, now numbering five and ranging in age from one to thirteen, rested alone on their own shelf. Randle had surrendered to fate and Father Time his goal of bringing a son into the brood, but Stahl sensed he had no complaints. Other photos showed Russ crossing the finish line at the Hawaii Iron Man Triathlon and both the New York City and Boston marathons.

Randle stepped from his office, sweat still seeping from his forehead and dripping down his face.

"Not sure why I bother showering." He grabbed his towel and buried his face in it.

"I never have that problem anymore." They both chuckled, acknowledging Mike's complete and unrepentant transition to the sedentary life. Stahl had forever dreaded exercise, but the burns and bullets had given him the ultimate get-out-of-jail-free card. He would occasionally stroll with Claire on the soft sand along Aunt Lydia's Cove, but even this sporadic routine interfered with his primary desire to sleep late, devour a huge breakfast, and read the *Herald* on his porch swing.

"Let's head to the lab. There's something you should see." Randle plucked two white lab coats from the coat rack, tossing one to Stahl as he maneuvered himself into the other. Mike had to double time it to match the marathoner's pace along the hall.

Maria Stennett and several other bodies lay on stationary autopsy tables in the sterling white room. Randle's medical examiners conducted autopsies at nearby work stations, the tiled floors and walls amplifying the medical devices' shrill grinding and whirring sounds as they separated bones and flesh. The hanging scales' metallic plink tapped at his ears as they accommodated the dripping internal organs plopping onto them.

Randle breezed past the long lines of sinks, walk-in refrigerators, and freezers until he reached his work station and Maria Stennett's body. Autopsy saws and blades, bone and rib cutters, and hammers and chisels rested beside her on the dissecting cart, still splattered with blood and matter. A deep Y incision closed up with heavy stitching desecrated her chest. The extent of her body's bruising showed much clearer under the morgue's brilliant light.

Randle handed Stahl a pair of latex gloves.

"Did you determine cause of death?" Stahl asked, snapping on the prophylactic over his sweaty palms.

"Suffocation, garroted with rope."

"So, she was alive when Abner Stennett hoisted her up to the ceiling?"

"Looks like it." Randle pressed his lips together.

Stahl gazed downward, shifting his weight from one leg to the other.

"As we prepared for autopsy, we found something. I want you to look closely here." Randle adjusted the overhead lighting, directing it onto the body. "The bruising." He pointed to the dark, purple patches along her skin. "Couldn't make it out in the basement."

Stahl leaned forward to scrutinize the repeated bruising patterns, the size and shape of small hands, around the throat, along the arms and legs, and across the stomach. He peered at his friend expectantly, awaiting an explanation.

Randle frowned and scratched his head. "Could be…when the husband came for her, the boy held onto her tightly, trying to protect her. Maybe caused incidental bruising."

Stahl failed to spot any conviction in his speculation. He closed his eyes and rubbed his neck. "Russ, if someone hoisted a living, naked body to the ceiling and tethered her to it, would you anticipate larger, hand-sized bruises?'"

Russ just shrugged. "That's what I would expect."

"Then how come I can't spot any?"

Randle stared at the body, the crack of a separated ribcage breaking the silence, echoing across the room. "Because they aren't there."

Chapter Nine

'Thy troubles are all ended—
Thy pains, thy sufferings done;
Thy parents still will love thee,
Thou dear; thou only son.'

In memory of **WILLIAM WALLACE**, died Feb'y 2, 1834
(Aged 1 year, 10 mo's & 17 days)
-Epitaphs from Burial Hill

June 21, 2019

Malachi

Malachi hovered above Larson Skoczek as he reclined in the stained Barcalounger in his one-room Hyannis hovel, located in a corner of town even a lost Cape Cod tourist would never discover. A muted television sent shards of scattered light across the young man's eyes, but his gaze focused elsewhere. A leaky kitchen faucet's interminable drip into a scum-laden sink breached the room's silence as he placed the bottle to his lips and took a long pull, dribbling foamy lager down his stubbled chin and onto his stained shirt.

Malachi scanned the apartment unseen, shaking his head, taking in the seventies era faux-wood paneling and roach-infested brown shag carpet matted with food. A humid breeze descended through the propped windows, augmenting the fusty odor permeating the cramped space. He slipped inside Skoczek, donning him like an old sweatshirt. He hated how the boy's body had changed over the years, maturing and growing in foul ways, but its familiarity and comfort outweighed his disgust. Malachi spoke to him deep inside his mind in the familiar ancient language that could double as Skoczek's native tongue. *"Love what you've done with the place, Lars."*

"Decided to tear yourself away from your new boy?" He rubbed the spot where Malachi had breached his chest. *"What the fuck do you want?"*

"And such nice language. Is this how you greet your old friends?"

The jumper paused, attempting to discern Skoczek's prevailing mood. He had gotten used to the young man's uneven disposition, content to accommodate him one day, fighting to expel him the next.

"What old friend?"

Malachi grinned, detecting no resistance. He had won this round.

"Don't take it out on me, Lars. I didn't make you who you are. That's how you've always been. And you have great things ahead of you." Malachi eyed the toppled beer bottles on the floor beside the recliner.

"Great things, huh?" Skoczek rose from the chair and padded

into the bathroom, relieving himself without flushing, his urine stream spattering the porcelain rim.

"You've always been a jumper, Lars. I sensed it the moment I entered you all those years ago. You can't blame me for revealing your destiny."

Skoczek raked a hand through his shoulder length hair. *"Well, thanks for that! Thanks for making my life a living hell. Now I get to look forward to death to turn me into a monster like you."* His arm shot forward, sweeping beer bottles and dishes off the kitchen counter to shatter on the Linoleum floor. *"My glorious destiny."*

"Oh, you'll be a formidable power in the next world." Malachi rubbed his hands together within Skoczek's human shell. *"But you don't have to wait for death to shower you with your blessings. Sure, you can deny who you are, living like…this."* Malachi wrinkled his nose at the squalor he beheld. *"Or you can embrace your true self and set out your journey now…with a job I have for you."*

"A job?" Skoczek paced the filthy carpet. *"I'm not ready to do what you do!"*

"Oh, really…" Malachi tapped Lars's mind, getting a front-row seat to the parading images creeping through the man's consciousness. He sensed Skoczek's fight against his own dark nature, the repressed rage simmering behind his eyes, the desire to kill flowing through his mortal veins.

"If a man inherits a murderer's heart but never acts on it, does it make him a murderer?" Skoczek challenged. *"I don't have to become a killer just because you say I will be some day."*

"Some day? You're not being honest with yourself. You need someone to show you who you already are…"

Malachi queued the images and played them in Skoczek's head, the ones the young man kept hidden, buried beneath layers of a forgotten past: a mother pressing her hand against a scalding griddle as a five-year-old boy brooded next to a plate of burned pancakes; two years later, a doddering grandfather's stumble into the moldy darkness from the basement's top step after swatting a willful boy on the rear with a folded newspaper; a once-attractive fifth-grade teacher piercing her face with a letter opener after she had sent a defiant boy to the principal's office. Fast-forward to his teenage years: Mary Ellen Colby's foot jamming the gas pedal to the floor along the narrow, winding country road after she had bolted from the movies with Jimmy Bliss instead of the boy who brought her.

"Anything ring a bell?" Malachi queried.

"I didn't have anything to do with those accidents."

"And you cried such crocodile tears at grandpa's funeral. A nice touch, if you ask me."

"Those memories you showed me…I imagined those things. You're showing me my dreams, nothing else."

"Dreams?" Malachi leaned back and chuckled. *"You were there, Lars, making it happen. Should I show you more?"*

Skoczek lowered his eyes and shook his head. *"You were in my head, too. You were there! I remember you with me."*

"Tsk, tsk, always blaming others." Malachi waggled a finger inside Skoczek's head. *"The way I see it, Lars, you've got a number of kills under your belt…even more if we count Mary Ellen. I mean, having to move yourself in a chair with a lever in your mouth? How do we score that one?"*

Skoczek buried his face in his hands. *"That's not who I am."*

"Oh, it's very much who you are. You're trying to fight it, sure. You keep to yourself…here," he pronounced, scanning the room, *"cut off from the human race because you're afraid your true nature will emerge."*

Skoczek lowered himself onto the grimy, fetid carpet, hoisting another tepid gulp of beer from a day-old, forgotten bottle.

Malachi glared at the man on the floor. When he first met Skoczek as a little boy, he had befriended him, slipped inside him one evening to hijack his body and take over his life. But the boy had expelled him with a fury equal to the darkest souls he had ever encountered. Malachi persisted, exerting his influence, and they eventually came to a mutual understanding. He had faced only one other soul with the raw, developing power Skoczek displayed—the woman caretaker from the dream. But she sought out the light, the other side's beneficence. He had read in her the desire to rescue his special children.

Someone would have to stop her.

"So, let's get down to brass tacks. The job I have for you...there's a woman who's interfering in my work. She and her husband are teachers. They have a beautiful baby boy." Malachi flashed their images inside Skoczek's head.

"So what?" he shrugged.

"I want you to slaughter them. Each one. You don't have trouble with children, do you?"

"How could you ask me to kill a child?"

"You're serious?" Malachi queued up the mind-film of a ten-year-old Skoczek, stepping off the school bus with a neighbor boy from across the street. He grasped the younger boy's hand and walked him down the hill through the McCormack's backyard, over a bowed, weather-beaten fence rail, across the field beside the pond, and deep into the woods. He spoke to the boy in hushed tones, making him giggle with his silly jokes. The shimmering afternoon sunlight fought to penetrate the dense woods' swaying pine needle canopy, scattering patches of uneven sunlight across the two forms holding hands and following the winding river bank. When the boy fatigued, they sank into the soft mossy ground beside the brook, huddling together to stave off the autumn chill, scaling rocks and sticks into the swift current. They talked about catching frogs when the weather warmed up and the boy's black Lab, Wiley, who slept on his bed each night.

As darkness fell, Skoczek returned alone.

"Stop! No more," Skoczek cried, burying his face in his hands.

"And I want you to take care of the child right in front of them."

"I won't do that." Skoczek doubled over, his wince betraying the gnawing in his viscera. *"I can't."*

"You want salvation?"

Skoczek swallowed, wiping his damp eyes with his palms. *"What are you talking about?"*

"A chance for redemption and a new role in the universal structure."

He shrugged. *"I don't understand."*

"You will. The man wears a gold band on his finger. His ring will change you, make you who you want to be. But, first, you must pit your fledgling jumper's talents against another emerging power. I have confidence you'll be victorious."

"And if I'm not? Well, no loss, right? At least you'll find out what type of adversary you're facing."

"Touché."

"Then you can spend more time with your…new recruits." The man turned his head, arms folded across his chest.

"I'm touched, Lars, but jealousy doesn't become you."

Skoczek reached for the chair and hauled himself up, leaning on the cushioned arm. *"So, there's a way out. I don't have to be like you after all?"*

"You can be whatever you want. You can rescue kittens from trees, read to the blind, save the world from rot like me…whatever you fucking want."

Skoczek rose to his feet. *"And this power…it's there for the taking?"*

"It sits on a finger, waiting for you."

"And all it takes is——"

"A little dirty work."

———

Mike

Mike Stahl folded the *Cape Cod Times* and rubbed his eyes as he leaned back at the kitchen table, the story about Kenny Farley's disappearance stabbing at his gut. Farley had gone to bed six days ago, and no one had seen him since. His parents only reported he was missing after the school called the second day, asking where he had been. He stood, wincing as he straightened his hip. *How could that be?* Didn't they feed him, get him off to school, and help him at night with his homework? A heavy guilt hung around Stahl's neck like a yoke for the unenviable notions he had entertained about Farley after learning he'd bullied Zach. If the only attention the boy ever received took the form of indifference and physical abuse, no wonder he had ended up taking it out on others.

Balancing the half-eaten sandwich in his palm, he dumped it in the garbage pail next to the pantry and brushed the crumbs from his hands into the sink. He shook his head. *It had to have been his asshole father who made him disappear.* He renewed his vow to go up to the guy and punch his lights out after he had arrested him.

Stahl squeezed a blast of Dawn onto the dishes bathing in the sink and turned the water to hot.

Whump, thwack!

The sound reverberated in his head. He surveyed the backyard through the kitchen window above the sink, a humid breeze rippling the seahorse curtains and sending a welcome coolness across his heated skin.

Whoosh, thwack!

Scanning the property from left and right, Stahl attempted to pinpoint the sound's origin.

"Zach, you out there?" he shouted. Stahl stepped across the kitchen floor and through the slider onto the raised deck.

Zach leaned over the deck's railing, gazing at the line of pine trees along the woods separating the property from their neighbor's.

"Whatcha doing, bud?"

The boy didn't acknowledge Mike's presence as he pulled his right arm back, cords and tendons straining against ropy muscles.

Stahl threw a hand to his mouth as he spotted the blue, web-like veins throbbing underneath his pale skin. He blinked to clear his eyes and stepped closer. Zach's behavior had changed recently, spending more time alone in his room, sullen and distant. A pall surrounded him as if he moved in perpetual darkness. But now the boy appeared older, like the time enhanced photo of a missing child. Stahl moved across the deck to observe him from a different angle, viewing a boy at an infinite number of ages, anywhere from eight- to eighty-years-old, some strange caricature of a child. Yet Zach's familiar face still remained visible under the shadow of the others. He jammed his eyes shut, and when he opened them, the shadows had disappeared like a mirage.

He remembered Abner Stennett. *Something inside pulsed against Nathan's skin, pushing, trying to get out…*

Whoosh, thwack! The warble of multiple birds taking flight pierced the calm as a whistling stone caromed off a tree trunk along the cluster of knotty pines and skittered across the woods' mossy leaf carpet.

He approached Zach. "What the hell have you got in your hand?"

Zach turned, a dark sheen clouding his once-blue eyes. He lifted his hand to reveal a slingshot, the dark and grooved wood resembling a petrified artifact.

"Pretty dangerous toy, Zach. You hit something with it, you're gonna kill it."

You know, eyes are like windows...

The ends of Zach's mouth curled into a grin, sending a shiver through Stahl's core.

"Your mom know you have that thing? Where'd you get it anyway?" He couldn't imagine Claire's approving of any such toy, but Zach's aiming it toward a living creature proved a greater surprise. For a kid accustomed to rescuing wayward frogs and carrying them back to the pond over on Ted Boyle's property, who fed their ducks and rabbits and left extra bread crusts from his half-eaten toast on the porch for the squirrels, something had changed.

"My friend gave it—" Zach's eyes widened as his mouth dropped, halting him midsentence. He cocked his head as if someone whispered something in his ear. "Never mind."

"What friend? Someone from school?"

...If you look deep into them, you can spot all sorts of things.

The boy turned away, loading up the slingshot's leather pocket with a stone from a pile he had gathered along the railing.

"What's the matter with you, Zach?"

Turning his attention toward the tree line, Zach pulled back the twin rubber tubes.

"Hey, I asked you a question." Stahl followed Zach's line of vision, honing in on the colorful bird hopping along the tree branch.

Zach squinted, taking dead aim. The bird hesitated, darting its head toward the deck as if it sensed a vague threat, its flapping wings ripping the air to take evasive action. The boy's tongue slithered along his lower lip as he released the tension on the rubber tubing, the stone hurling like a missile across the yard.

Whoosh! Thump!

Stahl winced as if punched in the gut, a plume of feathers

hanging suspended in the air as the bird plummeted to earth. He stood fixed in cement as Zach raced down the deck steps and stood over the quivering shape.

Stahl's descending commands to his lower limbs jumped the tracks, leaving his weakened legs wobbling like Jell-O. With gradual coaxing he ushered them forward, guiding them down the steps and across the backyard until he stood beside Zach.

Stahl crinkled his nose. A pungent odor wafted from the boy, stopping him in his tracks.

On the ground, the baby bird clung to life, the mysterious whatever-it-was within ebbing from its battered body. He had never spotted a bird with such markings before. Its vibrant feathers' interlocking spirals resembled a Technicolor suit of armor, a flying rainbow. Each iridescent sparkle and brilliant hue faded into the next with immaculate symmetry, from its blue- and black- toned head and neck to its bright yellow and red chest and wings. The bird's jet-black eyes darted back and forth between Zach and Stahl, as if beseeching them for help. The bird stopped searching when it locked onto Stahl's glance. Its left wing no longer moved, but the right fluttered in a rapid blur. One of its feet jerked, scraping the dirt.

Stahl knelt and met the boy's eyes. "Zach?"

"It's suffering. I need to put it out of its misery," Zach growled. He bent down to snatch a branch from the edge of the woods.

The bird lay helpless on its grass bed. It had stopped twitching, but its chest still heaved, its crushed lungs struggling to suck in oxygen.

"Wait!" Stahl shouted.

Before he could react, Zach hoisted the branch over his head like a sledgehammer. Stahl made the mistake of glancing at the bird, its gaze still locked onto his. Zach glared at his step-father as he swung the lumber over his head. He struck the bird with such force it shattered into pieces. Feathers flew upward like a plume of colorful smoke, fluid and innards jetting onto Stahl's pant leg.

He searched Zach's eyes, his mouth agape. The boy's eyes had gone black.

He looked like him, he even moved like him. But it wasn't him.

"Give me that thing!" Stahl attempted to snatch the slingshot from the boy's back pocket, but Zach twisted away.

"What's the big deal?" Zach's voice had dropped, words tumbling over his lips with a gruff lilt.

"The big deal?" Mike's hands dropped to his sides. "You just killed a living creature, Zach. For no reason."

"You've seen worse." The Zach-like boy stepped toward Stahl. "You know about death, don't you?"

"What?" Stahl's vision shifted, peppered with white dots. Flames simmered at Zach's feet. He pressed his palms to his eyes to stop the surge.

Zach cocked his head to the side and sniffed the air like an animal, his voice growling, "You've been places, haven't you?"

Stahl stood mesmerized by the absence of life, a soul... anything behind his eyes. "You're not Zach anymore, are you?" A wall of flames grew behind the boy, coiling into the shape of a monster. A charred, blackened body lay on the grass, writhing. Stahl attempted to block the images from his mind. *He's just inventing pictures, that's all. They're not really there.*

"You've been places no one else has seen." The boy circled. "You've faced my kind."

He recalled the dream Kacey had taken him into eighteen months ago, drawing him through a portal to witness a great evil, one following him home and leaving it in rubble. He glanced around, as if searching for answers. "I...Zach, how do you know any of this?"

"Tell me about the boy on the rocks," he pressed. "You found him, didn't you?"

Snap out of it, Zach…please. The sun beat down on Stahl's shoulders, but his muscles shivered uncontrollably. His pant legs ignited first, flames inching upward until his whole body was ablaze.

"Nathan…you found him, didn't you?"

You're not on fire, Mike. "Did you know him?"

Zach dropped the branch as he turned and headed toward the deck. "Know him? I was him."

The boy hiked across the lawn and climbed the porch steps as Stahl collapsed to his knees, hands pressed to his temples, *the rush* in full force.

———

RG

RG rolled the Legacy into the Cape Cod Community College's faculty lot and parked in the farthest corner. He would have a good five- to ten-minute hike to his office in the North Building and then to his class in the adjacent lecture hall, but he welcomed the extra steps. With supernatural storm clouds brewing, the first day of summer session had come at a bad time. But if he and Kacey were to pursue their destined paths as caretakers, nothing from this point on would ever fit a convenient schedule.

He unbuckled the shoulder harness, but remained seated, sunglasses balanced on his nose as he leaned his head back and reveled in the early summer sunshine filtering through the yawning moonroof. He had never grown accustomed to teaching summer session, especially now that he lived on the Cape. It seemed an affront to the natural order of things. But summer work paid well, and, with his financial portfolio on life support, he considered himself lucky to have gotten the gig. Still, on a day like today, any type of work was punishment.

He gazed through the side window at the West Barnstable campus, a modest-sized community college surrounded by picturesque beach towns and tourist destinations. It remained the only place in the country that had offered him a job. Teaching health science courses remained a far cry from RG's projected ascension at Boston University just two years earlier. With several million-dollar federal grants and a stable of research assistants, PhD students, and post-docs in his growing laboratory, RG Granville had been a rising star in the sports medicine field. But after the nationwide publicity surrounding his multiple murder charges and dismissal from BU, his professional opportunities foundered.

He had inquired at nearly every university in the country, reaching out to distant colleagues and collaborators, anyone he had met at a professional conference or seminar, desperate to get a foot in a rapidly closing door. After scores of rejections, his former PhD advisor from Northeastern had called in a favor and informed him the University of Missouri agreed to grant him an interview, but only if he would pay his own flight and expenses.

He had arrived in Columbia on a drab, winter morning, three days before Christmas, the university deserted during intersession. A light snow framed Jesse Hall's cupola and obscured the massive stone columns perched in the quad as he glanced at the campus map, struggling to pinpoint his destination. This wouldn't be the typical whirlwind, two-day interview process, touring laboratories, meeting faculty and students, and allowing the dean and administrators to wine and dine him. The hiring committee chair had granted RG a single, thirty-minute interview inside a crumbly building's drafty eighth-floor office on the edge of campus. The man did not introduce

RG to any colleagues, give him a tour of the facilities, or ask him any questions about what he could contribute to the department or school. As RG had described his research plans, the man had stood, checked his watch, and thanked him for making the trip, never bothering to remove his winter jacket.

And here RG found himself, his career in freefall, in a job with less money and little opportunity…on a perfect summer day. He exited his vehicle, reaching into the passenger side window and snatching what Kacey affectionately termed his 'professor bag' with the throw-over flap and buckles, her gift when he had earned tenure at BU. Though it contained nothing more than a class roster and a flash drive, he held it reverently, as if holding onto a piece of himself that no longer existed. It reminded him of what being a professor had been like.

Before cracking the Science Building's auditorium door, RG hesitated, garnering the courage to face a room full of indifferent millennials. The first few minutes of any class could make or break the course, setting the tone for the entire six-week session. The key was to establish authority yet appear approachable, inject humor and self-deprecation but exude confidence, and set high expectations without frightening anyone. By the time he had launched into his lecture, RG had confidence he'd won over the majority of his students, their faces visible through the auditorium's dim shadows and not illuminated by their smartphones' hazy glow. Small victories.

Ready to congratulate himself, a student's hand shot up in the first row.

"Is this gonna be on the test?"

Before he could respond, a young man appeared at the rear entrance in the back of the auditorium. Pausing to mitigate the heavy door's metallic crunch against the jamb, the student scanned the room, choosing a seat in the back corner, alone. RG squinted through the overhead row of glowing fluorescence. The slim figure slid into the last row without a backpack, notebook, laptop, or any other student utensil; he just sat, arms snaked across the adjacent seatbacks, staring at the dais, occasionally swiping a casual hand through his shoulder-length locks.

Late on the first day and oozing indifference. RG fought his spiraling annoyance, but conceded such students often turned out to be best in the class.

RG continued to lecture, but a visual flurry of thoughts and pictures mobbed his senses, streaking past him as if he stood in a field of fireflies. The room pulled away as images leeched from the stranger in the back row, dark and disturbing, pictures of death and violence, actions the man had witnessed up close.

When RG had first worn the ring his father had bestowed upon him, hidden images and deep thoughts from unsuspecting strangers had barraged him, a hundred different conversations vibrating in his ears all at once. He would hear their pleas, witness their sins and desires, their pain. But over time, as he cultivated his powers, he had learned to deflect the images into nothing more than white noise. But, the image salvo from the student in the back row had a force and persistence he couldn't repel. RG sensed a raw power inside the mysterious latecomer—not a caretaker's power, but a stormy rage lying dormant within, an unfamiliar gift the man had yet to fully embrace.

And if he wasn't a caretaker…

RG found himself staring, words no longer coming from his own mouth. He may have stopped lecturing; he wasn't sure. At that moment, the man's thought stream halted as if awareness prevailed. The lecture hall's lights resumed in RG's vision as he stood silent before his class. A deliberate cough from a student in the front row jolted him from his awkward trance.

"And so...um, research doesn't just fill useless journals and pad professors' curriculum vitae but filters down from practitioner to patient and ultimately improves healthcare delivery." RG killed the computer's projector as backpack zippers closed and folding arm tables clanked down, confirming class had ended.

"Okay, then. Any questions? I'll see you all on Thursday. Chapters one and three before then."

RG gazed toward the auditorium's back row, shielding his eyes from the glaring light aimed on the podium.

The back row sat empty, the figure gone.

———

Firing the Subaru's engine, RG pulled out from campus, cranking the air conditioning and cracking the moonroof to dispel the interior's summer bake. He had arranged to meet Kacey and Junior in Hyannis for some Chinese and late afternoon shopping. RG had only recently discovered Dragon Lite along the town's main drag, a restaurant emerging as a suitable replacement for China Palace in Watertown, the place that fed his family at least four times a week when they had lived in Beantown. The trip to the restaurant took about fifteen minutes from campus, a beneficial perk to working a stone's throw from JFK's hometown. Maybe he could talk Kacey into ice cream at Katie's on Main Street since he had done well this week with his exercise regimen.

From campus, he navigated the backroads into Hyannis and scored rock-star parking steps from the restaurant's front entrance. He located Kacey tucked in a corner booth, Kindle in one hand and an eggroll in the other

"Who needs China Palace anymore?" He kissed her on the forehead as he slid into the booth. "Where's Junior?"

"I left him with the sitter. Figured we could have an old-fashioned date where we actually talk to each other, maybe stare into each other's eyes like we used to."

"I like that idea." RG reached across the table and folded her hand inside his.

"How'd the first lecture go?"

"Never fails to terrify me, despite my years of teaching. But I'm guessing I won them over."

"Mr. Charming." Kacey rolled her eyes. "Remember the late-night calls you used to get when we lived in Boston? A distraught student—always female, of course—who just *had* to speak with you. Thank God we got you out of the city and packed a few more pounds on you. Now I don't worry as much about those pesky co-eds."

RG chuckled, thinking he may just get ice cream after all. "So, you've fattened me up to keep me all to yourself? Kinda selfish of you, don't ya think?"

"Yep! But now it's the summer of buff, so I might be in trouble."

RG glanced around the restaurant. "Have you ordered yet? I'm gonna get—"

"RG," Kacey whispered, cutting him off. "Keep looking at me, okay? There's someone eyeing us from across the restaurant. He came in right behind you and hasn't stopped staring since you came in."

"Okay. Where?"

"Opposite wall, four booths down."

"You want me to give a subtle glance, maybe like I'm searching for the waiter or something?"

As RG pivoted in his seat, a college girl appeared beside

the table, her order pad held in front of her. "Can I get you something to drink?"

"Too late," Kacey grinned.

"I'll have a Coors Light, and..." RG glanced across the table.

"Blue Moon."

"Okay, I'll be right back with your drinks."

"To hell with subtlety." He stood and nearly bumped into a young man with shoulder-length hair, the stranger now standing beside the table, the lecture hall's glare no longer hiding his stubbled chin and chiseled features. The man forced a smile

"I'm sorry, Dr. Granville." He held up his hands. "I spotted you, and I wanted to come over and introduce myself. Larsson Skoczek, I'm in your Tuesday-Thursday."

"Of course. Back row."

The young man nodded. "My apologies for coming in late today."

"Not a problem." He gestured across the table. "My wife, Kacey. Kacey, this is Larsson, one of my new students."

"Pleasure to meet you, ma'am, and please call me Lars." He flashed a smile, his eyes lingering over Kacey's form.

"Nice to meet you, Lars."

"Why don't you have a seat, share a beverage with us? Nothing like a beer to break the ice."

Skoczek pulled up a chair from the adjacent table and positioned it at the end of the booth. The waitress returned with RG and Kacey's drinks.

"Get this young man whatever he wants," RG directed the waitress.

Skoczek pointed to Kacey's bottle with a grin. "Blue Moon for me, too." He produced his ID. The waitress's prolonged photo examination betrayed an interest beyond just his birth date. In moments, she returned with his drink along with a frosty pilsner glass.

"Thanks." He returned her gleaming smile and combed a hand through his hair.

How come we didn't get frosty glasses? RG frowned.

Why do you think? Kacey replied inside his head.

"Well, cheers." He clinked bottles with Skoczek. "So, tell me, Lars, why did you choose to take my course? How'd you get interested in the health sciences?" He listened as Skoczek spoke, but only partially…"Well, I'm hoping to go into health management…" RG pulled into the man's mind, searching for the breach he had witnessed in class, attempting to recreate that moment when his dark imaginings bombarded him, when grisly scenarios flew from his open mind…"It's an up-and-coming field with good compensation…" the young man's voice droned on, muffled and distant as if seeping through a wall… "You're a professor with a great reputation…" he searched for a fissure, a crack in the wall he could exploit, get a foothold to kick open the door to his thoughts…"Cape Cod Community is lucky to have you, as are all of your students…" but the man had corrected his earlier mistake and sealed the entrance, masking his dark truths while engaging him and Kacey with his story.

He wasn't convinced Skoczek's presence in the same restaurant could be a complete coincidence. He had checked his class roster, and it didn't contain the name Larsson Skoczek.

The man had followed him.

"Well, it sounds like you have a good plan for your future," Kacey added.

"I don't recall your name on my class roster."

Skoczek's eyes drifted to RG's wedding ring. "I guess I have a bit of explaining to do. I have to get a course override, the reason I followed you here tonight. I understand how it might look, a bit sneaky, I admit, but I need to get into your course and it's full. We've had a beer together; there's no way you can turn me down now, right?"

RG chortled. "Not a problem, Lars. Just come by the office before next class, and I'll get you a permission number."

"Thanks, Dr. Granville. I appreciate it." Skoczek took one more swig from his sweating glass and stood up. "Well, I don't want to invade your time together. I'm sure you don't get much with a little guy at home."

Kacey's eyebrows lowered as she leaned against the cushioned booth. "How do you know we have——?"

"Your husband mentioned it in class today," he interrupted, a bit too quickly. "Said he had a wife and young son. Thank you for the beer, Dr. Granville, and nice meeting you, Kacey." He stood and reached for her hand, holding it for a moment before letting go. He faced RG. "I'll stop by before Thursday's class to get that course override. Thanks again."

Skoczek closed his hand over RG's left hand, resting on the tabletop, swaying a moment before steadying himself against the table.

"Sorry, must have gotten up too fast. Or the Blue Moon went straight to my head. Well, goodnight then."

RG leaned his head out of the booth as Skoczek moved between tables to the front door. The eager waitress stopped him with a smile as he passed the server station. Her body language revealed her hope for a moment of small talk, but he blew past her out the door and into the sultry evening air.

"Good looking kid," Kacey remarked.

RG grabbed the last eggroll off the plate and bit it in half. "Something about him concerns me. Didn't you sense it?"

"Other than he came across as hell-bent on getting into your course, I didn't sense anything."

"He came into class late today, settled in the back row, didn't pull out a pen, laptop, or appear to be paying much attention."

"What does that have to do with anything? You've just described all your best students." Kacey pried the remaining eggroll from RG's fingers and gobbled a bite.

"When I lectured, disturbing images flew at me from deep inside his mind. It threw me off, I even stopped lecturing."

"That's never bothered you before. I thought you had that under control."

"It's all white noise to me now unless I really concentrate. But this guy...his thoughts came at me like a runaway train. I couldn't stop them."

"What did you do?" She took a sip of water to coax the eggroll remnants onward.

"Nothing. I sputtered up there on the podium for a few moments before he caught on and pulled his thoughts back inside. From what I witnessed, I'm guessing he's no caretaker."

"If he's not—"

"Exactly!" RG pinched the final eggroll bit from Kacey's fingers and threw it into his mouth. He mopped his hands with the linen napkin in his lap. "I tried to get him talking tonight, hoping I could probe him."

"You're absolutely shitty at probing. Why didn't you signal me to do it?"

"I didn't want to give anything away," he said, jumping in. "But somehow, I gave everything away. Did you notice how he admitted things before I'd called him on it? I'm thinking in my head, he wasn't on my class list. The next second he says he needs an override. I said to myself, kind of a coincidence he'd be in this restaurant. The next second, he says he followed me. It's like he read what I was thinking, trying to head off my concern."

"Was he tapping you?"

"If he got in there somehow, I couldn't detect him."

"I must be getting rusty." Kacey shook her head. "I didn't even notice."

"Too busy staring into his baby blues, maybe?"

"Hard not to," she said, grinning.

The waitress returned with a scowl. RG assumed Skoczek's departure had torpedoed her enthusiasm. They ordered a plate of beef and broccoli and vegetable lo mein with a hot and sour soup to share.

RG scooped the last fried wonton strips from the oil-splotched bowl and shoveled them into his mouth. "I can't remember if I said anything about you and Junior today," he said between chomps, "but if I did, it happened *before* he wandered in late for class. I was already lecturing for Chris-sake. He knows something."

"Kind of odd how he touched your hand like that."

"No shit, and did you see his face? He touched the ring and his eyes rolled back behind his lids. Blue Moon, my ass. He sensed Morrow's power."

She placed her palm over his hand. "You mean, your power. Maybe his being in your class is a blessing."

"How?"

"Well, at least now you can keep an eye on him two days a week. You ever watch those *Animal Planet* documentaries about wildebeests and impala living on the Serengeti?"

RG drew his eyebrows in. "And this had to do with…?"

"Well, you'd figure the weaker animals would stay as far away from the lions as possible, but, in fact, they follow them."

"Why?"

"So they can keep an eye on them, get a sense of what they're planning."

RG leaned forward. "You want me to keep an eye on Skoczek?"

She shrugged. "Couldn't hurt."

"Are you saying I'm the prey?"

"Only if he's hunting you."

Chapter Ten

'Tis the blest hope that they shall meet
Their daughters in the skies.'

HELLEN died Sept. 4th, 1847 (aged 7 years)
LOUISA S. died Sept. 12, 1847 (aged 3 years)
Children of Edward & Salina Doten
-Epitaphs from Burial Hill

June 22, 2019

RG

RG pushed through the Boston Public Library's heavy wooden door, exhausted and defeated. He had arrived early in the morning to research the disappearance of a young boy from Plymouth who had died in a well sometime in the 1940s… maybe. He enlisted the skills of his old friend, Mariel, to refine and narrow his search and reacquaint him with the basement microfilm reader. But after rifling through hundreds of drownings on the South Shore from every New England paper from 1930 to 1950, he pushed his chair back from the screen with nothing to show for it. He checked his watch, hoping to get a jump on the late afternoon rush-hour traffic. Unfortunately, every hour proved to be rush-hour traffic in Boston, and RG resigned himself to an inevitable crawl south.

He slogged down the library's steep granite steps, the air-conditioned fortress's chill giving way to a late June's oppressive humidity. Pulling out his cell, he lowered himself onto the unforgiving stone surface, stretching his legs along the speckled descending slabs. He peered out across the city's unremitting mass exodus: herds of pedestrians running the gauntlet of cars, bicycles, and transit busses zipping along Dartmouth Street, a perpetual rumble emanating from Boston's downtown motorized chaos. Habituated to beach-town living, he couldn't imagine he had once thrived in such a hectic environment.

As he tapped Kacey's name on the iPhone touchscreen, an old man shuffled back and forth along the sidewalk, hands folded behind his back. His deliberate nonchalance stood out when juxtaposed with the jostling hordes fighting their way through and around each other. He glanced up occasionally in RG's direction.

"Hey, hon." Kacey's sweet voice oozed like a dopamine surge through his brain. "I haven't heard anything from you today. How'd it go?"

"Colossal waste of time. Didn't find anything." *Yeah, some researcher you are.*

"Nothing? No drownings?"

"Kacey, I read more about drowning and death today than I ever wanted to, but nothing about a boy in a well."

"No Malachi?"

"The only thing close…hang on a minute." RG stood,

pulling out an old movie stub, a few coins, and a crumpled scrap paper from his front pants pocket. "Here it is." He unfolded his handwritten note. "Some politician's kid, Malachi Pratt, swept out to sea off White Horse in 1946. Close, but not what we're looking for."

The old man had climbed up a few steps and leaned against the metal railing.

"That's gotta be it," Kacey insisted. "How many kids named Malachi do you imagine died around White Horse Beach in the 1940s?"

RG jammed a hand onto his hip. "You said he died in a well. That's a lot different than being swept out to sea, even if it happened near White Horse."

"Did you try his cousin's name, what was it—?"

"Elias," he said, interrupting her. "Kacey, I tried everything!"

"Damn. What now?"

"I dunno. I'm thinking maybe I'll head to Plymouth, try to corner one of the locals in the Shanty Rose or another of the wharf watering holes, or maybe hit the historical museum. Somebody's gotta be familiar with the case. With all the traffic heading out of the city, I won't be home until late."

"I'll give Junior a kiss goodnight for you."

A tug in RG's chest disrupted his breath. God, how he missed his boy, despite being away only a few hours. Since Junior had arrived, he had observed his world shrink, its perimeter tightening around home and family. He recognized the growing need to surround himself with the people he loved every minute now, and not be stuck in the world counting the hours until he could be home. And with his world contracting, his heart had countered with an exponential expansion. Before Junior, RG had secretly worried he would have to parse his love for Kacey between the two, like having to cut the last piece of pie into smaller slices to share with others, leaving everyone wanting more. But he had discovered love kept serving more slices and adding a tasty variety of toppings to each one.

He switched the phone to his other hand as he checked his watch. "Give yourself a kiss for me, too."

"Hmm, I'll wait up for that."

RG cracked a grin and trudged down the library steps. As he approached the sidewalk, the old man stepped in front of him, blocking his path.

"My name's Elias, Elias Ashton. I think you know my cousin, Malachi Pratt."

———

RG and Ashton faced each other in a high-backed booth in a forgotten pub on the corner of Newbury and Dartmouth, a couple of cold Coors Lights sweating in front of them. In the dim light, RG couldn't discern the man's age, his best guess would have either shaved or added a decade. A thick shock of white hair and sinewy frame betrayed a favorable genetic bequest coupled with good nutrition, and his clothing spoke to an earlier life's professional success.

RG waited for the man to answer the question.

"How do I know you're looking for Malachi? Let's just say there are things I know about you."

RG inspected the old man's face while fishing a greasy tortilla chip out of a paper-lined basket the waitress had just set before them, but he couldn't place him. "I've never seen you before, Mr. Ashton. How could you know a goddamn thing about me?"

"We've met before, although you're not aware of it. I've

been searching you out again for many years. Your notoriety as the 'Fugitive Professor' has made you easy to locate."

The gift that keeps on giving.

"You're a legend around these parts...the east coast's version of O.J. Simp—"

"Well, that's fucking great!" RG tore at the label of his beer and cursed under his breath. "Just what I want to hear."

"I must say, I almost didn't recognize you, though. You look heavier than your pictures in newspapers and on TV."

RG threw the handful of chips back into the basket. *This just keeps getting better.*

Ashton leaned forward, resting on his elbows. "But now having found you, I can fulfill my destiny."

"Destiny?" RG glanced around the bar. "What are you, a caretaker or something?"

"Caretaker? I'm not familiar with the term. But, I am flesh and bone, if that's what you're asking. I suspect you're a bit more than that, no? Same as your wife, Kacey."

RG choked on a swig of beer. "What do you know about my wife?" he uttered between coughs, decibel level rising.

Ashton waved his hand. "It's not import—"

"It's important to me, you sonofabitch!" RG shot forward in his seat, his sudden outburst drawing furtive glances from the joint's numbed patrons. "What the fuck do you know about my wife?"

Ashton ignored him with a sip from his beer. "What happened to you last year, Dr. Granville? Who really killed those two people they arrested you for? I'm aware there's far more to your story than what the media let on."

RG jabbed a finger across the table. "None of your goddamn business!"

"Whole country's business not long ago." Ashton grabbed

a tortilla chip and dipped it in the tangy salsa. "No one will ever be charged in those cases, will they?"

"What could you possibly know about it?" RG spat. "You're a nosy old fart, aren't you?" *Who the fuck does this guy think he is? Matlock?*

"Just curious, is all. I understand you…solve problems. Problems others can't?"

RG clenched his jaw. *Bastard must have come across the ads.* He leaned into the table, shoved the chips forward, and crossed his arms.

"The important thing is, I can help you with one of your problems. I know where Malachi lives. I can show you."

"Mr. Ashton, with all due respect, you're out of your league here."

"Am I? And by the way, call me Elias." He swirled his bottle in a lazy circle. "You don't have a goddamn clue where he is, do you?"

"Not yet, but—"

"Or *when* he is?"

"When?"

"You don't understand a thing." Ashton smirked. "You need me. Just as much as I need you."

RG leaned against the booth's cushioned back and drained his bottle. "And why do you need me?"

"As I've said, it's my destiny to meet Malachi again." Ashton pointed across the table. "You're gonna bring me to him."

"Bring you…why would I do that?"

"Let me ask you. Do you have any idea how to stop Malachi? To kill him?"

"Not yet. Just gathering information at this point—"

"You've gathered shit!" Ashton butted in. "You spent the entire day across the street and came up with nothing. Where would you have gone next if I hadn't come to you? You can't do this alone."

"No offense, Elias, but you're a smidge over the hill for this kind of thing." He scrutinized the man sitting across the table. *More like over the mountain!* "How old are you, by the way?"

"Turned eighty-three on June fifteenth."

"Well, happy belated birthday." They clinked bottles. "Sorry, I forgot to send you a card. I have to say, you're pretty spry for your age." RG tossed another chip into his mouth. "What's your secret? Pilates, hot yoga?"

Ashton chuckled. "I've made a small fortune in the health-care industry. One benefit has been learning how to stay healthy and strong, live longer to ensure I'd meet you and fulfill my destiny."

"You keep using the word."

"We all have a destiny, Dr. Granville. I happened to learn of mine early in life." He took a sip from his beer, wiping the froth from his mouth with a crumpled napkin.

"So, tell me about Malachi? You say you're cousins?"

Ashton nodded. "Malachi Pratt, son of state legislator, Emerson Alcott Pratt, and his wife, Sarah, of Chestnut Hill. He visited me and my family on the weekend of July Fourth back in 1946 and died at the bottom of a well."

"Hold on a sec." RG leaned to his side as he fished his hands through his front pocket. "Wait! I have it right here. I just found this today. Malachi Pratt, 1946, swept out to sea off White Horse Beach. He didn't die in a well, you sack of shit! If you're gonna lie, at least be aware who you're lying to."

"You're focusing on inconsequential details…" Ashton waved him off again.

"Listen, I'm just about done with this meeting. I'm not sure how you found me, or if you're trying to trick me into some-thing, but I don't believe a goddamn thing you're saying!" RG slammed his bottle on the table, reached into his wallet, and dropped a wad of bills onto the table as he slid across the booth.

Ashton tossed the crumpled napkin onto the table and leaned back in his seat. "Hear me out, Dr. Granville. Please."

RG stood and checked his watch. "I'm listening."

Ashton sighed. "Malachi has come to me several times over the years."

RG rested his palms against the table and leaned forward. "What do you mean, come to you? He's been dead for a long time."

Ashton halted him with a penetrating stare. "I suspect you understand what I'm talking about. After the accident, he would come to me in my dreams or through my childhood friends. I'd be asleep at night, and I'd sense him near me, in the room, inside my head with me. It resembled a dream at the time, but deep down I understood he'd been there…inside me. Know what I mean?" Ashton sipped his beer.

RG sank into the booth's spongy cushion. "Yeah, I follow."

"Then, I'd spot him within my friends...behind their eyes. Eventually, he would use them up. Their eyes would dim, you see. Go from blue or brown to jet black, like a shark's eyes. Dead. Lifeless. Then, the boys would slowly disappear inside themselves. Once I reached my teens, he stopped coming to me. He appeared…uncomfortable inside me at that point, with me grown up. Can't explain it."

RG recognized the same story from Molly Buckholtz. He reached for his bottle, but he had already emptied it. "Why did the newspaper article say swept out to sea?"

Ashton glanced at the table, wiping an imagined stain from its surface. "When it happened, I wasn't as truthful as I should have been. You see, my father had told me about buried wells and trenches in the field we'd crossed to get home, where Malachi disappeared. He warned me never to cut through it. I figured he would tan my hide if he found out I'd defied him." He picked up his beer bottle, but only moved it over a few inches. "Maybe with Malachi dead, I'd go to jail. I didn't know. I was just a kid. So, I didn't tell anyone."

The men sat in silence as Ashton sipped his beer.

"It's not something I'm proud of. I'm not sure they ever found him."

"They did, Elias, years later. Along with another."

"Another body?"

"They pulled two bodies from a well across from White Horse Beach in the 1950s, a child and an adult."

Ashton hesitated for a moment, then leaned back and nodded. "With the well hidden beneath the brush and tall weeds," he said, then cleared his throat, "it doesn't surprise me someone else ended up down there. Could have happened again, easily."

"So, why did Malachi visit you after he died?"

Ashton stared across the pub as if he hadn't heard the question.

The old fart must be getting Alzheimer's. "Elias?"

"Ah yes, woolgathering..." He smiled and took a gulp of beer. "At first, I figured he visited me out of anger. He's mad because I lived and he didn't, that kinda thing. Later, I wondered whether he missed me and wanted to play again like we used to...through the other boys. They gave him life. But, then the boys would disappear, no one would hear from them again. He took them back with him, back to the world he came from."

"How can you possibly know—?"

"Listen to me." Ashton cut him off, pushing himself up from the booth. "Malachi lives in another time. He has

Gunnar and scores of children he has been collecting for seventy years, in a far corner of the past."

RG drew a deep breath, his fingers pulling at his lips.

Ashton pushed the wad of crumpled bills toward RG and placed a larger bill onto the table. "It's taken me a lifetime, but I'm here to help you, to make it stop. It's time we brought those children home."

————

Kacey

Kacey stepped from the steaming shower and wrapped herself in an oversized towel. Swiping her palm across the frosty mirror, she leaned forward and inspected a new set of lines sprouting along the corners of her mouth. She grabbed the L'Oréal squeeze tube beside the sink, squirted a dime-sized, creamy mixture onto her fingertips, and slapped it onto her skin.

Age-defying, my ass!

Hedging her bets, she doubled down and rubbed the remainder of the product along her neck, shoulders, and legs, and tossed the empty tube into the wastebasket. With Junior sound asleep and RG due home soon, it would be a waste of time getting dressed; she would greet him in the towel. Grinning, she exited the master bathroom, giving the bedroom dimmer switch a quarter turn.

"Sure sets the mood." Larsson Skoczek balanced on the edge of the bed, one arm cradling a sleeping Robert Jr. in his lap, a large, jagged-edged knife in the other.

Her legs faltered, but she remained upright as her heart burrowed into her throat. "I had a feeling we might meet again, Lars."

"Yeah, I wasn't very convincing in the restaurant, was I?"

He swallowed, his Adam's apple bobbing up and down as his eyes wandered across Kacey from top to bottom. He reached for the vanilla scented Yankee Candle on the bedside table. "I'm guessing you're expecting someone?"

"Why are you here, Lars?" *Keep saying his name.*

He eased Robert Jr. onto the bed and stood, barely interrupting the boy's breathy snore. "You're a smart lady. You must have an idea." His hand tightened around the knife handle.

"I don't, Lars. Honestly." She attempted a probe, tap his mind's history to gauge the threat standing before her, possibly gain an advantage, but Skoczek's formidable defensive powers allowed nothing through his mind barrier.

He palmed the knife and slowly circled the room. "That's strange, I've heard you're one of the most powerful caretakers around, yet you don't have a clue why I'm here. You're not living up to your billing." His glance lowered to her towel, his tongue flicking across his lips. "In fact, you come across as pretty vulnerable right now."

She detected a brief thought-flow leach from his distracted mind, a younger version of Skoczek with Malachi.

"You see, I have a mission I need to complete for...an old friend. It won't be pretty, but it's something I have to do. You can understand, can't you?" His eyes burned another path along her body.

Another memory erupted as his breath rate increased. She latched onto the image of Skoczek as a child, kneeling beside a stream in the woods behind a neighborhood, piling leaves and sticks on top of another boy. At first, she figured the boys were playing a game, but...

"You're very beautiful," Skoczek whispered. More accidental images burst from his head.

Maybe the L'Oréal is working after all.

"I haven't heard those words in a long time." She feigned a smile.

"If I didn't know better, I might have suspected you were flirting with me the other night."

"Flirting's for kids." Kacey smirked, adjusting the towel to reveal a hidden swath of skin. She sensed his quickening pulse. A barrage of images detonated from his mind, flooding her consciousness as she breached his defenses...death and murder, Skoczek learning how to slip into others' bodies, punishing them for their wrongdoing. She stepped toward the bedroom dresser as Skoczek advanced toward her, his hand loosening around the knife's hilt.

She could sense different intentions now, a moment of pleasure before he would initiate the carnage...a vehicle careening out of control along a dark, country road, a teenage couple tossed about like clothes in a dryer as the vehicle tumbled down the embankment...With her back against the dresser, Kacey let the towel fall from her body, gripping it loosely in front of her as Skoczek reached a hand to caress her shoulder...an argument, Skoczek questioning his destined path, Malachi promising an exchange: the reversal of fate for a favor—slaughter the three and take the ring from the dead man's finger. He could undo his past, live in the light, with a power he couldn't fathom.

Skoczek reached a trembling hand for the sagging towel, hesitating as he craned his neck to follow the line of her arm tucked behind her back. She would have to act quickly, and she would have to bank on her hunch Skoczek remained a novice jumper who hadn't advanced far in his development.

Kacey whipped her arm forward, spraying Skoczek's eyes with the L'Oréal Longwear dry shampoo she had sneaked from the line of cosmetics on the dresser.

He dropped the knife, raising both hands to his eyes as she

leaned back and delivered an arcing kick to his midsection, towel spinning from her body. She exploded toward the bed, scooping up Robert Jr. to take her one shot at escape. If she had any chance to save her child, she would have to open her mind and flip worlds, tumble into the abyss. But, the only way she had ever slipped through the portal before had been to fall asleep. Now she would have to make it happen immediately, like turning a key in a cold engine and hoping it would turn over. She closed her eyes and concentrated.

Nothing.

She pictured the place of her childhood dreams. Her world gave a lurch forward, pulling away slightly as she cradled her son.

Skoczek struggled to his knees, blinking and dabbing furiously at his swollen eyes. "Fucking whore! You're gonna pay…"

The engine fired, the portal opened, silence enveloped her as she shifted. Lingering a moment between worlds, she transitioned.

"Hey, get back here!" Skoczek leaped for the knife resting on the floor in front of the dresser. Grabbing the hilt, he scrambled toward the bed on all fours, slashing an arc through the air in the spot where Kacey had initiated her shift.

She sensed the knife pass through her, like a gentle breeze, as she dropped into the next world. She tumbled in silence through the calm, swirling vortex, finding herself seated in the Pancake Man with a sleeping Robert Jr. clutched in her arms, the frenetic activity of the restaurant soothing her as if she had returned home. She glanced across the aisle to observe a younger version of herself in French braids sitting with her parents getting ready to order. The little girl mouthed a complicated incantation and waved a magic straw across a mound of fried potatoes, distracting her father long enough to steal a bite of his apple and cinnamon pancakes. Trickery? *So that's where I got it from...*

Kacey emptied her lungs, collapsing against her favorite booth's worn red cushions, stark naked but safe, a wide smile growing across her face.

Oh, the wonders of L'Oréal.

Chapter Eleven

'Affection lives beyond death's dark and withering will.'

EMMA M., daughter of S.S. & R.M. Howland, Died Sept.
15, 1867 (Aged 15 y'rs, 12 ds.)
-Epitaphs from Burial Hill

June 25, 2019

RG

RG and Kacey shared drinks with Morrow in a quiet sidewalk cafe along a busy thoroughfare, a short distance from Morrow's home. The umbrellas shielding the outdoor patio tables provided a comfortable shade as they waited on Morrow's friend, a fellow caretaker who would be arriving shortly. Morrow and Kacey shared a peculiar colored wine while RG reluctantly sipped on ice-cold water.

RG had tried on several occasions to enjoy the different

beers of his father's world, but he couldn't stomach them, each fermented from a host of unfamiliar and foul-tasting grains and fruit sugars. He had grown accustomed to the glaring differences between his world and the next, but an afterlife without any satisfactory suds might be a fate worse than death. RG served as a mule to satisfy Morrow's post-mortem chocolate fix; maybe after he died, he could work out an arrangement with someone from one of the major breweries.

If not, I'll just slip back and forth for happy hour.

As he scanned the busy street, the vivid sounds, smells, and colors overloaded his senses. With his feet in multiple worlds, RG could still sense visual auras lingering in his domain as apparition-like figures shuffled before him through this parallel existential plane. Like an animated double-exposure image shifted askew, vague earthly silhouettes moved in unison with their otherworldly counterparts, piercing the boundaries of overlapping souls in a macabre supernatural tango.

Morrow's booming voice jolted him from his distracted musing. "We have a few minutes before Mr. Wilder is due, why don't you take a look at the menu. The food's quite healthy on this side." Morrow's eyes met Kacey's, nodding his head toward RG.

RG folded his arms. "I saw that, you know!"

Kacey breezed through the menu, but RG struggled with the next world's written parlance. While universally understood in spoken form, the language's text took years to master for those in subsequent worlds.

"It goes this way." Kacey spun RG's menu right-side up.

"Ah, much better." He rolled his eyes and flipped it back over again.

"You need to spend more time with the language," Kacey said, taking a sip from her wine. "It's like I'm with a two-year-old, having to read everything to you all the time."

"Sorry, I haven't had time to master the hundred letter alphabet. Maybe I'll get to it this weekend."

She gave Morrow a shrug and spoke into his mind. *"See what you missed all those years."*

"I heard that." RG peeked at them over the menu. "Even if I could read this thing, what difference would it make? I still wouldn't recognize what I'm eating." He tossed the indecipherable list onto the table. "If anything here tastes like chicken, order it for me!"

Morrow leaned forward and removed his glasses, wiping them with his napkin. "Robert, learning to read our spoken language will make you more at home in this world...and others. Kacey has picked it up quite readily—"

Kacey blocked Morrow's view with her hand and stuck her tongue out at RG.

"—and I'm sure you will, too. We also have wonderful literature on this side, you know."

"There are too many books I haven't read in my world yet. I'm happy waiting until I'm truly dead before I add another world of writers to my Kindle queue."

"He's planning on remaining a two-year-old for the near future, I guess." Kacey elbowed RG's ribs with a playful poke.

"Speaking of two-year-olds..." Morrow nodded toward Junior, seated at the end of the table, "at least one of them isn't acting his age." Immersed in his coloring book, his pink tongue danced along his lip. "No babysitter today?"

"Not after what happened a few days ago," Kacey said. "He won't be leaving our side anytime soon."

"It's too bad, really," RG said, smoothing an eyebrow. "He'd gotten attached to the indifferent, teen-aged babysitter we found on Craigslist, and he had just about mastered the essential life skills of Snapchat and Instagram."

"What else does a child need to know?" Morrow smirked. "Ah, Ian has arrived."

RG's jaw dropped as the man approached the table, blow-dried locks tumbling to his shoulders, form-fitting, bell-bottom trousers hugging his hips, and a glittering shirt buttoned to midchest, showing off a perfectly coiffed chest-hair patch. He had expected someone like Morrow, a gentleman of a different generation, in a tailored suit and crisp, fitted shirt. But Wilder appeared more like an early seventies Glam-rocker than a supernatural protector. Viewed in the next world's Technicolor glow, Wilder exuded a touch of Ziggy Stardust without the androgyny and radiated a disarming sensuality.

What the hell kind of people does my father hang out with over here?

Morrow made introductions as RG and Kacey rose to greet him.

"I'm in the company of royalty," Wilder ranted in his rich Cockney accent. "I've heard a lot about the two of you! Terrific work with Victor Garrett, Reggie."

Reggie? "Um, it's RG."

The man spoke with his entire body, all parts moving at once. "Oh, bullocks! I misunderstood, mate. You and your lovely wife have been the talk of the realms since Victor's downfall. I'm truly chuffed to meet the lot of you."

Chuffed? He shot Kacey a bewildered glance.

Wilder gave his hand a firm shake, then took Kacey's hand in his, giving it a gentle turn. "And for the lass," he said, pressing his lips to her knuckles.

"You're too kind, Ian," she said, a blush migrating across her cheeks.

Ian? What the fuck?

RG glared at her as if she had stood him up at the prom.

Morrow eyed RG and cleared his throat. "I've asked my old friend to join us because he's had experience with the jumper, Malachi. His knowledge could be useful in our endeavor. Mr. Wilder, would you brief my guests on what you know?"

"I'll give it a go." Wilder swiped a hand across his scalp like a comb, his lustrous locks falling into place in feathered layers.

This guy's way too fucking pretty to be a caretaker.

"I first met Malachi when I protected a young lad from your world, back about forty years ago, your time. Bloody wild decade, mate, the swinging seventies!"

No wonder the getup…he's a refugee from Studio 54!

"Anyhoo, I recall Malachi had a playful streak to him, like a child. He fancied tricking caretakers, invading their charges after he'd distracted them, catch them napping. He'd do a quick jump in and out for the fun of it, laughing the entire time."

"I saw him in a dream, recently," Kacey recounted. "He's lost whatever childlike qualities he had then."

"Well, now he's a bit of a wanker, I'll admit! As he's gotten older, he's turned more violent and unpredictable."

Kacey frowned. "Why do you suppose?"

Wilder scratched his head. "Bloke's getting on in years, but he's still a pint-sized bugger. One look will tell you. He understands he's not a child anymore, but he still longs to be one."

"What happened with your charge?" RG asked.

"It's not easy to admit, but Malachi bested me, invaded him in a moment of distraction. Before I could react and challenge him for the boy's control, he transitioned and took him away."

"Where?"

Wilder's face crumpled. "Not where…*when*. Malachi didn't just take him to a different place, he took him to a different time. I've only been able to view the lad from a distance for the past forty years."

"I'm sorry, Ian." Kacey put her hand on top of Wilder's. "What's the boy's name?"

"Travis." From his neck, Wilder pulled an ornate locket swinging on a gold chain and caressed it with the reverence of a family heirloom. He flipped open the latch and passed it around the table. RG expected to view a photograph pasted inside but instead witnessed Travis's living image, a miniaturized motion picture of a boy trapped somewhere.

Different place, different time. That sonofabitch Ashton was right.

RG's sympathy for Wilder bloomed, condemned to viewing the captive boy in real time, but unable to do anything to help.

"Is this how caretakers keep tabs on their charges?" Kacey asked.

"Caretakers have many ways to check in from different worlds: looking glasses, mirrors, numerous objects projecting the soul." Morrow rubbed his chin. "Similar to how you two use the ring to communicate with me across worlds when you need my help. Mostly when you need someone to watch Junior," he chuckled.

Don't worry, old man, you already played yourself out of a job.

"I don't mean to be rude, Mr. Wilder," RG challenged, "but—"

"Please, luv, call me Ian." He took a sip from his ale.

Luv? "Sure thing, Ian. Why don't you just go and get him?"

"Unfortunately, Reggie, I'm not blessed with the power of time transition."

"It's RG, Ian. R…G…"

"Ah, bloody hell! I'll get it, mate."

"All caretakers have different capacities, Son," Morrow interjected. "Like how Kacey can witness the future and alter destiny, but you can't. Ian's blessed with the ability to stop time."

"Only for a few brief seconds," Wilder said, shrugging. "Unfortunately, I can't travel backward or forward in it."

"Stopping time? Must come in handy for a caretaker, giving the mind a few more seconds to react when encountering a threat," Kacey stated.

Wilder leaned toward her. "True, there's that, luv." His eyes darted to RG with a wink. "But it's a lifesaver around the birds, eh? Gives me those critical extra seconds in the pub to come up with something witty when I'm on the pull!"

Good lord, Morrow handpicked this guy to help us?

Wilder picked at the complimentary breadbasket on the table. "The only caretaker I ever met with the power of time travel sits beside me. Reggie's father."

RG didn't bother correcting him. "Hold on a minute." He straightened in his chair, locking eyes with Morrow. "So, if you could travel through time…"

Morrow nodded. "Then you can, too. When I gave you the ring, it retained the power to transcend different epochs, and that power now lives within you."

RG threw up his hands. "So, I'm the one who's stuck having to fix this thing?"

"You're looking at it all wrong, mate," Wilder chided. "You're the one with the opportunity to save scores of children and put an end to Malachi."

RG gave a half-hearted shrug.

The waitress struggled to the table beneath a massive tray, a vivid assortment of colors and textures reflecting the next world's different palette of edible life balanced across a hunched shoulder. As she distributed the plates, RG crinkled his nose, prodding his meal with his fork.

God, what I'd give for a burger and fries.

"Ian, what else can you tell us about Malachi?" Morrow asked.

Wilder chomped his sandwich. "Malachi lives in a two-day time loop he's constructed from his childhood."

"A time loop? How's that possible?" RG asked.

Wilder pressed his hands together in a steeple, rubbing his index fingers against his chin. "Imagine time like one of your old record albums. The needle plays the album from beginning to end, just as time has a beginning and an end. But remember when a song would skip, how the needle would catch in a groove and replay the same song patch over and over?"

RG nodded, lamenting early technology's simplicity. "Until you tapped the needle and the rest of the song would play."

"Used to dig that about your world, luv. The records." Wilder leaned back in his chair, gazing upward. "Bowie, the Stones…they don't make music today like they did back then!"

"Aerosmith, the Doors…"

Wilder narrowed his eyes. "Wrong side of the Atlantic, mate. Led Zeppelin, the Who."

"Allman Brothers, Springsteen—"

Kacey jumped in to squelch the sparring match. "Hang on, I'm confused here. The skipping record is the time loop?"

"Just like a skipping record, time can sometimes get caught on itself and repeat over and over. Malachi has gone back in time to make the record skip, creating this repeating loop. It's his own little room in the past where he likes to go and reminisce, watch the world the way it used to be."

"So how come we're not all stuck in the past if time is looping over and over?"

"Time exists on many planes simultaneously," Morrow offered, "just like the different worlds we can transition into. The past, present, and future are all happening at the same time."

"But they're not exactly separate from each other, either," Wilder said. "They're side by side, but they're dependent on each other. Just as the past determines the present, the present determines the future. It can be a bit confusing."

RG pressed his fingers into his temples. "So, Ian, where… or *when* does Malachi live?"

"Depends on which Malachi we're talking about."

"So, are there more than one in this scenario?" Kacey bit into something resembling a taco, covering her mouth to catch the crumbling shell.

Wilder nodded. "The 'old' Malachi, the jumper you seek, lives in your world sometimes, in the boys he abducts, and sometimes in the time loop he's constructed. The 'young' Malachi, he's the nine-year-old boy who died in the well a long time ago."

"And where…or *when* does he live?" RG asked.

"He also lives in Malachi's loop. You see, the loop repeats the same two days, over and over. July Fourth and fifth, 1946—"

"The day before and the day of the boy's death." RG interrupted, taking a hesitant bite from the unfamiliar meat resting between his vividly colored sandwich bread.

"Spot on, mate! How'd you know?" Wilder inquired.

"A man came to me. Malachi's cousin, Elias. He told me Malachi died visiting him at the beach that weekend in 1946."

"He's bloody right, but why did he come to you?"

"Somehow Elias caught wind of my mission to find Malachi."

"How did he figure that out, you suppose?" Kacey asked.

"Not sure. But he told me he could bring me to old Malachi…the jumper. Only we'd need to return to the well at the moment of his death in 1946 when he was a boy. Elias is the only one who knows exactly where that happened."

"What is Elias's stake in all this?" Wilder raked fingernails through his chest hair jungle.

"He wants to stop Malachi as much as we do. He used to haunt Elias, visiting him in his dreams or through his childhood friends. He told me Malachi has taken children away with him for seventy years. He's convinced it's his destiny to end it."

Morrow frowned, wiping his mouth with his napkin. "Why would Elias want to go back to the moment of young Malachi's death?"

"He told me if old Malachi, the jumper, witnessed what happened at the well, it would stop him."

"Sounds a bit dodgy to me." Wilder ran his fingers across his cheek. "Bloke has a lot of knowledge for a human. You trust him?"

RG sighed. "The guy's stayed alive for seventy years trying to find me, and he's motivated to make sure he helps end Malachi's reign of terror. My gut tells me to trust him."

"How could he know the things Malachi has done?" Kacey asked.

RG shook his head.

"Maybe he's stayed connected to him somehow," Morrow offered.

"The fact he's Malachi's cousin could be your advantage," she added. "Seeing Elias after seventy years might catch Malachi off guard, rattle him a bit. Could give you the edge you need."

"Edge?"

"To stop him."

RG folded his hands on the table. "And what's your brilliant plan to rattle him?"

"I'm not sure how yet, but you have a way of rattling

people. You sure rattled the burning man. The strategy worked against him. We're one-for-one."

RG rolled his eyes.

"I'm concerned about his insistence on going back to the well." Morrow put down his fork. "It sounds as if he might try to alter the future to stop Malachi."

"What do you mean?" RG inquired.

"Prevent the *young* Malachi from falling in the well."

"Ah, yes!" Wilder washed down a bite of food with a swig from his ale. "If the boy doesn't die in the well, he never turns into the bleedin' jumper. We erase seventy years of tragedy. Brilliant! Might be a strategy worth considering."

"Absolutely not!" Morrow boomed. "No greater violation to the tenets of our universe exists than to alter time. If young Malachi doesn't die the way he's intended to, it would change the course of history."

"But it would save countless children," Kacey pleaded.

"We understand nothing about the children Malachi has removed from earth's history. As callous as it sounds, the world's proceeded without them, the way destiny determined, whether they deserved it or not."

"So, if young Malachi doesn't die in the well, all those abducted children would carry out lives they weren't meant to live?" she asked.

"Not just the children," Wilder offered, "but every person Malachi interacted with from July fifth, 1946, onward would disrupt the events leading to today."

"Time is like a spider's web. You pull on one corner and you disrupt the whole structure," Morrow sighed.

"So, if Malachi opens the door for a woman and initiates a conversation," RG asked, tapping a fist against his lips, "he may cause her to miss meeting her future husband—"

"Or, he causes her to meet someone not meant to be her future husband," Kacey interrupted. "Children are born who weren't meant to be born…lives sent in unintended directions."

"Heaven knows what you'd return to?" Morrow pointed to RG. "He might come back to find you don't exist, or the world you recall might be radically changed."

RG's eyes widened. "But it could be changed for the better. Maybe we will have cured cancer or eradicated wars and conflict?"

"Or maybe some madman will have taken office and dropped another bomb." Morrow waved his hand. "Knowing human nature, it would be too risky. Robert, to rescue those children, you must bring them back individually through the portal to this time and place. Do not try to erase the past. Young Malachi *must* die the way nature intended!"

"But how do we handle Malachi, the jumper? Elias maintains he can stop him somehow at the well."

"Then let him try, but only after young Malachi falls into the well. He mustn't interfere with the boy's destiny or the world's fate will be compromised."

"I don't get this time-loop thing." RG put down his fork. "If Malachi lives in a two-day loop, wouldn't everything happening in the loop be contained? Even if we interfered, wouldn't everything just keep repeating forever in that separate universe?"

"Time loops are tricky, mate." Wilder grabbed a chip from RG's plate and tossed it in his mouth. "They're not separate from time, they're just a hitch in time's flow. You disrupt history in a time loop and you break the loop."

"And everything happening from the disrupted moment carries forward, altering the future," Morrow added. "The loop can be broken safely two ways: if Malachi shuts down the portal leading to it, or he dies."

RG threw up his hands. "Piece of cake!"

"But either way, you don't alter history." Wilder signaled the waitress, pointing to his empty bottle.

"Listen to me and listen carefully." Morrow leaned forward, aiming his fork across the table. "You must exercise extreme caution if you enter a time loop. The way I view it, your mission will have two objectives. First—"

"Bring the children back," Kacey jumped in.

"Absolutely. Once you escort the children through the portal, it doesn't matter if you can or cannot kill the jumper. They will be back in the present, safe and sound."

RG leaned back in his chair. "But if we don't kill Malachi, he's free to continue to abduct new children."

Morrow sighed. "An inevitability we can't control. But at least you give those suffering children a chance at a new life.

"So, we trade one set of lives for another." Kacey frowned. "Doesn't seem right."

"Why bother bringing the children back at all? They'd be sixty, maybe seventy years old by now. Their lives are over."

"Not so fast, Reggie," Wilder interjected. "They've been living the same two days over and over, some for many decades. I look in on Travis daily. Each day he's doing some-thing different, but he's never gotten any older."

"Are you saying he's been through forty years of hell, but in reality, no time has changed?" Kacey held her hands to her face.

"Hard to tell how the children perceive the passage of time. It may feel like two days or forty years to Travis. Can't say. Either way, it's time to get him home."

"But I witnessed an ancient Malachi in my dream," Kacey pointed out. "How's he aged but not the children?"

"He doesn't operate on earth time. He ages according to our time," Morrow replied.

"So, I bring the children back to a world where their parents, siblings, and family might be long dead, but they're still children? What kind of life would they have?"

Wilder rested a hand on RG's forearm. "They deserve the life Malachi's deprived them from having, don't you think?"

"RG, imagine how many mothers like Molly Buckholtz have prayed for one more hug and haven't given up hope it's still coming?"

RG nodded his head, reaching for Kacey's hand. "You're right."

The conversation paused as waitstaff approached the table and cleared dirty plates and refilled empty glasses.

Morrow tossed his napkin on the table as he leaned back in his chair. "Your mission's second objective...kill Malachi. His death will end the time loop, and history will proceed as destined. But it's critically important not to interfere with the course of time before he's stopped."

"If you bump into someone on the street, you step in front of a moving vehicle forcing it to slow, the future will be affected in ways we can't predict," Wilder said.

RG dropped his head into his hands. "It's impossible. It can't be done."

"It's being done as we speak. The last thing Malachi wants is to change his precious time loop, the memories of his former life. He's found a way to navigate undetected in the loop, and with numerous children. You can, too."

"I'm not ready for this one." RG raked his nails through his hair. "I can't do this alone."

"You are ready." Morrow clasped his hands together. "And you don't have to do it alone. Others can join you."

"Well, that's a relief."

"Maybe to you, but once you've opened the portal and traveled through it, you're the only one keeping it open."

"So, what if something…happens to me?" RG swallowed.

"The portal closes," Morrow replied, "and they're stuck in the 1940s forever. There's no getting back without you."

RG rested his elbows on his knees, his eyes boring a hole through the pavement at his feet. He didn't like his options. He would need Kacey's skill for this mission, no doubt. Still learning to navigate his power's depth and capacity, he would be at a disadvantage against a jumper with over seventy years of experience. But if she came on the mission, he would be putting her in danger again. And if neither of them made it home, Junior would grow up without a father *or* mother. Too much risk.

"I hope you'll consider letting me go in with you, mate." Wilder placed a hand on RG's shoulder. "Only you can get us in, but I need to save my boy. It's selfish of me, of course, to focus on Travis considering how many other children need you, too."

"I just need time to process all this."

"Just don't take too long, Reggie. Time loops are different than full time travel. You can only get into a time loop on the particular days it spans, in this case July Fourth or fifth, and it's coming up soon."

"Doesn't give us much planning time, like a week and a half!" Kacey exclaimed.

Fuck me.

Wilder frowned as he stroked his intentional five o'clock shadow. "It's not your typical portal either, mate. It's Malachi's portal, and it'll recognize when someone else uses it."

"The portal understands who's in it?"

Wilder gave him a nod.

"Portals are living extensions of their creators and take on their temperament." Morrow tossed his napkin on his plate and bridged his hands in front of him. "They can be stubborn."

"What about the portals I've been using? I haven't detected any resistance."

"You wouldn't," Morrow countered. "The portals separating different realms have existed for millennia and accommodated countless transitions; they can't distinguish who they answer to anymore."

"How about the portal I've created to the next world?" Kacey pondered.

Morrow grinned. "Your portal knows when you use it to go from the Pancake Man to my world, but it also recognizes when Robert and I are its guests. It welcomes us because it understands our relation. Malachi's won't be as…agreeable."

"And it will alert Malachi to your presence," Wilder added. "He could shut it down and basically bugger the both of you. You'd both be stuck in 1946."

"Would he do that?" Kacey wrinkled her nose.

"Not likely. He likes to play in your world. It'd be easier if he just kills Reggie there." He turned to RG. "So, you want to watch for that, mate."

RG slumped in his chair. *Good tip, Ringo.*

"Oh, and one more thing, Son," Morrow raised his finger. "If you're able to kill the jumper, the portal will die with him. It will perceive his death, weaken, and eventually collapse. There won't be much time. You must get everyone out before you attempt to handle Malachi."

"Get everyone out…except for me."

Morrow nodded, a somber expression crossing his face. "Except for you. And you must race back to the portal if you're successful."

"Or else?"

Morrow leaned back and removed his hat. "It could be a one-way ticket."

Kacey leaned her head against RG's shoulder and rubbed his back. "Then we get the children back and forget about killing Malachi. There's no other choice. I can't lose him, and Junior needs him. It's too dangerous."

"Then we do what we can," Morrow concurred.

Wilder placed his empty ale glass on the table and stood. "Right! Well, Reggie, let me know if I can be of further assistance. Cheers, mate!"

RG stood as Wilder gave his hand a firm shake and clapped him on the back.

Turning his attention to Kacey, Wilder raised an eyebrow. "And you, luv, an honor to make your acquaintance." He leaned forward to kiss her cheek.

"All right, enough, lover boy!" RG grabbed Kacey and pulled her toward him.

"What're you doing, Reggie…er, RG!" Kacey stammered.

Wilder stepped back, palms out in front of him. "Okay, luv. Don't throw a wobbler, everything's groovy."

Groovy?

Morrow leaned toward Wilder. "You must forgive my son, Ian. He still retains the previous world's primitive emotions, jealousy, and insecurity. He lost his job, pretty much ostracized in his profession, and—"

"I'm sure he gets the picture, Dad!" RG interrupted.

"Ah yes, I recall your world very well…like yesterday. No offense, mate."

"None taken, Ziggy. Just a lot on my mind here, that's all."

Limey bastard!

"Completely understood. Your world needs you again, Reggie. We need you, and we're here to help. I trust you'll step up. Good day!"

Morrow, RG, and Kacey stared as Wilder pranced along the sidewalk like a polyester Travolta reborn into a parallel realm.

"So, how do we proceed?" Morrow asked.

"Yeah, what do you think, Reggie?" Kacey smirked, folding his hand in hers.

"I think I need a doughnut, luv."

Chapter Twelve

*'Can the human heart remain untouch'd
With tender feelings when an Infant dies.'*

In memory of THOMAS JACKSON, died Decr 24, 1788
(Aged 31 days)
-Epitaphs from Burial Hill

June 28, 2019

Mike

The drive up Route 3 to Plymouth took less than an hour, but the last five miles took almost half that, traffic grinding to a standstill as the skies opened in a late June downpour. Mike Stahl edged from the right lane and scooted the last two hundred yards through the breakdown lane's standing water, pulling off the Long Pond exit. Sheets of rain pelted the Crown Vic as Stahl swiped his palm across the foggy windshield. Craning his neck to peer through the glass's diminishing porthole, he searched for the entrance to the Plymouth County Correctional Facility, invisible through the squall. He fumbled with his cell and pressed the warden's number.

"Tom Gooden." The warden's thick south Boston accent bit into his ear.

"Tom, Mike. I'm pulling in now."

"We got him set up for you. They know you're coming. Just check in at the desk, and one of my guys will walk you down."

"I appreciate it, Tom." Stahl pulled into the closest parking spot he could find, but the space sat at least fifty yards from the entrance.

"I don't know what you did to him in Chatham, but he's in no fucking mood to see you."

"I may have been a little cranky."

"Well, I don't know how much you're gonna get out of him. Just giving you the heads up."

"Thanks again, Tom. I owe you…Mexican."

"Chipotle, not that Taco Bell shit."

"Deal." Stahl disconnected. Scanning the sky through the driver's side window, he calculated he would be drenched before he reached the entrance. He eyed the crumpled handicapped tag jammed between the seats and the blue-lined parking space nestled beside the front door.

Too young for that shit.

He fished beneath the front seats for a miracle, a forgotten umbrella, windbreaker or circus tent, finding nothing but fast-food wrappers and soda cans.

"Fuck it." Stahl threw the door open and hurried across the parking lot lake at a double-time limp, his shoes completely submerged by the time he had cleared the Vic's rear quarter panel. Halfway to the entrance, he slowed; what was the point?

It wasn't as if he would be any less soaked by the time he mounted the stairs to the entrance.

At the front desk, a corrections officer greeted him with a towel and a hot coffee, a sturdy build pushing at the man's shirt seams. "A little something from the warden."

Mike smirked. *Sonofabitch knows me too well!*

Stahl swiped the towel across his face and neck before rubbing it through his hair. He followed the man along the prison's intricate labyrinth. Their footfalls echoed along buffed cement floors, but sanitizers and cleansers failed to mask the desperate human odors permeating the corridor.

The guard unlocked a visitation room and ushered Stahl inside. The detective eased around a circular table taking up most of the square footage in the claustrophobic room, the correction officer's massive frame sucking up the rest. Stahl's preference for an interrogation would not have included such closet-sized accommodations, but he couldn't be choosy. His gaze settled on Abner Stennett who glared at him with the eyes of a killer, his hands shackled to the bar on the table, his withering frame taut in his chair.

Compared to the other men, Stennett appeared almost childlike in his orange prison jumpsuit. Its sleeves rode down his hands and the shirt squeezed his midsection, obviously tailored for a larger, leaner man, not a soft business owner from a sleepy seaside town. Stahl had a fleeting moment of sympathy for him. How would a man like him survive in such a place? Especially after they found out he was a child killer...

"Just my fucking luck," Stennett mumbled.

"Glad to see you, too." Stahl turned to the second guard and pointed to Stennett's restraints. As the man reached for his keys and uncuffed the prisoner's hands, Stahl nodded toward the door. "Give us some privacy. I'll be fine."

When the two men were alone, Stahl reached into his shirt

pocket and pinched the cigarette pack between his fingers. He fought the urge to reach across the table and pound the bastard for his previous sins, but he had come for information, and he needed to do whatever he could to get it. His son's life depended on it.

"These might be a bit wet."

Stennett scanned the soaked detective from head to foot. "No shit?" Stennett retracted a dry stick from the crumpled pack. "This is a no smoking corridor. Think they'll tack on a year or two for violating policy?"

"Not gonna matter much for you." *Be nice.* Stahl shook his head as he struck a match and lit the butt pressed between Stennett's lips.

Stennett pulled a deep drag. "I don't get it, detective." He let out smoky breath. "Why aren't we talking over a telephone, through three inches of glass, surrounded by other prisoners? I'm thinking…you may not want anyone to hear what you have to say to me."

"Or what you have to say to me."

His eyes darted about the room. "No audio, no one-way glass?"

"Just two people talking."

Leaning back in his chair, he dragged a hand across his two-day stubble. "So…talk."

Stahl dropped into the chair opposite Stennett and rested his elbows on the table. "I need to hear you say you killed your wife, Maria."

"They've already charged me with her death," he said with a shrug. "What difference—"

"It makes a difference to me." Mike held his gaze.

"Why?"

"I need to know if you're crazy or not."

Stennett exhaled a gray smoke plume toward the ceiling.

"Two weeks ago, you had no doubt. Why does it matter now?"

Mike leaned forward, chin resting on clasped hands. "Because."

"Why would you believe anything I have to say?"

"Just tell me about Maria."

Stahl pushed himself back from the table, but his eyes never wavered from Stennett, studying him to gauge his truthfulness, his eye movements, consistency in his body language with each response.

"You have a son, don't you...about Nathan's age? I saw him once at the Card & Candle. Both of you. He was looking for a special gift for his mother's birthday, if I recall."

"Don't change the subject. Did you kill Maria? You admitted to killing Nathan. Why won't you admit to killing Maria?"

Abner tucked the cigarette between his lips, taking a hefty drag as if it might be his last smoke. "Because I can't. I didn't. You know that now, don't you?"

A distinct resignation in Stennett's voice made Stahl sit up and drop the cigarette pack clutched in his hand. "If you didn't do it, who did? Who had the strength to hoist Maria up to the ceiling joists when it took three of us just to get her down? If you know something..."

Stennett stubbed out his cigarette as the last wisp of smoke wafted upward and hung suspended like the storm clouds behind the window glass. "I was in denial for a long time, but I came around. You will, too."

"Come around to what?"

"That some things...things not of this world...can't be explained." Stennett glanced up, eyeing a distant spot on the ceiling.

"Like what? Demonic possession?"

Stennett's gaze darted back to Stahl's with eyes of fear.

"Worse than any demon…"

Stahl could have sworn the room's temperature had dropped. "And this…this *thing*…goes by the name Malachi?"

"Like I said, you wouldn't believe me anyway. Hell, I didn't even believe it myself. Still not sure I do."

"Suppose I do. What can you tell me about this Malachi?"

Abner settled back, let the room whisper in a prolonged silence. Stahl could tell he still needed prompting. "What if I told you I might have seen this Malachi?"

That got Stennett's attention. "Heaven help you, if you have."

"What is that supposed to mean?"

Pressing closer to the table and leaning over as if he didn't want anyone to overhear him, Stennett parted his lips with an apprehensive sigh. "He lived inside my boy, and what that evil creature did is worse than anything you can imagine. You can't fight a monster like that. You just can't…where do you think you saw him?"

Stahl debated his answer, Stennett's revelations sounding more like the rantings of a lunatic making things up as he goes. But if he expected him to share his experiences, he had to do the same. "Behind my stepson's eyes…"

Stennett shook his head, meeting Stahl's gaze with eyes of sympathy. "I wouldn't wish that on my worst enemy…but you better take my advice…"

"Advice?" Mike stifled a reaction he might regret. He continued to play it cool. "Whatever you can tell me, I'm listening."

"Malachi moved into my son's body…pretended to be his friend. He took over Nathan's soul, turned him into an evil child we couldn't recognize. At first, the behavior changes were subtle…but then he became unmanageable. It was like Malachi siphoned every last bit of our boy away from us. We tried everything...psychiatrists, medication...our priest, you name it."

"Where did you hear the name Malachi? How do you know that's his name?"

"Nathan told me. He had a lucid moment before his death, almost as if he was trapped in a room but had found his way to an open window to cry for help. He blurted out a number of things before he disappeared again. He told me about Malachi. Said he would either take him away or kill him...that Malachi hadn't decided yet. I guess Nathan had been fighting him pretty hard the whole time, trying to stay...relevant."

"Take him away? Where?"

Stennett fished through the battered cigarette pack, finding a partial smoke he could work with. He lit it with the crushed butt's last glowing ember. "Back where he goes. Who knows? My take on it... Nathan figured his time was up soon and made a last-ditch effort to communicate with me....tell me what he knew."

Stennett tapped his ashes into Stahl's empty Styrofoam coffee cup and deliberated a moment before lifting his gaze. "Way I see it...you got three choices. You either kill your boy and hope that you take out Malachi. You watch him die on his own. Or you watch him disappear when Malachi takes him away. None of them great options. I know you'll find this impossible to accept, but I had to kill Nathan...out of compassion. But I failed. I killed the host but didn't kill the parasite." Stennett pressed his palms against his eyes. "Don't let it come to that."

How could this be happening again? Stahl could feel *the rush* beginning. *Not here, not now!* From frigid to warmth, Stahl tugged at his shirt collar, fighting for air. "But if you couldn't kill Malachi without killing Nathan...what am I supposed to do? Couldn't you have found another way?"

"After I found Maria, mine was the only way."

RG

RG stared into the Dell's seventeen-inch monitor and entered the afternoon's final quiz grades into Canvas. Leaning back in his chair, he folded his hands behind his head as the grin spread across his lips. His students had crushed the first of his challenging quizzes, leaving him pleasantly surprised. A twinge of guilt gnawed at him for his low expectations. After a full semester under his belt at Cape Cod Community, he should have known better than to underestimate his students' capabilities. A lingering arrogance continued to encourage his perception community college students would somehow be less apt than those he had worked with at a major, private university. Truth was, with the value of a university education in question, the brightest now opted for two years of community college, transferred to a name school, and came out with a prestigious degree and little to no debt. Students with such savvy acing his assignments should be a no-brainer.

He dragged his hands down his face before extricating his cramped body from behind his desk. The reclining chair's squeal pierced the office's tomb-like silence. On a June afternoon, the health sciences department lay empty, its faculty off for the summer and staff long gone for the day. RG twisted kinks from his back and hobbled along the hallway to the vending machine, his shoes echoing along the buffed, tiled floors. He leered at the assorted sweets and candy bars.

...*Maybe just a minor dietary detour.*

Identifying the two-digit code for the Peggy Lawton chocolate chip cookie three-pack, RG aimed his fingers carefully to ensure he wouldn't select the healthy fiber or multi-grain bar on either side by mistake.

As if through divine intervention, the machine spiraled out an extra cookie package from the top shelf. RG grinned as he fished through the take-out port and stuffed the crinkled cellophane packages into his pockets and headed down the hall to the restroom.

As he stepped through the creaky wooden door, a set of boot tips, visible beneath the third stall, startled him, positive he had been the only soul in the office.

Must be Peterson from statistics again.

RG had learned from his years in academia faculty never took a dump in their own floor's restroom, as if the olfactory discovery of some prandial indulgence would force them to appear before their department's committee on colonic offenses and have their mugshot displayed in the faculty lounge. Either that, or they were too cheap to spring for a tin of Yankee Candle scented room spray. Shaking his head, he positioned himself in front of the *Globe's* sports section tacked above the urinal, making it through the entire MLB box score page before his bulging bladder had finished showering the porcelain.

Giants' Sandoval goes four-for-four. Why can't we get guys like that?

RG flushed, stepped to the sink, and scrubbed his hands. Leaning forward, he splashed his face, closing his eyes as plump liquid droplets peppered the basin with a rhythmic plink. He reached blindly for the paper towel dispenser, pressing the sand-paper brown parchment to his still-dripping face. As he stood up, a figure in the mirror loomed behind him.

His eyes tracked to the baseball bat held taut in Larsson Skoczek's clutches.

An explosion rattled RG's temple, putting out the lights.

RG awoke with cool restroom tile pressing against his cheek and his head buzzing as if filled with bees. His eyes fluttered, spots of light clearing the blackness away, the slightest movement igniting a searing fire ricocheting from the frontal lobe to the base of his skull. Scuffling feet beside him and persistent tugging against his hand alerted him to another's presence. He must not have been out long.

He tried to rustle his limbs, but the scrambled brain signals petered out long before they reached their destination. Shifting his head to the left, his eyes rolled back in his head as the room spun, nausea rising in his throat. He snapped his eyes shut, successive swallows keeping the bile at bay. Cracking his eyelids, he viewed Skoczek beside his arm, tugging against his hand, struggling to free the wedding band from his finger.

"Son of a bitch!" Skoczek pushed back from RG and knelt beside him. He pressed his arms against his thighs as if reevaluating his strategy.

A smile crept across RG's face, a glimmer of vindication for his pudgy fingers. His grin receded as Skoczek rummaged through his pockets and pulled out the instrument, the words Handi-cut stenciled on the handle. He wasn't a wizard when it came to the Craftsman family of tools, but it didn't take a genius to figure out what a stainless steel blade attached to a spring-loaded handle could accomplish.

"Wait a minute. Just stop…" he mumbled, another wave of nausea flooding his senses.

Skoczek smirked as he knelt on RG's arm, pinning it against the bathroom floor. He clicked off the Craftsman's safety catch, allowing the gleaming jaws to spring wide open.

"Don't…please," he begged.

The tool carved through RG's ring finger with a sickening

crunch, the only sensation a burst of warmth flooding his hand and a copper iron smell as a warm liquid pooled around him. Skoczek grasped RG's finger and slipped the ring off from the jagged end, tossing the digit beside his face. It twitched and curled with a ratcheting cadence as the volley of impulses burned out along severed nerves.

"Thanks, professor." Skoczek examined the ring pinched between his thumb and index finger. Pulling RG's head upward with a grasp of his hair, he displayed the ring in front of his face before releasing his grip, bouncing his forehead off the unyielding floor. The impact initiated a third nausea tsunami, a vomit burst ejected across the tiles. RG's eyes fluttered shut.

Malachi

Malachi slipped inside Larsson Skoczek as he sat on his tattered sofa, the bloodstained ring resting on the scarred table before him. Skoczek gave a brief wince as he accepted the jumper's familiar shape, a mass pressing against his chest and interrupting his heartbeat, then a freeing burst of oxygen into his lungs.

"Miss me?" Malachi said inside his head.

Skoczek ignored him. *"I can smell him on you."*

"Who?"

"The new boy."

Malachi sometimes underestimated the jumper and host's complex relationship. The physical overtaking, if done at the appropriate developmental period, spawned an emotional need in the dominated soul, a dependence difficult to break. Despite Malachi's inability to control Skoczek physically—no jumper could control another—the young man rarely expelled him, his emotional need for Malachi greater than the desire to exert his independence. He had been part of Skoczek his whole life, the voice in a lonely boy's head, the partner in his internal dialogue, the soothing presence to a child crying in the night. He remained his one and only friend, father figure, tormentor…pick one.

"Envy is such an ugly emotion." Malachi shifted inside him, grimacing at the spacious borders of Skoczek's adult human suit. *"You failed in your mission. I instructed you to kill them to get the ring."*

"Change of plans."

"She outsmarted you, didn't she?" He chuckled. *"Typical of the breed, but you've left me with a lingering problem. I'm still faced with a formidable opponent you failed to deal with."*

"I'm done with your dirty work."

"For now…" Malachi eyed the object resting on the table. *"Why do you stare at the ring like that?"*

"There's something wrong with it." Skoczek searched for Malachi inside him. *"When I put it on, I can picture things, people's thoughts bombarding me from every direction. But it doesn't show me anything good."*

"Whoever said humanity was good?"

"I witness their evil, their sins…things they've done. It makes me sick to be walking among them. They do terrible things to each other."

"Like…killing a child, for example?" Malachi raised an eyebrow.

Skoczek lowered his head. *"I exude evil now, more than I could ever witness in the human rabble. It leeches from my pores like a dirty sweat. On the street today, a child grabbed for his mother's hand, a woman crossed to the opposite sidewalk rather than approach me, and a man turned his head and averted his gaze as I passed."*

"That's because they fear you. Something inside their reptilian brain

senses your dominance, makes them bow at your altar and cower before you."

Skoczek stood and ambled to the icebox. He pulled a cold beer and popped the top. *"But the worst part is…an explosion happens inside me each time I put on the ring. It rises up from a place…I'm not sure where."*

"From the darkness." Malachi closed his eyes.

Skoczek leaned back for a deep gulp. *"I expected the ring to give me the power to help people. But all I feel is revulsion when I view their faces. I want to kill them all."*

Malachi smirked. *"Maybe you should."*

"You lied to me!" Skoczek turned and fired the half-finished beer can across the room, golden foam soaking the walls and curtains.

"Just a teensy white lie. What, did you imagine you'd be good all of a sudden? The ring would cleanse the disgusting things you've done from your soul? You're a fucking child murderer, a monst—"

"And you're not?" Skoczek interrupted.

Malachi shrugged. *"The past is the past. I've learned to nurture and protect my children. If you imagined a ring would change your dark nature, you're more naïve than I suspected. You disappoint me."*

"Like I care what you think." He collapsed onto the couch.

"I wanted you to have the ring because I hoped it would wake you up to its power, entice you a bit. Don't you see? Your powers are indefensible now, and it's time to embrace your true self."

Skoczek toyed with the ring, sensing the power pulsing from its edges. But it gave off a resistance, jumping away from his touch as he poked at it on the table. Malachi took control of Skoczek's hand, clutching the ring and jamming it onto his finger. The sensation forced Skoczek's eyes closed.

"It clears the mind doesn't it, Larsson? It takes away the worry, the anxiety and remorse for the things you've done in this world. No reason for guilt anymore."

Skoczek pulled at the ring, but Malachi stopped him, controlling his hand from within. *"Leave it on a while longer, get used to it."* Malachi could sense the burst of pleasure chemicals coursing through Skoczek's bloodstream, like a heroin rush to a junkie, removing pain and emptiness from the soul, leaving nothing but the indescribable. The ring could be his opiate, remove doubt, and reveal the truth. The longer Skoczek wore the ring, the sooner he would understand it was the way. The only way.

"I'm gonna need another favor from you."

"No more favors!" He sprung from the couch. *"I'm done with you, Malachi. You didn't give me what I wanted."*

"I've done you a tremendous service. You're just not aware yet. You have more power than you could ever imagine. But you can't stay here any longer."

"Why not?"

"By now the Granvilles will have alerted the authorities to you. They'll be looking for you soon. You could fight them when they come, but you aren't eternal yet. You can still die."

Skoczek leaned against the window sill, gazing absently through the smudged pane. *"I'll take my chances."*

"Besides, I could use you. I'll be having visitors soon. They'll be coming for the children…and me. I'm sure at least one of them will be pretty pissed off his winter gloves aren't gonna fit right anymore."

Skoczek crossed the room and picked up the jettisoned beer can. He threw his head back and drained the last swallow of suds.

"The other made you look like a fool," Malachi taunted, whispering inside his head. *"Be nice to run into her again, maybe teach her a lesson?"*

Skoczek paused a beat. *"Maybe."*

Malachi grimaced as he read in Skoczek's thoughts the vengeance he envisioned for the woman.

Skoczek used his sleeve to wipe the foam from his mouth, a foul grin slipping across his face. *"Definitely."*

———

RG

RG steered the Subaru with his good hand, the road spinning before him, alternately opening and closing each eye in an attempt to cancel out the double vision. His mangled hand lay in his lap, wrapped in a near-crimson gym towel and secured with a bungee cord from the trunk. He used the makeshift tourniquet to dab at the blood leeching from his open head wound.

Securing the wheel with an elbow, he arched his back and corralled the cell phone in his rear pocket with his good hand. Pressing the home button, Siri's comforting voice beckoned.

"Call Kacey!" he directed, aiming his voice into the speaker.

"Calling Kacey."

The phone went to voicemail. "Kacey, meet me at Cape Cod Hospital," he slurred. "I had an interesting visit from Larsson Skoczek. He's got the ring...and then some."

Pulling into the Seven-Eleven just past the Route 6 overpass, RG aimed for the handicapped parking space in front of the Food Center.

He held up his hand. *If this doesn't qualify, nothing does.*

Throwing it in park, he grabbed his severed, sunbaked finger off the dashboard.

"Welcome to Seven-Eleven," the stoned teen mumbled in unison with the entrance door's electronic ping, not bothering to raise his head from his magazine. RG grunted reflexively, refusing to abide the corporate-mandated give-and-take posing as conversation. He pressed his hand to his left eye, allowing his good one to focus and steer him through the narrow aisle toward the rotating Slurpee cup towering over the refreshment center at the store's rear wall. Clutching the back counter to maintain balance, RG grabbed a sixty-four-ounce Big Gulp and jammed it against the ice dispenser, filling it to the top. Inserting his maimed finger deep into the frozen shavings, he turned and stumbled back toward the door.

"Sir, that's ninety-nine cents for the Big Gulp," the kid behind the counter stammered, his wide eyes reflecting shock at the man standing before him, blood dripping onto his shirt from a pulsing head wound, a leaking bloody towel secured around his hand.

"But I didn't fill it with anything, I just need the ice."

"Holy fuck! What happened to you?"

"Just a little accident. I gotta get myself to the hospital." RG turned toward the door.

"It's still ninety-nine cents, drink or no drink. You pay for the cup."

"Are you fucking kidding me?" RG blinked.

"It's my first day, mister. I could get in trouble. Help me out, won't you?"

Sonofabitch!

RG staggered toward the counter. Placing the Big Gulp on the counter, he fished into his pockets for loose change. He pulled out a crushed package of Peggy Lawton cookies and placed it on the counter.

The teen frowned. "It's a dollar-twenty-nine for the cookies." His fingers flew across the cash register buttons adding up RG's purchases.

"Wait, that's mine. Look, I have another one right here. He pulled out the second crushed cookie package from the opposite pocket with his good hand but knocked over the Big Gulp, sending his severed finger skating across the counter top along a sheet of ice.

Fuck me!

The teen added another buck-twenty-nine to RG's tab but hesitated before he totaled the purchase. "Listen, why don't you just take your snacks and your…finger…and get out of here, okay?"

RG grabbed his stuff, shoving cookies into pockets and his finger into the cup's remaining ice. He covered his left eye with the bloody gym towel to refocus and aimed for the exit, leaving a trail of red droplets across the dirty stone floor. Pressing his bruised shoulder against the glass door, he staggered into the parking lot.

"Thank you for shopping at Seven-Eleven," the teen muttered in response to the electronic ping.

––––––––

Ten minutes later, RG swerved through the hospital's emergency entrance where he fell out the open front door, engine still running, and dragged himself into the emergency room, Big Gulp clutched to his chest. The gleaming white facility blended efficiency with outright chaos, emergency responders wheeling patients on gurneys through sliding glass doors, while doctors and nurses dashed back and forth across buffed, spotless floors to examination rooms tucked away behind white curtains. No one appeared to be in charge, yet everyone knew just where to be and what to do. Large windows ringed the structure's high walls and bathed the main floor with generous natural light.

Within moments of arriving on the floor, two nurses in colorful smocks seated him along a row of oversized cushioned chairs and tended to his head wound, while a third unwrapped the towel around his hand with caution. RG handed the nurse his Big Gulp and pointed inside. Minutes later they had stitched the gash along his head and irrigated his ragged finger socket and severed digit. An MRI would reveal a pretty nasty contusion, but no skull fracture or hemorrhaging.

After wheeling him from radiology, the medical team transferred him into an exam room and prepped him for finger reattachment surgery. The Versed dripping into his vein flushed him with warmth and relaxation. RG eyed the youthful doctor staring at X-rays on a sizable computer screen.

Kid looks like Doogie fuckin' Howser.

RG whipped his head around, searching for the nurse. "Doth the doctor thave yet?" The IV drip slurred RG's words into a soupy mixture.

The nurse tilted her head, poking her tongue against her cheek. "Shave yet? You mean the bone? Well, he'll have to shave it down a bit, but he hasn't done it yet. We need to let the IV work a bit longer." She smiled.

After a few minutes, the anesthetizing drug left him with thoughts of how nothing in the world could possibly matter, not even the fact a teenager who didn't even shave yet readied himself to perform surgery. But when the nurse led Kacey to his bedside, he understood how much everything did matter.

"We need to wheel you up to surgery, Mr. Granville," the nurse reminded him. "But you can have a few minutes with your wife."

"Is he gonna lose his finger?" Kacey asked.

The doctor extended his hand to Kacey and introduced himself. "I'm Doctor Howser."

RG opened his mouth, but nothing came out. *We gotta call this thing off.*

The doctor invited Kacey over to the computer screen and repositioned his glasses. "It's a clean separation, which lends itself to a very good prognosis. There's not much damaged tissue to remove, and we may not need to trim much of the bone. We'll insert a few plates and screws, reattach the tendons, then repair the nerves and reestablish the blood supply. What we don't know is how much sensation and movement he'll have. It helped he got the finger on ice so quickly."

"Big Gulp…" RG mumbled, the Versed's effects now garbling his neural pathways.

Kacey nodded. "What the hell happened, RG?"

He struggled to speak, pointing to his clothes piled on the chair. "Chead on my diet."

"Huh?" Kacey shrugged, pulling out a crushed package of Peggy Lawton cookies from his khaki's pockets.

"No more thummer of buff…"

"He won't make much sense from here on out," the nurse said with a smirk, "and he won't recall a thing when he wakes up." She busied herself checking his lines and securing the gurney's side rail latches before calling for an orderly.

A thick man in blue scrubs entered the room and wheeled RG into the hallway and toward the elevators. As the car eased them to the hospital's surgical center on the upper floor, Kacey stood beside him, holding his good hand. Exiting the elevator, the man pushed the gurney down the hall, stopping at a set of double doors.

"When we're done…" RG mumbled, lifting his head.

"What is it?" Kacey leaned her ear to his lips.

"…I promith… you can hold…either hand." He squeezed her palm twice and dropped his head onto the pillow.

The nurse stopped Kacey at the door to the OR. "We'll take him from here. It will be a few hours for this type of surgery. Have a seat in the waiting room and keep your eyes on the monitor for updates." She pointed to the LCD screens mounted on the walls with patient ID numbers in columns beside their choice of surgery. "We're here if you have any questions. It'll be okay." She gave Kacey a reassuring smile.

Kacey peeled open the crushed chocolate chip cookies and poured the crumbs into her mouth as they wheeled RG through the double doors.

————

"Okay, Mr. Granville, we're going to help you sleep now." The anesthesiologist tinkered with the IV, increasing the Versed and infusing a dose of Fentanyl to alleviate the upcoming pain.

A rush of warmth filled RG's veins, and his eyes fluttered shut.

Surrounded in a cloak of unyielding dark, RG's body rose and fell along a floating current, a gentle tumble along a swirling channel.

He had been here before, numerous times, the landmarks as familiar as his own street.

He glanced ahead, spotting the Pancake Man's recognizable outline. He hurried through the crowded restaurant and out the front door to the next world, momentarily tempted by the cherry cobbler resting under glass beside the register. Picking up speed, he flew through the unearthly silence until he landed at the edge of a grassy field. A rumbling stream flowed beside him, leading toward a distant, tidy house. The older man reclined on a porch swing, staring out over his world's heightened color spectrum and vivid texturing, as if appreciating a visual gift he had taken for granted. Nature's sounds awakened RG's senses as he traversed the meadow, from the clicks and whistles of birds and field insects to the magnified swish of the swaying grass against his legs.

"So, this is what retirement looks like." RG held his arms out.

"Robert, what a surprise." Morrow stood and embraced his son, ushering him to the porch swing. "Please, sit. It's good to see you, Son."

RG dropped onto the cushion beside his father. "I'm not sure what I'm doing here, Dad. Did something happen during the surgery? Am I…?"

"Dead?" Morrow laughed. "Of course not. You don't die from finger reattachment surgery."

RG glanced at his hand, his ring finger still attached. "Then how come I've got my finger back?"

Morrow peered over the top of his glasses. "You don't. Not yet, anyway. You're just here in your mind. Your body's still back on a gurney. The surgery's going quite well, by the way."

"I've lost your ring, Dad."

"I'm aware," Morrow acknowledged. "Ian's kept me up to speed on the most recent happenings. Skoczek has become a fly in the ointment, it appears. Turns out he has a history with Malachi. You see, he's a fledgling jumper, a duckling about to turn into a swan. Much like Kacey at his age."

"A swan?" he countered. "Skoczek's going a different way, I suspect."

Morrow nodded. "And the ring will take him to dark and unimaginable places, hastening his development."

"How is he acquainted with Malachi?"

"He once tried to collect him, put him in his stable of children, but he couldn't. No jumper can fully control another, but a bond formed, and Malachi has tried to nurture his dark side. Skoczek stole your ring with the belief harvesting the powers of a caretaker might help erase his dark urges, help turn him toward the light."

"So, he had good intentions?"

"At first."

"What happened?"

Morrow gritted his teeth. "His dark urges proved more powerful than the light, and the ring simply enhanced the evil already inside."

"So, Skoczek's with Malachi now?"

"It appears that way, one more obstacle you'll have to tackle. By the way, I hope you take Ian up on his offer to assist in your upcoming mission. An extra caretaker never hurts when—"

"Upcoming mission?" RG cut him off. "We're grounded, Dad. I'm not going anywhere without the ring. I'm powerless without it."

"You found your way here, didn't you?" Morrow asked.

RG cocked his head. "I guess I did. How did I get here without it? Did you have a hand in this?"

Morrow shook his head. "You know I can't help anymore. It appears you're still holding on to a bit of mojo despite the ring's absence."

"So, I don't need it anymore?"

"I didn't say that. Unlike Kacey, you do not come by your gifts naturally. Without the ring, the power will fade; it does as we speak."

"How can I hold onto a power I don't possess?"

Morrow paused, swiping a hand across his jaw. "It's like stepping off a boat after being at sea. When you reach dry land, you still sense the ocean's sway. You'll continue to sense the ring's sway, too, but it will eventually subside. If you don't get the ring back soon, you will lose it all." Morrow stood and leaned against the porch rail. "This poses a serious conundrum for your mission."

"So, how much time do I have?" RG absently pressed and prodded his ring finger.

"Days? A week maybe before you'll return to your meek

and powerless original form." Morrow raised his hands. "No offense."

"None taken." *But thanks for twisting the knife.* "We're supposed to leave in the next few days."

"You'll likely have enough juice to get everyone there and back."

"And if I don't?"

Morrow stared off toward the woods surrounding his home. "Best not to imagine the alternative. Remember, you'll only be there for two days—"

"Hopefully," RG interrupted, "and that's the best-case scenario."

"What other choice do you have but to remain positive?" Morrow stared at the floor as he scuffed his shoes along the porch floorboards. "I'm sensing your heart is not fully in this."

RG lowered his head. He pushed his feet against the floor, initiating a squeal from the swinging chain links. "It's important to Kacey, so I'm—"

"What? Doing her a favor?" Morrow interjected. "You have to find the importance for you, or you'll never succeed."

"Listen, I'm not a caretaker!" RG sprung to his feet. "I'm a professor, or at least I was. I'm still hoping things might turn around for me sometime…" His voice trailed off.

"That life is over, Robert. You've been lingering in no man's land between your past and future for over a year now. I know you didn't ask for it, but you have the power to change lives. And until you believe you're a caretaker, you never will. You'll never gain the advantage of the ring. It will sense your reluctance."

"What difference does it make, I don't have the ring anyway."

"That may not be as important as you think."

RG threw his hands out to his sides. "Well, what the hell

does that mean?"

"It means the power is yours if you want it."

"Well, then I'll think about it." RG grimaced as a gripping sensation seized his midsection, a pull from his world. "I'm getting the feeling I'd better leave now."

"They're bringing you out from the anesthesia, I suspect."

The tug intensified, pulling against him. He gazed out over Morrow's splendid meadows, captivated. "What if I didn't... respond to the call? You know, just stayed here a while longer."

Morrow crossed his arms. "Why do you entertain those notions?"

"I'm not...just wondering."

"You would die. The body can't exist without the mind, and vice versa. They're calling you back now. You'd best be on your way." Morrow stepped forward. "Listen, Robert. Before you go, promise me you'll contact Ian, get him on the team." He jammed his hands into his pockets and eyed the floor before meeting RG's gaze. "Do it for me."

He could sense Morrow's helplessness, his need for assurances there would be a backup weapon. "I will, Dad. I promise."

RG closed his eyes and relinquished himself to the pull, floating back through the portal to his body, painkillers and relaxants coursing through his blood to relax and warm him. He peeled his eyelids open to find Kacey staring at him.

"We weren't sure you'd be coming back to us." She blotted her eyes with her sleeve.

He gazed around the hospital room, his shared soul seated bedside, Junior's arms slung around his chest. He glanced at his left hand, the gauze's shape confirming the presence of flesh and bone. He wiggled it.

"It's been a long day, I just needed a few more minutes of sleep."

Chapter Thirteen

'So fades these lovely blooming flowers.'

WILLIAM THOMAS, died Nov. 30, 1830 (5 mo. 5 ds)
THOMAS, died Jan. 25, 1844 (17 ds.)
HIRAM, died March 7, 1845 (2 y'rs 3 mo.)
Children of TH^s & Maria Tribble
-Epitaphs from Burial Hill

June 29, 2019

Malachi

Zach drew the covers to his chin and spoke inside Malachi's head. *"I don't wanna be your friend anymore."*

"You don't have a choice in the matter." Malachi had gotten used to his new life, the new body, and he wasn't ready to let it all go yet. But he could tell the boy was disappearing. He gazed at the stucco patterned ceiling through Zach's eyes. The boy's

voice came from such a great distance now, and Malachi could taste the bitter odor; his body had made its choice. He would have to move him soon or he would lose him.

"I don't like it when you take over and make me say things I don't want to. And you made me kill that bird." Zach wiped his charcoal eyes, a pair of tears slaloming down his cheeks.

"It's just a bird, you wuss."

"You're not being a very good friend anymore. We used to laugh all the time, but now you keep me hidden away from everyone. I miss my mom and dad." Zach's lip quivered. *"Please, let me go now."*

"Hey, I have an idea. How'd you like to go on a little trip with me?"

"I don't wanna go anywhere with you."

Zach's words stung. *"I can show you where I live, and you can stay with me for a while. I'll let you out."*

"Let me out! Now!" Zach strained against Malachi's presence, expelling the jumper partway from his body.

Malachi dangled from Zach's body before reasserting himself within the boy.

"Let me out, or I'm gonna yell for my mom!"

Fucking whiny little shit. Why do they always change? *"Well, your mom can't help you anymore."* Malachi guided Zach's hand to his throat and squeezed. He clutched the boy's windpipe long enough to send a jolt through his tiny frame.

Zach coughed and sputtered as Malachi released his grip.

"She doesn't take care of you anymore; I do. Maybe you should start appreciating me a bit more." Malachi squeezed again.

"I can't breathe, Malachi. Stop!"

"Are you gonna shut your fucking trap?"

With a percolating rage, Zach pushed against Malachi as hard as he could, ejecting him like a human cannonball.

Pushing himself up from the floor beside the bed, Malachi struggled onto shaky legs, stunned that the boy had bested him.

Zach sat bolt upright and bellowed, "Somebody! Hel—!"

Malachi quickly threw himself inside Zach, wrenching a hand across the boy's mouth to stifle his cries, but he kept fighting, resisting him.

"You little shit!" He had never encountered such ferocious opposition before. He had underestimated this one, a mistake he wouldn't make again. Malachi picked up Zach's body and hurled it against the wall, crunching him face first against the windowsill. Blood dripped from his nose down the wall and onto the bedding, a crimson splotch gathering on his pillow.

Malachi released his internal grip on the boy. *"So, are you coming with me?"*

Zach nodded as tears swelled in his eyes.

"I thought so."

———

Mike

Patrol vehicles rested around Mike Stahl's Seaview home, the lawn trodden in a haphazard yet oddly uniform arrangement, like something from a CSI episode. Lightbars scattered sharp blue electric strobes across the leaf canopy nestled above as an army of cops and detectives moved back and forth to the house. Inside, they dusted for prints and photographed the scene as Mike and Claire huddled like zombies at the kitchen table. But with clues failing to support a kidnapping, skepticism grew across stern faces, glances, no longer furtive, accompanied whispers once under breath.

Claire awoke early to find Zach's room empty and a blood trail leading from the open window to his bedding. Before her screams could rouse him, Claire had hijacked Mike's cell and rallied Chris Daniels and a team of Chatham investigators to the scene. But Stahl knew deep down this was no kidnapping. Thoughts migrated from the dark corners of his mind, from places he hadn't allowed himself to fully accept...until now. He had held off their onslaught, but now he couldn't stop them. Malachi had made his decision about Zach before he'd had a chance to act. Now Stahl would have to play along until he could contact the only two people who could really help him.

Claire's SOS had also assembled battalions of cops from Yarmouth to Eastham and most of the towns in between in record time. The show of solidarity initially buoyed Stahl, convinced that his brethren in blue had put aside their suspicions surrounding Falmouth Police Chief Chuck Brennan's mysterious death in the detective's home, as well as his association with accused murderer RG Granville. But he soon suspected the overwhelming response reflected the desire to find or witness the key piece of evidence to tighten the noose around his neck.

Just after noon, Daniels entered the kitchen, his eyes failing to meet Stahl's. He grabbed a chair and straddled it, fidgeting to get comfortable.

"Spit it out, Chris. What've you got?"

Daniels tapped his fingers against his thighs. "Nada."

"What does that mean?"

"There's nothing there."

Stahl's throat tightened. *It really happened. Stennett had it right all along.* But he had to be sure. "There's always something, Chris."

"Oh, we collected some trace evidence. But I got detectives with twenty-five years in the trenches shaking their heads, and it's the cleanest crime scene I've ever observed."

"How can that be?" Claire demanded. "Our child's gone. Someone had to have been in the room with him."

"We didn't find a single print in there."

Claire's glance darted to Stahl, as if he had the answer. The answer he had wasn't going to fly. "There must be prints, hair, fibers, something on the windowsill——"

"Nothing, just the…blood," Daniels interjected.

Stahl raised his palms. "So, what are you saying?"

"I'm not saying anything yet. We'll get what we have to the lab and see if they can match anything to someone other than you, Claire, or Zach." Daniels lowered his voice. "I'm gonna be frank with you. It doesn't look like a crime scene, okay? I'm just telling you how the prevailing winds are blowing in here."

Stahl squeezed his eyes shut. Daniels' insight confirmed everything Stennett had told him. He should have known the moment he sat with that bastard in the police station, the day he searched the house, when an unholy presence triggered a series of flashbacks plaguing his waking moments, the day Zach had plucked that bird off the tree. Deep down he had known. The truth had been right in front of him the whole time, but he had been in denial. Now his son had paid the price for his inaction.

Disentangling himself from Claire's desperate clutches, Stahl excused himself from the kitchen and stepped down the hallway, fishing his cell from his back pocket and tapping the number.

Just as he was about to disconnect, Kacey picked up.

At one time, the sound of her voice would rock him like a bare-knuckled punch to the jaw, igniting a memory bombard-ment that left him woozy for days. But now he could visualize the incoming punch in time to sidestep it easily, Claire's love helping him dodge and weave the past, leaving it where it belonged.

"Michael Francis Stahl, to what do I owe the——"

"Kacey," he interrupted. "Zach's missing,"

Silence. "What?"

"When we woke up, he was gone."

"Oh my God, Mike. What happened?"

He dragged his nails through his hair. "I'm not sure...but I have my suspicions."

"Are the police looking for him?"

"Not that I can tell." Stahl cupped the cell and whispered, "but there's about fifteen of them looking directly at me."

"Why would they be——?"

"Listen, Kacey. I'm thinking you and RG may have some...expertise in matters like this."

More silence filled his ear.

"Kacey, you there?"

"I'm here. Can you get away?"

Stahl slunk further down the hallway, lowering his voice. "I dunno. Cops have been here all morning. No evidence of a break-in...no prints, nothing. There's a trail of blood, but thankfully no...no body." Stahl's voice cracked, his professional demeanor finally giving way to suppressed emotion. He had held it together all morning, detached as he witnessed the investigation, going through his mental checklist, asking Daniels for updates. Now, an undeniable reality had set in. He grasped the wall for support as knees bent like a folded jackknife. Zach's sweet face loomed in his vision as his lungs heaved. "Oh Christ!"

"Stay with me, Mike."

A heavy sigh. "The way these guys are whispering to each other, I'm not sure they're gonna let me just walk out of here right now."

"Then we'll come over. Just a couple friends coming by to comfort you guys, right?"

Stahl closed his eyes. "Thanks."

Five minutes later, RG and Kacey's Outback skidded to a stop along the shell driveway, a plume of dust enveloping the vehicle. Stahl opened the deck's sliding door, running the gauntlet of officers congregating on the deck. As he stepped onto the yard, two officers followed, arranging themselves at the property line along Seaview, their subtle positioning divulging their suspicion.

Kacey hugged him as they met in the middle of the lawn. "I'm so sorry, Mike."

He nodded to RG. "Thanks for coming guys. We gotta talk."

"What are you thinking, Mike?"

"What I say might sound crazy, but…"

"We've already done crazy," RG reassured him. "Everything else is just normal now."

"Let's put distance between us and curious ears." The three ambled slowly toward the woods along the property's south side, stopping to gaze across the Boyle's moss-laden pond.

A single tear shimmered in Stahl's eye. "Zach's gone. He'd been acting strange lately. I'm not sure he…was himself."

RG and Kacey exchanged a glance.

Stahl scuffed his foot against a patch of dirt. "You heard about Nathan Stennett?"

"Oh my God, yes! His father killed him…and Maria, too."

Stahl scratched his head. "I'm not sure Abner Stennett did kill his wife. And even though he killed Nathan, he was trying to kill someone else. You see, Abner Stennett told me a story. I thought it was nuts at the time. He told me Nathan wasn't his son."

RG rubbed his face. "What? He wasn't the boy's father?"

"No, no! He meant the boy had changed. I didn't believe him at first, but then Zach changed. Same things Stennett described in Nathan."

"Like what?"

Stahl glanced up. "His eyes."

"What about them?" RG probed.

"Darkness crept into them, hiding their color, and Zach… didn't seem to be behind them anymore." Stahl pivoted, throwing up his hands. "God, I've been thinking about this for the past week or so, tossing and turning. I even drove up to Plymouth County Correctional and had a conversation with Stennett to confirm my suspicions. Still, it all sounds plausible at three in the morning, but in the light of day it just comes off as crazy."

"Never mind that," Kacey interrupted. "Go on."

Stahl placed his hands on his hips. "His behavior changed. He went as far as to kill this beautiful bird with a slingshot. I mean, he'd never harmed anything before in his life."

"What did you say?" Kacey's eyes widened.

"I said he'd never harmed anything—"

"No, before." Kacey cut him off. "Did you say slingshot?"

"Yeah. Zach told me a friend gave it to him."

"Did he tell you his name?" RG interjected.

Stahl stroked his chin. "No. He tried to, but then he stopped."

"Or maybe someone stopped him." RG glanced at Kacey. "Sounds like Malachi."

Stahl opened his mouth, but nothing came out. He swallowed. "That's the name of the demon…or spirit Abner Stennett said controlled Nathan. Who is he?"

"He's a boy who died back in the forties," RG explained. "Appears he's been coming back and living the life he missed through bodies of children he befriends."

"As in…inside their bodies?" Stahl asked.

"Hard to believe, I know." RG blew out a breath. "Different from most jumpers. When a jumper invades for an extended time like Malachi does, the competing souls force the body to choose. A body can't hold two souls at once. The weaker soul fades away and disappears, and the body begins to change."

Kacey grabbed his arm. "Then he abducts them. We've been looking for him."

Stahl raised his eyes, glaring at the blue sky. "Jesus Christ, not again."

"Twenty years ago, a woman in Brookline lost her son when the boy was taken from his bed and never found. No evidence whatsoever. The woman also described the boy as disappearing inside himself before his abduction."

"We've been losing Zach for the past week or so. Both Claire and I have noticed. My mind kept spinning back to Abner Stennett's interrogation. I should have known. I should have done something."

Kacey placed a hand on his arm. "How could you have known, Mike?"

"Because I've been to that place, Kacey, remember?" His raised voice drew attention from the nearby officers. "I've been fooling myself, though, living in denial it ever happened, eighteen months building a new life, trying to forget the past. Trying to forget where I'd been…the fire." He closed his eyes as *the rush* built up behind his eyes, like a wave rolling to the shore. He reached for RG who steadied him, the simmering flames burning out in his mind.

"You okay?" RG propped Stahl's sagging body against his.

"Yeah." Stahl's hand absently rubbed the grafted skin behind his neck as he blew out a breath. "I should have known something wasn't right the minute I spotted the changes, the minute I interrogated Stennett."

RG rested his hand on Stahl's shoulder. "Don't beat yourself up over it. You couldn't have known."

"I met Malachi in a dream," Kacey began. "He had a slingshot hanging from his back pocket. Do you still have it?"

Stahl nodded. "I took it away from Zach the other day."

"I need to see it."

"Sure. Hang on a minute."

He loped across the yard until he had reached the deck, taking the steps two at a time before disappearing into the house. When he returned, he handed the toy to Kacey, the thick rubber tubing wrapped in loops around the dark wood handle.

She turned the slingshot in her hands. Pressing a finger into the ancient grooved wood, her nail slalomed in a jagged pathway along the grip. On the bottom, a crude 'M' had been carved into the base.

Now it was Kacey's turn to swoon, her body swaying on shaking legs. The slingshot dropped from her hand as her eyes fluttered in their sockets, her knees folding beneath her.

Kacey

At the same moment she fumbled the slingshot, her mind plunged into the familiar void. Pulled through the unearthly stillness, Kacey emerged into blazing late-afternoon heat, the sudden glare forcing her hand to shield her eyes. She stood in a knee-high grass field, rotting board remnants scattered beside a deep hole in the ground.

The well.

She advanced toward the edge, peering over the rim into blackness, the slosh of water tickling the wall's mossy edges echoing from a hundred feet below her.

"Be careful, ma'am. It's a long drop."

Kacey's heart lurched in her chest as she pivoted to face

the voice behind her, heels licking the well's stony brim. A young boy stood before her, his lobster-red skin a near match to his bathing trunks, a shock of black hair standing out against the brilliant azure sky. Kacey sensed her mind deceiving her—the boy had already dropped into the earth. She had heard his splashing from deep within the well.

How can he be standing before me?

"What do you want, Malachi?" Kacey fought to maintain her equilibrium as she glanced over her shoulder deep into the earth.

He nodded toward the object gripped in her fist. "I want my slingshot back. You see, I lent it to a friend, and he forgot to return it."

"Your friend…Zach?"

The boy nodded and held out his hand.

Kacey held the slingshot out of reach. "Did you take him away, like the others?"

"Take him away? What do you mean?"

Kacey narrowed her eyes. "You know what I'm talking about."

"I don't," the boy said, shrugging.

"Then let me talk to…the one who does."

They stood facing each other for a long moment, the buffeting wind whipping through the grass with a hiss, underscoring the silence. "I don't know who you mean."

The sun warmed her skin, countering Malachi's chilling presence. She waited, anticipating what would follow. The transformation erupted at his mouth first, the corners turning upward in a cracked, toothless grin, his thick black hair shedding from his grizzled scalp. His youth receded before her eyes, splotchy purple and blue veins pulsing against his dermal shell like a roadmap, tendons and cords straining against his thin, ropy arms. The ogre-like beast stood before her, the folds of skin piling up along his forehead as he raised his eyebrows.

"Don't touch my stuff." He snatched the slingshot from her hand and shoved it into his back pocket, the rubber tubing jiggling as he wavered on spring-loaded haunches.

Kacey hadn't noticed at first, but another man appeared behind him. Dressed in black, his long, shoulder-length hair rode a left-to-right air current, a familiar gold wedding ring glistening on his left hand.

She pointed. "You've got a hell of a nerve showing up with that ring on your finger, Skoczek!"

The man twirled the shimmering band with his opposite hand as a grin parted his lips. He blew her a kiss.

"You bastard!" Kacey bolted toward Skoczek as he backpedaled, his eyes wide. Malachi threw himself forward like a linebacker, knocking her backwards into the pit. She fell, weightless against gravity's inevitable pull toward the fetid water.

Not again!

Kacey's shout resonated across Mike Stahl's lawn, drawing the stares from the cadre of police officers meandering about the house. She had wound up in RG's arms, half-standing, half-leaning against him as he steadied her.

"Oh my God, I still sense him inside me." Her stomach clenched as bile erupted from her throat. "His taste, smell…it's all over me." She ran her hands over her body as if she could scrub off the stench.

"Who?"

"Malachi. I just saw him…back at the well."

Stahl searched the grass in front of her. "Where's the slingshot?"

"It's gone," she said, followed by a long groan. "Malachi has it."

"How is that possible?" Stahl asked.

She turned her attention to RG. "He also has your student with him. He's wearing your ring."

"Motherfucker!" RG clutched his bandaged hand.

"God, I'm dizzy." Kacey pressed a shaky hand against her forehead.

RG positioned her arm around Stahl's shoulder. "Just lean on Mike for a second." RG jogged toward the car, returning with her aluminum water bottle.

Kacey found her feet again after taking a long glug.

Stahl wedged his hands against his hips. "Listen, Kacey. You say this Malachi, he abducts children. Where does he take them?"

Kacey gave him the rundown on the situation. "We're going in next week to get them out."

"How?"

RG folded his arms and shifted his legs. "We're not sure yet."

"I mean, what's your plan."

"We don't have one," Kacey sighed.

Stahl scrunched his face. "You sure you don't want to map something out before—"

"We don't have time, Mike," RG interrupted. "We can only go into the loop during its corresponding time period, so we don't have a hell of a lot of time to plan."

"But we're going in anyway," Kacey added.

Stahl gazed up at the throng of detectives milling about the deck.

"Well, you're not going anywhere without me."

———

Mike

Chris Daniels descended the deck steps and strode across the lawn toward Stahl and his circle, a barrel-chested police officer creeping behind him like a shadow.

"Who's the bulldog with Detective Daniels?" RG mumbled.

Stahl gritted his teeth. "Guy named Berrelli, but he's more like a pit bull. Been with the Chatham PD for over ten years but hasn't made it past the rank of patrol officer. Suppose if he didn't make a habit of beating up the tourists, it might help his career trajectory."

Calling the pug-nosed Matt Berrelli a time bomb would be an insult to the complex explosive, Berrelli's wiring not nearly as intricate. Still, no one had yet figured a way to defuse the man once ignited.

"Guy's a member of Team Brennan," Stahl whispered, "used to be a drinking buddy. He won't be happy to find you here. Best to keep your mouth shut."

Daniels sauntered up to the group, giving Stahl's elbow a quick squeeze. "Mike, you have a minute?"

"Yeah, what do you need?"

Recognition dawned in Daniels' eyes as he surveyed the group. "Dr. Granville, I didn't recognize you. You've...um..." Daniels placed his hands over his belly.

"Yeah, that's the general consensus."

"Granville? Well, well. If it isn't the 'Fugitive Professor,'" Berrelli barked. "It's like meeting a celebrity, O.J. Simpson...or maybe Robert Blake. Hey Daniels, we're in the presence of greatness."

RG bit his tongue, folding his arms across his chest.

Berrelli inspected RG from head to toe, a twitch flaring across his lip. "People seem to be in the habit of getting killed around you. That makes you a problem in my book."

Stahl glared at the officer. "That's enough, Berrelli."

He stepped forward into RG's personal space. "We have a nice interrogation room waiting for you, Granville, if you ever need to get anything off your chest. Seriously, anything you wanna confess. Take this as a personal invitation." He turned his head. "You too, Stahl."

"Fuck yourself," Stahl snarled, taking a step toward the cop.

Daniels stepped between them. "All right, all right, just relax you two."

"You know, there is one thing I'd like to get off my chest, officer." RG eyed the human attack dog in front of him. "You see, I've been wrestling with a bit of guilt."

"Here we go," Berrelli sneered. "Let it out."

"I never got the chance to thank your pal, Brennan. If he hadn't been so inept trying to frame me for murder, leaving a trail of clues leading right to him, the courts might have actually found me guilty. Could you thank him for me? Oh, wait, he's dead, isn't he?" RG shook his head. "Go figure."

Pulsating blue cables grew from Berrelli's neck and temple as he lurched toward RG. "You motherfucker!"

Stahl jumped between them as thunder erupted from the deck, a parade of feet pounding down the steps toward the altercation.

Daniels inserted himself into the melee, one hand on Berrelli's chest as he absorbed a couple of the man's flailing roundhouses. "You're out of line, Berrelli! Step back!"

Rough hands grabbed Stahl from behind, allowing Berrelli to bulldoze RG to the ground, a handful of officers wrenching his arms behind his back.

"Fucking cop killer!" Berrelli snapped as he drove a knee into RG's back.

"Get off him, asshole!" Kacey shouted, grabbing a fistful

of Berrelli's hair and round housing him with her aluminum water bottle, denting the frame on the bridge of his nose.

As one of the officers reached for Kacey from behind, Stahl drove his shoulder into him, dropping the man onto his back. He lay on the grass, straining to catch his breath as Stahl hovered above him. "Don't touch her."

The woozy Berrelli rose to a seated position and spit on the lawn, a line of blood dripping from his nose from Kacey's well-aimed blows.

"You're finished, Stahl. You should have been in jail for protecting this piece of shit." He tossed a thumb toward RG, buried under a pair of struggling bodies. "But a missing kid? Bye-bye, asshole."

"That's enough everyone." Daniels' voice boomed from the center of the storm as he pushed and pulled officers off the humanity pile in the middle of the lawn. "That's a civilian you're engaging, and he's injured. Let him up."

The chaos slowly ebbed as the combatants struggled to their feet and wiped the dirt and grass from their clothing. An animated Berrelli trudged toward the deck stairs, flanked by his comrades, spitting venom and holding a sleeve to his flowing nose.

RG rose to a knee, Kacey helping him to his feet, the top two buttons dangling from his shirt and his collar partially torn. Someone had rolled across his surgically repaired hand, the unwound bandage exposing a blotch of fresh blood.

Daniels straightened his tie as he backed away from the crowd. Stahl followed him.

"What the fuck was that, Chris, bringing Berrelli over here? Guy's a goddamn loose cannon!"

"I'm sorry, Mike. The guy's way out of line. I didn't bring him down here to rile things up. I just had a message to deliver." Daniels jerked his head, signaling for Stahl to follow him as he headed to his vehicle, slapping at his pant legs to dislodge the clinging grass.

Daniels leaned against the front quarter panel and blew air from his cheeks. "So, this is how it's gonna go down. We gotta question you and Claire, separately." He raised his hands in front of his chest. "It's protocol, Mike."

"Jesus Chris! Our son's missing—"

"And there's blood on his sheets."

"We've been answering your questions all morning, Chris."

"Yeah, and the only reason you're not in cuffs right now is because they can't find the Farley kid across town either. We gotta get it on record, Mike. By the book."

"You're gonna put me in front of the one-way glass? Claire, too?"

He had asked the question, but already anticipated the answer. They always interrogated the parents when a child went missing. He had been on the other side of the glass on more than one occasion. But Claire didn't deserve to go through the grueling procedure and suffer any more grief, especially now that he recognized who had abducted Zach.

"I don't make the rules, pal."

"Goddammit!"

Daniels sprung away from the vehicle. "Hell, I know you didn't have anything to do with it, but how would it look for the department if you did, and we didn't bother getting your statements on record? Press would have a field day."

"So, it's just a formality? Don't tell me no one thinks we had anything to do with this."

Daniels hesitated. "I didn't say that."

"Great."

Daniels put a hand on his shoulder. "I'm on your side, Mike. Let's get this over with. You'll be home before dinner."

Stahl inhaled deeply a few times to calm himself, preparing

for what he could control, cops and statements, his world's immediate minutiae.

Just get through it Mike, get through the bullshit and prepare for the real battle.

Stahl's chest tightened, and his breath came in bursts as he visualized his son in some godawful place, a world away from the people who loved him. He had promised him on the beach he would jump in front of a train for him and protect him from the monster in the closet. He figured he had meant Kenny Farley, but the boy had encountered every child's worst fear, a living, breathing nightmare. Zach had given Mike his trust, and he had failed him, the monster had won.

Stahl clenched his teeth, his jaw muscles flexing.

Zach's coming home, dammit!

He nodded toward the house. "Which one of my supportive colleagues up there gets the honor of sweating me under the lights?"

Daniels shrugged and shook his head.

"Listen, Chris. There are cops in this town…Christ, cops in my house," Stahl said, gesturing toward Berrelli and his comrades making their way up the deck steps, "who figure I harbored a killer, who suspect Granville's a murderer."

"You understand how it is with unsolved murders, Mike. You ended up clearing Granville's name."

"Because he was innocent."

Daniels crossed his arms. "And Brennan ended up dead in your house."

"Because he was dirty."

"Hell, Mike, everyone knew about Brennan. Most cops don't think he should have died for it."

"Guy killed one of his lackeys, tried to kill me. Still got two of his slugs in me."

Daniels shifted his weight from one foot to another. "Some

view it differently, is all. Figure there's more to it. Things you never told anyone. Hell, you haven't even let me in, Mike. I don't have a fucking clue what went down! I'm the one defending your ass every day."

"I appreciate it, Chris."

"Ah, fuck 'em!" Daniels wiped his forehead with his arm. "I'll drive you downtown. Claire's gotta go separately."

"I understand."

Stahl headed around to the passenger door, then glanced up at Daniels, eyes lowered and nodding toward the vehicle's backseat.

Sonofabitch!

Daniels opened the sedan's rear door and Stahl slipped in, secured behind the mesh cage.

———

Mike and Claire returned home from the Chatham Police Department late in the afternoon, their grueling interviews leaving them both shaken and silent on the short taxi ride home, courtesy of the Chatham taxpayers. A red sticker affixed to the front door alerted them to the Chatham PD's right, under Massachusetts General Law, to revisit the home in the course of their investigation.

Stahl ripped the sticker from the front door and crushed it in the palm of his hand as he flung open the front door. The house exerted an eerie stillness, the immediate heaviness of Zach's absence quashing the relief and comfort of being home.

"They assume I had something to do with his disappearance, Mike. They're not even looking for him!" Her body shook like a hooked fish, her legs giving way until she collapsed in tears onto the kitchen floor, smudged with the footprints of Cape Cod's finest. "How could they?"

He sank to the floor with her, trying to fathom a loss he couldn't describe or imagine, isolation and helplessness wrapping its vile arms around the two like a cement cloak, augmenting gravity's pull. A beam of late afternoon sunlight bisected the kitchen like a shiny glass wall, a blizzard of particle dust darting back and forth from darkness to light and back again. Leaning against the kitchen island, they sat, clutching each other, their rhythmic breath sounds hypnotizing them in an exhausted trance.

"What do we do, Mike? Where's our boy?" Her damp eyes pulsed with fresh tears.

He got to his feet and helped her up, guiding her across the kitchen and over to the living room couch. "I might have an idea."

She stopped. Her mouth opened but no sound escaped.

"Claire, you need to listen to me. Sit." He dropped onto the couch beside her, folding his hand around hers. "There are things..." He hesitated. "Things I never told you."

"What things?"

"Things about the accident."

"What does that have to do with Zach?" Her eyes beseeched him for a miracle, as if he could solve her son's disappearance with his words.

"It's all connected." He gazed at the floor as he prepared to finally let her in. What he would give if RG and Kacey could magically appear and corroborate his story. "First, let me say, I'm pretty sure I know what happened to Zach, and right now he's all right."

Claire sprang from the couch and whipped around to hover in front of him. "Then let's go get him, why are we waiting here—?"

"Because he's not in a place we can get to," he said, cutting her off. He stood and crossed the floor, peering through the bay windows onto the battered front yard, the evidence of law enforcement vehicles carved into the flattened lawn. What he would say would sound insane, but he had to come clean. He would be going after Zach in a few days and the truth had to come out sooner or later.

Claire's eyes glossed over as her face went stoic, her eyes piercing his with the fierceness of a mother's angst. "What are you saying? You know where he is, and you don't say anything until now? Why would you do that? What have you done with him?"

Mike grabbed Claire's fisted hands and held her steady. "I haven't done anything."

Jerking her hands out of his, she stepped backward, revealing a woman he didn't recognize. She shook her head and guttural sounds penetrated the space around them. "But you just said he's all right. How can you know that?"

"Just listen, Claire. I need to start at the beginning."

She took another step back. "You're scaring me, Mike."

He raked his fingernails across his head. "During the 'Fugitive Professor' case, I witnessed things I wasn't meant to see." He explained all he had been through with RG and Kacey eighteen months earlier, caretakers, jumpers, and their battle with the burning man. His words had the tone of a crazy man's ramblings, and he prayed each phrase tumbling from his lips would somehow sound more convincing, prompt a look in her eyes hinting at belief. But when he described how Malachi had abducted Zach and taken him to another time, Claire's glassy stare seethed with a mounting darkness he had never glimpsed before. "I'm leaving in a few days to get him. To bring him back."

"Where is he, you sonofabitch!" She was screeching now,

and Mike realized he should never had said anything at all, just reassured her, comforted her, held her for a while before making an exit to charge out into the world and bring Zach home. Why did he think he needed to go there, drag her into a mess no one could fully comprehend unless they had been there and witnessed what he had been through? He should have thought twice about burdening her with the truth, left her innocence intact, let her remain under the sky and stars of simplicity. Life on earth was complicated enough.

"The cops were right about the evidence, or lack of it, weren't they?" Tears spilled onto her cheeks. "What did you do with him? Did you hurt him? Just tell me, please." She buried her face in her hands.

Stahl's throat closed, he couldn't swallow. *She thinks I did it.* "Claire, I love Zach like a son, he's—"

"Don't you say his name, you fucking bastard!" She scooped her keys off the counter before storming out the back-door and onto the deck, sprinting down the steps and across the lawn. Stahl hobbled after her, catching up with her in the driveway as she jumped into her Toyota and snapped the lock switch, the mechanism catching as he grabbed the door handle. She jammed the keys into the ignition, the engine roaring to life. Her body shook as she struggled to put the car in gear, a glazed look clouding her eyes.

"Claire, please!"

She threw the car into drive and stood on the gas, spinning tires spewing brightly colored shells onto the flattened lawn as she sped away.

————

RG

The pounding door jolted RG from his nap, sending a cattle prod into his core. Three more staccato bangs followed.

"Hang on," he mumbled, dragging himself from the living room couch toward the entryway, blinking himself back into consciousness. He cracked the front door to find a distraught Claire Simpson pacing along the porch like a caged animal, the nervous energy seeping from her in waves.

"Claire? What're you—"

"Mike's gone and done something to Zach," she interrupted, crying and wringing her hands. "He must have had a complete break with reality."

"Come in, come in." RG pressed the door shut and ushered her into the living room.

He tried to tell her things, I bet, tried to put her mind at ease…

Bringing someone into his and Kacey's reality took subtlety and tact, as well as proof. When he had informed Stahl about the presence of caretakers, jumpers, and other worlds eighteen months ago, Stahl had already borne witness to the dark evil. Kacey had brought him to the next world in her dream, giving him a front row seat to the unexplainable. RG had simply filled the gaps to a mind craving closure. Claire couldn't accept the reality-bending truth after the jolt of losing her son, and she questioned the source. How could she not?

"Please, sit. What did Mike say?"

Claire remained on her feet, moving and shifting in a haphazard dance along the carpet. "He told me a story about you and Kacey. Something about a dream and vengeful souls…jumpers… from the next world—"

"Claire," Kacey interrupted, stepping from the hallway.

She gnawed at a tattered cuticle below her thumbnail as her words picked up speed. "And he said one of them kidnapped Zach and brought him somewhere we can't get to.

He said you guys are involved, that you're planning on going through time to find Zach, and—"

"He's telling the truth." Kacey reached out a hand to steady her.

She swatted it away. "You're all fucking mad!"

"He's not crazy, and neither are we. In a few days we're going through time to bring Zach home."

Claire's gaze bore a hole in the living room carpeting. "This can't be," she stammered. "It's not true, no one can visit other worlds, travel through time." She dashed toward the front door.

RG intercepted her as her fists flailed against him. "It's true, Claire. You need to listen!" He wrapped his arms around her like a straightjacket and eased her to the floor beside the couch.

"Get your hands off me, you fucking psycho! Let go of me!"

RG held her immobile as she struggled against him, her body jerking like a live wire, frustration driving a wave of tears across her cheeks. "Claire, you need to forget everything you've learned about everything," he said, straining through clenched teeth. "Forget your Sunday school lessons. Forget what you've ever imagined about life and death, heaven and hell. There's a war between good and evil waged beyond earthly boundaries, and it spills into this world every day. A few of us can sense it, fight it."

"You're in on it, too, aren't you? You're in on this with Mike?"

Kacey dropped to her knees beside them on the floor. "Nobody's in on anything, Claire! We're trying to help."

RG leaned forward to speak in Claire's ear as he fought to hold her. "We're gonna get him home."

"Tell me you didn't hurt Zach, you bastard!" Claire's breathing picked up as she battled to free herself.

"Stop it, Claire! If you stop fighting me, I'll let you up. You can run out of here if you want, but you can't run from what I've told you. It's time to face the truth."

Claire's breathing slowed as her body calmed, but her eyes remained lit up like a pinball machine, darting back and forth. RG could sense the fight coiled within her muscles, taut and ready to spring. He relaxed his hold, gauging her reaction before he committed to letting her go.

"Promise me you didn't do anything to Zach. Promise me he's alive."

The front door slammed against its hinges as Mike Stahl burst through it. "Claire! Are you here?"

"In here, Mike!" RG shouted.

His eyes darted with a mad obsession until he spied her in a heap on the floor, wrapped tightly in RG's grip. "What the hell's going on here? Let her go!"

Stahl graduated to the living room with caution as RG relaxed his grip. Claire attempted to rise but her numbed limbs kept her pinned to the floor.

"Claire…" He approached her with cautious steps.

RG sensed Stahl's uncertainty whether he stared into the face of love and trust or a complete stranger.

Claire stood, raising her head and meeting Stahl with glassy eyes.

"Claire, I—"

In an instant, her fists exploded from her sides, pummeling Stahl's face and bloodying his nose. Her well-aimed shoe tips sent him to the floor, hands clasped to his shins.

Eyes oozing venom, Claire stormed from the house, slamming the front door so hard it rattled the frame.

Chapter Fourteen

'Heav'n knows What man
He might have made. But we,
He died a most rare boy.'

F.W. JACKSON, died March 23, 1799 (Aged one year &
7 days.)
-Epitaphs from Burial Hill

July 4, 2019

RG

Resting his elbows on the sticky tabletop, RG grazed on what remained of his fingernail nubs, chewed to the quick over the past fifteen minutes. He surveyed the team assembled in the Pancake Man's cushioned, back booth resting against the Wurlitzer juke box, a dead seventies glam rocker, an octogenarian, and a hobbled cop with two bullets lodged inside him.

Oh, and Morrow, with no residual powers left to make much of a difference. In moments they would jump seventy years into the past, unprepared for what lay before them, with no coherent plan to achieve their objectives. Kacey remained optimistic as usual, but RG couldn't mask his trepidation. She grinned at him from across the table, the softness in her eyes calming his frazzled nerves.

The previous year, when RG had confronted the jumper, Victor Garrett, he had studied his history, learned his weaknesses, his vulnerability. But he knew nothing about Malachi, much less how to find him and the children or how to kill him. His ringer, Elias Ashton, assured him he had the solution to Malachi's demise but would provide no details. The team had two days in Malachi's time loop to pull off a miracle, restore the lives of countless children, and stop a powerful jumper bent on keeping them enslaved.

As team leader, RG didn't bring much to the table. His left hand proved useless, a bulky gauze keeping his severed digit attached to his paw, his caretaker power waning and resting on the finger of another—a fledgling jumper with a ruthless streak and a growing darkness invading his soul. The chance of stranding the entire team seventy years in the past loomed as a solid possibility. The risk of altering history remained a near certainty, five future-dwellers stumbling blind through the streets of 1946 Plymouth, but what choice did they have? No trial run or reconnaissance mission would help them find their targets or an extraction point. They'd wing it. The opportunity to hijack Malachi's portal had arrived by way of calendar, not through adequate planning, and it was now or never.

Kacey's childhood restaurant bustled with activity on a July Fourth morning, servers racing through the aisles with trays of steaming hot breakfast plates, jostling with patrons hoping to nab an empty table or booth. Noises clambered from the kitchen. Spatulas and wire whisks clanked against the sizzling griddle as hash slingers flipped and scrambled the food, bells dinging with each plate slung onto the pick-up window shelf. Wilder had fed quarters into the jukebox all morning, singing along with the entire catalog of ABBA songs, reveling in the music of the seventies after a forty-year absence.

"Agnetha and Anni-Frid's singing voices," Wilder sighed, "like honey over melted butter." He wiped the corner of his eye with his napkin.

Kacey glanced at RG and stuck a finger in her throat.

RG gave Wilder the once-over, the caretaker sporting a pair of form-fitting, polyester-flared trousers with a silk shirt opened to the third button, as if he planned to go clubbing. But his outward appearance belied a stony resolve. Earlier, he had stood with him as he flipped open the locket around his neck. He had set his jaw as he viewed his charge, Travis, behind bars in a crude cage, huddled with the other children. Tilting the locket had revealed Zach Simpson on the cell's cold stone floor behind Travis, shivering and dirty, but very much alive. Stahl's breath had caught in his throat as Wilder leaned over and draped an arm across his shoulder.

"No way we're coming back without your son."

As RG leaned back and gulped his coffee, Morrow slid from the edge of the booth and stood in the aisle, nodding for RG to join him. He slipped off the seat and stood beside his father as eager patrons jostled through the crowd, hustling along the aisle in anticipation. But when they observed other team members remaining in their seats, an audible murmur emerged with their scowls as they trudged back to the waiting area.

"What is it, Dad?" He had to raise his voice over *Dancing Queen's* maddening chorus.

"I won't be coming with you."

RG tipped his head to the side. "What?"

"I've given this a lot of thought, so hear me out." Morrow folded his arms. "You see, Robert, I'm the only one who has no useful role on this trip."

"Of course you do. There are lots of things—"

"Name one," Morrow interrupted, raising an eyebrow. "What purpose would I serve? My powers are gone, I can't protect anyone. I'd just be in the way."

"How can you say that? We're a team."

"I'd just be one more person who could inadvertently disrupt history."

RG rested his hands on his hips and stared at the floor.

"Listen, Robert. Once you recruited Ian for the mission, I found I could step back. He'll do everything he can to protect you and Kacey, something I can't do anymore. The team is small, tight, and everyone has a mission. You don't need dead weight."

RG lifted his gaze. "But I need you."

"The children need me more. Who's going to meet them at this end? The portal will disorient them, and they won't know where they are. They may try to leave the restaurant and wander off into the next world. They'll also need a good breakfast in them, and I used to whip up a pretty mean batch of chocolate chip pancakes back in the day...when chocolate was easy to get."

He grinned and took off his hat and dark suit jacket, hanging them on the coat rack by the door. "Someone has to stay."

"Well, whatta ya say, mates?" Wilder rose from the booth, raking a hand through his blow-dried locks. "This little shindig has been knees up, but I figure it's time we make our jump."

RG placed a hand on Morrow's shoulder as he spoke up. "Okay, it's time everyone. Five of us will be making the trip:

Mike, Kacey, Elias, Ian, and myself. Morrow will remain here in the restaurant as the children arrive through the portal, keeping them together and making sure they get something to eat before we get them back home."

RG grinned at his father, sensing his frustration at the circumstances relegating him to childcare on such a critical mission. But he had been right. Someone needed to stay behind, and the children would be in good hands with him. Still, after all the sacrifices he had made to keep RG and Kacey alive and help defeat the burning man, he longed for him to have a bigger role in the mission. Morrow had passed the mantle of power to his son, but even on his best day, RG couldn't hold a candle to him.

The crew slid from the booth and sidestepped the hungry patrons as they worked their way to the entranceway. At the door, RG faced the team for a final debriefing. "It's critical to keep your thoughts masked, your minds closed during the jump. Malachi will recognize our presence in his portal, but he won't know what we're up to. We can't betray our intentions."

"Reggie's right. If he knows why we're coming, the mission's a damp squib."

The others looked to RG, who gave them a shrug, having abandoned his English-to-Wilder dictionary.

"All right, let's head out."

Stahl elbowed Kacey. "It had to be Plymouth." They both smirked as if sharing an inside joke.

Before RG could interrupt, Wilder sidled up beside him and threw an arm around his shoulder. "Don't forget, mate, this portal will be like nothing you've ever traveled. It will try to deter you, make you envision things you don't want to. If you don't stay focused, you'll get us all lost in there, and we'll never make it back."

RG nodded. *Thanks for the pep talk.*

Kacey faced Wilder. "We're heading to a packed Plymouth on Independence Day weekend. What happens if someone sees us? Shouldn't we wait until dark?"

"We need as many daylight hours as we can get if we're gonna find the children. And it won't upset the course of history if someone glances our way. But it will if we interfere with someone's progress, someone stops to talk with us, bumps into us, anything…history will change forever. It's best to keep hidden, though…travel through the woods or empty fields whenever we can."

"Remember, Plymouth isn't as populated as it is today, it still has lots of undeveloped land and open spaces," RG reminded her. "Probably best if we leave our cellphones here, though. Besides, they'll be useless without cell towers."

"And if anyone from 1946 got hold of one, I wouldn't want to imagine the kind of world we'd return to," Kacey ventured.

"Imagine if this kind of technology gets a sixty-year head start." Ashton turned his cell over in his hand. "Consider how history would have changed."

"The 'summer of love' might be remembered as the 'summer of likes.'" RG welcomed the throaty chuckles from the team, defusing the growing tension. Soon, everyone had relinquished their devices, piling them on the hostess's lectern.

"We'll pick these up on the way back."

"Are you sure they'll be safe?" Stahl asked. "My whole world's in there."

"These are my people, Mike," Kacey acknowledged, scanning the restaurant. "Everything will be just as we left it. I promise."

"Your gun, Mike." RG held out his hand.

"It stays with me." Stahl crossed his arms, steeling himself for a confrontation. "I'm bringing my son home, and I've got a little something for the motherfucker Malachi."

With Claire gone, Stahl resembled a man with nothing to lose. She hadn't called the cops on him yet, so she either believed him and needed time to cool off, or she had figured her story might land her in the slammer with him.

"Mike," Kacey said, stepping between the two men, "you can't kill a jumper with a bullet. You already tried that once."

"And a gunshot will bring people running, alter human trajectories, change history," Wilder added. "Won't do, mate."

Stahl unsnapped the retention strap of his shoulder holster and relinquished his sidearm to Kacey. She held the piece at arm's length between two fingers as she dumped it on the table with the rest of the electronics.

"Best to keep it here."

"All right, Mike has provided a couple two-way radios with a twenty-mile range in case we need to separate." RG raised them above his head. "These might end up being our lifelines since we won't have another way to communicate." He clipped the first onto his belt and tossed the second to Stahl.

RG waved everyone toward him until they huddled together by the door. He grasped Kacey and Ashton's hands, wincing at the old man's grip on his damaged hand. "Okay, everyone, join hands in a circle. Since I'm the only one who's able to travel through time, we need to go as a unit. Once the portal's open, it'll be open and operational as long as Malachi stays alive and my powers hold out. If I run out of juice or we don't get the ring back, we may be staying awhile."

Each fished for the person's hand next to him. Kacey leaned over and whispered to RG. "When's the last time we didn't spend July Fourth on the Cape?"

He grinned. "Hey, we'll be in Plymouth, close enough for me."

Morrow stepped over and quieted the group. "Listen to me, no matter what you see or hear inside the portal, don't let go of your partner's hand. The portal could throw you into another time or another place. We don't fully understand its capabilities."

"One thing for sure, it won't be friendly." Wilder gave RG a nod. "All right, Reggie, it's your gig."

"Everyone ready?"

The team nodded their heads.

Everyone's ready but me, then.

Morrow folded his hands behind his back as the team stepped through the Pancake Man's front door.

RG closed his eyes, drawing on the power once wrapped around his finger. It sputtered, then caught, like an engine firing. He gave a nervous glance toward Kacey as the five dropped from the world.

A moment of disorientation and confusion greeted him as his body adapted to the pathway, each portal's idiosyncrasies manifested in differing degrees of turbulence and physical discomfort challenging the body's inner sensors. He had gotten used to Kacey's portal, a coiled pathway sending him through a swirling stillness in a soothing absence of sound or light, bathing him in warmth like a return to the womb.

But Malachi's portal oozed a hellish fury.

Dropping into the yawning chasm between worlds, a cacophony of screeching sounds rattled RG's teeth. He forced himself to continue grasping Kacey and Elias's hand instead of succumbing to his instincts to shed them and clasp his hands over his ears. A thumping backbeat pounded in his chest as if a fist slugged his midsection with every heartbeat, the blinding light and faint death and decay odors overwhelming his senses. But the voices in his head proved the worst, triggering his brain to conjure excruciating images, brutalized children, slaughtered families, mass killings—a roadmap of Malachi's atrocities over the past seventy years, moving images sliding past his vision like a blurred subway station's mural, viewed from a speeding trolley. He couldn't discern whether Malachi had implanted these pictures to deter interlopers or to celebrate his life's work, but RG forced his eyes shut and clutched the hands beside him with more intensity. He kept his emotions walled off, confined to his inner mind, but he struggled to contain them. He glanced at Kacey and Wilder to his right, Stahl and Ashton to his left, viewing the pain splayed across their visages, witnessing their internal struggle, wondering whether they beheld the same horrific scenes or others Malachi conjured in their minds.

Just as RG had reached his breaking point, when he could no longer shield his mind, a furious jolt ripped Ashton's hand from his grip. RG, Kacey, and Wilder tumbled headlong from the portal. Their bodies rebounded off a massive four-post bed and crashed onto a thickly woven carpet in a spacious room replete with high ceilings, a fireplace, and ceiling-to-floor windows adorned with thick, flowing drapes.

Stahl and Ashton were gone.

———

Malachi

The rumble spread through his body like a train thundering through an underground station as Malachi steadied himself against the drafty dwelling's stone wall. Images flashed before his eyes, his defiled portal allowing him glimpses of the intruders. Their faces reflected the terror his portal inflicted as he strained to tap into their thoughts and intentions, but he couldn't find purchase within their minds.

They've come prepared.

But Malachi didn't have to steal their thoughts to understood why they had come. He sensed the woman. Her presence in the portal told him everything he needed to know.

Malachi dashed toward the stairwell leading to the holding area below, Skoczek following at his heels.

"They're on their way," he said, growling. He turned and jabbed a gnarled finger at Skoczek's face. "The two I instructed you to kill, I might add, and they've brought others. Come with me."

Malachi pushed his grizzled form down the stone steps. Hewn into the earth, the cavernous clearing extended hundreds of yards through dirt and rock, forged on the backs of generations of children. Positioned along the circular space's perimeter and scattered throughout the grounds, barred cages teemed with weakened, dirty children. A walkway wound through the cells, giving Malachi a view of the children when he took his regular strolls through the cages. He would survey his trophies, smelling the fear from the cells' occupants as he passed, picturing his loving mother close beside him, holding his hand like she used to when they strolled through the Franklin Park cages.

At night, the children's desperate wails penetrated the stone ceiling into the main chamber where Malachi slept and continued upward, seeping through the earthen layer into the graveyard above the buried fortress. The colorful explosions bursting above the harbor every other night, raining red and blue streaks across the sky, nearly disguised the faint cries, but Malachi could still hear them when he wandered through Burial Hill. Had anyone ventured from the bustling town square's comforting arms to the chill of the ancient cemetery, they might have attributed the ghostly wails to the sounds of the dead buried around them before beating a hasty retreat from the Hill. But now others *had* come and would be listening closely for tell-tale sounds of suffering.

He would need to silence their wails.

The loudest cries belonged to the newer arrivals, the boys still clinging to the hope they would one day find a way home to their parents and not have to dig into the solid earth each day or sleep in cages come night. Like the new boy, Farley, whose whimpering lit a raging fire within the jumper. Unlike the other boys brought there out of love, Malachi had snatched the bully to punish him for what he had done to Zach.

He was expendable. The others…well, he would have to make tough choices.

Malachi's arrival into the pit triggered wary movements from the caged children, torches ringing the hollow's perimeter projecting writhing shadows against the far stone walls. Tonight, the sounds from the cages had escalated, as if the children could sense the coming intrusion.

"You're weak, Zach," Malachi muttered, spitting as he wandered past the boy's cell. He couldn't understand why Zach would sit with Farley, share his food with him, and comfort the trembling bully. "I save you from this blubbering hunk of shit, and you watch over him like a mother hen. Why?"

"Because you don't understand anything. You may be older than me, but you don't know much."

Malachi's blood boiled as Zach's words peppered him. "Maybe I'll jump back inside and teach you what I do know."

The cave's echo only served to mock his empty words. He could read in Zach's eyes the boy sensed his bluff. The boy wasn't born with special powers like Skoczek, but somehow Zach had figured out how to defend against him, learned to expel him, and he didn't want to give the boy any more confidence. He had already embarrassed him once, and he didn't want to appear weak in front of Skoczek or the other children.

The boy had bested him, which made him expendable, too.

Malachi attempted to recover. "Or maybe I'll jump into your friend over there, and he can teach you for me."

"That's just like you, isn't it?" Zach sneered. "I used to think Kenny was the bully, but it's you. You're the bully, and you'll be sorry because my father's coming to get me."

"Your father…" Malachi smirked.

"He promised he'd protect me from monsters like you."

"And I'll make sure when your father arrives, I will kill him right in front of you. Or maybe I'll kill you in front of him. What do you think, Skoczek?"

"Either one works," Skoczek laughed, twisting the ring on his finger.

"I'm not afraid of anything anymore. Not of him," Zach said, pointing to Skoczek, "and not of you. I'm not afraid of monsters."

Malachi leaned against the bars and growled. "Maybe you should be."

Grabbing Skoczek, the jumper stepped away from the cells. "You're to remain here and keep the children quiet. Do what you must to silence them. Tomorrow, I must go to the well."

"But…you died there."

"Tomorrow, it will give me life. I want you to stay here and wait for the trespassers to arrive. I want them dead." Malachi pointed to Zach. "I want the boy and his father dead."

Skoczek stepped toward the cage and closed his eyes, raising his head to sniff the foul air. "He's…the one, isn't he?"

"What one?"

"I can smell him." Skoczek's hands trembled as he turned to face Malachi. "I can still smell him on you."

Malachi sensed the jealousy erupting inside Skoczek, hoping to twist it into a rage he could use to his advantage. "Oh, he's the one. He's like no other. You failed me before, but now you can show me your loyalty. I want him and his father dead. And anyone else who ventures in here tomorrow. Can you handle that?"

Skoczek sneered as he advanced to the cage and pressed his face against the bars. "It would be my pleasure."

———

July 4, 1946

Mike

Mike Stahl bounced across Plymouth Harbor's marble-blue water like a skimming stone, hurtling toward the shoreline. His twisting body cartwheeled against the rocks with a stunning impact, his flailing arms doing little to protect himself. A gash opened across his scalp as his head glanced off the stone embankment; but the two-way radio on his belt took the brunt of the collision, imploding between his pelvis and the wall of stones abutting the shore. As he struggled to his feet, pinpoints of dazzling light shimmered across his vision. Raising a shaking hand to his bleeding head, he pressed his hands to his skull, grateful it hadn't shattered like a melon against the rocks. He gaped at the useless electronic components and plastic shards scattered on the sand beneath him.

Separated from the group…and no way to reach them.

Stahl found himself in no-man's land between Plymouth Bay and dry soil, resting on a steep embankment below a walkway along the harbor's banks. A hundred yards to his right, Plymouth's familiar weather-beaten waterfront businesses and storefronts bustled with activity. July Fourth vacationers and tourists paraded along a clogged Water Street, darting in and out of restaurants and gift shops or stopping to gaze at the brave souls traversing the uneven jetty circling Plymouth Harbor. Observing the sleek, torpedo-shaped automobiles and the revelers' dated short sleeve dress shirts and knee-cut, patterned dress styles, Stahl had no doubt he had been cast into a long-forgotten decade. Perched below the sightline of wandering eyes, he remained safe for the moment. But a passerby's curious glance over the embankment and history might change forever.

Dazed, he glanced out across the harbor. Ashton swam toward him with confident strokes, creating a nearly infinitesimal wake. The old man's entry point to this time and place appeared to have opened yards offshore. Stahl bristled at the image of what may have happened to an eighty-year-old body if he had grasped RG's hand a few seconds longer and met the unforgiving stone shoreline.

"You're bleeding." Ashton pulled himself onto the rocks beside Mike.

"I'm grateful to still have a head. You okay?"

"Rough impact, but I'd sure as hell rather be in the drink than caught in that ghastly portal." He glanced down at what remained of the two-way radio. "Looks like we're screwed."

Stahl nodded.

"If we don't find the group, we may be stuck—"

"Yeah, yeah, I got it!" Stahl kept his thoughts in control, no need to ratchet up his blood pressure envisioning 1946 Plymouth as his permanent home. At least a crowd hadn't gathered to help them from the water, marveling how a packed waterfront hadn't witnessed either of their bizarre water dances. "First things first. We gotta get out of here without drawing attention."

"There are too many people. Too many chances for an unintended interaction."

"God, it's busy down here, even for a holiday."

Ashton checked his watch. "I have two o'clock? Could that be right?"

"What? We left about nine. It only took minutes to get here."

Ashton clambered to the top of the embankment and peeked above the earthen lip, careful to remain undetected. He glanced at the clock tower looming over Water Street, confirming their missing hours. "We must have lost time along the way."

"So maybe we wait it out until dark, then we sneak across—"

"It's July Fourth, Mike. Thousands of people are already trickling into town with more arriving in the next few hours. Hundreds will spread blankets and lawn chairs along the green right above us to watch the fireworks. The kids will climb down here and sit on these rocks to get a better view. We won't have a chance; we gotta get out now."

Stahl joined Ashton at the embankment's edge, eyeing the throngs of residents and visitors crowding the narrow walkways, dodging the steady parade of motorized traffic as they dashed across Water Street to restaurants and gift shops.

"We gotta get across that street. What should we do?"

Ashton turned to Stahl. "I have a really bad idea."

Stahl tossed his hand in the air. "Well? Don't be shy."

"How long can you hold your breath?"

Chapter Fifteen

'Surely life is, as a vapour that appeareth
For a little time and vanisheth away.'

THOMAS, born July 18th, 1799, died Nov[r] 9th, 1800;
WILLIAM THOs, born April 14th, 1801, died Sep[r] 24th, 1801
Children of Cap[t] Thomas & M[rs] Margaret J[s] Bartlett
-Epitaphs from Burial Hill

July 4, 1946

RG

A suitcase lay open on a luggage rack beside the bed. A shower's hiss and puffs of heated steam greeted RG, Kacey, and Wilder from the cracked bathroom door.

Wilder shook the cobwebs from his head and gained his feet. "Where's the rest of 'em?"

"The old man's hand ripped from my grasp. I couldn't

hold on." RG cradled his damaged hand, rewinding the stray bandages.

"Bullocks! When did you lose them?"

"Right before we fell, seconds ago."

"Well, that's gonna throw a spanner in the works. Should be all right, mate. I'm guessing they're somewhere close." Wilder scanned the room. "Where the bloody hell are we?"

"Shhh!" Kacey raised a finger to her lips, gesturing toward the bathroom. "Looks like we're in some kind of hotel room," she whispered, "and someone's in it with us. We better get out of here."

"God, this room's beautiful." RG's eyes swept the chamber, darting among the hardcover classic literature tomes filling the mahogany bookcase from floor to ceiling, vases stuffed with flowers, and an assortment of chocolates and teas assembled on the desk. "Sad the only draw at hotels today is HBO and WiFi?"

"What's a WiFi, Reggie?" Wilder scrunched his face.

"Never mind, luv."

Kacey grabbed the leather-bound binder from the ornate wooden desk beside the window and gazed across its gold-embossed cover. "John Carver Inn, Plymouth, Massachusetts."

Racing to the window, Kacey fumbled with the heavy velvet drapes until she could observe Main Street and a banner strung across it. "Welcome to America's 170th birthday."

"1946," RG said, his tongue darting against the corner of his mouth as he quickly did the math.

"We're here." Wilder pressed his hands together.

"Wait a minute…John Carver Inn." RG rubbed his chin. "Rumor has it this place is crawling with ghosts."

"What? It's haunted?" Kacey scratched at her temple.

"Well, a bloody portal from the future leads right into it," Wilder shrugged. "I'd say that qualifies."

"What room number is this, Kacey?"

She inspected the key on the table. "Says 309."

"That's the one. Travel magazines recommend spending the night in this room if you have a spirit of adventure. Lots of guests have reported disturbances, lights going on and off, things going bump in the night."

"Your hubby really knows his onions." Wilder grinned at Kacey, raking a hand through his hair. "I'm living proof there's at least one ghost here."

The hissing water from the bathroom halted. Shower rings clinked as a curtain slid along the metal runner.

"Let's go," Kacey whispered. "Now!"

She hustled to the door and cracked it open just enough to peer into the crowded hallway. Men, women, and families milled about, making their way to their rooms and stopping to discuss the July Fourth festivities. They created a formidable gauntlet to their escape plans.

"Fuck me," RG muttered, rolling his eyes. "Wouldn't it figure, people in 1946 actually talk to each other in hotels?"

"No WiFi, I guess, eh, Reggie?" Wilder smirked.

As the bathroom door swung open, the three time travelers scrambled in different directions. RG dashed into the open closet, Kacey hurled herself under the bed, and Wilder slipped behind the window's velvet drapes. A rotund man's bare feet padded across the carpet toward the closet. He dropped his towel, standing full Monty before a cringing RG, the man's hanging clothes a tenuous linen barrier separating the two. He reached into the closet and fondled his bathrobe, knocking it off the hanger and sending it to the floor in front of RG's feet. He stepped back as far as he could into the recesses of the spacious closet, careful not to jostle the wire hangers dangling around him. The man groped along the closet floor until he gripped the robe, his fingers tickling RG's shoe tips. Covering himself, the man wrapped the sash around his waist and shuffled into the bathroom. The clink of shaving supplies deposited onto the porcelain sink and slosh of running water drifted through the half-open door.

RG dashed from the closet and threw back the drapes. "Let's go, Ian!"

Kacey shimmied out from under the bed as RG threw open the door to 309. The last of the congregating throng lumbered to their rooms at the hallway's far end.

The three race-walked along the thick carpeting to the staircase in the opposite direction. The twenty-yard stretch extended for an eternity. RG's heart throbbed in his throat, expecting at any moment for a room door to swing open or someone to appear from the looming stairwell door. As they reached the end of the corridor, RG held out his arms to slow his companions. Peering around the edge of the adjacent corridor to his left, he waved them forward.

"All clear. Come on, let's go."

Glancing inside the stairwell door, he craned his neck back and forth. "Let's head to the basement and find a backdoor out of here. We'll be safer outside in wide-open spaces."

"But people are out there," Kacey said.

"They're in here, too."

They traversed the wooden steps to the basement. While RG's and Kacey's sneakers muffled their footsteps, Wilder's high-heeled platform shoes emitted pained thumping clomps.

"For chrissake, Ian. Your disco shoes are gonna get us nabbed and change the course of history."

"Wouldn't be the first time disco changed history, luv."

Fuckin' Limey!

As they reached the basement landing and hustled toward the rear exit, a man threw open the stairwell door behind them, his voice booming.

"What the hell are you doing in my hotel?"

———

Mike

"How long can I hold my breath? What does that have to do with anything?"

"Take a look across the street," Ashton remarked, pointing, "behind all the businesses on the waterfront. It's nothing but trees and woods. We can regroup there, figure out our strategy."

"But we can't get over there."

"Yes, we can. There's a drainpipe underneath Water Street. It starts at the harbor and comes out across the street at the edge of the woods behind the waterfront businesses. As a boy, my schoolmates and I would play inside it. We crawled through it all the time to get from the harbor to the woods. We'll pass right under everybody."

Stahl squinted toward the pier. "I can't spot any drainpipe. Where is it?"

"It's about a hundred yards that way." Ashton pointed toward the marina and wharf in the distance to his right.

"But with the crowd down there, won't someone spot us?"

"Just keep close to the rocks. When we get near the harbor wall, we can slip into the water and swim to it. That'll keep us out of sight. Doesn't look like anyone's hanging over the edge right now staring into the harbor."

Stahl rubbed his forehead. "But even a casual glance over the railing will cause a commotion, and we'll be fucked."

"We'll have to be quick. It's the only way."

Stahl's hand shielded his eyes from the glaring sun as he gazed toward the wharf. "How come I still can't see the drainpipe?"

Ashton blew out a breath. "Because most of it is underwater."

"What?"

"Well, it's high tide. We'll have to swim through it."

Stahl steadied himself against one of the larger rocks and lowered himself to a seated position. Resting his elbows on his knees, he cradled his head in his hands, rubbing his temples in slow circles.

"What's the matter?"

Stahl raised his eyes. "I can't swim."

"You live on a goddamn island for chrissake!"

He gave Ashton a quizzical look. "It's not like I have to swim back and forth to it."

"Look, you'll be able to pull yourself along the bottom, you don't need to swim. You'll just need to hold your breath."

"How long?"

Ashton rubbed his chin. "Shouldn't be more than forty-five seconds...tops."

He glanced across Water Street, hoping for another option, but even more people seemed to have streamed into downtown since the last time he took inventory. He pulled a deep breath. "All right then, let's get this over with."

Stahl and Ashton navigated a careful route over the treacherous stone embankment. He kept a discerning eye on the old man, one hand ready to lunge and catch him should he stumble. But the man's balance and dexterity surprised him, and Stahl found himself lagging behind. As they crept closer to the heavily populated waterfront, the rocky embankment gave way to a fifteen-foot-high seawall, topped with an iron railing, a popular spot for tourists promenading along the waterfront to halt their leisurely jaunts and gaze out over the harbor.

When Stahl finally caught up to Ashton at the base of the seawall, the old man turned to him.

"This is where my friends and I used to play at low-tide, when it was nothing but sand, shells, and horseshoe crabs. The drainpipe's at the other end of the seawall."

Mike gazed at the wall, extending fifty yards or more along the harbor, separating Plymouth Bay from the shops and businesses along the wharf. The briny, barnacled edifice revealed a high water mark several feet above their heads. Today, they could stay hidden by crawling along under the waist-deep water until they reached the drainpipe boring through the sea wall at the other end. Luckily, the sea hadn't completely submerged the pipe yet, but they didn't have a lot of time before it would.

"We're fortunate high tide hasn't peaked or the whole pipe would be flooded." Stahl could sense his anxiety leveling off. "That means we can just crawl through and keep our head above the water then."

Ashton frowned. "The pipe doesn't go straight across the street, Mike. A network of pipes branches off the main artery, some kind of ingenious engineering for back in the day to keep the waterfront from flooding. We still have to swim. Sorry."

Stahl's face crumpled. "You mean—like a maze. Great." Mike's heart pounded in his throat. "You sure we'll fit?"

"We'll be fine. Trust me."

Panic flared in Stahl's voice. "Famous last words."

———

RG

RG, Kacey, and Wilder stood transfixed by the figure glowering at them from the doorway to the basement stairwell. They had violated the one admonition Morrow had begged them to heed, and God knows what type of world they would be returning to.

"I said, what are you doing in my hotel?" The man inspected Wilder from head to foot, eyeing his blow-dried coif and loud regalia as if he had just met someone from outer space "You, sir, I don't imagine hail from these parts."

"I'm guessing you don't either." Wilder flipped the man's shirt collar. "Looks more like seventeenth century than twentieth. How many hundreds of years you been rattling the chains in these halls, mate?"

RG tilted his head to the side. "What are you talking about, Ian?"

"He's a ghost, Reggie. This place is haunted, remember? I'd say he may be one of the town's original settlers." He turned to the ghost and gave a quick salute. "Name's Ian, luv."

"You sound like a damned Brit," the ghost grumbled. "Risked my life to leave that godforsaken land…" He extended his hand. "Name's John Carver."

"Chuffed, mate." Wilder shook the ghost's hand. Rubbing his chin, he turned to RG. "Why does that name sound familiar?"

"Um, because we're standing in his hotel," RG whispered.

"Sir," Kacey said with a hard swallow. "Are you *the* John Carver? Original settler from the Mayflower?"

"First governor of the New Plymouth Colony," he replied.

Wilder leaned forward, peering at the ghost. "Are you aware you haunt your own inn, mate?"

Kacey slugged him on the arm. "You've just met one of America's founding fathers, and that's all you can come up with?" She turned to the ghost. "We're honored to make your acquaintance, sir."

"And who is the beautiful lass?" A wide smile blazed across Carver's face.

RG cleared his throat. "My wife, Kacey."

Carver stepped toward her and took her hand. "You have

the eyes of the sea, or is it the summer sky, perchance? You remind me of my second wife, Katherine." He stooped to kiss the tips of her fingers.

Christ, not another flirting ghost.

"And the fortunate swain, you're…Reggie, I believe I heard? Short for Reginald?" Carver asked.

"Well, actually, it's…never mind, Reggie's fine."

"How have you come to my inn, Reggie? From whence have you traveled?"

"From another time, mate," Wilder chimed in. "Listen, we're looking for a bloke about the size of a small rotary engine—"

"What dross tumbles from your lips, sir?" Carver cut him off. "Do you even speak the King's English?"

"Mr. Carver, if I might." RG stepped in front of Wilder. "There's a powerful spirit living here in Plymouth. He's the size of a child, but he—"

Carver held up his hand. "I know of whom you speak."

"You do?" Kacey asked.

"The native Wampanoag spirits call him Chepi, the Manitou of Death. He's unlike any spirit I've encountered, somehow alive, yet unquestionably dead. He's an abomination to the honorable dead inhabiting this town, my inn."

"Mr. Carver," Kacey said, locking gazes with the ghost, "we've come back to save children this spirit has taken from our world. We need to find where he's holding them. Can you show us?"

"I know not where he dwells, but I can inquire of my spirit brethren. His presence is strong, and—" Carver stopped midsentence as if losing his train of thought. "Say, what hour approaches?"

"Pardon?" RG tilted his head.

"The time, man, what's the time?"

"Can't be later than ten or so." RG pulled back his sleeve to check his watch. "What the…? I have five of three."

"Me, too," Kacey said.

"It's easy to lose half a day during a jump back and forth in time, mate," Wilder pointed out. "I mean, we lost seventy years already, eh, what's another four to five hours?"

Carver bolted toward the door. "Well, I must be on my way then."

"Wait! Where are you going?" Kacey asked.

"I cannot help you just now."

"Why not?" RG launched a flustered shrug.

"I must revisit a tale about a man in the insurance trade."

"Huh?" RG scrunched his face as his gaze darted between Kacey and Wilder. "But we need your—"

"The man falls for a wicked woman," Carver interrupted, his eyes lighting up. "The two plan her husband's death—who, I must say, is quite a rube. They conspire to collect payment on an insurance policy. An altogether dark tale, I must say."

What the fuck is he talking about?

"Sounds like the plot of a movie or something," RG mumbled to Kacey from the corner of his mouth.

"Yeah, the old black and white movie with the lady from *The Big Valley*, Barbara…what's her name?" Kacey frowned and rubbed her chin.

"Stanwyck, my lady!" Carver nodded. "Good call. But I'm not sure of which valley you are referring."

"You're familiar with Barbara Stanwyck?" RG probed.

"They are showing a wonderful film of hers across the street at the Bijou. I haven't seen it in several years. The matinee begins at three o'clock. I must be off. You are free to join me if—"

"Wait a minute!" RG stepped in front of him, blocking his way "We have just a few hours to free your world from a dark and evil spirit and save the lives of countless children, and you're going to watch *Double Indemnity?*"

"I wish you well in your endeavor." Carver stepped through the basement stairwell, throwing the hotel door open.

"You're heading to the movies?" RG's jaw dropped.

Carver turned. "Sir, I've dwelled here nigh four hundred years, and the one thing that has brought my life meaning has been the photoplay, a truly amazing discovery."

"And this guy wrote the Mayflower Compact?" Kacey frowned.

"Mayflower...?" Wilder scratched his head. "What's that, some Yankee thing?"

"It's our country's first governing document," Kacey explained, "written aboard the *Mayflower* before the settlers claimed the land."

"Didn't William Bradford write it?" RG asked.

"No, no, no!" Carver spun from the open door to rejoin the conversation. "That horse's arse didn't write it! Bastard forever gets the credit. I wrote the Compact, but it ended up getting lost somewhere."

"But I've seen the document. It sits under glass in the State Library of Massachusetts," Kacey countered.

"That's the one Bradford rewrote...his signature right at the top, the wanker," Carver seethed.

"Well, it's an amazing document, and I'm sure yours reads even more beautifully than his," Kacey smiled.

"Hmph! The written word's dead. Film's the way to go these days. All stories should have pictures with them. It's truly something to behold. My favorite thus far has been the one in color. It had a fearful lion and a man of tin. Can't recall the name of—"

"Please, sir," Kacey pleaded, "before you go, can't you help us? I'm sure there's another showing."

"We'll talk about Chepi later," Carver said. "Come, join me. You just won't believe how this film ends."

"Already streamed it on Netflix, Governor." RG rolled his eyes.

"So be it." Carver disappeared through the rear exit, his coattails stirring in his haste.

"That's one of your founding fathers?" Wilder deliberated a moment and shrugged. "Not surprising really."

"So, what do we do now?" RG threw his hands up.

"Well, we can wait around here until the film is over, or we can try to contact the others. RG, get on the radio."

RG fired up the two-way but encountered nothing but static. "What the hell. Could they have turned it off?"

"Maybe it doesn't work in this realm," Wilder concluded.

"Here give it to me, RG. Let me try it out of the stairwell. Maybe it only works outside." Kacey pushed the heavy door open and stepped into the late afternoon shadows behind the inn. Moments later she returned, shaking her head. "Nothing but static."

"Maybe theirs broke," Wilder offered. "They may have had a rougher landing than we did."

"Well that's just fucking great!" RG dropped onto the bottom step and ran his hands through his hair. "Now what do we do?"

"We'll just have to find them," Kacey suggested. "We can't do this without them."

"And how are we gonna do that?" RG raised his head. "We have no clue where they are."

Kacey remained silent for a moment. "No, but I have an idea where they might be heading."

"How could you know?"

She chewed on the end of her thumbnail. "Since you're

not gonna like my answer, how 'bout I tell you when we get there."

———

Mike

Hugging the seawall, Stahl followed Ashton underneath the waist-deep water, trying not to struggle and splash during their swim to the cement drainpipe's opening, despite his distress at being submerged. He held it together until they arrived at the pipe, protruding at a ninety-degree angle from the seawall, already partially submerged with the rising tide. The men climbed in, struggling to position their heads above the water, necks bent at near ninety-degree angles. Claustrophobia mobbed Mike's senses, imagining his body twisting through jet-black, underwater corridors with a lungful of air to keep him alive. His breathing grew more rapid, as if his lungs understood these might be the last breaths he would ever take.

"The drop-off is coming soon." Ashton's voice echoed off the drainpipe's ceiling.

"Drop off?"

"There's a pipe…it goes straight down about five feet. If we go head first, we'll be aiming in the right direction when it straightens out. It'll be about twenty feet straight ahead, then there's a branch point to the right. You'll feel the exit hole if you keep your hands on the wall. If you miss it…well, don't miss it."

"Good safety tip, thanks for that! And then what…"

"Once you're in the branching pipe, go about ten feet… really not far…then the pipe bends around to the left…"

Mike made a pointing motion leftward with his hand.

"…that's when you'll be directly under the street. You follow it to the other side…"

Mike aimed his hand forward, still following the directions tangibly to commit it to memory.

"...after you get to the end of that pipe, you'll see a metal ladder..."

"Ladder," Mike muttered.

"Climb up and you're home free." Ashton turned to start the journey.

Home free? Isolated from the group, window of time closing, possibly stuck in 1946 forever. Guy's way too optimistic. "Oh hell...wouldn't it just be easier if I follow you?"

"Stay close. You have to keep your head about you. It's gonna be pitch black down there."

His breath came in waves, spots forming in front of his eyes. "I'm not sure I can do this, Elias."

"Yes, you can. Do it for your son. He's waiting for you."

Stahl shut his eyes as his heart's tempo picked up, pounding in his ears. He could all but hear it echoing off the drainpipe walls. He pictured Zach, imprisoned in a jumper's hell. The monster had come out of his closet and took him away, and he promised he would come for him. And Claire wouldn't ever accept his story unless he came home with Zach. He couldn't go back without him.

I have no choice. I gotta do this.

Ashton moved forward into the dim tunnel. "Here it is, the drop-off. I can touch it with my foot. Let's hold our breath a couple of times to get ready."

Down, straight, right...left...then what?

He inhaled the drainpipe's fetid air, but his constricted throat could barely pull anything into his lungs. His hammering heart forced the remaining air out with each beat. He sucked in a rescue gulp of breath after only ten seconds.

"Relax, Mike. Take another deep breath. Hold it in."

This time, Stahl relaxed his windpipe enough to drag more

air into his lungs. His heart had fallen to a steady thump, still elevated, but more controlled. After half a minute, the spiraling pressure forced an exhale, a burst of glorious oxygen filling his lungs.

The pipe's rising water now licked his chin.

"One more time, Mike. Then we'll be ready."

Stahl gazed at the old man in front of him, head cocked to keep it above water, about to swim through a labyrinth of underwater drainage tubes. A wave of embarrassment rolled over him as he considered the man had almost fifty years on him and remained calm as a Zen master. He suspected if he checked the old man's pulse, it wouldn't have budged but more than a few beats over resting rate. Stahl's ribcage expanded with gradual ease as he filled his lungs. Counting in his head, he didn't release the air until he had reached forty-five seconds, and he still had a puff or two held in reserve.

"You're ready, Mike. Let's do this. Stay close."

The rising tide forced Stahl to lean his head back further, his lips nearly kissing the pipe's mildewed ceiling. Soon they would be unable to suck in any more air before the water swamped them.

He repeated the route in his head, down, straight, right, left, straight across. *I got this!* "Okay, Elias. Lead the way."

Before he could say another word, Ashton took a deep breath and dove straight down through the drainpipe and into the abyss.

Chapter Sixteen

'Her heart was folded deeply in ours.'

Darling ALMA MAY, daughter of J.S. & M.B. Butler, died
Dec. 17, 1888 (Aged 9 y'rs, 2 mo's.)
-Epitaphs from Burial Hill

July 4, 1946

Mike

Stahl drew an extended breath before diving through the
narrow pipe into the inky blackness, the dark unlike anything
he had experienced before. It clung to him like a wetsuit, a
complete absence of light, rendering him unable to gauge his
body's orientation. He had read once how pilots flying through
clouds or the black of night without instrumentation experienced such disorientation they didn't know they had been
flying upside-down or sideways. The subterranean cave had

provided the same effect; he would have to locate the exit pipe to his right, but now he couldn't be sure his body's inner senses had him properly oriented to find it with his groping hands.

How far did Elias say it would be?

Stahl continued to pull himself along the pipe, ten, twenty, thirty feet? He had no idea how far he had traveled without visual cues.

No opening to the right.

Had he traveled too far, or not far enough? Maybe panic fooled him, the rapid hammering in his chest tricking him. His lungs ached. How could they beg for oxygen this soon?

He kept moving, extending his hands in front of him until the pipe narrowed against his torso, but he couldn't recall whether Elias had said anything about the tube tapering.

Then, the cylinder turned upward ninety degrees.

This can't be right.

He crunched his forehead against a cement barrier, reflexively taking a breath, anticipating the cold sea flooding his lungs. But instead, a magical puff of stale oxygen filled his pleading lungs, an air pocket materializing at the end of the capped tube. Panic flooded his brain, a dead end underneath the earth.

Okay, Mike…think.

"Elias? Can you hear me? Where are you?"

Nothing but his own words rushed back at him. How could Elias abandon him like this? Whatever happened to team work? The buddy system?

He stared into the murkiness, but he saw nothing, heard nothing but his own fibrillating heart resounding against the swoosh of water and metal tubing. He tried reciting Elias's instructions, an easy task for a police detective, or at least it should be, but the constricting enclosure pounded his nerves with an unforgiving force, robbing him of his clarity.

He would have to reverse direction, back up until he found the opening to the right. Stahl took a deep breath and pushed himself back along the pipe feet first, groping with his right hand for the branch point. If he didn't find it, there would be no way out.

The narrow pipe widened as he pushed himself backward. Farther and farther he backtracked into the pipe until he felt the yawning hole of the drainpipe's branch point to his right. Stahl pulled himself along until he came to a short jog to the left. The oxygen from his stale puff of subterranean air had dwindled, an ache thumping in his chest. It would be a straight shot along this pipe until he would hit the ladder. He concentrated on his possible location, his placement below the stores and restaurants across Water Street, its distance from the harbor.

Just keep swimming.

As he crawled frantically along the cement pipe, out of breath, out of strength, a faint hint of light found his eyes. He blinked them open to a scintillating halo piercing the brackish water fifty feet in front of him, an inkling of daylight. He could almost make out the ladder's metal rungs embedded in the concrete. Starved for air and unsure whether he had the energy to pull himself along another foot, Claire's image appeared before him. She reclined on the porch swing at the Seaview house, wearing the seahorse and shell spangled summer dress he loved so much. She balanced a sweet tea in her hand, Mike massaging the foot she had swung into his lap while Zach romped in the front yard.

He had stopped moving in the pipe, content to be beside her again, the warm, salty breeze from Aunt Lydia's cove misting their faces. He perceived her beside him, warming him through the icy-black water, as if she were alive in the pipe helping him breathe.

He glanced over at her, panic erupting in her eyes. She burst across the swing and grabbed the sides of his face with both hands, the tendons and chords in her neck straining as she screamed at him, *"Swim!"*

The image shattered in an instant and drew him back into the bleakness of an underground world filled with darkness. Her voice spurred his reflexes, forced a massive intake of seawater into his lungs, leading to a frenzied thrashing. He pulled himself along the pipe, his lungs filling with water. He could detect faint light shimmering through the murky haze, getting strong, glinting off the ladder's metal rungs. The pipe finally ended, but he was out of air and drowning. He inhaled another burst of water into his lungs as his hands grasped the first metal rung.

He had gotten close but recognized he couldn't make it any farther. His journey would end here, under the road in Plymouth, fifty miles—and seventy years—from home.

As his muscles relaxed and he succumbed to an indescribable peace, a pair of hands grabbed his collar and hoisted him upwards. Stahl's oxygen-starved brain envisioned an ascension into heaven, but when he hit the water's surface it graduated into hell. The inhalation of fresh air triggered a reflexive, violent expulsion of water from his burning lungs. Ashton labored to pull him up the ladder and out through the sewer grate, laying him on ground and hammering his fists against his chest until the salt fluid evacuated his lungs. Staggering coughs erupted from his core, straining his ribs.

He lay along the woods' perimeter, blinking open his glassy eyes to glimpse his surroundings. Between buildings, he could make out the harbor's rich blue water, so close he could have hurled a stone halfway across. How had it seemed so far during his blind swim? He rolled on his side, thankful to be alive.

"Thanks, Elias."

"Let's get deeper into the woods before someone…" Ashton's voice trailed off, his eyes widening. He signaled to Stahl, who crawled toward him, both men ducking out of sight behind a downed tree trunk at the wood's edge.

A woman draped in a food-stained apron exited the building's rear door, her hair pulled back in a bun, a few wispy stragglers escaping the pack. She struggled with a bin of discarded food scraps as she shuffled toward them, aiming for the line of garbage cans along the parking area. Shaking the refuse into the metal drums, she hummed to herself, pausing to swipe a wrist across her forehead.

Stahl glanced at Ashton. The blood had drained from the old man's face and he struggled to catch his breath.

As the woman disappeared into the building, Stahl tugged the old man's shoulder. "What's the matter? You look like you've seen a ghost."

Stahl followed Ashton's eyes as they tracked to the dented cans resting in front of them. He squinted to read the words painted on the side.

Property of Ashton Delicatessen.

———

Ashton skirted from behind the tree trunk, stepping tentatively from the woods as his mother slipped inside the building through the deli's rear door. He strode across the dirt parking lot toward the back of the building as if guided by an unknown force, his limbs pumping like a speed walker on the last leg of a race.

"Elias!" Stahl's voice wavered between a shout and a mumble, attempting to draw Ashton's attention but no one else's.

The old man kept walking.

Sonofabitch! Stahl rose on wobbly ground, not having fully recovered his sea legs. He hadn't taken his first step before sinking to his knees, his head still spinning and limbs aflutter. Spots hurtled across his vision as he buried his head between his knees. Nausea bloomed, and a burst of salt water emerged from his throat.

The old man had reached the deli's rear entrance, his neck craning to peer through the open backdoor.

Stahl struggled to find his feet, hoisting himself up against the felled tree and orienting himself to a sudden, awkward gravitational pull. Recovering his balance, he stumbled across the parking area, eyes scanning the lot with caution. If two men traipsing across a parking lot, soaked from head to toe in twenty-first century garb, didn't draw attention in this town, nothing would.

Catching up with Ashton at the backdoor, Stahl grabbed his shoulder and spun him around. "Elias!"

The old man's eyes hung vacant in their sockets, Stahl's chest serving as the focal point for his unfocused stare. But as he raised his head, the color resumed in his eyes and he shook his head, as if trying to empty his head of the vision he had just witnessed.

"I'm sorry, Mike. That's my…"

"I know."

"She gets cancer in a few months." He spoke with the impatience of a ten-year-old boy. "She's dead a year from now."

"Elias, she's been dead for seventy years."

The old man's eyes sharpened. "Not today she isn't! She's here, right now. I understand we have a mission, but I…I need a moment with her."

"You can't have it, Elias. You'll interfere with—"

"I need to see her one more time," he interrupted, looking squarely at Stahl. "She's alive, Mike…she's…."

Stahl pictured his own mother, taken from him by a drunk driver years earlier. How many things about her he missed, her comforting presence never more than an arm's length away in a blank stare over coffee or momentary daydream at a red light. If he had the chance to glimpse her one more time like Ashton did, her delicate soul moving in a living, breathing body, what would *he* do?

"You walk into that restaurant, and she'll spot you. All this will be for nothing."

Ashton checked his watch. "Mike, listen. Right now, she's sitting out front with a sweet tea. I can stay hidden, spy on her from the back room. I just need a minute."

"How do you know that?"

"Because it's July Fourth, 1946, and I'm out there with her! I made her the sweet tea."

Stahl fixed Ashton with his best cop's gaze, but he didn't expect to dissuade him. The man had saved his life, and he would let him have a moment with his mother. "I'm going in with you."

The two men slipped quietly through the backdoor into the cool of the deli's storeroom, maneuvering around stacked boxes and crates of fresh produce. Canned vegetables and dried goods rose beside them, shelved floor to ceiling in the cramped space. A chill crept through Stahl's body, whether the blistering July sunshine's sudden absence or fear of discovery, he couldn't tell. Sweet scents from homemade cakes and pastries drifted through the drawn curtain separating the restaurant from the storeroom. The men stepped past the walk-in cooler, halting within the narrow corridor leading to the store's front room.

Ashton pulled back the curtain, a soft smile lighting his

face as he peered at familiar walls. Sausages and kielbasas hung above the glassed-in cases housing assorted deli meats and cheeses, a massive Toledo grocery scales perched on top. Stahl imagined how the images storming Ashton's senses must pop compared to the past seventy years' hazy recollections.

Elias's breath caught as he fixed on his mother through the front window's stenciled glass. Resting at a sidewalk table, she sipped her cool drink and brushed hair from her eyes. A young boy sat beside her, the two chuckling over something shared, long forgotten.

Ashton peeked at the living memory playing out before him like a heartsick voyeur. Fate had delivered him the opportunity to rise above the strange disconnect between the person living life and the one observing it from within, springing him from his own flesh prison to witness it firsthand.

He moved with measured steps, advancing through the curtain separating store from storeroom, but Mike placed a gentle hand on his shoulder.

Ashton nodded, forcing an exhale from his lungs.

"It's time to find the others." As Stahl leaned forward to close the curtain, a nine-year-old Elias burst through the deli's front door.

"I'll get 'em, Mom," he shouted. "They're in the back."

"Christ!" Ashton mumbled, eyes darting about the storeroom. "Into the cooler!"

The men scampered into the walk-in as young Elias breezed through the curtain and into the storeroom, the boy's footfalls reverberating through the insulated wall.

"Don't let it close all the way," Ashton whispered, pivoting to reach the door.

"What?"

"Keep it cracked or we're trapped. There's no handle on the inside."

Stahl's hand shot forward, halting the weighty door's progression moments before the latch clicked into place. He breathed a sigh of relief, resting a steady hand on the door.

"Close call," Stahl exhaled, frosty breath visible in the icy air.

Ashton clasped his arms around himself, his damp clothes magnifying the abrupt temperature change. "We'll be safe for the moment, I wasn't allowed in here back then. Let's wait a minute or two for me to leave, then we can slip out the back."

Stahl listened for movement through the door, the cooler's whine obscuring the sounds from the storeroom. "You're doing something out there," Mike breathed, "I can hear you moving things around."

As Stahl leaned closer, the door slammed against his ear, driving his head in the opposite direction. "Sonofabitch," he blurted under his breath, grasping his bruised ear. "What the fuck happened?"

"I must have bumped the door on my way back to the store up front."

Ashton pushed gently against the door, then with all his weight.

It wouldn't budge.

Chapter Seventeen

'The infant smiles in lisping speach,
And in the grave in silence sleaps.'

In memory of ESTHER COOPER, died Sep^t 9th, 1803 (Aged
2 years & 2 months)
-Epitaphs from Burial Hill

July 4, 1946

RG

RG threw open the inn's backdoor and led Kacey and Wilder through the woods behind the First Parish Church and up Burial Hill, one of the oldest cemeteries in the country and home to the bones of many *Mayflower* travelers and their descendants. No human soul occupied the deserted graveyard as the town gathered along the distant waterfront for the Independence Day celebration. A humid breeze whistled through the bowing grass.

When they had reached the top of the hill, Kacey led them to a tree, lines of ancient headstones surrounding it. Kneeling in the warm grass, she brushed the grime from one of the slabs.

"Look at these." She pointed to a pair of matching grave markers standing side by side, the words 'mother' and 'father' chiseled across the whitewashed stones.

"'Parted below,' 'United above,'" Kacey read aloud. "That's so beautiful. I wonder who they were."

RG glanced across the gravestones on either side of the dirt path. "Those two are like the only ones without names on them."

"And over here." She jumped to her feet and padded to the next row of markers, placing her hand against her cheek. "This one's so sad. 'Stop traveler and shed a tear, Upon the fate of children dear. In memory of Four Children of Mr. Zacheus Kempton and Sarah his wife.' God, these are incredible. I've been up here before, but I don't remember these."

"Why'd you bring us up here?" RG asked. "I assume we're not here to take etchings on our little Plymouth vacation."

Kacey rose to her feet. "Mike will find a way here. I'm sure of it. We need to wait for him."

"Why here?"

She reached for RG's hand. "This spot..." Kacey announced, pointing to the tree shading them, "represents a piece of our history."

Wilder sidled up beside RG. "Ooh, this sounds like it's gonna be good, luv."

RG shot him a cutting stare.

"Back in high school, we had a field trip to Plymouth. Mike and I weren't dating yet, just flirting a lot. We sneaked away from the group and climbed up to Burial Hill. We had our first kiss on this spot."

"Oh, for chrissake!" RG threw his hands up. "Is this thing ever gonna end with you two?"

"RG, please! Don't even..." Kacey crossed her arms.

"So, was Mike planning a little reunion up here, maybe relive the past?"

Wilder grinned at Kacey. "Don't want to come off all gobby here, but...you and Mike?"

"A long time ago." She turned and stepped away.

He threw an elbow into RG's ribs. "This assignment keeps getting better and better."

"Butt out, Ian!" RG barked.

"Listen to me, RG. Mike's in love with Claire. Can't you recognize that? He's here fighting for his family, and you're making it all about you!"

RG rested his hands on his hips, staring at the ground.

Kacey approached him, lifting his chin with her finger. "In the Pancake Man this morning when you mentioned Plymouth, I glanced over at Mike and smiled. We shared a moment, two friends laughing about the past. Nothing more. Our innocent exchange may end up salvaging this mission. It's the only place I can think of any one of us has in common. I'm not standing here because I want a trip down memory lane."

"She's making sense, Reggie," Wilder offered. "In fact, I'd say you're the one unable to stop reliving the past."

Thanks, Dr. Phil. "So, how long do we wait here? The longer we're out in the open, the greater the likelihood someone sees us."

"We wait here until they find us," Kacey replied. "What other choice do we have?"

Wilder threw an arm around RG's shoulder. "We can't

spend the weekend inside, mate. We'll never find the children that way, either."

"Well, how are we gonna find them anyway?" RG eyed his watch. "Our only hope won't be done at the movies for at least another hour!" *This is impossible. This whole thing is…* RG paced the dirt path along the line of headstones, swiping his good hand through his hair. *I can't do this. I don't have my father's power, I don't…*

Thoughts swirled through RG's mind as he pressed his palms against his temples. He forced himself to concentrate on his father's fading gift. He would need to maximize the powers he had nurtured and studied if they had any chance of success. A numbing heat filled his head as his visual field narrowed, black dots marching toward his pupils like a river of ants. He swooned, steadying himself against a crumbling headstone before falling to his knees. Leaning forward, he rested his forehead on the grass as if a magnetic force had drawn him to this exact spot for a reason.

Kacey dropped beside him, arm wrapped around his shoulders as she spoke into his ear. "What's the matter, hon?"

"The ring. I can sense it."

––––––––

Mike

The frigid air stiffened the men's damp clothing against their bodies, their breath hanging in icy puffs before their faces.

"We've gotta get someone's attention, Elias. If not, we'll freeze." Stahl's teeth chattered as he paced back and forth in the confined space, his shivering muscles failing to generate enough heat to counter his plummeting body temperature.

Wrapping his arms around his core did nothing to thwart the biting chill.

"What do you suggest? The store's empty. We've all gone to the Kingston depot to pick up Malachi. We can bang all we want, but no one's gonna hear us."

"When does the store re-open? Tomorrow?"

Ashton's shoulders sagged. "Tomorrow's Sunday. We're closed."

Stahl dropped to the icy floor and rested his back against the hand-built wooden shelving, the frozen goods' icy burn not registering against his numb skin. Reality had set in. They wouldn't survive the night, let alone make it until Monday morning. He wasn't sure there would be a Monday morning in this fucked up time loop.

Either way, we're screwed.

"So, I guess that's it then."

Ashton settled on the floor beside him. "I'm sorry, Mike. The others will get Zach home. I'm sure of it."

"Thousands of people out there on the waterfront, probably less than fifty feet from us." Stahl threw his hands up. "If our predicament wasn't so tragic, I might actually laugh."

First drowning, now freezing to death. This would be a banner last day for Mike Stahl. How many people stare death in the face twice in one day? Had to be a record. Or maybe not. He had known too many cops.

The drowning hadn't been as bad as he imagined. Peace and love had surrounded him. Claire's gentle touch, pushing him to survive, had comforted him. But what would she do if no escape existed this time? Would she shrug her shoulders and settle in beside him, brush the icy hair from his eyes—like she did a thousand times a day—one last time? Or would she cry from the sheer absurdity? Who loses a husband in a freezer on July Fourth in a place that didn't even exist? Stahl closed his eyes and waited for her to come. At least she would be with him. He knew it for sure.

Maybe he would comfort her this time.

Stahl allowed himself one more shot at optimism. "How about deliveries…anything scheduled for—"

"It's July Fourth, Mike. No one delivers on…" Ashton gazed upward as he trailed off, lost in thought.

"What?"

"Well, Mr. Brigham, maybe," the old man mumbled.

A cautious elation welled within Stahl. "Who is Mr. Brigham?"

"Runs the ice cream shop next door. He drops off some goodies we feast on after the fireworks tonight, but he may have already been here. Could have been yesterday. I don't know."

Ashton's uncertainty deflated Stahl as reality reasserted itself, the temperature appearing to drop even further. The cold fatigued them. Frost formed along their noses, the tops of the ears, crusted around their fingers while their damp clothes stiffly encased their bodies like Plaster of Paris. Paris… wouldn't that be nice about now? Or better yet…ice cream, despite the cold. Stahl strained to exert even the weakest effort now, struggling even to keep his eyelids open. But his faltering body didn't stop him from picturing himself digging into a carton of French vanilla…*for chrissake, Mike, you're dying. How about going out in style*…okay, fudge swirl. He licked his lips as he succumbed to the cold…quit thinking, stopped fighting…

At some point, Stahl awoke to a shuffling sound outside the cooler. He shook the fog from his head, immediately reacquainted with the bone-numbing cold. What about Paris? Must not have been important.

He tilted his head to shift the acoustics, once again hearing a faint scraping outside the door. His muscles had grown sluggish, and his attempt to spring to his feet resembled a slow-motion replay.

"There's someone out there, Elias." He stumbled toward the door. His shoulder slammed against the wall as he teetered, catching him before he fell.

Ashton graduated to his feet, tipsy at best. "What are you doing?"

The shuffling sound grew louder, feet pounding the floor in the storeroom. "I'm gonna bang on the door…get us the hell out of here!"

Stahl raised his arm and swung it forward, but Ashton grabbed him. "You can't, Mike. This is history we're talking about. It can't be disrupted."

"You don't suppose someone finding our frozen bodies in here come Monday morning will disrupt history?"

"No one will find our bodies, Mike. There's no Monday morning here."

"This is fucking insane. What? Do you want to die?"

"I've stayed alive my whole life to take this trip. I'm the last guy who wants to die. Maybe in my failure, I can do something positive and not disrupt history's intended course."

"Well, I wasn't meant to die in any freezer. I gotta save Zach!"

Stahl glared at Ashton, expecting a fight. But a ray of hope flashed across the old man's face, his eyes glowing like candles.

"It's got to be him," Ashton muttered, pulling Stahl behind the shelving next to the freezer door.

"What are you doing?"

"If it's Mr. Brigham out there, he'll be opening up the freezer any second."

Stahl twitched with renewed energy, wiggling and dancing about to resuscitate his frostbitten limbs.

Ashton held up his finger over his mouth. "If he sees us or hears us, it's over."

As the freezer door clicked open, the men pressed themselves against the wall behind the heavy wooden shelf adjacent to the door, hiding behind stacks of frozen foods packed from floor to ceiling. Mr. Brigham propped the heavy freezer door open with a produce crate and entered with a tub of sherbet in his arms, resting it on the only empty shelf. Stahl and Ashton pushed themselves as far back against the wall as they could, the man's icy puffs of breath floating toward them. Brigham slapped his hands together and turned toward the door, a scraping sound ripping the air as he pulled the crate away from the door.

Stahl's muscles tensed. He would have to time this perfectly.

Dashing from behind the shelf as the solid door swung closed, Stahl skidded on the icy flooring and dropped to a knee. The door accelerated toward the latch. He forced his numbed limbs to propel him toward the door before it slammed shut again and pronounced certain death. With lagging muscles, he lunged for it like a baseball player reaching to tag a runner. He rammed his right hand into the jamb moments before the door settled onto the latch. His crushed mitt sent shooting, painful bolts up his arm, but before he could cry out, Ashton wrapped his hand around Stahl's mouth, muffling the sound.

Ashton waited a moment, listening for footsteps outside the cooler before pushing open the heavy door and extricating Stahl's mangled hand from the jamb. The two men stumbled into the storeroom, the humid warmth bathing them like a tropical shower.

Stahl winced as he cupped his damaged hand with his

good one, scanning the jumbled metacarpal bones protruding at odd angles. "Damn things broken for sure."

"Better than the alternative."

"How the hell did he get in here? Does he have a key?"

"A key?" Ashton chuckled. "This is 1946. No one locks doors around here."

Stahl smirked. "Come on. It's time to find the others."

"I'm not sure we ever factored eating into this crazy plan. How about we grab a quick bite, bring back something for the team?"

"Assuming we find them by some miracle."

Ashton shook his head. "If anyone should believe in miracles today, it's you."

They crept to the front of the store. Hunching down to avoid detection from the throngs of people traipsing along the sidewalk, the men slipped behind the counter and grabbed fistfuls of shaved meats and cold cuts from the display trays, wrapping them in parchment and stuffing them deep into their refrigerated pockets, stuffing their faces with a few chewy bites to take care of the overflow.

"Okay," Ashton wiped his hands," that should do it. Now what's the plan to find the others?"

"Follow me." Stahl nodded toward the back door. "One miracle down. Another one to go."

RG

"The ring," RG repeated, burying his head in his hands. "I sense its power."

Wilder knelt beside him. "You're nearer to the ring than you've been in a long time, Reggie. It's calling out to you, and you're sensing its pull. It knows you're close."

RG raised his head. "Mike and Elias…they're on their way. I can see their thoughts…God, I can see everything. But cold cuts?" His obsession with food had to end.

Wilder helped him to his feet, throwing his shoulder under RG's arm to support his dead weight.

RG's eyes fluttered as his mind evoked activity taking place on the harbor and in Ashton's deli. As he concentrated, a fluid pitch of blackness enveloped him and ignited a sense of claustrophobia he had never experienced before. He inhaled deeply but couldn't breathe. Claire Simpson's voice sounded close, a soft rhythm with overwhelming love caressing Mike's feverish skin. Then a cold, bone-chilling freeze dispelled the warmth. A second vision rocked him. Bread and meat aromas wafted through his senses as he gazed at a mother and a little boy at a sidewalk table. His heart swelled with emotion, an overpowering childlike need directing him toward the woman. The ring had reignited the familiar sensations, the onslaught of unrestrained thoughts and visions leaking from unguarded minds, with RG unable to corral them. He stumbled, but Wilder caught him.

"Grab his other arm, Kacey. Let's get him back to the inn."

"No," RG mumbled. "They're coming…any minute now."

He turned to Kacey. Her boundless love glowed around her like a corona, billowing from her soul untethered, not confined to thoughts or pictures, but limitless. Shapeless and indefinable. With a front-row seat to her mind's private viewing room, RG attempted to deflect the onslaught, uncomfortable peeking into her head and violating her secrets. But he couldn't fight the ring's potent will, and he succumbed to it like a powerful opiate. Butting against her thoughts, her earlier words 'Parted below' and 'United above' sang like a mantra in his head, providing a scaffolding to a new stream of flowing imaginings leeching from her subconscious.

Kacey and Wilder acted like crutches for the legless RG, supporting his body on either side. He snapped his head back and forth, willing the images from his mind, his eyes pressed shut to lock them out. *'Parted below, United above.'* The color returned to his face as the onslaught diminished, the happening over. He opened his eyes to a world shifting back into view, Stahl and Ashton trudging up the path toward them.

"Thank God." Mike greeted them with a wave as his head crested above the path leading up the hill. "I don't have a clue where we would have looked next." He glanced at the distraught form hanging between Kacey and Wilder. "Everything okay?"

"Reggie's having a bit of a dizzy spell, that's all."

"He'll be okay, Mike. What happened to you guys in the portal?" Kacey asked.

"We ended up in the harbor," Stahl muttered with a distinct scowl. "It took us a while to make sure we could get away unseen. Lucky guess, this spot, eh?" He grinned at Kacey, gesturing to the tree. "I figured since we laughed about it earlier…"

"You're completely in love with Claire," RG mumbled, sounding a bit drunk and appearing hungover from his recent episode.

"Huh?" Stahl shrugged. "Of course, I am. Why would you ask that?"

Kacey waved her hand. "Never mind him." She squinted to inspect his shattered hand and open gash across his forehead. "What happened to you, Mike?"

"It's been a rough day."

"Let's go," Wilder suggested. "Maybe the old ghost is back from his movie."

"What ghost?" Ashton chimed in.

"Just follow us." Kacey gave a lurch as she repositioned herself under RG's arm. "There's someone who may be able to help us find Malachi. If we find Malachi, we'll find the children."

"He's at a movie?" Stahl shrugged.

"Apparently there isn't much for ghosts to do in this town." With the help of his supports, RG navigated along the scuffed, dirt pathway winding down Burial Hill.

The team slipped back into the John Carver Inn through the rear door. Before the door rested against its hinges, the ghost appeared before them in the stairwell.

"Jesus, Governor," RG declared, slapping his hand over his heart. "You scared the shit out of us."

"Pretty foolish for you to be gallivanting around town, don't you think?" He folded his arms across his chest.

"Well, the only one who could help us decided it was Barbara Stanwyck day." RG raised an eyebrow.

"Listen, mate," Wilder said, leaning toward Carver, "we need to give this man his rest. Do you have a vacant room where we could hole up for a while?"

Carver rubbed his chin. "The boiler room in the basement. That's the only place you'll be safe. No one will have need of its service this weekend. Follow me." Carver led them through the twisting basement corridors and down a short flight of stairs deep into the building's bowels. Looking up at the shrubbery through a small corridor window revealed their positioning below ground level.

"Who is this guy?" Stahl whispered, jabbing a thumb toward the ghost.

"John Carver. First governor of the Plymouth Colony," Kacey replied with a grin.

"No shit?"

"And primary author of the Mayflower Compact," Ashton proclaimed.

Stahl cocked his head. "Didn't William Bradford—?"

"For the last time," Carver blasted, wheeling around to face Stahl. "It wasn't the horse's arse Bradford, you knave!"

"What did I say?" Stahl raised his hands, searching Kacey and RG for answers.

Carver led the group into a stuffy room, the humidity leeching through the damp, moldy walls. Broken and outmoded furniture littered the floor, and perilously stacked boxes formed natural mazes throughout the space. Above, water dripped from soft, brown splotches, and spiderwebs cascaded from cracked wooden beams crisscrossing the wide ceiling, undulating in the updrafts of the room's stale breath.

The group collapsed onto the furniture, unleashing dusty clouds as they stretched limbs and rubbed tired eyes.

Ashton withdrew handfuls of cold cuts folded in parchment from his pockets, placing them onto the wobbly table resting before the tattered sofa. "We figured you guys might be hungry."

"So that explains it..." RG grabbed a fistful of turkey, throwing down a massive meat swallow.

"Explains what?"

"Never mind."

"Well, that takes care of half the food for the next two days," Kacey sighed.

"Don't worry, Kacey." Stahl removed the remaining meats from his pocket with his good hand, adding them to the impromptu buffet. "We have plenty."

As the team divided up the comestibles, RG addressed the ghost. "So, Governor. Can you help us find Mal...what did you call him, Chepi?"

"As much as I'd like to, Master Reggie, I and my spirit cousins have no answers for you."

"You talked to them already?"

"We all ended up in the cinema balcony. They, too, enjoy a good film noir."

My God, what's the spirit world coming to?

"The Wampanoag spirits will not reveal Chepi's whereabouts to any natural soul."

"Why not?" Kacey inquired.

"They fear him too much. They believe Chepi will bring nothing but suffering. In their lore, the Manitou of Death plays terrible tricks on the living. They say he pulls off eyelids to steal the body's sleep or twists the feet to make one lame. If they reveal his whereabouts, they believe he'll punish them even worse. The spirits themselves will not cross him."

"But Malachi's not Chepi. He's a jumper," Kacey explained. "He doesn't play those tricks. He steals children…"

"Do not dismiss the spirits' beliefs. If they believe your Malachi is their Chepi, it doesn't matter what he does or doesn't do. It only matters what they believe. They will not betray him."

"And you don't know where he is either?" RG inquired.

"Even if I did, I would not betray my Wampanoag spirit cousins and anger their Chepi. I am sorry. They are my people now."

Kacey dropped onto the musty couch beside RG. She leaned her head against him.

"We got nothing. We're back at square one." RG rolled and stuffed another meat slab into his mouth.

"Did we ever get to square two?" Kacey inquired.

RG raised an eyebrow.

"Maybe we just concentrate on trying to kill Malachi. We

can't find the children without help, and we're running out of time."

"And what happens to the children if Malachi dies, and we can't find them?" RG whispered, guiding Kacey from the couch and navigating the box maze to a quiet corner of the room. "They're stuck in their cages with no food or water. Whether we like it or not, they'll die without him."

Kacey rubbed her forehead. "I didn't think of that."

"It's all about the children now. We owe it to Molly Buck-holtz…and we owe it to Mike."

"Mike?"

"As much as I've questioned Mike over the years, his intentions, his motives, even hated him at times, I owe him. The man singlehandedly proved my innocence in the 'Fugitive Professor' case. Every time we walk hand in hand on the beach, or I read to Junior at night until he falls asleep, I have Mike to thank. I owe him for pulling you out of a burning house before it blew up. Claire's gone, and he's got nothing if he doesn't return with Zach. I'm gonna find those children, and I'm gonna find Zach. I need to do something for him now."

"We can only do what we can."

"Mike's not gonna return to Chatham without his son, and neither am I."

RG and Kacey sidestepped the clutter as they joined the group, an animated Founding Father acting out Fred MacMurray's demise to a rapt audience.

Kacey dropped onto the couch, but RG continued out the boiler room door and into the hallway.

Kacey shook her head, catching up with him at the end of the dim corridor. "Where are you going?"

"I'm going back up the hill. Something happened to me up there, and I need to find out what."

Chapter Eighteen

'Parted below, United above.'

-Epitaphs from Burial Hill

July 4, 1946

RG

As the sunset edged daylight from the sky, RG meandered among the more than two-thousand grave markers lining Burial Hill's five acres, one-hundred sixty-five feet above sea level. He had wandered the Hill for nearly an hour, but no longer sensed the ring as he had earlier. It had shown him something today, signaled to him. He recognized now the ring contained more than his father's power, it held a universal dominion, a gift from the heavens greater than any individual possessing it. It never belonged to Morrow, nor would it ever belong to RG or Skoczek.

But it had preferences.

Today the ring had beckoned him, deemed him its authority's true caretaker, and it wanted its rightful possessor to reclaim it. RG had glimpsed a third goal of this mission, satisfying the arbiters of this grand design's insistence he reclaim the ring's power as its chosen host.

RG stepped through the grave markers and headstones, pausing to peruse the faded, chipped epitaphs grooved into the marble facades, their muddied patina reflecting the fickle elements' unrelenting, four-hundred-year assault. Approaching the tree where Kacey and Mike had shared their first kiss, RG knelt beside the mother-and-father matching gravestones she had discovered earlier, triggering the words from her mind again and again, 'Parted below,' 'United above,' hammering his brain like a pop ditty he couldn't shake.

He shuffled on his knees to the next marker in line, a stone dedicated to the Thacher children, aged one and three years: 'Early Bright Sweet As Morning Dew They Sparkled, Were Exhaled and went to Heaven.' RG's breath hitched at the thought of losing one child, let alone two. No pain or loss could be greater. He imagined a numbing winter chill in seventeenth century Plymouth, a child's cough worsening, the light leaving its eyes, a pint-sized coffin resting beside a frozen hole in the ground. He leaned forward, squinting at the name James and Susanna Thacher through the gravestone's weathered layer. They had lost their children, stood on this exact spot as they lowered their dreams into the ground with the remains of their ripped souls. He clutched his chest, his heart pierced with a universal ache. The next marker in line also lamented the loss of an infant child: 'Receiv'd but yesterday the gift of breath, Now call'd to slumber in the arms of death.'

God, another one.

Raising his head, RG counted the rows and columns of

headstones surrounding Kacey's kissing tree, hundreds scattered about the spot. On a whim, RG stood and slogged to the farthest stone, kneeling in the grass and wiping grime off its epitaph. Another lost child, another message: 'An empty tale a mooring flower, cut down and wither'd in an hour.' The next one in line: 'And must thy children die so soon.'

What the fuck?

Springing to his feet, RG raced from headstone to headstone, marker to marker, each one bearing a grieving message to another lost child. He had stood too quickly, salt and pepper dots creeping into his periphery, picking up speed. He clamped his eyes shut and dropped to a knee on the soil, a single phrase reaching a crescendo in a symphony of cluttered thoughts and images crowding his mind.

Parted below, United above.

His eyes snapped open as his head's swirling maelstrom receded to silence. The evening breeze whooshed through the kissing tree's leaves, its sturdy branches providing a protective umbrella over the hundreds of markers beneath them, sheltering lost children. Today, the same tree Mike and Kacey had found twenty years ago—and had shared their first kiss beneath—had united the team traveling back in time to rescue lost children.

His jaw dropped. *United above...*

He glanced at the tree's leafy canopy. He tracked one craggy branch, thicker and more gnarled than the others but pointing toward a crumbling mausoleum. A metal railing surrounded the building and cobblestones led from the dirt walkway to a black, heavy wooden door, cracked with age and dislodged from its hinges. The wayward tree branch scraped against the structure's roof, beckoning, emitting a repetitive shriek with each gusty breeze bursting across the Hill. Stepping toward the broken door, RG peered inside, a set of stone steps leading deep into the earth.

The ring pulsed deep within his core, like a second heartbeat. It called to him again, pulling him forward like a dog on a leash. In the still of the crypt, the moans and howls resonated from below, voices in pain crying for salvation. The ring lay somewhere below in the darkness, as did the children, separated from their loving parents.

Parted below...

Taking a deep breath, RG descended into the tomb.

———

Stepping into the mausoleum, RG inhaled death and decay's overpowering stench. As a flurry of grim images cavorted across his vision, shrill voices screeched all around him from pain and despair, a horrific sensory barrier Malachi had constructed to deter the curious. But unlike the portal's grisly sounds and imagery, mass slaughter and brutalization, his current visions arose from his own memories. Malachi manipulated RG's mind-film and tacked on his own brutal scenes in a gruesome director's cut.

RG witnessed the butchered remains of Kacey and Junior splayed across the kitchen floor in their Chatham home. He watched the most important people in his world writhe in agony and call for him, the pictures playing like a Herschell Gordon Lewis film, looping over and over. RG pounded his palms against his head to shake the assault, pull the plug on Malachi's splatter film homage.

He descended deeper into the vault toward the stairs. He pushed against what felt like a living membrane, confining him as he advanced forward. His gait slowed as if he trudged through waist-deep water. False images elongated and stretched into a tight barrier, preventing his passage. He kicked his legs through it and ripped the barrier apart. RG's momentum catapulted him onto the crypt's dusty floor with an uncontrollable skid until he smacked into the opposing wall.

A torrent of gruesome pictures flashed in RG's mind, one final assault, a last stand to repel the interloper, but the images weakened and faded. RG rubbed his eyes, giving them flight, his heartbeat resuming its customary rhythm. He drew a deep breath, hoping his breach of Malachi's psychic security system hadn't tripped an alarm, alerting the jumper to his presence. He rose from the grimy stone floor and faced the stairwell.

Nothing I can do now. He either knows I'm here or he doesn't.

He used his hands to sift dust from his pant legs as he hovered at the stairwell's edge. The path carved a tight spiral into the earth, coiling downward through inky darkness like a corkscrew. Guiding himself into the abyss with his good hand, he caressed the cold stone and stepped blindly into the nothingness. Countering the fear he would freefall through a hidden void, RG graduated downward, scraping the tips of his boots along each step until a breath of light waxed across the stone wall.

Stepping from the stairwell, frightened voices bloomed in his ears, escalating in volume. He traversed the dim corridor, muting his footsteps' echo on the stone flooring. Despite the surging heat from flaming torches spaced along the wall, a piercing chill penetrated his bones. He continued forward until he came to a stairwell to his left, veering away from the light. Muffled voices crescendoed, but he couldn't discern their source. To his right, a second stairwell led downward, opening onto a sprawling excavation. The area resembled a crumbling, ancient arena constructed from dirt and rock with barred cages carved into its earthen chamber.

Sounds of agony floated from below.

RG stared into the pit with a hollowed-out gaze. He leaned forward on hands and knees and exhaled with a sigh of sadness and disgust. He had found them. His overwhelming grief forced his eyes closed, the sight before him too great to comprehend. It brought to mind a medieval colosseum, but with children being thrown to the lions. He had to wonder if they had forged this place from their own sweat and toil, digging through earth and rock day after day for over half a century.

He gazed at the children, robbed of their lives and separated from loved ones, deprived of everything they had ever known and forced to live like caged animals. But in that moment of despair, a truth struck him like a hammer on a rail spike. He had the power to give them their futures back. *He* had brought the team through the portal, not Morrow, not Kacey or Ian. And the ring had called to *him*, directing his steps to this place. Without him, no one would have ever found them. What had seemed like a burden for so long now blessed him with a purpose. It no longer mattered that he had lost his career or that his reputation had suffered. He had chosen to wallow in his self-pity too long, but there would be no more lamenting the life he once had; it had vanished with one glance at the sea of huddled bodies below. Nothing mattered but to free them from the ogre who incarcerated them, to give them their lives back. So what if the world continued to snicker and stare, judge the man they believed a murderer. So what if no one ever knew what he had done, and would continue to do, in his role as caretaker. None of that mattered any longer. The children would know, as would their families. And everyone else he would help from this day forward.

He advanced to the stairs with new found determination. Wooden torches provided a dim glow to the clearing, flaming barrels keeping the chill at bay. Children massed together in cages, many sleeping, others pacing back and forth, their dirty faces and haggard bodies reflecting a life of work and struggle. The children's empty eyes stared through him, their demeanor indeterminate, unable to assess whether his interloping presence helped or hurt them. Their eyes told him they didn't want to commit to hope's possibility—as if maybe they had once dangled such optimism before having it dashed against the stone walls along with their spirits.

A buzz arose from the children's throats as eyes drifted upward, words tumbling from desperate lips… "help us, mister,"…"let us out, please"…"kill the beast"…RG pressed a finger to his lips to quell the voices' chorus gathering in strength.

With urgency, RG sprinted down the steps to the bottom of the clearing, bursting at the seams to do something, anything. Comfort them, free them, wait for help, he wasn't sure. His muscles hummed as his eyes darted about the space, his feet turning in a 360-degree turn.

What can you possibly do with two jumpers lingering above and your own powers leaking out of your skin like sweat?

He would be lucky if he had enough juice to get everyone home by tomorrow evening.

Pacing the cavern floor, he calculated his unfavorable position within the filthy pit, caught in the crosshairs of two jumpers patrolling the floors a hundred feet above him.

You and General Custer should compare notes.

RG paced the foot path twisting from cage to cage, the positioning of wooden benches outside each cell a telltale sign someone took time to revel in the human suffering.

He had entered a human zoo with children as the main attraction.

The tenor of the children's voices grew more desperate, their pleas echoing off the walls.

"Shhh, all of you! Keep it down! You'll alert Malachi. We're coming for you tomorrow, I have a team——"

"Mr. Granville, is that you?" A whisper floated from one of the cages. RG whipped his head around searching for the source.

"Over here, Mr. Granville."

RG peered through a human mass in a centrally located cage. "Zach?"

"You remembered me," the boy smiled.

"Of course, I do." RG embraced the boy through the bars, giving his hair a tousle. He squatted until he had reached eye level. "I've only seen you about a hundred times when I visit Mrs. Granville at school."

"My dad says you're a magician. Is it true?" The boy pressed his smudged face against the bars, hands grasping the cold metal on either side.

He smirked. "Kind of, but it's your dad with the powers, Zach. He's here, and he can't wait to see you."

Zach's grin spread across his face like a cresting wave. "He's here?"

"You bet, and he's gonna help you get out of here tomorrow, same as all the boys. You gotta give them a message, real quiet like, you tell 'em to be ready tomorrow. We have a team that's come to take you home, but we have to wait until Malachi's gone. Tomorrow afternoon, that's when we're coming. You spread the word…from cage to cage. You tell everyone to be ready. Can you do that for me, buddy?"

"You bet I can." Zach's grasping fingers opened and closed along the cage's vertical bars.

Another buzz of voices arose as whispers spread among the cages.

"Shhh! Everyone." RG dashed from cell to cell, his hands raised in front of him. "If Malachi finds me, there won't be any rescue. Keep it down. We'll be back tomorrow to get you out. You gotta hang in there one more night."

RG turned and hiked toward the stairs.

"Please," a voice whispered from the back of Zach's cell, "don't leave us." His vacant eyes betrayed a prolonged, suffering existence.

RG stepped toward the cage, catching sight of a lanky, wobbly boy underneath a layer of caked dirt. "I can't get you all out of here by myself. I wasn't sure you were all here until a few minutes ago."

"Well, now you know. Help us, please."

"I will, I promise. How long you been here, son?"

"Only a couple days, I think, but it seems like forever." The boy turned to a friend lying on the floor beside him. "Hey, Frankie, how long we been here?"

"Two days, maybe three, I'm not sure," he responded.

They have no idea...

"Listen to me, son. We're gonna get you home tomorrow, understand? You hang in there, okay?"

"You promise?" The boy pleaded.

"Cross my heart." RG made an X on his chest and ruffled the boy's shock of red hair.

The boy smiled at him, matching dimples blossoming on his dirty cheeks.

RG squinted, inspecting the boy's face more closely, striking looks replacing, in an instant, his haggard appearance.

He's a looker, she had said.

RG swallowed. "You a Sox fan?"

"What?"

"The Red Sox. Who's your favorite player?"

The boy gazed upward, tongue poking from the corner of his mouth. "Mo Vaughn."

"The 'Hit Dog.' He's my favorite, too." *Guy hasn't played for the Sox in twenty years.* "So, are you from Brookline?"

The boy nodded.

"Then you're…Gunnar?"

"Gunnar Buckholtz. How'd you know?"

RG closed his eyes and leaned his head back. "You're the reason we're here, Gunnar. I promised your mom I'd find you."

"My mom?" Tears pulsed from the boy's eyes, leaving cleansing streaks along his smudged cheeks.

"She's waiting for you to come home. You just sit tight, Gunnar. One more day, I promise."

Zach pressed his face against the bars. "Mr. Granville, Malachi's not alone. There's another."

RG nodded. "I'm aware of the other one. We'll be ready for him tomorrow."

Zach smiled, but it quickly diminished as his eyes drifted toward the stairway. RG tracked his gaze, spying the gnarled shape at the top of the stairs freezing him in his tracks, his knotted face sending spiders flitting along his spine. He resembled a demon carved from stone. Kacey had described him, but no description could have prepared him for what he beheld, a grizzled corpse, an otherworldly abomination, one of hell's gargoyles stuffed into a child's body. He wore an old pair of tattered brown knickers, a roadmap of blue and purple web like veins pulsing against pale skin crisscrossed his ropy calf muscles. He wore no shirt but covered his upper body with a grimy ash-colored button jacket, sleeves and pockets torn. The chafed skin pulling across his scalp had split in places, revealing hints of skull and congealed exudate. RG dropped to all fours and scrambled behind the cage, relying on the clusters of children for camouflage.

He searched for a more permanent hiding place as the

stunted monster descended the stone steps but encountered nothing more than open space.

Fuck me.

"Quiet down, you rabble!" Malachi bellowed, the rock walls and ceilings amplifying his voice through the hollow. A hundred feet above, Skoczek appeared on the mezzanine, leaning forward with his hands against the stone railing like a preacher at the lectern, surveying his trembling congregation. RG's blood simmered as his thoughts drifted to their last encounter, his finger stinging with a pop as it detached from his hand. He rubbed his bandaged appendage, sensing the ratcheting pulse in his resurrected digit. He resisted the urge to dash up the stairs and fly at the fledgling jumper, take back what rightfully belonged to him.

As Skoczek moved his hand, the fires' glowing light caught the ring, reflecting across RG's face and bursting through his corneas like an oncoming vehicle's searing high beams. RG twisted away from the pulsing orb illuminating his darkness. The ring's power flooded him, sending energy and recharging his dwindling powers.

As Malachi sauntered toward the center cage housing Gunnar and Zach, RG threw himself to the ground and pressed himself flat. He didn't have the firepower to engage Malachi tonight, especially with Skoczek present. Something told him whatever fate awaited him with Malachi was destined to happen at the well. He would have to stay hidden.

Zach whispered to the other boys huddled around him. They pushed their bodies together, blocking Malachi's line of sight through the cage.

RG surveyed his surroundings. It would be challenging enough to remain hidden from Malachi's piercing eyes, but if he let his thoughts leak from his mind, he would give himself away for sure. He concentrated, Skoczek's ring pulsing out more power as if it sensed RG's need, or maybe RG pulled the power from the ring, he couldn't tell. Shuttering his thoughts, he sealed them off inside his brain.

The beast surveyed his caged prizes with a hunter's pride, as if perusing a wall of stuffed antler heads, but the boy's behavior in the prominent center cage drew his attention.

"Ah, but you now stand before me," he marveled. "This is how it should be, don't you think?"

The boys remained silent.

Malachi lowered himself onto the wooden bench facing the cage, inspecting his flock. RG lay prone in the dirt, but he could make out Malachi's partial form through the boy's legs. His gnarled hands fondled an old slingshot.

Rubbing a palm across his dome, Malachi rose from the bench. He bent over and snatched a stone from the ground, positioning it in the slingshot's pouch. Circling the cage to his right, he forced RG to skitter across the dirt in the opposite direction. The boys drifted left to counter Malachi's movement.

Pulling back the rubber cords taut, Malachi released the stone, sending it hurling through the weapon's prongs and high along the rocky surface a hundred feet above. The impact rained shattered, pebbly shards and embedded dirt from the cave wall onto the children.

"Oh, what I'd give for a bird or two to stray from the flock and find its way down here," Malachi lamented.

He stepped around the cage, forcing RG and the boys' mirrored movements. RG had slithered far enough around the back of the cage to position himself within Skoczek's line of sight. If the young jumper happened to glance into the pit, he would have a clear view of him. But Skoczek continued to stare off in another direction.

"Tomorrow, we have to make room for new arrivals. You

will be in charge of the culling. I figure it's time I give you more responsibility here."

Culling?

"Tomorrow, I must face an enemy bent on breaking up our family and stealing you away from me. They won't succeed, of course, and they'll pay the ultimate price for their arrogance." He circled the cage. "Once they're dispatched, I'll bring new boys here—new friends—but we need to free up those cages against the wall."

"Which cages?" Zach spoke up.

Malachi turned toward the wall, pointing. "The ones where the wailing children are housed, on the opposite side of the benches."

Zach glanced at RG and nodded toward the stairwell. RG gazed upward, Skoczek no longer loitering at the top of the stairs.

"What do you mean...free up?" Zach asked, drawing Malachi to the cage.

While Malachi engaged Zach on the cage's opposite side, RG had one shot at the stairway. He crawled across the dirt, inching toward the steps.

"I mean free up, liquidate, finish!" Malachi growled. "What else would I mean?"

"You're nothing but a monster," Zach shouted. "I hope you die tomorrow."

Enraged, Malachi flew at Zach, smashing against the metal bars, the boys scattering in all directions inside the cage. He pointed a bowed finger at Zach. "It's you who'll die tomorrow...and your father, too. Not me."

"We'll see," Zach snarled. "My dad's a cop!"

Zach's courage buoyed RG, and he scrambled in silence up the steps. Scanning the upper hallway for Skoczek, RG fixed a clear path toward the stairwell to the mausoleum and freedom.

He gazed into the pit, ashamed of his retreat, fuming he had to leave the children for one more second with such a monstrosity. He found comfort that at least his impulsiveness hadn't blown the mission. He could have just as easily gotten himself killed tonight, and how would that have helped anything? He owed the children a chance at freedom, but it couldn't be tonight.

He dashed across the stone corridor as Malachi loped up the steps from the cavern. By the time Malachi had reached the upper hallway, RG had disappeared out of sight.

———

July 5, 1946

Kacey

The team spent the night huddled together in the dank boiler room underneath the John Carver Inn. Firework pops and whistles penetrated the basement walls and pitched colored bursts of light through the smudged windows. Despite their exhaustion, the team didn't get much sleep. RG had told them what he had discovered—finding Zach, Gunnar, and the rest of the boys interred beneath Burial Hill. Wilder and RG had to wrestle Stahl to the ground to restrain him from attempting to rescue Zach, a sure suicide mission.

"We need to get them *now!*" Stahl had shouted, struggling to a seated position on the floor with two bodies draped over him. "We know where they are...why are we waiting? This is why we came here!"

"We already talked about this, Mike." Kacey did her best to calm him, his raw emotions roused. "Malachi believes we're here to rescue the children, but he also knows we'll try to kill him, too. The most logical point of attack is at the well, and at some point he'll show up to try to save himself, make sure the young version of himself falls in. But when he does, he will leave his domain vulnerable. That's when we make our move."

"I know, but—"

"We have a much better chance of springing the children if we only have one jumper to face, and a novice one at that."

Even though Stahl eventually agreed to the plan, RG and Wilder camped close to the door, sleeping in shifts, ready to intercept him if he had a change of heart sometime in the night.

In the morning, they finished the rest of the rations from Ashton's deli and withstood the interminable wait, standing vigil until the sun commenced its gentle descent from the sky. When Ashton checked his watch and nodded to RG, they all stood and teamed up with their groups.

"You'll be careful with Skoczek," RG pleaded, grasping Kacey's hand. "God knows the power he possesses."

"It's two against one." She smiled, nodding toward Wilder. "Plus, we'll have a pretty pissed off Mike Stahl."

"Maybe we should have let him bring the gun," RG smirked. "Are you guys clear on your roles…what you're gonna do when you get there?"

"We've been working it out all morning. Ian will engage Skoczek. Mike and I will free the kids, get them to the inn, and take them through the portal. According to the governor, room 309 will be open until early evening, so we should be fine. Once the kids are through, I'll go back and make sure Ian's okay, help him with Skoczek."

"He's still human. He can die. Whatever it takes, don't hesitate. Hit him over the head with a fucking rock if you have to. And make sure you get the ring back, or we may not be going anywhere."

"What about you? Has Elias clued you in to his plan?"

"He says he's seen Malachi's death, and I have to trust him. He's pretty sure of himself. After learning how he swam through the city sewer, saved Mike from drowning, and survived a deep freeze, I figure I'm in damn good hands."

She leaned her head against RG's chest as he wrapped his arms around her.

He kissed the top of her head. "When I first met Elias in Boston, I had a feeling about him. One of those things you can't explain, like pieces had fallen into place. You know what I mean. I'm not sure just how we're gonna defeat Malachi, but he's the key to this whole thing. Remember, the most important thing is getting those children out of the pit. If we can keep Malachi occupied long enough to make it happen, we win. And I'm ready to do whatever I can to see it through. You'll understand when you get down there."

"Don't go dying on me again, RG."

"Ahem." Ashton sidled up beside the couple. "I hate interrupting these moments, but we'd better be going. Time's short and we have to cover several miles on foot. We can't miss this window."

"I understand, Elias. I'm ready to go."

The old man reached for Kacey's hand, fitting his palm into hers with a gentle pat from his opposite hand. "You be careful, young lady."

"You, too." Kacey nodded her head toward RG. "And keep an eye on this guy for me."

"He'll be fine, I promise," Ashton smirked as he ambled off. "It'll be the walk that kills him."

Kacey grinned as Ashton moved across the room to say goodbye to Wilder and Stahl, repeating his gentle two-palm handshake like a preacher after Sunday services.

When they were alone, Kacey lifted her gaze to study RG's

face, like she had done countless times before when he slept or when he kissed her, even when they fought. It hadn't changed much since they met twelve years ago, a bit fuller as if he had needed more time to grow into it. His wavy, coffee-colored hair still provided the perfect border, like a picture frame impeccably chosen to complement the colors and themes of the featured art. She traced a finger across his ear, lingering on the maze of creases and infoldings, curving like a roadmap to her heart. Her hand continued across his face until it reached his lips. Brushing her fingertips against them, he gave her his smile, and a view of that one single tooth, her favorite, turned just a fraction inward. One of his perfect imperfections. She glanced into his eyes, some indeterminate hue marbling through his milk-chocolate iris, his left one anyway, a color she had never spotted before.

How could that be?

She silently wished for another tomorrow together, so she could continue where she left off, focusing on the other features she had yet to ponder.

RG glanced toward Ashton. "I gotta go." He stepped away, keeping her fingers entwined in his own until they stretched to their ends. With a gentle pull, her hand fell to her side, suddenly cold.

Please don't die on me.

Chapter Nineteen

'What did the Little hasty sojournr
Find So forbidding & Disgustful in
Our upper World to occation its
Precipitant exit.'

In memory of EZRA THAYER JACKSON, died Novr. 23^d,
1783 (Aged 25 days)
-Epitaphs from Burial Hill

July 5, 1946

RG

RG and Ashton trudged through the woods bordering the
main roads, careful to remain hidden as Independence Day
travelers filed from Plymouth, anxious to reach Route 3 and
points north. RG struggled to keep up with his spry
companion as they skirted rocky shorelines, hiked up slippery

hillsides blanketed in leaves and knotty pine needles, and navigated downed trees, brambles, and tumbling streams. He had visited Plymouth a number of times, but couldn't believe how beautiful it once had been, miles of rich woodland bordering unending oceanfront, now littered with houses, condos, and nuclear power plants.

As if reading his mind, Ashton turned and grinned. "This is the Plymouth of my youth. Reminds me of being ten years old again."

Sonofabitch has the energy of a ten-year-old, that's for sure!

After traversing Warren Cove's soft white sand, the two men struggled along Rocky Point's treacherous shoreline. They stepped carefully over the slick, misshapen boulders dotting the sand to avoid an icy dip into the waist-deep seawater. But the breaking waves cascading over the rocks still showered a misty spray across their path. At Priscilla Beach, with the last of the weekend stragglers still traipsing through the surf, the two bypassed their intended route, hoisting themselves up the grassy bluff and disappearing into the thick woods. They emerged from the wooded shade into a tall grass field near Bartlett Pond across from White Horse Beach.

Pausing to catch his breath, RG leaned over at the waist and rested his hands on his thighs. If he ever saw Kacey again, he would have to tell her he'd gotten way more than the ten thousand steps she pestered him about. He gazed at the expanse of land before him, soon to welcome row after row of clapboard houses along Elm, Beach, Pearl, and Hilltop, streets not yet in existence and still unnamed.

"We're here." Ashton waved his hands across the thigh-high beach grass, his fingers closing over the soft spikelets attached to the stem tops, a faint smile playing on his lips.

The two men proceeded across the field, the land's pitch taking them up a gradual embankment. Their cadence found a singular pattern as the whoosh of their threshing limbs against the grass fell into sync. White Horse Beach rose like an artist's rendition along the horizon. The roar of the pounding surf carried on the humid breeze, meeting their ears in alternating crescendos. RG closed his eyes, the sound so close and crystal clear he could have been wading in the surf.

"Be careful now." Ashton scanned the field before him. "It'll be difficult to spot in the tall grass."

"What'll be difficult to—" Ashton grabbed his arm as RG quickly stepped to his left, teetering a moment before steadying himself. Directly in front of him, a line of rotting planks interrupted the sea of waving grass rolling across the hill.

Their eyes met as RG exhaled a quick breath.

"That would have thrown a monkey wrench into the weekend," the old man chuckled. "Let's continue up a ways, find a place to observe."

The two continued to the top of the hill, settling behind a line of large, flat-iron rocks jutting from the hilltop's edge. Ashton swiped a hand through his hair, closed his eyes, and tilted his head toward the late afternoon sun, a peaceful expression radiating across his face. Unlike RG with stomach in knots and blood pressure spiraling, Ashton's manner belied no fear, no sense of dread at the specter of facing his long dead cousin.

The old man lowered his head and opened his eyes. He pulled back his shirtsleeve and checked his watch. "It won't be much longer now."

They waited.

———

Malachi

Positioned behind a small copse of trees, Malachi eyed Granville and the old man trudging up the hill toward the well. As he scanned the field, his younger self and Cousin Elias crossed Taylor Avenue from White Horse Beach, heading toward the field, their shortcut home. They would be arriving at the well in minutes. If Granville and the old man interfered, Malachi the jumper would never exist—and he couldn't let that happen.

He pressed his eyelids together, recalling the chafing salt grains powdering a young boy's lips, a sea taste flickering in his recollection, flushed skin savoring the late afternoon sunshine. His mind drifted to Mr. Brigham's diner and late-night ice cream cones, the colorful light explosions over the harbor, the kindness of Mr. and Mrs. Ashton. He had chosen to inhabit this loop in time because of these memories, reliving the joy of that magical weekend with Cousin Elias over and over. But now another memory tarnished his reverie, surfacing unannounced. It hijacked his consciousness and reverberated like a pinball in his head—a chilling darkness at the bottom of a watery pit, no escape from gravity's force pulling him under. In all his time inhabiting the loop, he had never come back to the well to revisit the moment of his death. Now, the memories had come. Watching his ten-year-old self moments from his fate, a painful gnawing ripped at his core, giving him pause.

What if I had lived?

He tried to shake the troubling notion from his head. What if he hadn't plunged into the well, but instead caught the train back to North Station and met his mother on the platform. He imagined jumping off the train and leaping into her arms, blissfully tolerating the rapid kisses she would pepper across his cheeks as he searched for the small X she had carved in the dust. They would pile into the Rolls, the wind whipping through his hair, his head hitting his pillow later with Jiggs at the foot of his bed. Maybe they would stop for a sundae on the way home or stroll around Chestnut Hill reservoir like they were wont to do on summer evenings. A vision of his mother holding his hand once more brought a flutter to his chest, a forgotten sensation somehow jostled from its long-dormant hibernation.

He ran his hands from the top of his head to his chin, wincing at his gnarled scalp and misshapen features, his stunted posture. He could read in his boys' eyes the horror and fear when he finally would reveal himself to them. He didn't have to be like this; he could still be a boy if he wanted. He could have a life again. But then he pictured his boys, huddled on the cold stone floor of his hutch, his friends. They needed him. He fed them, clothed them, and disciplined them. It wouldn't be fair to turn his back on them.

This is the world I've created. This is who I am.

There could be no turning back.

Malachi's eyes snapped open to find Granville and the old man had graduated past the well and had lowered themselves onto the grass behind a rocky outcropping. He crawled on his belly, the tall grass shielding his pint-sized body as he eased closer to the men. The swirling afternoon breeze buffeting the swishing grass masked the rustling sounds of his approach. Malachi stifled a chuckle at the men hiding from him, waiting until the boys came closer to the well before they intervened. *They must think I'm a fool.* Didn't they recognize he would be expecting them, that his defiled portal would have appropriated their hidden intentions?

Lifting his grizzled mug above the high grass, he spotted the boys halfway up the hill about a hundred yards from the well. He lowered his head and crept through the concealing grass until he had advanced mere feet from the two men.

"There's no stopping the past," he growled, springing to

his feet, "or changing the future. Today, the boy dies, just like he has every other day for the past seventy years. And you're both about to join him."

————

Kacey

Kacey, Stahl, and Wilder slipped out the inn's backdoor, pausing to stare through the woods at Burial Hill before readying themselves for the task ahead. Stahl had champed at the bit all morning, agonized his son rested so close yet so far, imprisoned a few hundred yards from him beneath the earth. He had rummaged through the boiler room and found a mallet and peg to break open the cells—and by the look in his eyes, maybe a jumper's head if the chance presented itself.

Kacey sensed tension in the Brit, less talkative than usual, jaw squared. The time had come for his contribution to the mission, and he was in pre-game. He hadn't once checked his hair or run a hand through it, but paced the hotel basement corridor, peering into the locket hanging around his neck. He had skin in this game. He had traveled across time for the boy he'd lost forty years ago, and his steely eyes communicated he wouldn't be leaving without him.

"Well, whatta ya say we quit taking the piss and get those kids home?" Wilder jutted his chest forward and advanced up the hill with purpose, leaving Mike and Kacey scrambling to keep up.

After a short hike, the three reached the cemetery's outer boundary. They eyed the crypt beside the kissing tree, a late afternoon breeze scattering freshly mowed grass and fallen leaves. They had taken their first steps from the woods when Wilder threw his arms to his sides, halting their advance.

"Bloody hell!" he cried.

In front of them, a man and woman strode along the cemetery's walkway. They held hands, their eyes locked onto each other's, but in moments they would glance forward and witness the three standing directly in their path.

"Time for a bit of magic." Wilder grinned and extended his arm as if halting traffic, then twisted his hand into a fist.

Time crunched to a halt with a brake-like squeal, as if the world ran along a rail and reached the end of the line. The air thickened like syrup. The falling leaves hung suspended in midair as the couple's gait halted midstep.

"What the fuck's going on?" Stahl's eyes darted back and forth, his voice sounding flat and distant, failing to carry through the stagnant air.

Kacey grabbed his arm. "He can stop time," she shouted, struggling to hear her own voice, as if the words migrated through wet cloths to reach her ears. She turned to Wilder. "Tell me that's what you just did."

He nodded, raising his eyebrows in quick succession. "But we don't have long, maybe a few seconds. We gotta get out of sight."

They struggled toward the crypt as if in slow motion, struggling against the dense air.

"I can hardly move," Stahl barked.

"When time stops, everything stops," Wilder shouted. "Every molecule of air is suspended before us. It's like pushing against a wall. It's hard to hear because sound has trouble traveling through it, just like we do. Don't stop, keep pushing forward."

They labored with each dogged step, passing through a world devoid of movement, the air like a lead blanket pressing against them. The absolute silence alerted Kacey to an infinitesimal ringing in her ears she had never heard before, hidden beneath the cacophony of daily life. Curiously, she reached for a stationary leaf in midflutter falling from the kissing tree. Her fingertips pushed the leaf against the spongy air but couldn't dislodge it from its intended trajectory.

The halted world vibrated in a spiraling sound crescendo, picking up energy and mobbing the team's ears, physical laws battling against an unplanned disruption. The earth's rotational kinetics, the sun's radiant energy, gravity's pull, the laws of motion all fought to reestablish their mathematical and scientific certainty against their unknown oppressor.

Reaching the mausoleum's battered black door, the three crept inside. Wilder finally released his trembling fist. They worked their jaws, swallowing, attempting to pop their ears as the world's natural sounds resumed, air's bulky mass pulling from their shoulders. Kacey peeked from the crypt toward the couple strolling along the walkway, oblivious to their lives' momentary disruption as they disappeared over the hill and out of sight.

"Close call," Stahl muttered.

The renewed volume in Kacey's ears surprised her as she rubbed her heated legs, burning with lactic acid from her battle against the resistant air. "God, it's like I've just run a marathon."

"Not the most pleasant experience I admit, but as a party trick it's quite the dog's bollocks!"

The vault hummed with an electrical grid's crackling voltage, an otherworldly energy tangible within Kacey's core. She locked gazes with Wilder as they both sensed the familiar power percolating from the darkness below. As they stepped deeper into the vault, Malachi's defensive mind tactics hung a veil of heinous images to repel them.

"Keep moving," Kacey shouted. "They're like images from the portal. They're not real."

Stahl had taken the brunt of the visual assault, still recovering from the stoppage of time. His mind couldn't handle the sensory blitz as easily as his companions. He dropped to his knees, clutching his head to squash Claire and Zach's tortured images.

Wilder and Kacey knelt beside him and hauled him to his feet. They linked arms as they struggled through the image barrier holding them back, like a hellish curtain they had to pass through. As they pushed forward, Kacey sensed a yielding, a tear in the cosmic fabric, propelling them forward to the crypt's dusty floor.

"Is everyone okay?" Kacey glanced at Mike, kneeling on the floor and pounding his forehead with an open palm, attempting to dislodge the pictures from his overwrought mind.

"Oh my God, what the...?" Stahl massaged his temples.

"Just a small deterrent. Malachi trying to queer our pitch," Wilder replied.

"Okay, let's move." Kacey stepped into the darkened stairwell.

They groped along the pitch-dark spiral staircase until the torchlight illuminated the stone corridor leading to the subterranean pit. At the top of the stairs, the three stared in horror at the scene below, children packed into cells and huddled together for warmth. Stahl scanned the cages for Zach, his glance darting wildly back and forth.

"Travis...I see him," Wilder mumbled.

Kacey spotted the boy from the locket. He leaned against the cell bars along the perimeter, lifted his head, and returned her gaze.

"Does he see you?" Stahl inquired.

Wilder lowered his eyes. "He might, but he doesn't know who I am. I wasn't visible in his realm, so he's never seen me before."

"Well, he senses you, that's for sure," Stahl grinned.

"How does a child ever recover from this?" Wilder's voice thickened.

They don't, and they'll never be whole again. Ever.

Kacey groped for the stone wall as her quivering legs faltered, pinpricks of light shimmying across her vision. Stahl and Wilder raced to her side as she dropped to her knees, an emotional dam bursting within her.

"I'm sorry," Kacey muttered, blotting a sleeve against her eyes.

"It's alright, luv." Wilder helped her to her feet, brushing the dust from her pants. "Let's get them out of here."

By the time they had turned around, Stahl had already dashed down the stairs into the clearing.

"Mike, wait!" Kacey half shouted, not wanting to announce their presence.

"Go with him. Get the children out. I'll search the upper floor and take care of that bastard Skoczek!"

She dashed toward the stairs, glancing over her shoulder. "Be careful, Ian."

"I'll see you back at the inn," he said, leaving her a wink as he sprinted up the stairwell.

Kacey raced down the steps as Stahl zig-zagged from cell to cell, calling for Zach. When he reached the center cage, Skoczek stepped from behind it, gripping Zach in front of him, one hand clutching his neck, the other aiming a long, jagged knife at the boy's jugular.

"Looking for this one?" he said with an ominous grin.

Stahl froze, his eyes searching. "Just relax, man. Take it easy. Zach, you okay?"

"I'm fine, Dad." He struggled against Skoczek's grip, kicking at his shins. "Let go of me, you freak!"

Skoczek gripped Zach's neck tighter, silencing him.

"Appears we have an attitude problem with this one...the one Malachi loved so much. The one he thinks is so special." Skoczek sneered at the boy. "You're nothing."

Stahl waved the mallet in front of him. "Let him go!"

"Hit him in the head, Dad!"

Skoczek pressed the knife against Zach's skin.

"Lars," Kacey spoke, her tone soothing. "You can stop this. You have the power."

"Well, look who's here," Skoczek growled at Kacey. "Pretty clever trick you pulled to save your little boy." He turned to Stahl, repositioning the knife. "Not gonna help with this one."

"I've seen inside you, Lars. It doesn't have to be like this."

"This is who I am!" he shouted, eyes burning. "Malachi told me this is all I'll ever be."

Kacey took a step forward. "I understand you've done things in the past, but the ring's amplifying the evil."

"It's just showing me my true self."

"You fought it for years. You controlled the evil inside you. You don't have to give in to it now. We can all make choices about good or evil, whether caretaker or jumper."

"What do you know?" Skoczek's hand jerked away from Zach's neck as he pointed the knife at her.

"I denied my powers for years, Lars, buried them deep inside me, just like you did. I brought them back when I recognized my calling, my—"

"This is my calling, too!" Skoczek interrupted. "The ring showed me."

"Lars, listen to me. It's like a magnifying glass, making things look bigger than they are. You can put the powers to sleep, let them lie dormant. Let me help you try to right the ship. You can have a life, a good life."

"Yeah, and then what? When I die, guess what I become?"

"You have a choice."

Skoczek glanced up, a grin playing across his face. "I've made my choice. Now, let me show you."

Skoczek drew the knife under Zach's chin this time.

"No!" Stahl shouted, rushing toward him with mallet raised.

An explosion rocked Skoczek, knocking him forward. The knife launched from the jumper's hand and propelled Zach into Mike's arms as Wilder pierced the jumper's body from behind. The two writhed inside Skoczek's shell, battling for control, the body morphing back and forth like an amalgam of the two, each man's distinct form surfacing briefly as the internal struggle raged.

Stahl pulled Zach close, whisking him away from the melee. "Hang on, Zach. I'll be right back."

Stahl charged toward the jumper with mallet raised, a guttural cry spouting from deep inside. Just as his arm initiated its violent descent, the hammer in direct line with the top of Skoczek's head, Kacey bolted forward, throwing her arm beneath Mike's shoulder from behind. Her split-second disruption upset its preordained pathway, the hammer falling awry, drawing sparks against the dirty stone floor.

"What're you doing, Kacey? I had him!"

"You kill the host, you kill Wilder, too."

"Jesus!" Stahl dropped the mallet and stepped back, his breath coming in waves. "Sorry, I knew better than that."

Zach yanked on Kacey's sleeve. "Why can't my dad just hit him with the hammer, Mrs. Granville?"

She leaned forward, putting herself at eye level with the boy. "There are two lives inside the one body, Zach. If you kill one, you kill them both."

Zach crinkled his nose. "If your friend spits out Skoczek, we can kill him?"

"That's right, Zach, but it's hard to tell who's inside who

right now, and we can't wait around for that to happen. We gotta get you and your friends out of here now."

Stahl rescued the mallet and waved it in front of Zach. "What do you say we open up these cages?"

"Can this one be the first?" Zach gave the center cage's bars a rattle.

"You bet, bud. Hey, I need your help. You have to hold the metal peg against the lock, and I'll bust it open. Can you do that?"

Zach glanced at Mike's mangled right hand. "What happened to you, Dad?"

"Nothing I can't handle. But you gotta help me, okay?"

"I knew you'd come get me. I told everyone you'd come, and you did!"

He placed his good hand on Zach's shoulder. "I made you a promise, didn't I?"

"Dad…" Zach positioned the peg against the cage's lock and gazed into Stahl's eyes. "I'm not afraid anymore. I'm not afraid of Kenny Farley or Malachi or the long-haired freak over there. I'm not afraid of anything!"

"Then I'm putting you in charge of all the boys. Let's get 'em out of here."

Within minutes, Mike had shattered the cage doors while Kacey and Zach had corralled the children up the steps and out of the pit. Their physical condition made it slow going. Zach half-carried Kenny Farley to the upper floor, going back and forth to help others to the landing.

When everyone had assembled in the corridor above the cavern, Kacey glanced below where Wilder battled Skoczek. The shared form spun across the floor in a bizarre dance. She was unable to determine which form dominated the other or who controlled the skirmish. The two flipped into the air and remained suspended, defying gravity. The cavern shook as earth and rock tumbled from the ceilings and walls, plinking off the metal cages and littering the cave floor. She considered jumping into the fray to give Wilder a hand, but the shifting stones beneath her feet pushed her forward. Getting the children to the portal remained her first priority.

Stumbling through the mausoleum's broken door, Kacey and Stahl whisked the boys through the cemetery and into the woods. When they reached the inn, John Carver stood at the backdoor like a seventeenth-century doorman, hustling the boys into the basement stairwell. With the stealth of a military operation, they led the children quietly up three flights of stairs and into a packed room 309 where Stahl gathered the children at the portal's entrance.

"All right, everyone." Stahl raised his hands. "It's time to go home."

Shouts and whoops erupted from the boys.

"Quiet down, now! Listen up." Stahl couldn't hide his grin. "This tunnel will take you to a breakfast restaurant. Go through the front door and find yourself a seat. They're ready to serve you a big breakfast. You guys hungry?"

With another burst of joyous cheers, the boys crowded together, pushing forward.

"Hold on to the hand of the boy beside you, and don't let go. I'll be following from behind." Stahl ushered the children into the portal until only Zach remained.

Kacey sensed no volatility in the portal or any malice directed toward the children. The portal appeared to understand Malachi's attachment to them. It would be a different story for her and RG when the time came for their return trip.

"Is that everyone?" Kacey asked.

"All accounted for." Stahl shook his head. "Fifty-two children heading home."

"We did it, didn't we?"

Stahl hesitated as he stepped through the portal, Zach's hand held tightly in his. "Don't take this the wrong way, but our first kiss may have saved my son's life."

Kacey grinned. "You better get going. I'm going back to check on Ian. We'll be right behind you."

Stahl jabbed a finger at her. "You be careful. I'll save a booth for you and RG." He peered deep within the portal at the rows of children moving toward the Pancake Man. "It's gonna be crowded in there."

It's always crowded in there. "Don't forget to order me the silver-dollar pancakes."

"They'll be waiting on the table." Stahl gave her a wave and disappeared into the portal.

Time to check on Ian. As Kacey dashed across the hotel room and grasped the handle, the door exploded, knocking her backward. Skoczek flew into the room, piercing her body with a sickening fury.

"Well, well, well," he purred inside her head. *"Finally, the alone-time we've been waiting for."*

Chapter Twenty

'Yet with delight you drew your balmy breath
And the first pain you seem'd to feel was death.'

In memory of CONSIDER BRADFORD, died December
25, 1826 (Aged11 mo. & 17 days)
-Epitaphs from Burial Hill

July 5, 1946

Malachi

At the other end of Plymouth, Granville and the old man pivoted to face the diminutive jumper poised on his coiled haunches, ready to pounce.

"The portal told me you were coming." Malachi grinned as he exploded through the caretaker's chest, overtaking his body, hijacking his internal workings.

He sensed the Granville losing the battle almost immediately, his dwindling power offering nothing against Malachi's overwhelming strength and experience.

"Thought you could stop the past and change the future?" Malachi barked at him inside his head.

The caretaker attempted to expel him, but Malachi's size made it impossible to confine him. His body didn't altogether fit inside Granville's human suit, and the caretaker couldn't pinpoint his position. Malachi swallowed back rising bile, repulsed at inhabiting an older, more developed body than the children's frames to which he had grown accustomed, but he had no choice. He would put an end to this weakened caretaker and move on to the rest of the team.

"You call yourself a caretaker? You're nothing without your ring. You're powering down like an old battery," Malachi hissed, *"running out of juice."*

Granville squared off against him. *"I've faced opponents a lot tougher and bigger than you."* He scanned the miniscule jumper from head to toe. *"Come to think of it, I just bought my son a little Cabbage Patch doll about your size."*

A blinding rage spiraled and burst inside Malachi. He sent a bolt of stabbing pain through the caretaker. He opened his mouth to let out a wail, but Malachi stifled his cry from within.

"Just need to keep you quiet for another minute before I dispatch the two of you...wouldn't want to alert the boys, now would we? Afterwards, I'll take my time with you...and your wife."

Malachi craned Granville's neck to peer around the rocky edge as the boys advanced closer to the well, steps away from sealing a fate destined to repeat itself every two days until the end of time.

Before he could turn away, the younger Malachi stepped through the ancient well's rotting wood covering and tumbled headlong into the silent void, the hungry earth swallowing him like a pill. Before scampering away, young Elias shouted to him from the top of the well. "Malachi, Malachi! I'm going for help!"

"Aww, too late to change history now. What a team you two turned out to be, a pretend caretaker and…" he glanced at the old man, *"the walking dead. You overestimated your worth, don't you think?"* Malachi sent another burst of pain burrowing through Granville. *Who's the old fart, by the way? Your ace in the hole?"* he cackled.

The pretender clenched his teeth, as if determined not to give Malachi the satisfaction of witnessing his pain. *"He's an old friend. He wanted to see you."*

The jumper studied the old man, who had risen to his feet. A spark of recognition flit through his churning mind as he exited the caretaker with a violent shove, smacking him against the rocky wall and dropping him to the grass in a heap at his feet. Granville clutched at his chest and gasped for air as he writhed in the grass.

Malachi stepped toward the other man. "I know you, old-timer."

"You do. Or you did." He straightened, hands clasped behind his back.

"Elias?" Malachi peered into the old man's face. "Such irony…*you* coming to visit *me* in Plymouth now. You got old, cousin."

Ashton flashed a grin. "So did you, Malachi."

Malachi stretched his lips into a menacing grimace. "It's been a while. Have you come back to relive my death and enjoy it a second time, or to stop it? Neither choice makes you look very good right now, cousin."

"I wanted to come back and save you."

"Save me? Kill me you mean!" He sneered at the old man. "And I thought family took care of each other…"

"I don't like what you've become, and it's my fault."

"Your fault?"

"Come with me, Malachi. You need to see something." The sun hung low in the sky as Ashton and Malachi stepped out from behind the rock and advanced toward the well.

Standing at the brink of the pit, Malachi leaned over, cupping an open hand behind his ear, listening to the splashing and wails from the dying boy below. His lips descended into a frown, a small quiver tugging at one end. "I'm going down for the final time now," he whispered.

"I'm sorry, cousin," Ashton replied.

The jumper's heart lurched as he pictured himself in the brackish water below, shouting for help, reaching for the soft, moss-sodden walls to keep his head above water, a part of him still linked to the ten-year-old boy who never emerged from his watery grave.

"It's my fault, Malachi." Ashton placed his hands on his hips and stared at his shoes. "It's my fault you stole children from their families, destroyed innocent lives. I'm here to make things right."

"Destroyed lives? I take care of those children. They're my friends."

"No, Malachi. They're your possessions, and you're their nightmare. I've stayed alive long enough to come back and show you something, something you won't want to see." He pointed over the crest of the hill at a lone figure perched in the grass a hundred yards below the well. Across Taylor Avenue, the setting sun had given birth to a watercolor burst across the sky, but the figure remained seated, eyes glued to the ground, unmoved by the beauty surrounding him.

"Who's the boy down there?" Malachi demanded.

Ashton folded his hands behind his back again, shifting his weight from one leg to another.

Malachi squinted his black eyes toward the bottom of the

hill, fixing on a boy still wearing the swim trunks from a day at the beach, sobbing, head in his hands.

"Elias…is that you?"

He nodded.

Malachi's face fell, as if a curtain had dropped behind his eyes. "You mean…"

"I never went for help."

Malachi's knees folded, steadying himself against his cousin before he slumped to the ground. "How…how could you…my *best* friend…just leave me down there to die? Elias!"

The silence pressed between them.

"I was nine years old, Malachi. I knew we weren't supposed to cross through the field. I thought they'd send me away, maybe put me in jail if they found out it I'd been at fault. I wasn't thinking straight. I made the wrong choice, and I've had to live with the decision my whole life. I made you what you are. I'm responsible for everything."

"You let me die down there!" Malachi's arm shot out and pointed at the hole in the ground behind them, pulsating veins jetting boiling blood beneath his pallid skin. "All because you were afraid of getting in trouble? Too worried about yourself to care about me. My life?"

Conflict erupted inside the jumper as the internal battle raged between the life he missed and the life he now possessed. Malachi's memories pelted him like sleet in a winter wind, his mother's face silhouetted against the hallway light, leaning over for a goodnight kiss; his stunted form shivering in the mausoleum on Burial Hill, the moans from the boys below sending shards of icicles through his black heart; Mr. and Mrs. Ashton's arms draped across his shoulder as they strolled under a canopy of colorful explosions falling from the heavens; his mother kneeling in front of him at North Station, marking an X on the dusty platform. The image of a blue-eyed boy with a shock of jet-black hair gave way to a ghastly caricature in a fractured window's reflection, a grizzled gargoyle with eyes of stone and skin like parchment. Malachi clasped his arms around himself and bent at the waist, bellowing a wounded animal's guttural cry.

The boy at the bottom of the hill peered over his shoulder toward the commotion at the well.

Malachi gazed at the boy with venomous intent but transferred his rage to the man he'd become. "You made me what I am," Malachi cried. "You took everything from me!"

"I'm ready to pay my penance, cousin." Ashton peered toward the sky, twilight's slow dismount throwing the day's last light onto a boy's eighty-year-old face.

Ashton closed his eyes, as if ready for what would come.

———

RG

RG drew himself to his knees, the wind still knocked from his lungs. Stars streaked across his visual field and orbited his head as Malachi and Ashton ambled off toward the well. He grasped his chest where Malachi had exploded through him, the pain as fresh as if a lance had pierced him.

He couldn't shake the image of young Malachi and nine-year-old Elias strolling across the field, unaware of the precipitating event that would destroy countless lives, like watching a doomed airliner awaiting takeoff, knowing it would never reach its destination, yet being unable to do anything about it, to scream at someone, anyone, to stop for a moment and hit reset. He was also about to view an individual tragedy, his sympathy going out to a young boy whose life had ratcheted down to its final moments. And now he would view Ashton's death...unless he could get to him in time. He rose to his feet but stumbled and pitched headlong into the grass. Clambering to his knees, he crawled after them.

As he got to within twenty feet of the pair, Ashton leaned his head back and closed his eyes, a faint smile playing at the corners of his mouth. Malachi growled and exploded through the old man's chest, toppling him to the ground, ravaging him from the inside. RG rose on unsteady feet and took a running leap at Ashton, now perched on a single knee. He had no idea whether he would have enough power to enter him and wrestle Malachi for his body's control or whether he would bowl him over a second time with his momentum.

I guess we're gonna find out.

He penetrated the old man's sinewy frame with ease, as if he had fallen into water, entering him with the same cool energy of his father. He faced Malachi's overwhelming power once again, unable to counter his spiraling anger and vengeance. RG's dwindling strength made it difficult to limit his thoughts, but he fought to protect the rest of the team and their mission. If he had to die today, he'd have to die; but Kacey, Mike, and Wilder would escape with the children. Molly Buckholtz would hold her boy again. As would Claire. But he needed to stay alive long enough to keep the portal open.

With blinding speed, Malachi gripped RG, shaking him like a Rottweiler with a rat in his powerful maw, tossing him against Ashton's internal human shell with a bone-jarring force, leaving him battered and disoriented.

He spoke to Ashton inside his head. *Pretty sure we won't be getting out of this one, old man. Forgive me.*

"*I've got this, RG. Talk to the boy, tell him what to do.*"

"*The boy?*" RG fought to stay connected as Malachi turned his attention to him.

"*Go now,*" Ashton shouted. "*This is my destiny.*"

Malachi commandeered Ashton's hand and pressed it against his throat. He rattled RG with another violent shake, expelling him from Ashton's damaged shell and hurling his battered body to the ground. Lifting his dazed head from the soft, grass bed, Malachi turned and spoke into his mind.

"Once I'm done with my traitor cousin, it's your turn, caretaker."

The hairs on RG's neck lifted as he grasped his life's dwindling timeframe. When would he and Kacey share souls again? Which lifetime? *It wasn't long enough. I didn't get enough time with her.* His mind drifted to Robert Jr., the boy who would never get to know his father. Kacey would show him pictures, of course, tell him all about him. But, he would grow up just like *his* father had, listening to his mother's sobs through the bedroom door, his empty heart longing for something forever missing, the void he would be unable to fill. RG hoped he had infused enough love into the boy during their short time together to leave a trace of himself, something that might spark a fleeting moment of peace while Junior played in the surf or someday gazed at the ocean trying to remember his father.

He struggled to his knees, promising himself he would be on his feet when Malachi came for him.

Malachi

Ashton's bloodshot eyes bulged in his head as Malachi worked his limbs like a maestro conducting an orchestra. He directed the old man's hand to tighten around his windpipe, weakening him.

Malachi's eyes simmered with ire. *"You were my family once, but that was a long time ago. I don't regret what I have to do. In fact, I'm starting to enjoy it."*

Ashton fought his way to a knee, then pushed himself to a standing position.

"There, there, just relax, cousin. No need to struggle anymore, it will be over soon."

"Sooner than you think." Ashton gave a quick glance behind himself. He locked gazes with Granville and threw him a grin.

Malachi swallowed. *What are you up to, old man?*

Ashton closed his eyes and stepped backward into the well, dropping through the earth like a cannonball.

The jumper's emotions swung from surprise to panic in the microsecond it took for his equilibrium to change. His breath caught in his throat as Ashton's plummeting body hurled him for a second time into the abyss. Malachi's childhood fears manifested in a high-pitched scream exploding from his throat, initiating a reflexive paralysis as the world fell away. His predicament's magnitude rushed past him like the well's glistening, sod-covered stones. How long did it take to fall from the well's opening to the stale water? He remembered it as an eternity, but it must have been only a matter of seconds.

If he remained trapped in Ashton's body when he hit the water, he would die, plain and simple. The wind rushed past Ashton's weightless, freefalling form, throwing Malachi into a disoriented state. Sensing the fleeting time, he could only react in slow motion, the well's blackness, the pinprick of light receding above, and the deep earth's confines reviving his darkest terror. As he recovered and hurled himself against the internal dimensions of Ashton's body in a desperate attempt to flee, the old man slammed against the water, killing him instantly.

———

Kacey

In room 309 of the John Carver Inn, Kacey's body turned inside out as a bloodied and battered Skoczek slammed her to the floor, stretching her body's seams with an excruciating deliberateness as he fitted himself inside her. He stunk of the grave, as if he had wrenched himself through rotting earth. His dark thoughts peppered her mind unimpeded, the jumper no longer maintaining a ruse to keep them hidden, his intentions for her obvious and final. She attempted to hold him inside her, expel him, but he overpowered her and pinned her against the carpet.

"Ah, I've always wondered what it would be like with a real woman." His lips curled into a malicious sneer as he guided Kacey's hand across her skin, her nails magnifying in length before her eyes, cutting grooves across her stomach. She twisted her body to escape his assault, her nerves screaming as if gleaming scalpels had raked her skin.

"Did you expect me to be gentle with you?"

Her throat went dry, sensing his invasion would be time-consuming and painful. Her only hope rested with Wilder and the odds he had survive the cave…well, there weren't any odds.

Skoczek remained secure inside her, moving against her with an animalistic fury. She couldn't move as he had taken full control of her limbs, slicing her skin with a hand's gentle stroke, her body on fire. He manipulated her other hand and forced it to her throat, squeezing the breath from her, snowy spots forming in her vision as she hurtled toward unconsciousness.

Then the other hand joined, increasing the pressure on her windpipe.

With the ring's powers coursing through him, Skoczek's face morphed into Morrow, then RG. Their black eyes burned through her as they took turns throttling her, their presence within the ring perverted into a raging mishmash of love and terror. RG slammed her head against the carpet, and Morrow dragged her from side to side, veins thick as cables protruding from their temples, faces burning crimson. Skoczek grinned as he conjured residual images before her, depraved reflections of their gentle souls, designed to fill her final moments with horror, the hands of those she most loved coiled into fists and carrying out his brutal vengeance on her.

Grasping at consciousness, Kacey perceived the first rumblings from inside the portal, sensing it dying, a flickering of lights in an interworld's last call. The knowledge RG had somehow killed Malachi buoyed her, and she fought with renewed vigor against her attacker. She dislodged her own hand from her throat and swallowed a few breaths of precious air. But another thunderous vibration rattled the building, and she accepted the unthinkable: RG had run out of time, he wouldn't make it to the portal before it ceased to be.

The rumbling portal weakened Skoczek's grip on her constricted airway as he roared in anguish. The oxygen inched toward her lungs again. She latched onto his thoughts, the truth of Malachi's death flooding through him. The connection between them abruptly severed. His façade shattered at the loss of his perverse mentor, his father figure, leaving him curled in the fetal position inside her as he let loose a second anguished cry. Taking advantage of his momentary weakness, Kacey pushed with all her might, dislodging him halfway from her body, but he held tight, maintaining his hold on her from within.

Another explosion billowed from the portal. There wasn't much time.

She struggled against Skoczek's control, her mind still locked onto his thoughts and intentions. She sensed his resolve to continue Malachi's work, to return the children to Burial

Hill and re-populate the empty cages, to reign over the innocent and pay an eternal homage to his creator and savior. As
his thoughts emptied around her, a darkness fell. A vision grew
from her center lobes and drowned out everything happening
before her. It bathed her in fear, reached into her soul, and
twisted things around for good measure.

In the vision, she and RG had aged a few years, Robert Jr.
maybe five or six now. He appeared to be asleep, his
wondrous, boyish face sharing the fragments of heredity and
DNA that would someday reproduce his father's familiar
features, the careless hair, dark eyebrows, and fading freckles
scattered across his nose. She grinned at her boy, but as the
image pulled back and she visualized the entire scene, sadness
and dread diminished her smile. The boy drooped in Skoczek's
grasp. His hand encircled his throat, squeezing the life from his
gentle body. Kacey lay bloodied and still on the floor, her head
pummeled and resting at a terrible angle.

A wounded cry escaped her lips as the hotel room resumed
in her vision, the emotional assault overwhelming Skoczek's
physical battering. She drew every ounce of anger and energy
she possessed, her protective, motherly instinct kicking in as
she pushed again to expel him. He flew across the room and
smashed against the wall beside the portal. She sprung to her
feet, throwing herself inside him with a viciousness that
surprised her. Tossing him from floor to ceiling, Kacey
shredded his insides like a predator disemboweling its prey.
Battered and bruised, Skoczek fought back, expelling her with
a powerful thrust.

He stood beside the portal, bent at the waist, leaning his
hands against his thighs and gasping for air. Kacey faced him
from the opposite side, ready to strike. He glanced at the quivering portal as another colossal rumble shook the room,
knocking them both to the floor.

"Hope you enjoy it here. Looks like you might have to request the extended stay." The building shook as the air sucked from the room and funneled into the portal. Skoczek hurled himself inside, disappearing as a final vibration rattled the walls.

———

RG

The mind connection between RG and the jumper severed with the abruptness of a phone slamming into its cradle as Malachi died his second death at the bottom of the well. Placing his weight on unsteady legs, RG turned from the well to find nine-year-old Elias Ashton standing behind him.

"Can you save my cousin?" the young Elias pleaded, eyes riveted on RG.

The blood drained from his head as he gazed at the boy, the gravity of the situation hitting him like a blow to the skull. He had interfered in the past and had irrevocably altered the course of history. The life of the young man standing before him would move forward, forever altered.

Fuck me.

RG whipped his head back and forth, searching for a place to hide, as if that would help. Maybe if he just bolted, his interference would not affect the boy's life too much. He clenched his jaw, rubbing the back of his neck.

Nothing I can do about it now.

Stepping toward the boy, RG dropped to a knee. "I can't, Elias. It's too late for him."

The boy jammed his hands against his hips. "How do you know my name?"

"It's kinda hard to explain."

The silence stretched between them. "I thought I saw a monster."

"You did, but he's gone now."

The old man's words resounded in RG's ears. *Talk to the boy, tell him what to do.* His heart hammered in his chest as his energy rebounded. It dawned on him he hadn't altered history, he was about to create it. The boy standing before him would orchestrate it and set it in motion from this moment on, and it was RG's job to guide the young Elias toward making it happen. RG's presence in this place, right now—and what he would tell the boy—would ensure history would proceed as intended. When, or if, RG made it back to the portal and returned to 2019, he would find everything the same. He will have met Kacey at Johnny D's Independence Day shindig, the Sox will have thrice won the World Series, although that ground ball will still have dribbled through Buckner's legs…

Maybe we could hope for at least one piece of disrupted history.

But, Ashton would be gone, having stepped back in time to die in a well in 1946, found almost ten years afterward with a young boy's bones beside him, two cousins born a year apart, but separated in age by over seventy years.

"Who was the old man?" Elias scratched his head. "Did the monster kill him?"

"Actually, the old man killed the monster. You killed the monster."

Elias sat cross-legged on the grass and gave RG a curious glance. He lowered himself onto the grass beside the boy.

"I heard the old man talking to the monster and the monster talking to him." The boy's voice hitched, and he wiped away a tear spilling over his eyelid. "I heard them clear as a bell from the bottom of the hill, just as clear as I'm talking to you right now, like the way cousin Malachi and I used to talk. I climbed up the hill because I thought Malachi might still be alive."

"Listen to me, Elias. The monster *was* Malachi and you heard him talking to you. When Malachi fell into the well and died, he came back…changed, angry."

"But he *just* died."

"Actually, he died a long time ago."

"You're not making any sense, mister." Elias stood to leave.

"Wait, please." He grasped the boy's hand.

"The old man told you to talk to me, tell me what to do. Do what?" Elias plucked a string of grass, picked off the dirt, and chewed on the end. "And who was he?"

"The old man was you, Elias."

"You must be cracked!" He turned to leave. "My mother and father told me not to talk to crazy people."

RG jumped to his feet. "Wait, Elias!"

The boy stopped, peering at the ocean across Taylor Avenue.

"Please listen. This is gonna sound a bit crazy, but you came back here seventy years from now to stop a monster, a monster snatching children from their families. It had been your life's mission. *You* were the old man. How else could you have heard Malachi's voice in your head talking to you?"

Elias lowered his gaze, staring at the grass. Then he took off in a dead run down the hill.

"Wait!" RG dashed after him, grabbing him by the shoulder and wrapping his arms around him.

"Hey, let me go! Let me go, you looney tune!" The boy kicked and stomped at RG, connecting against ankles and toes.

"Ow! Wait a minute. Just stop! Listen to me, Elias." He relaxed his hold on the boy bit by bit, gauging whether he might bolt. He wasn't convinced he had the energy to catch him again. "You saved the lives of countless children when you stepped into the well. You took the monster with you."

Elias turned. "But that can't happen. There aren't any monsters."

"You just saw one, didn't you?"

"I guess."

"Some things seem impossible until they happen." RG knelt beside the boy, placing a hand on his shoulder. "You ever read any books or go to the picture shows on Saturday mornings?"

"Yeah, my mom takes me when we have a good week at the deli. And I read lots of Edgar Rice Burroughs and H.G. Wells."

"Stories about men rocketing to different worlds and traveling through time, right?"

Elias nodded.

"I read those books, too, when I was your age. Where I'm from those things have happened, we've traveled to the moon. And you've traveled back in time." RG fixed the boy with his gaze. "Seems impossible until it happens."

Elias shook his head. "So, in the future I travel through time to stop the monster?"

"Yes. But you have to come find me again if you're gonna be successful. When you're an old man, you have to find Robert Granville...that's me. Read the newspapers. You'll spot my name. I can help you get back here to save those children."

"Robert Granville? I'll try to remember."

RG grasped Elias by the shoulders. "No, you *have* to remember!"

"Robert Granville," the boy repeated. "This is the place where I'm gonna die, isn't it?"

RG nodded his head. "It's a long, long time away, a lifetime really. You'll have a full life. You'll be ready when the time comes."

"It's okay, then." Elias gazed across the field toward White Horse Beach, the crystal blue Atlantic water scattering the last of the sun's radiance across it. "It's a pretty place to die, I guess."

RG marveled at the pluck of a nine-year-old boy coming to terms with his own death—and the impossible.

"What do I do about cousin Malachi?"

"You tell your dad whatever you must to keep yourself out of trouble, okay?"

"Robert Granville, right?" The boy rose to his feet and held out his hand.

RG shook it.

"I guess I'll be seeing you around."

RG had sensed the portal's rumblings during his conversation with young Elias, its dying groans echoing its creator's demise. He would have to hurry. Missing the portal was not an option. If the doorway between worlds closed, he wouldn't have the juice to construct a new one. The sand had picked up speed through the hourglass, time fading away. If only Wilder were here to perform his magic, slow things down a bit, RG might have a chance to make it back to the inn.

He broke into a sprint across the knee-high grass field as he aimed in the general direction toward Plymouth center. Dusk had fallen, keeping him partially hidden from other living souls and reducing potential interactions as he bound through wooded areas and empty fields into town.

He hadn't given it much thought until now, but if the portal closed, everything he had accomplished might be for naught. He had set the future right with Elias, but that future depended on his riding the pipeline back to 2019. His main concern up until now had been how he would live if stranded in the time loop, how he would remain hidden from Malachi until someone got him home. He figured he'd avoid humanity by learning their patterns, taking advantage of the repeating days. He could find a house, empty for the holiday weekend, maybe next to the ocean. He could remain hidden, fishing the waters for food. He would get by. But Malachi's death had broken the time loop. Human behavior would have no predictable pattern now, nothing he could study and master. Even if he could hide away forever, his luck would run out at some point, he would eventually run into someone.

He had believed nothing mattered, not even his own salvation, when compared to Elias's understanding of his role in stopping Malachi. But by setting the future right with Elias, he had set himself up to destroy it.

More stellar planning, RG.

Arriving in town, RG crept along Market Street, bathed in sweat and wheezing, his whooshing blood pressure pounding against the back of his eyes. *Didn't they say to increase exercise gradually?* He ducked into alleys or disappeared into the shadows when someone approached or threatened to pass him on the street. He snuck behind the old court house and approached the inn from the rear. As he pried open the back door, he flinched at the looming shape in the doorway. Jumping back into the shadows, RG flattened himself against the hotel's outer wall.

"Is that you, Reginald?" John Carver leaned his head out the door, scanning the darkness.

RG placed his hand on his chest, leaning over to catch his breath. "You scared the shit out of me, Governor."

Carver grinned. "No such compliment a ghost would

rather receive." He hustled him into the rear stairwell. "But you haven't much time. The guests will be arriving soon, and room 309 will not be vacant much longer."

"Did the children get through?"

Carver nodded. "Your companions were successful in their endeavors."

RG closed his eyes, covering his mouth with a hand. The children safe, Malachi dead. After all they had encountered, after all the uncertainty raiding Plymouth without a plan; somehow, they had accomplished the mission. Now all he had to do was get Kacey back to the Pancake Man.

"Unfortunately, the strange looking Brit didn't accompany them back."

RG dropped his head, staring at the floor.

Carver placed a translucent hand upon his shoulder. "In all worthy endeavors, some will be lost."

RG pictured Burial Hill, the names of those who didn't make it through the first year in the new world, including Carver himself. If anyone understood sacrifice, it was the ghost standing before him.

"Make haste, Reginald, before your opportunity is lost."

He shook John Carver's hand and hurried up the stairwell, taking the steps two at a time until he reached the third floor. He cracked the stairwell door and peeked his head out to check for guests. He sprinted along the hallway to room 309.

As he threw open the door, Kacey sprang off the bed and rushed into his arms, burying her head in his chest.

"The portal…it's gone."

Chapter Twenty One

'Sleep lovely babe thy toils are o'er
Why do we weep why should we mourn.'

To the memory of MERCY M. BRIGHAM, died June 18th,
1827 (Aged 9 mo. and 5 days)
-Epitaphs from Burial Hill

July 5, 2019

Mike

Mike Stahl slipped through the Pancake Man's front door, grasping Zach's hand firmly in his own. He scanned the restaurant, every table, booth, and counter seat filled with a dirty child downing pancake stacks, fried potato mounds, omelets, sausage, and bacon. The regular customers had vacated their tables, giving up their seats to the famished hordes. Many of them dashed from table to table, helping the waitstaff carry plate after plate to the hungry children. Morrow had manned an apron and spatula and worked the kitchen griddle, slinging steaming dishes onto the stainless-steel service window, tapping the bell for pickup.

"You hungry, Zach?"

"Like, starving!"

"Why don't you have a seat with your friends, and I'll get you something."

"Can I sit with you instead?"

A squeeze fluttered through his chest as he ran a hand along the back of Zach's head. He couldn't keep his hands off the boy, as if by touching him, it assured him Zach had made it back. He was real again. "I spot a couple of empty seats in the back. Come on. Follow me."

Stahl dropped the boy's hand as he navigated through the narrow aisle.

He grinned, taking in the children's glowing faces, the hearty breakfast food adding life and color to their dulled features and pallid skin. But in an instant, their beaming smiles shrank, eyes reflecting a terror he had witnessed in the cave. The comforting restaurant sounds, forks and knives slicing against each other, plates and glasses jingling together, voices echoing from the kitchen, reduced to silence. Stahl pivoted, his breath diminished as Skoczek appeared at the door, hand resting on Zach's shoulder.

"I'm back," he growled.

Morrow stepped from the kitchen. "There's nothing for you here, Skoczek?"

The jumper scanned Morrow from head to foot, white apron strung behind the old man's neck and back, stained with grease and egg yolks. "Who are you, the cook?" he sneered. "And I disagree…everything's here. I've come to take the children. Malachi's dead, so they belong to me now."

Stahl eyed the cellphones stacked at the service station beside Skoczek, the spot where the team had left them before entering the portal the previous morning. The raised handle of his HK45 nestled among them drew his immediate attention.

He's still human, a bullet can kill him.

"Malachi filled your heads with lies." Morrow folded his arms in front of his chest. "The ring has made it worse. It doesn't belong to you, and you've perverted its true power. Take it off, Skoczek, and you'll find out who you truly are."

Skoczek rolled his eyes. "God, I'm fucking tired of everyone telling me who I'm supposed to be. The ring has shown me the truth. Why am I bothering to listen to you, old man?"

Morrow's fists clenched underneath his folded arms. Stahl sensed in him the deep desire to once more possess the elusive power resting on the finger of the man before him.

"The ring calls to another, not you," Morrow informed him.

"Well, the *other* is stuck in Plymouth for the time being. The portal's gone. The ring's mine, and I can build my own portal anywhere."

Stahl stepped forward, his glance darting to the server's station. "Let the boy go. If you're pissed off, you should be pissed off at me. I'm the one who rescued the children. Take it out on me."

"Oh, don't worry. I will."

"Malachi deceived you." Morrow stepped closer. "He came to you when you were a child, like these children here. He made you do things."

"You're wrong!" Skoczek shouted. "I did all those things. Malachi loved me. He was…all I ever had."

"He didn't love you. He loved me," Zach chimed in. "At least that's what he told me."

Stahl widened his eyes, attempting to get Zach's attention. *Don't do it, Zach. Don't antagonize him.*

"When did he tell you this?" Skoczek spun Zach to face him.

Stahl sidled closer to the server's table, still ten feet to his left, a line of tables blocking his access.

"He told me every day," Zach said, beaming. "He'd also laugh and tell me what a loser you were."

"You lie!" Skoczek shouted.

"It hurt you when he chose me as his friend, didn't it?"

Stahl froze, locking eyes with Morrow. *What the fuck is he doing?*

Skoczek regained his composure. "Nothing hurts anymore, not now. But you're gonna learn what it's like to hurt."

"Maybe if you'd been with him, he wouldn't have died. You ever think of that? Maybe you're responsible for his death."

Skoczek's face fell. "Shut your mouth!"

"He's dead now, Skoczek," Morrow began, "It's time to move on, recognize your life can still have purpose."

"Oh, it does. His death *has* given me purpose. His death will be honored with all your lives, starting with this one here."

Skoczek lunged for Zach, but he spun away and sprinted along the aisle toward Mike.

As Stahl threw himself forward to shield Zach, Skoczek pierced the boy's body like a lightning bolt, stretching the boy's limbs as he worked himself inside the smaller host. Zach's skin and bone outer shell stretched and elongated with a crackling sound as the jumper conformed to the boy's dimensions. Zach fought, jerking his body back and forth, kicking his limbs, and hurling his elbows, as if slam dancing in an invisible mosh pit.

Stahl stood motionless, unsure what to do, imploring Morrow with a stare.

"Talk to him!" Morrow shouted.

Stahl nodded, recalling an earlier conversation he'd had with Zach as the sun set over Lydia's Cove, skimming stones into the yawning surf. "Remember what we said about bullies, Zach?"

A hint of recognition dawned in the boy's eyes but disappeared in an instant as Skoczek's dominating presence overtook him.

"We said when you encounter a bully, you have to push back. Sometimes a bully needs a good smack in the mouth!"

Zach writhed on the ground as Skoczek directed the boy's hand toward his throat. Stahl shot forward, grasping Zach's wrist to prevent it from cutting off his air, but Skoczek used it to swat him away, knocking him onto his back.

Stahl raised himself on all fours and crawled next to his son. "You have my permission to push back, Zach. Push back hard!"

A cry arose from Zach as his muscle's contracted, his fingers scraping against the tiled restaurant floor, a harsh grating sound. Skoczek's surprised face appeared beside Zach's, like a double exposure image lying marginally askew, the boy's effort partially expelling the jumper.

"Dad, help me!" Zach cried.

"You push back, Zach. Harder this time. You have my permission!"

The boy's eyes burned into his father's as he struggled.

"Remember what Mrs. Granville said back in the pit," he coached from beside him. "If they get spit out, we can kill them. You can do it, Zach. Do it now!!"

Zach gave a powerful push, every muscle in his body appearing to contract in a synchronous wave from the top of his head to his feet. Skoczek flew from the boy and slammed against the Pancake Man's opposite wall, shattering the mirror above the register. He tumbled to the floor, dazed, rubbing his head, blood seeping between his fingertips.

"You little shit!" Skoczek howled. The jumper rose to his feet, ready to spring toward Zach, ready to pick up where he had left off.

Stahl rose from the floor and leaped across the line of tables separating him from the server's station. But his bad hip minimized liftoff, his lead foot catching a chair back, cart-wheeling him over the tables and onto the floor. He landed hard on his back, fireflies streaking across his vision. With the wind knocked from his lungs, he dove toward the server's station and grabbed the HK45, rolling onto the ground and popping up in a shooter's position. The shot went wild, the room still spinning from the floor's impact. The bullet rico-cheted across the restaurant as a jolt of searing pain radiated along his arm, his broken hand unable to control the weighty firearm. A cry arose from the restaurant's stunned patrons as they hit the floor, shielding the children as they covered their ears and dove under tables. A young girl in French braids shouted to the other customers as they hustled the boys out the back door.

Skoczek turned his attention to Stahl.

Struggling to draw air, Mike cried out as he squeezed off another shot, its report echoing in the rapidly emptying diner. A bolt of lightning radiated from his hand down his arm as a second wayward bullet splintered the wood paneling a few feet over Skoczek's head.

"Your turn!" Skoczek aimed himself at the primary threat, his frame blurring as he transitioned for a bodily invasion.

Stahl transferred the stopper to his left hand, for the first time aware how awkward it felt on the opposite side, like trying to brush your teeth with the wrong hand. He shifted his stance to compensate for the uncustomary grip on the HK45. With

Skoczek bearing down on him, he steadied both hands on his gun, its weight suddenly cumbersome. His fingers curled around the trigger. He had one shot, one chance to deliver the deadly bullet. He couldn't miss.

The firearm's blast rocked the room a third time, gunpowder smoke wafting through Mike's nostrils. Skoczek's body dropped in flight, barreling to the floor against chairs and tables blocking his path. His body twitched, rasping sounds rising and falling silent as he took his last breath.

Mike remain posed, unflinching, watching Skoczek's lifeless form lay clumped in a mass. With no sign of movement, he slowly lowered his weapon, took short steps toward Malachi's unfortunate, misguided victim.

Inspecting the body, he observed the bullet's disciplined entry just to the left of the sternum, having pierced the heart.

As Zach rose to his feet, navigating overturned tables to get to his father, Morrow bounded to intercept his advancement. "Keep your eyes on me, Zach," Morrow shouted, blocking his view of the body on the sticky tiled floor. "Don't look down. Look at me, Zach. Look at me."

"Yes, sir." The boy averted his eyes as Mike hobbled to his son and kneeled beside him, throwing his arms around his neck.

"You did it, Dad," Zach cried.

"No, Zach, you did! You lured him inside you knowing you could push him out, didn't you?"

"I pushed Malachi out a few times before he got mad at me. I figured if I could push him out, the other guy would be easy."

Mike craned his neck toward Morrow, the caretaker kneeling on the floor and draping a tablecloth over Skoczek's crumpled body. "We should round up the children before they get lost out there."

The old man rose from a knee. "They're in good hands with Kacey."

"Kacey? But she's stuck back in—"

"True," Morrow interrupted, "but everyone in here is part of her, every patron, every server."

"The little girl with the French braids?"

"Her especially," Morrow smirked. "Kacey didn't want the boys to witness another death. She made sure they wouldn't suffer any more trauma." He reached for Zach's hand and led him to the red-top spiral counter seat and served him a piece of cherry pie with vanilla ice cream. Stepping toward Stahl, he glanced at Skoczek's body. "Now let's put this one with the trash out back before the children get back. They don't need any more nightmares."

———

Grabbing Skoczek's arms and legs, the men heaved the body from the floor. Stahl winced as he struggled to navigate the jumper's shifting dead weight, his hip and shoulder sending piercing reminders to his brain. He blinked back the next world's blinding light as they stepped through the front door.

"I see some of the children wandering by the dumpster," Morrow said, dropping Skoczek's lower half. "Let's leave him here for now until I can get them back in their seats. Meet me inside."

Dashing around the building's perimeter, Morrow corralled the wayward children like a Border Collie in a sheep field, reuniting them with the group and escorting them through the rear entrance into the restaurant. Stahl helped the waitstaff right the upended tables and deposit a slice of pie with vanilla ice cream at each setting. When the children had settled into their seats, Morrow voice rose above the growing murmur.

"Listen to me, boys. Both monsters are gone, I assure you. You are safe now. No one is taking you back to the cages, no one is taking you anywhere...except home, of course." A burst of chatter surged from the boys, relief morphing into smiles and laughter as they grasped forks and spoons and inhaled their desserts. Morrow glanced at Stahl, nodding his head toward the front door.

Stepping outside, the resumed their disposal of Skoczek's corpse, hauling the body around the side of the building to a surprisingly modern looking dumpster.

Morrow tossed open the metal impact lid, letting it crash against its rear hinge. "You suppose we can swing him up and over?"

"Wait a minute." Stahl dropped the bottom half of Skoczek to the pavement and placed his hands on his hips. "Shouldn't we call someone or something? I mean, I just killed a man. Don't I need to report it to someone?"

"We operate on different rules over here."

"But to just throw him in the dumpster."

"Don't worry. No one will stumble upon him back here. In fact, this place doesn't really exist except in Kacey's mind."

Stahl nodded, attempting to wrap his head around Morrow's logic.

The old man knelt beside Skoczek's body and removed the ring from his finger.

"What're you doing?"

"This doesn't belong to him." He placed the ring in his pocket and grabbed Skoczek's wrists. "What do you say, on three?"

On cue, they heaved Skoczek upwards. Lifeless limbs hung suspended as the body tumbled over the dumpster's railing, landing on a pile of plastic garbage bags and roiling spoiled food odors into the air.

Stahl followed Morrow to the front entrance, his mind racing. With two dead jumpers, Stahl's thoughts shifted to Abner Stennett, set to rot away in prison for the rest of his natural life. It could just as easily have been Stahl fitted to a six-by-eight cell were it not for RG and Kacey's help and experience. Who's to say he wouldn't have chosen the same path if he were in Stennett's shoes? He would pay the man another visit soon with a carton of smokes, let him know Malachi had been real and was now gone, permanently erased. The truth would not free him but might allow him to come to terms with Nathan's loss and the action he had taken.

Stahl opened the door for Morrow. "What's gonna happen to Skoczek?"

"The same thing that happens to everyone." Morrow held the door for Stahl as the men entered the restaurant. "And he'll move on to his next phase."

"But he's a jumper. Won't he come back?"

"Difficult to say," Morrow frowned, rubbing his chin. "He had powers, true, but Malachi filled his head with many lies. And the ring augmented his dark side, made him into something he believed he'd always been. I don't expect we'll ever truly know what he was."

Zach scampered toward the front door with a plate in his hand, blueberry pie swimming in melted ice cream. "I saved you a slice, Mr. Morrow. Would you like one?"

He grimaced at the soaking pie. "I'd love one, Zach. But I have one more job to do before I get to eat."

He pulled the ring from his pocket and pressed it into his palm, grasping it with his fingers. A smoldering light pulsed from his fist, the outline of Morrow's carpal bones evident with each glimmering throb. Stahl grabbed Zach and pulled him closer. Placing the glowing ring on his finger, Morrow closed his eyes as a warming light circulated inside him, flushing through his body like liquid phosphorescence. As the circuit completed, the iridescent glow surrounding him ebbed, and he opened his eyes.

"Are you okay, Mr. Morrow?" Zach's blueberry pie plate pitched at an ever-increasing angle, vanilla ice cream forming an expanding puddle at the boy's feet.

He squeezed the boy's shoulder. "Good as new, Zachary. In fact, better than new. I feel more…old, than new." He chuckled.

Zach scrunched his face and scratched his head. "That doesn't make any sense."

"Mr. Morrow," Stahl interjected. "What's gonna happen to RG and Kacey now the portal's gone?"

Morrow brushed the lint from his pearl-white shirt. "They're coming home."

"But they don't have a way back."

The old man stepped to the coatrack and threw an arm through his tailored black suit jacket. As he strode to the door, he lifted his hat from the rack and positioned it on his head. Pushing open the restaurant's front door, he tossed a glance over his shoulder.

"We'll just see about that."

RG

Kacey leaned against the four-post bed in room 309 while RG paced the floor. Carver had alerted them they had only twenty minutes before arriving guests would claim the room.

"What do we do, RG?"

"Well, we can spend another night in the boiler room—"

"I'm not talking about tonight!" She sprang upright against the bed pillows. "I'm talking about the rest of our lives! We're stuck in 1946 with no way home." She ran both sets of hands through her hair, clasping them behind her neck.

He stepped to the bed and sank beside her into the feather mattress, wrapping an arm around her waist and scooting her toward him. "Everything we've faced until now, every challenge...from Victor Garrett to Malachi...we've been successful. We'll find a way back. I'm certain of it."

Kacey glanced around the room. "Not feeling so successful right now."

"Kacey, you've already built a portal...to the Pancake Man. And you did it as a child."

"But it took years to make. We can't be here *that* long."

"What about the children you just freed from here? They've spent decades in a hell we couldn't possibly imagine. We can do it. We just need to stay positive and find solutions."

Kacey stood, pacing the room before pivoting to face him. "You're forgetting I can't travel through time, the ring's gone...and you're out of juice. I can't build a portal to another time without someone who can travel through time."

He shrugged. "How can you be sure? You didn't recognize the powers you had when we battled Victor Garrett. They just kind of came alive at the right time. You're still evolving."

"Sometimes you just know, RG." She folded her arms across her chest. "You understand what's inside."

"Tell me at least you'll try."

"Of course, I will. But it's gonna take time...and a miracle. What do we do in the meantime?"

His shoulders slumped. "We find a way to stay hidden."

"Where?"

"We'll figure it out."

She threw her arms to her sides. "Maybe we'll find an old mausoleum to inhabit…"

"I didn't say that."

She lowered her gaze, eyes fixed on the carpet. "The thought of never interacting with another person again is about too much for me. How lonely would that be?"

"Hey, we'll have each other." He stepped toward her and put his arms around her waist. "That's always been enough for me."

"That's not what I meant."

"We can always accompany the Governor to the movies." He flashed her a lame smile. "I'm pretty sure we'd have Burial Hill to ourselves on July Fourth each year. We could sit below your kissing tree…maybe we can make it our kissing tree… watch the fireworks together."

"You make it sound like a vacation."

"It could be. Like another honeymoon."

Kacey paced the carpet. "How will we eat? Can't really relax with a bottle of wine at the waterfront restaurants, can we?"

"You should talk to John Carver. His people came here in the dead of winter four hundred years ago and found a way to stay alive. We can do it. If Mike and Elias could sneak cold cuts out of his family's deli, we can, too."

She paused a beat, breaking from his embrace and dropping onto the bed. "What about Junior…" Her words faded as tears shimmered in her eyes.

My boy. His son's name delivered a gut punch to his already churning stomach. "I have to assume Mike and Claire will—"

"No!" Kacey sobbed, burying her face in her hands. "He's our son."

"They'll raise him like their own. And he could do a lot

worse than having Zach around. I'm sure he'll take care of him, be a good older brother."

"That's not the point."

He approached the bed and sank into the mattress. He studied her eyes, the solid blue broken up with hints of green and brown, a color spectrum growing deeper and wider with every exploration. He steeled himself for what he would say. "It'll be a lot harder on us than on Junior. With time," he choked on the words, "he'll come to recognize Mike and Claire as his only parents…" His eyes burned as he tried to prevent the rising tears. "He'll be fine."

"Maybe, but what about us?"

A vibration shook the hotel as the room yawed to the left, sending Kacey stumbling toward the mattress and RG to the floor.

"What the…?" RG struggled to a knee.

A light swirl penetrated the wall in a vortex above the bed, growing like a vibrant blossoming flower. Color infiltrated the room as the hotel wall disappeared, a lush, tropical garden extending miles toward the horizon replacing it. The next world's textures and unfathomable hues appeared like a drug-fueled hallucination. In the distance, Morrow approached with a smirk, arms held at his sides as if embarrassed at his over-the-top entrance.

He stepped into the room.

"Rather gaudy showing for a 'white-with-black-shutters' kind of guy, wouldn't you say?" RG grinned, stepping forward to embrace his father.

"I thought after your last trip through the portal, it might be nice to enjoy a more scenic route home."

"This one does look a bit more pleasant," Kacey added, hugging the old man.

"Hello, my dear," Morrow beamed, pecking Kacey's

cheek. "You both did wonderfully. You accomplished both mission goals."

"We lost Ian."

Morrow removed his hat and stared at the floor, running a hand through his hair.

"He engaged Skoczek and saved Zach's life," Kacey explained. "He held him off long enough for Mike and me to get the children into the portal."

"He helped get them home then?"

"In the end, he's the reason they made it home." Kacey swallowed.

RG glanced at the portal, then the ring on Morrow's hand. "How did you do all this?" he asked, gesturing toward the missing hotel wall.

"The ring called to me, invited me to use its power again." Morrow held up his hand. "I guess it missed me."

"I sensed its pull in the time loop, whenever I got close to Skoczek. It leaked its power to me, just enough to get the job done."

"It called to you, too. It knew what you needed." Morrow deliberated a moment. "And it appears to have given us both unexpected gifts."

RG grinned. "Are you…?"

"Back?" Morrow pondered. "We'll see."

"Won't the Tribunal…or the Elders…whatever, the guys who stripped you of your powers, won't they be pissed if you come out of retirement?"

"I have no more assignments as a caretaker. What I do on my own time is up to me now." Morrow smirked. "People in retirement take up different hobbies all the time."

Kacey placed a hand on Morrow's arm. "Is everyone back at the Pancake Man?"

"Just waiting for you to get us the rest of the way home."

Kacey grinned. "With all the talk about making sure we didn't change history, haven't we done just that by bringing all the children back?"

"Disrupting the past would have changed an existing history, but in the present, every single act impacts what will become history. We're changing a history that hasn't happened yet, a history undetermined. Whatever lives these children forge is meant to be from this moment on."

"So, it's okay?"

Morrow smiled. "It couldn't be any other way."

"And what happened to Skoczek?" RG inquired, raising an eyebrow.

"He's in the dumpster behind the Pancake Man."

RG opened his mouth to speak, but nothing came out.

"Now, are you guys ready to come home?" Morrow folded his hands behind his back.

"So much for our second honeymoon," Kacey lamented.

Morrow turned toward the portal. "I could come back another time if—"

"Uh, that won't be necessary." She grabbed his jacket collar, pulling him backward. "I'm more than ready."

"Oh, I have something for you, Son." Morrow removed the ring from his finger, placing it in RG's palm. The ring gave you powers even when it sat on someone else's finger. It sought you out. Now I can't be sure, but I'd imagine when your time comes, it may want to go along for the ride."

RG grinned as a calming peace descended his face.

"It's time you put this back where it belongs."

RG slipped the ring onto his right hand, swooning with thoughts and images from hotel guests, maids, bell captains, and people passing on the sidewalks. Hidden secrets, haunted voices, silent pleas flooded him like a tsunami. "Holy shit!"

Morrow steadied him as he shut his eyes. The moment

passed as his mind quickly adjusted, managing the turbulent onslaught he was experiencing.

"I think I got this," RG opened his eyes, blinking away the lingering residues. "I forgot what that was like."

The door to 309 clicked as a key rattled in the keyhole.

"Time to go, come on!" Morrow hustled RG into the portal, the hotel door opening too late for the guests to observe anything but another beautiful suite in the John Carver Inn.

————

RG and Kacey strolled arm and arm through the portal, Morrow following close behind. Stepping through the Pancake Man's entrance, the three stopped to appreciate the sight before them, a sea of laughing children, sharing their rich desserts with their friends and jabbering in anticipation of getting home to their families.

RG scanned the room with a sigh. The children didn't know it, but they would be returning to a world much different than they had left, some about to face more than a half-century of change, things they couldn't anticipate or prepare for. How do you tell a child their loved ones may be gone? The unspoken understanding reflected in Kacey's eyes, tempering the moment.

He grasped Kacey's hand, her eyes closed as the restaurant's comfortable sounds swelled in her ears, busy waitstaff hustling back and forth between tables, clearing dishes into plastic bins, voices booming from the kitchen, and dinging bells signaling orders slung onto the server's window. Just as she always imagined.

"Welcome back, guys." Stahl stepped from the crowd of children, an arm draped around Zach's shoulders. "Haven't you figured out a way not to cut these missions so close?"

"Just trying to keep things interesting," RG smirked.

Stahl threw a paw around RG's shoulder and pulled him away. He let out a breath. "Listen. I owe you…everything. You killed the jumper that stole my son. Zach's free from him forever. I'm not sure I can ever repay you."

"You're part of this team now." RG nodded toward Morrow and Kacey. "No doubt there'll be other missions where we'll need a good cop. That's how you'll repay me."

"I thought so," Stahl frowned.

"I also want you to look around, Mike…at what you've done here."

He cast his eyes over the crowded restaurant.

"Morrow told us how you took out Skoczek. Kacey had a vision he would have come back to harm Junior. You see, you saved my son, and I'm not sure I can ever repay *you*, either."

"You can let me give your wife a hug; how 'bout that?"

For the first time he could remember, RG's suspicion and distrust of Stahl had taken wing. He no longer braced himself behind the raging fortress he had constructed. Having been inside his head and witnessing his devotion for Claire, he understood him in a way he could never experience before. He often wondered if he could ever be his friend. But maybe he already was.

"Deal." He slapped Stahl on the back. "But I'll be watching."

Mike stepped to Kacey and welcomed her back with an embrace.

"I have to tell you, when Skoczek stepped through that portal instead of you…" He shifted his weight from one leg to another.

"You must have thought the worst."

Stahl lifted his gaze. "I decided he had to die."

"You and me both. You just saved me the trouble. You did great work over there, Mike."

"Thanks. But where's Elias? He's the one I need to thank." Stahl raised his head, scanning the restaurant. "If it weren't for him, I'd either be drowned or frozen. I didn't see him come in with—"

"He didn't," RG said quietly, shaking his head.

Stahl rubbed the back of his neck. "For chrissake! And Ian?"

Kacey pressed her lips together and shrugged.

"Dad!" Zach's shrill voice broke the pressing silence. "Dad, I have something for Mr. Morrow."

Stahl knelt beside his son, staring at the gift, an arm poised on the boy's shoulder. "He's gonna love it, bud."

Zach pulled on Morrow's coat sleeve and handed him the soggy pie he had been saving for him, melted vanilla ice cream saturating the once crispy crust three quarters of the way up the blueberry filling. "You said you'd have a piece when you got back."

"I did, didn't I?" He rolled his eyes at Mike.

Morrow took the plate and carved off the smallest possible bite he could manage with his fork, sliding the wet paste into his mouth with a hidden grimace.

Zach glanced up at him, waiting. "Well?"

"Mmm! That's good."

"See? Aren't you glad you're back?"

Catching his reflection in the mirror over the counter, Morrow smoothed the collar on his crisp dark suit and straightened his hat.

"Damn straight."

Chapter Twenty Two

'God called thee home,
He thought it best.'

GEORGIE
-Epitaphs from Burial Hill

October 17, 2019

RG

Kacey and RG strolled along Plymouth's waterfront, rummaging through the John Alden gift shop for rock candy and saltwater taffy, tee-shirts and novelty toys for Junior—a much less stressful Plymouth second honeymoon than they had envisioned several months earlier. Morrow had agreed to watch Junior, forever cherishing his time with his grandson, but RG sensed his father was gearing up for bigger roles now.

After ice cream at Ziggy's, they trudged up Chilton Street

and spent the afternoon poking through the antique shops along Main. They checked into the John Carver Inn...and spa. RG chuckled, wondering whether the ghost would approve of the addition to his namesake, as well as the *Mayflower*-shaped indoor waterslide and fitness center.

They had reserved room 309, the Carver King, featuring the four-post bed in the online photo. It may have been the same one they bounced off of seventy years ago, but no one seemed to know for sure how long it had been there. They dropped their packages onto the bed as they inspected the room, an assortment of dark chocolates and teas beside the gold embossed leather-bound binder on the ornate wooden desk under the window. RG grinned.

Somewhere, some things never change.

They lounged on the pillow-top mattress, flipping the channels of the flat screen mounted on the opposite wall, enjoying the novelty of doing the same things they did at home, but in a different place.

Kacey reached over and rested her hand on his stomach, patting it and giving it a squeeze. "So how many pounds is it now?" she asked, chuckling. "I sort of miss the rest of you."

"Twenty-five and counting," RG bragged. "You didn't think I had it in me, did you?"

"Frankly, no. But I'm proud of you."

"So, when do I get my *DDperks* card back?"

Kacey smiled and interlaced her fingers with his, his ring brushing against her. She grabbed his left hand, turning it over back and forth. She leaned closer and squinted, inspecting his ring finger, the golden band glowing at its base. "How is it possible?"

RG glanced at the digit, nothing different about it than before the accident. It remained the exact same length as the finger on his opposite hand, despite the surgery. No scars were visible from any angle, and he could sense her fingertip's briefest brush against it. Then he reached down and removed the ring. In an instant, the finger changed, the life draining from it before their eyes. Healed stitches crisscrossed the discolored skin, choked by a limited blood supply. The extremity shriveled slightly and appeared blunted, and he could no longer sense Kacey's hand wrapped around it.

"I've only just scratched the surface of the ring's power." RG slipped the golden band back into place. "It holds more secrets than I could ever access, more depth than I could ever grasp."

After another half hour channel surfing, RG could read in Kacey's features a distant angst, her fidgety body fighting a persistent pull, a summoning.

It came from the Hill. RG sensed it, too.

He gripped Kacey's hand and squeezed twice. "What do you say we check it out?"

"I thought you'd never ask."

They hopped from the bed and threw on their jackets. As they paced along the corridor, RG jumped as a couple emerged from the stairwell and stepped toward them. They nodded, a look of concern in the couple's eyes as they passed, trying not to focus on the man flattening himself against the wall.

"Christ almighty, RG. It's not 1946 anymore."

"This place still makes me a little jumpy."

They reached the end of the hallway and pushed open the heavy wooden door leading to the stairs. When they had climbed down the three flights to the basement stairwell, RG paused a moment as Kacey continued out the rear exit.

She snagged the swinging door before it settled against the doorframe and peered into the stairwell. "What are you waiting for?"

RG strained an ear, listening as he scanned the tight corridor. "Nothing."

Their steps took them past the First Parish Church and up Burial Hill. When they reached the top, they wandered along the walkway until they found the headstones scattered beneath the kissing tree.

"They're not here?" Kacey scratched her head.

RG stepped to her side.

"The mother-and-father headstones," she said.

"'Parted below,' 'United above.'"

Kacey jammed her hands against her hips. "Could they have moved them?"

"They can't do that in an historical cemetery. For centuries, experts have been documenting each grave plot's location and epitaph."

"Then, where are they?"

They scanned the epitaphs beneath the kissing tree, searching for the Kempton children, the Thacher children, the hundred others that lead RG to the discovery of the missing children below ground. But they were no longer clustered together beneath the tree. They found the familiar epitaphs scattered across all corners of Burial Hill.

"It doesn't make sense." RG combed his fingers through his mane. "I'd have never put it all together if the markers hadn't been sitting side by side underneath the tree. How did—"

"The ring called to you that day. Maybe it showed you what it wanted you to see."

Kacey eyed the mausoleum behind the kissing tree. "Come on, I wanna check something."

They stepped around the grave markers until they stood before the heavy wooden door of the vault. It no longer hung off its hinges, a restoration having repaired it at some point since their last visit.

He tried the handle, expecting it locked, but the door glided open as if waiting for their return, welcoming them back. Stepping into the crypt, RG held his hands out, anticipating the impenetrable wall of air, Malachi's mind tricks, but all he sensed was the stuffy vault's stale, mildewy odor.

"Should we?" Kacey asked, glancing toward the stairwell.

RG pulled out his iPhone, swiped the screen, and tapped on the flashlight app. The tomb appeared to shrink and coil against the invasive unnatural glow. Kacey stepped forward along the twisting stone staircase, RG following.

They approached the bottom of the stairwell, earth and rock packed together before them, creating an impassible barrier into Malachi's ancient lair.

RG pushed against the unyielding barricade. "The ground must have collapsed at some point."

"I remember when Skoczek and Wilder tangled, the whole place shook, rocks and dirt rained off the walls and ceiling and came down all around us."

"Maybe the ring tried to erase this place's evil or finish off its oppressor."

"It got the wrong guy," Kacey uttered with a frown.

They climbed the steps in silence, grateful for the burst of fresh air as they cracked the mausoleum's door and stepped out onto Burial Hill. The night had turned brisk by the time they returned to the inn.

Later, with Kacey sound asleep beside him, RG reclined wide awake against the headboard, remote control in hand. The television's electrical flashes bathed the room in alternating light and shadow, like heat lightning on a still summer night. He clicked the power button as he swung his legs over the side of the bed and shuffled to the door.

"Where you going?" Kacey rolled onto her side.

"Just wanted to check something out. I'll be right back."

"Don't forget your key or you'll be sleeping in the hall."

RG smiled as he closed the door. She meant it. Kacey wouldn't get out of bed for anything once she settled in. Padding down the hallway to the stairwell, he descended the three flights until he reached the basement landing.

He stood, listening. "Governor?" Silence.

RG shouldered the door open and wandered into the corridor, facing a wall of vending machines. A sign directed guests to the pool, spa, fitness center, and game room, arrows aiming in different directions along the thick carpeted hallway. He traversed the corridor toward the boiler room, the recipient of at least one thorough renovation since he had last set foot there. The room now resembled an arcade with whirring sounds and beeps coming from the electronics lining the walls, a pop-a-shot, air hockey, and the requisite alien annihilation games featuring oversized killing devices mounted to the machines. Several deep leather sofas faced a seventy-two-inch flat screen television flickering above an old-fashioned Wurlitzer juke box, Judge Judy about to render a legal judgment against a soon-to-be humiliated plaintiff.

Someone must have left this thing on.

As RG picked up the remote, a voice piped up from behind him.

"Oh, do wait a moment, Reginald." A figure rose from the recliner. "The barrister will soon determine whether the man owes his betrothed the bail money he needed before he left her for her best friend. Ooh, such scandalous behavior!"

His jaw dropped as he examined the Founding Father standing before him. He had abandoned the seventeenth century garb for form-fitting polyester flared trousers with an oversized shiny belt buckle, the word 'Pimp' across it in raised, shiny block letters, and a silk shirt buttoned to midchest. His feathered locks tumbled to his shoulders in waves.

"That's quite a different look you're going for, Governor." He extended his hand.

Carver shook it. "It's good to see you again, Reginald, and where is the lovely Kacey?"

"Well, I couldn't sleep."

"Ah, but she could."

RG nodded.

"I saw you'd reserved room 309. I was hoping to run into you again."

"I thought you might be down here somewhere. So, you're a Judge Judy fan?"

"Ms. Sheindlin proves again and again she is one of the great legal minds of this, or any, century."

"I thought you were a movie guy."

"Pfffhh!" Carver rolled his eyes. "No better entertainment has arisen in the past fifty years than television. And films come right across the screen all hours of the day and night. No need to travel to a crowded theater anymore."

"So, where did you get the clothes?"

"Well, I felt it was time to update my wardrobe, experiment with some of the more recent styles."

Recent? He's only about forty years behind. "How are the shoes working for ya?" He gazed at the white leather platform shoes anchoring Carver's feet to the floor.

"A bit ponderous, I admit, but your friend Mr. Wilder told me they were, how did he say it, 'the dog's bollocks.' The Brit's been a godsend when it comes to fashion—"

"Wait a minute," RG interrupted. "Ian's here?"

"No, no, he's not here, but he comes back from time to time."

"How can that be? Isn't he...?"

"He is what he's always been. He's just on to the next thing."

RG recalled Morrow's words when he had first met him. *There's always something on the other side of the door.*

"Where is he?"

"That's the question, isn't it? Where are any of us? It gets confusing sometimes."

RG rubbed the back of his neck.

"Here." Carver produced a quarter and pressed it into RG's palm. "You seem in a quandary. Go to the music machine and press D15."

RG rolled the quarter into the Wurlitzer, only to hear 'Dancing Queen' blare from the speakers.

"ABBA cannot help but lighten the mood." Carver blotted the corner of his eye with his frilly sleeve. "Just listen to those voices."

"You *have* been hanging out with Ian."

"Oh, I almost forgot. The Brit gave me something he wanted the lass to have." Carver pulled the locket from his pocket. Dangling the magic jewelry by its chain, he poured it into RG's outstretched hand.

RG glanced down, folding his fingers over it. "Thank you, Governor. When you run into Ian, tell him—"

"Sir?"

RG raised his head. The hotel desk clerk stood in the room's entranceway, the name Colleen embossed across her gold nametag. Her eyes darted about the room.

"Excuse me, sir, is someone in here with you?"

He whipped his head around, but Carver had vanished. He positioned the chain around his neck and tucked the locket under his collar. "Um, no. I couldn't sleep. I was just walking around."

"It sounded like...oh well. I heard the music, so I figured I'd check..."

"Oh, I didn't play it, I can't stand—"

"No need for embarrassment," she interrupted, nodding toward the Wurlitzer. "They had some good songs." She checked her watch. "Anyway, this floor is closed to guests after ten, along with the pool, fitness room, and spa."

"I was just leaving."

She reached for the remote in RG's hand, powering off the flat screen before slipping her hand behind the jukebox and silencing the four Swedes.

"Hey, you look familiar." Colleen instinctively took a step backward, arms hugging her body. "Aren't you..."

RG shrugged and nodded.

Her eyes darted about the deserted basement hallway. "Didn't you—"

He held up his hands. "No. I promise. I was cleared of all charges."

"So, they got the guy who did it?"

"Not yet."

She continued to backpedal. "Well, goodnight, sir."

"Night."

He waited until Colleen had gotten a head start before following in awkward silence along the empty hallway. She turned to check his position over her shoulder as she reached the stairwell, her best service industry smile masking the worry plastered across her face.

He paused, listening for her footfalls to subside and the first-floor door to shut before climbing the stairs to the third-floor corridor. Swiping the key in front of his door's electronic reader, he paused for the green flashing light before turning the handle and slipping into the pitch-black room. He let his eyes adjust to the darkness before throwing on his sweats and climbing into bed, careful not to wake Kacey. He assembled the pillows like a wedge behind his back as he scooted up against the headboard. Pulling the locket from around his neck, RG held it to his ear, as if expecting to hear a whisper or a wail, someone living in terror and needing their help. He swallowed and flipped open the ornate front panel.

Nothing.

———

In the morning, they packed their things and descended the two flights to the main lobby. RG spotted Colleen at the front desk pecking away at the computer, an oversized mug of Dunkin Donuts coffee beside her as she dragged through her shift's final leg.

"Good morn…" She glanced up, her voice trailing off. "I'm sorry I had to kick you out of the game room last night, sir."

"Oh, it's fine. I shouldn't have been there after—"

"And for bringing up…you know, the other thing," she interrupted, lowering her eyes.

"It's okay, really," he assured her.

"Here, let me make it up to you." She reached into her pocket and produced a quarter. "For torpedoing 'Dancing Queen.'"

Kacey's eyes widened as she turned to Colleen. "That's his absolute favorite song, you know."

Colleen dug deep into her other pocket for additional coins, pressing a handful of loose change into RG's palm. "Again, my apologies."

Kacey leaned over the counter. "He simply lives for ABBA." She gazed at RG, then back at Colleen. "Don't we all?"

"Let's go, hon." He grasped her elbow and led her from the front desk. "We're gonna be late for…something." *Anything.* He hustled her through the front doors.

Aiming the Subaru through the Dunkin Donuts drive-thru across from the inn, RG loaded up a Styrofoam tray with three to-go coffees, two jelly donuts, and a dozen munchkins. They had one more stop to make before heading home to the Cape, a visit they'd put off too long. But before hitting Route 3, they made a quick detour along the waterfront, savoring one more view of the shimmering harbor and historic *Mayflower*, ropes and tethers cascading from its majestic wood masts like ancient spider webs.

As they rumbled along Water Street, RG shuddered as he imagined Mike Stahl's desperate journey through the narrow, meandering pipes below their wheels, how he had braved the icy cold, pitch blackness pressing against him, lost, starved for oxygen. All for Zach. And now, all for nothing, it seemed…

"So, how's Zach adjusting to…you know." He didn't even want to say it. "Mike not being around so much anymore?"

Kacey blew out a breath. "Not so good. Kid's been through a lot, and he needs his father right now. They shared something no one could ever relate to. He'll talk to me sometimes, but Mike's the only one he feels safe with."

"Mike and Claire couldn't survive it, could they? The loss of trust."

"Hard thing to overcome." Kacey draped her arm across his shoulder.

RG tapped his fingers against the steering wheel. He couldn't imagine if the shoe had been on the other foot and Kacey's eyes had harbored the residue of accusation, a fleeting but indisputable belief he had harmed Junior. Even with Zach safe at home, the weight of Claire's distrust would be burned into Mike's memory. And how could Claire gaze into Mike's eyes and not see the monster she had created in her mind, if only for a moment. Yet how could it have been otherwise? When confronted with stories of otherworldly abduction and travel through time, how could she have viewed him as anything but insane? Claire was a scientist and Stahl had spoken the language of a madman.

"I guess it would be hard to overcome." Losing both the woman he loved and the son he almost had, collateral damage compounding the loss of Wilder and Ashton—as if that hadn't been enough.

"And now that she knows the truth about where Zach's been, she may not want him anywhere near Mike, or us, or anyone associated with that world. She's a mother first, RG. She wants a safe, normal upbringing for her boy. It's a miracle she hasn't left this place behind already, knowing what she knows about our strange connection to the world beyond. It's an awful lot to process."

Junior's image crept into RG's mind. "God, the separation must be killing him."

"How could it not." Kacey cracked the Styrofoam lid of her coffee and took a sip. "But he's there, every morning at drop off. He gets a few minutes with him before the bell rings. And Claire lets him take Zach in the afternoon. They're talking...there's still hope."

RG and Kacey wrestled with their thoughts as they continued along State Road until they arrived at White Horse Beach. They pulled up along Taylor Avenue, exited the car, and wandered through the beach shacks dotting the powder sand. The brisk fall morning fomented a stiffening wind along the flat beach, the tumbling waves a constant roar in their ears as they trudged toward the water.

RG turned and gazed toward the rows of clapboard beach houses lining the hill on the opposite side of the road, the once-empty field where Malachi had twice met his fate. RG scanned the hill for the rocks he and Elias had hidden behind, but he couldn't locate them, likely removed to make room for an additional carbon copy one-family dwelling.

"Hard to believe it all happened up there." RG shielded his eyes from a sunshine burst seeping through the cloud cover. "It seems so peaceful now."

"Strange to think how someone's house probably sits right over that sealed hole in the ground."

"Or it's under someone's backyard, where children laugh and play." He considered the odd juxtaposition of time and tragedy.

As they continued along the beach, Kacey halted, resting a palm against her forehead.

"What's the matter?" RG asked.

"Just a little dizzy, that's all." She bent over at the waist and blew out a breath. Straightening up, she grasped the locket hanging around her neck, cradling it in a death grip. Her opposite hand extended from her body, then twisted into a fist.

The air thickened as the waves' roar ground to a whisper, a metallic screech burgeoning from the deathly silence as the world's activity ground to a halt around them. The waves slowed and stopped midpeak, foamy spray suspended midair, the sun's rays bisecting them and leaving a rainbow corona exploding from the mist. The whipping wind died to nothing, but RG could barely move through it.

"What the...?" RG's focus skimmed the horizon, his voice failing to carry, the words sounding as if they came from behind a wall. He stepped toward Kacey, but it was as if he advanced against an opaque barrier, a cloak of heavy air coiled tightly around him.

"He did it," she shouted through the eerie silence. "He gifted me his power."

"So, now I can travel through time—"

"And I can stop it," she added. "One more tool to add to the arsenal."

RG had planned on a detective joining their team, but now wondered what type of asset Mike Stahl would be.

His curiosity piqued, RG stepped toward the ocean, his dry feet wading on top of the cold spongy surf. He pressed against a wall of water about to crash to shore as if it were a giant Jell-O mold, its molecular structure and physical properties frozen in the world's fleeting new reality.

"RG!" she shouted, her voice faltering through the stilted air as she weakened. "Get out of there!"

A vibration rumbled across the beach as the earth's physical laws reasserted their dominion. Trembling, Kacey's fist unclenched as her arm dropped to her side. A frigid October water wall towered over RG, pummeling him like a strawberry in a blender. He lugged his bedraggled body from the surf as he sputtered and hacked a lungful of saltwater. The cold wind picked up and the waves' roar resumed their fevered pitch as RG limped toward Kacey, arms wrapped around his frozen body.

"We gotta be careful of these powers, RG. We don't want to overestimate our abilities."

"Lesson learned." He stood shivering as the breeze picked up.

"That's what you get for trying to walk on water."

———

RG

ARE LOST CHILDREN RETURNING HOME?
—Boston (AP)—Ten-year-old Gunnar Buckholtz disappeared

from his Brookline home without a trace on May 23, 1996, but multiple reports suggest he may be back. Some have called it the greatest internet hoax since the 2008 rumor onions could power iPads, but dozens of reports from New England detail the reuniting of missing children with their families, in many cases, decades after their reported disappearances. And while such news should be a cause for celebration, the reticence of families to confirm or deny the rumors have left the issue shrouded in mystery. Adding to the intrigue, reports suggest the children haven't aged a day since their disappearances. A neighbor living in the same apartment complex as the Buckholtz family for over twenty-five years, wishing to remain anonymous, told the *Herald* she's positive Gunnar Buckholtz is back: "There's no doubt who the little boy is. Used to go to school with my son, used to play together on the sidewalk every day when they got home. Same kid. It's Gunnar, and somehow he's back." Other neighbors dismiss the reports as folly. "The talk is ridiculous, it's like something from a Stephen King novel. How insensitive do people have to be to drag the names of missing children back into the news after all these years? I can't imagine the pain the families are forced to relive." The *Herald* has learned Molly Buckholtz, 54, a person of interest during the original investigation, enrolled ten-year-old Gunther Buckholtz in fifth grade at Brookline Elementary School this fall, listing her relation to Gunther as the boy's aunt. Mrs. Buckholtz did not respond to repeated requests for comment. The Buckholtz case isn't the first report of this phenomenon. A neighbor of Bud Bateman, missing from his home in Methuen since 2006, says the Bateman family moved away almost immediately after a child resembling Bud appeared in the neighborhood last summer. "I know who the boy is. The Bateman's moved away to protect a secret, something big." The *Herald's* investigative team has confirmed new elementary school enrollments for thirty-six families of missing children in New England just this fall alone. In addition, sixteen families of missing children have moved from their towns during the same time period. The *Herald* has reached out to each of the fifty-two families, but none agreed to comment.

———

RG tossed the paper on the Subaru's console as he stared at the Brookline playground from the vehicle's side window, Kacey sipping a Dunkin Donuts regular in the passenger seat. He tapped the heater, coaxing the warm air from the vents, struggling to melt the chill from his bones after his unplanned dip in the sea. He estimated his clothes were roughly sixty percent dry, but he remained one-hundred percent frozen, despite the two coffees he had downed on the trip up Route 3. The late morning clouds whisked across the city's skyline, painting a swirling gray patina against the shadowed sky. Racing up and down the clay court, the boy heaved up three-pointers into the blustery wind. His mother rested on the weathered bench beside the walking path, tightening the scarf below her jacket's collar as the breeze picked up. She kept a close eye on him, her serene visage reflecting the blessings of second chances and fate's inevitable uncertainty.

RG and Kacey unfolded themselves from the vehicle and traipsed across the flattened grass between the parking lot and the chain-link fence surrounding the park, the Styrofoam tray balanced on Kacey's palm. As they approached the wooden bench, recognition sparked in Molly Buckholtz' eyes, a grin welcoming them forward.

"Oh my, you two." She stood. "What are you doing here?" Molly put her hands to her cheeks as she stepped forward and threw her arms around Kacey, then RG. "And why are you all wet? Decide to go swimming with the Chatham sharks this morning?"

"Something like that," Kacey said with a slight shrug.

"We've come to check in with our one-and-only client, make sure our services met with your satisfaction," RG quipped.

"Are you kidding? You brought my son back." She gazed across the basketball court. "He's truly back."

"Kinda cold out here. Figured you might need one of these." Kacey lifted a cup from the tray and handed it to her.

"You're so thoughtful. Thanks."

"We gambled on a coffee regular."

"You gambled right." She took a hearty sip. "Mmm. Cuts through the chill."

Not so much.

"How's he adjusting?" Kacey stared at Gunnar across the court.

Molly exhaled, gripping the Dunkin' Donuts hand warmer in her fists, as if in prayer. "Truth be told, he only recalls being gone a couple of days. But he remembers a lot, more than could have occurred in a weekend."

"The other children are reporting the same things. They haven't perceived any passage of real time."

"Until they've gotten back. He's confused. He's not sure why everything has changed as much as it has. He doesn't understand why I'm ancient, where his old friends are, why I'm calling him Gunther now. I'm not sure what I'm supposed to tell him. There isn't much precedent for something like this in the parenting books."

"What *are* you telling him?" RG asked.

"We're calling it a kidnapping, and he understands something's happened. He said you took him through some tunnel, a place he thought was…Hell. He says he's seen the devil." Molly blotted the corner of her eye with her sleeve.

"I can't imagine getting any closer to either than he did," Kacey said.

"There's a lot I'll have to explain. It's gonna take…years for everything to sink in. For now, we're just enjoying being together. We go to church now, sometimes in the middle of the week. Maybe it will help him come to some kind of understanding someday. Right now, it comforts him."

"You been okay? The publicity and all?" Kacey buried her neck into her jacket collar to stave off the gusting wind.

"I'm guessing you've read the *Herald*."

"*Globe, Cape Cod Times*, internet, too." RG held up his iPhone. "It's all over the place."

"It's been hard having people confronting me with suspicions, accusing me of things. If I tell the truth, they'll either label me a lunatic or hound me the rest of my life. There's nothing else to do but say 'no comment.' That's what we all agreed on."

RG tilted his head, pressing his eyebrows together.

"The other families. A detective from the Cape…Starr, maybe?"

"Stahl?" Kacey offered.

"That's him. And what a looker that one." Molly waved her hand in front of her face like a fan dispersing a swell of heat.

RG glanced at Kacey, rolling his eyes.

"He provided the other children's names and addresses. The families who have…how should I say this? The ones who have come to terms with things, accepted the truth this *really* happened…well, we've been in touch."

"What about the families who haven't accepted the truth?" RG asked.

"I've heard a number of them just picked up and left town." Molly hesitated as she savored a warming sip of coffee. She shook her head. "God, I can't imagine trying to get through this hell alone."

"Maybe they're in denial?" RG bounced from leg to leg to keep the blood flowing.

"How could they not be," Kacey chimed in. "We didn't give much thought to the psychological impact of this. We focused on getting the children home, and we didn't do much to prepare the families in advance."

"That wasn't your job. You left to get Gunnar...oops, Gunther," she said, cracking a smile, "and came home with fifty others. You did what you had to do." Molly grasped Kacey's hand. "In any case, I've talked to a number of the families surviving this thing, mostly the mothers, and the ones doing the best are those that view the world as one big miracle. This situation...just confirms what we've known all along."

Kacey sighed and reached for RG's hand.

"The families set up a private Facebook page to work through the issues we're facing, things we couldn't have prepared for."

"You think social media's a wise choice right now?" RG pressed.

"We're pretty careful, coding our posts so as not to raise suspicions. It's been a godsend when someone needs to reach out, break out from the isolation. A few of us have gotten the kids together again. It's helped them, knowing the others are close. We meet in out-of-the-way places where suspicions won't be raised."

"That's smart. The press would have a field day if they found missing children hanging out together all of a sudden." Kacey turned her back toward the wind, her chin dropping to her chest.

"It'll all come out one day. It has to. We've kept the lid on it for a few months now, but people are starting to dig."

"Have the authorities contacted you?" RG gulped his Joe.

"About a month ago. Damn if the same detective from twenty years ago didn't come to my door. I must have looked pretty guilty, shaking as hard as I did. Can't imagine he didn't recognize the red flags."

"Everyone shakes when the cops come to their home," RG responded, his own experience fresh in his mind. "They don't give it a second thought."

"What did the detective say?" Kacey pressed.

"Says he had to rule out reports of a missing child in my home. He asked to see Gunnar. Dammit, Gunther!" Molly tapped her index finger against her head. "That's what'll get me pinched. He asked his name, why he's staying with me. Gave him the standard 'distant family' excuse all the families are using. He gave me his card…and this is the funny thing." Her eyes drifted downward. "He said…how did he put it? He said, 'in case there's anything you want to get off your chest.' I think he has a hunch something isn't right."

"Guy's just doing his job," RG insisted. "He checked the box and now he's on to something else. Besides, most people suspect this thing's a hoax. It'll die down, these things always do with a twenty-four hour news cycle."

Molly chuckled, turning to watch Gunnar swish his final shot. The boy strode to the bench and gave his mother a hug.

"I'm cold, Mom. Can we go home now?"

"Of course, babe." She put an arm around his shoulder and pivoted him toward RG and Kacey. "Do you remember Mr. and Mrs. Granville?"

The boy's face lightened as he gave them a nod. "How could I forget them? Thank you both…for helping me and my friends." He tilted his head as he studied RG. "Are you wet?"

"Not as wet as I was." RG leaned forward, extending a bag of Dunkin Donuts munchkins. "You went too long without these things. You need to make up for it."

Gunnar gave RG a full-dimpled smile as he reached into the bag.

"You doing okay, big man?"

Glancing up at his mother, the boy replied, "Yeah, I'm just real glad to be home."

RG tousled his hair.

"And thanks for taking us for pancakes and ice cream afterward."

"You can thank Mrs. Granville for that."

No one said a word for a moment as the wind whistled through the park.

"Well, we should be going." RG tossed the coffee tray into the rusty garbage can beside the bench and thrust his hands inside his pockets. "Just wanted to stop by and see how you were coming along—"

"Mr. Granville," Gunnar interrupted, tugging on his jacket sleeve.

"What's up, Gunnar…oops, I mean Gunther?" He winked.

"Are there any other monsters out there?"

RG's voice grew soft. "Well, there might—"

"There's nothing out there anymore," Molly announced, summoning a weak smile. Grabbing Gunnar's hand, she turned and exited the park, throwing a rearward glance over her shoulder. "They're all gone now."

RG's breath caught in his throat as he and Kacey shuffled toward the car.

I wouldn't bet on it.

THE END

Acknowledgments

They say 'It takes a village to raise a child,' but they might as well have been talking about writing a book. It takes a brother bandying about an idea over the phone, a friend with a suggestion over lunch, a daughter with a vigorous head shake at the dinner table, a sister-in-law's two-page email. I cringe at what I would actually submit to my editor without such amazing input from the people closest to me. I don't thank you enough for your support, so I will here…Thank you, Mike, Kaylee, Chris, Jack, Kim, Tina, and all the friends who have read the work and provided such overwhelming support. Another big thank you!

I also owe the success of this series to my former agent, and current editor, Linda Kasten at Fix-It-Write.com. She has been a champion of the story from the moment I pitched it to her, and she has immersed herself into my world to help shape my ideas into stories to be proud of. Thank you for joining me on this ride and applying a steady hand to the wheel.

I am also so pleased to be part of the talented group of writers at Hydra Publications. A big thank you to Michael Liguori for his support, Stuart Thaman for his patience with a new author (and all his questions), and Tony Acree for showing me how to sell books. Honored to be part of the team.

About the Author

Stephen Paul Sayers grew up on the sands of Cape Cod and spent his first thirty-five years in New England before joining the University of Missouri as a research professor. When he's not in his laboratory, he spends his time writing and devouring his favorite forms of genre fiction—horror, suspense, and thrillers. His debut novel, *A Taker of Morrows*, was published in June 2018 to excellent reviews and became an Amazon Best Seller in the horror suspense category. His short fiction has appeared in *Unfading Daydream* and *Well-Versed*. *The Soul Dweller* is the second entry in the Caretakers series.

Throughout his journey, he has accumulated five guitars, four herniated discs, three academic degrees, two dogs, and one wife, son, and daughter. He divides his time between Columbia, Missouri and Cape Cod, Massachusetts. Visit his website: https://www.stephenpaulsayers.com or reach out on social media:

Made in the USA
Coppell, TX
12 February 2021